MW00931359

EMBARGO

ON HOPE

EMBARGO

ON HOPE

JUSTIN DOYLE

atmosphere press

© 2021 Justin Doyle

Published by Atmosphere Press

Cover design by Ronaldo Alves

No part of this book may be reproduced without permission from the author except in brief quotations and in reviews. This is a work of fiction, and any resemblance to real places, persons, or events is entirely coincidental.

atmospherepress.com

I'm so thankful for my wife Michelle, who gave me the love and long hours needed to craft this novel. I also want to thank my parents, brother, and grandmother, for supporting and encouraging me on this long journey.

A special thank you to my beta readers, Dave, Jordan, EJ, and Jenny, who brought my writing up a notch or two.

Speaker Nivian of Olav: The final tally on the resolution Embargo on Member Vastire: seventeen in favor, twelve against, with one involuntarily abstained (Vastire).

Each planet is pledged to deliver one cruiser class ship and four fighter class ships from their fleet to Vastirian orbit within one quarter Amicrux Year. The purpose of these ships will be to block all goods and services, nay all ships other than P.A. negotiators, in transit to Vastire. A commander chosen by Senator Shuka of Yiptae will direct the fleet.

To lift the embargo, member Vastire must demonstrate drastically improved conditions of the Olan-Har caste. The Senate has noted Vastire's grounds for complaint: the caste system is nearly 450 local years old, ordained by their gods. However, the Senate has ruled that the following must be remedied:

1.   Provide ample access to basic needs: nourishment, safe shelter, and health care.

2.   Allow freedom in housing, schooling, employment, travel, and other restrictions.

—From the transcript of Planetary Alliance session 614-6

CHAPTER ONE

"Think anyone would've noticed another dead orphan?" I asked as I dusted off the sooty stone residue.

I had nearly slipped off the edge of the crumbling roof, but Pavlar reeled me in with a sure hand. He gave me a motherly "be careful" look, then flashed a too-perfect smile for a guy like us.

He shrugged. "You might've lived. It's an even match between your head and the stone."

I peered over the edge of the building, down into the gloomy slums called Hargonla. The town withered away beneath our feet, even as the spectacular skyscrapers of downtown Ziphyr glittered to the south. This whole part of the city seemed like a relic of the past, with cobblestone roads, no motor vehicles, and people bartering what meager goods they had under tattered makeshift tents.

Pavlar yanked me away from the edge. "Darynn! You empty between the ears? They're looking for us, you know. We don't have enough plates, or chairs, for guests."

I subconsciously touched the scar behind my ear as I thought about the raid we failed to pull off in the Diterian Sector, west of here. "Not enough food either. Thanks to you."

"I get hungry. Can't help it." Pavlar was the most selfless person I'd met, maybe other than my mother, except for when it came to food. Not that there was enough for either of us—or anyone in the slums—even with us stealing and distributing from the quasi-weekly shipments.

I looked ahead. The sun, called Windoon's Star, seemed lower than it should have been. "We need to kick it into gear."

He nodded, and we continued our trek east from rooftop to rooftop, dodging crumbling smokestacks and rusted vents and sharp antennas. Any gaps too large to jump we'd bridged with a beam of metal or wood. This part of the city was like a graveyard, except the headstones were bunched too close together.

"It still hits me every time, just how bad it's gotten," Pavlar said as he stared despondently into the streets with his honey-brown eyes. The bazaar below used to be a flurry of activity, but now it hummed like a funeral service, and it smelled like neglected sewers and rotting flesh.

It was hard to see him this way—he was always so upbeat and resilient. Sometimes I wondered if my pessimistic attitude was wearing on him.

"In my humble opinion," I said, mocking a local politician with my arms open wide, "the P.A. embargo isn't working." Reflexively, I looked up to the sky, as if I would be able to see the hundreds of spaceships that formed the blockade around our planet.

The P.A. wanted to help slum-rats like Pavlar and me, since we have about the same rights as sheep, but those bureaucratic idiots didn't realize that an embargo would just mean things would get worse for the Olan-Har. If I looked hard enough, I was sure I would see someone letting out their dying breath right now in the alley below.

At least the Alliance had made some attempt to fix that problem: periodic relief shipments—like the one we were about to rob—for the Olan-Har. Unfortunately, we weren't the only ones robbing them, and it wasn't nearly enough for everyone.

After some time of hopping, tight-roping, and zig-zagging,

with Pavlar stopping every few minutes to survey the roofs around us, we finally reached the docks sector. The change from the Hargonla slums to the affluent docks was near-instant. Muddy cobblestone roads morphed into smooth, crystal-laced concrete; immaculate steel, composite, and glass buildings replaced the crumbling stone and wire; sun-collecting panels covered the roofs instead of water-logged tiles. Even the people had changed—from the dirty Olan-Har to the lively, careless bourgeoisie. A little bit farther on, water diverted from the shining green ocean into beautiful waterfalls and fountains. The stink of death was washed away by the inviting scent of a fresh ocean, and low, crashing waves created a soothing backdrop of sound to the humming vehicles below.

We jumped to the last roof before the Coastway, a broad freeway with a central magnetic railway that ran the length of the eastern seaboard. Robotic vehicles in aerodynamic teardrop shapes zipped north and south. Just beyond the Coastway lay the shining jetties of the docks, shooting out into the mint-green ocean, while a few cargo ships sailed sluggishly across the horizon in the calm, sparkling sea.

It was easy to spot Pier 19, the longest dock in view. A perimeter of dock guards, wearing the ocean green and jet black of the Ziphyr lord, surrounded it. I pointed to a group of lightly armored soldiers already loading the shipment onto the cargo hovers. "It's early."

"Mostly RF Sabs. Must be expecting a crowd," Pavlar pointed out. Even at this distance, it was clear the guards' forearms were wrapped with the ten cylinders that indicated they were armed with quick-firing, high-scatter Rapid Fire Solid Arm Blasters.

"Or they can't shoot," I countered with a quick smile.

As the last boxes, each inscribed with the symbol of the Planetary Alliance, were loaded onto the hovers, another Militia man exited the ship. This was no regular: he wore shining silver armor bearing the marks of a Captain, a glittering ring on one hand, and a short black cape with the five-pointed, ocean green shield featuring a great black shark.

A docks official whose pearl white pants and silver overcoat shaped him like a bowling pin bowed and announced something, but the Captain completely ignored him. The Captain was a monster of a man, towering over the others with broad shoulders and long arms that suggested his mother was a gorilla. Finally, after a thorough scan of the area, he responded to the official in a booming voice, though we couldn't hear the words over the whir of passing vehicles.

Pavlar grabbed my shoulder and squeezed hard. "Look at the size of that guy! I bet you this one makes it."

"You wanna take that chance? Sometimes you have the courage of a Castamere. I'll handle him if it comes down to it."

"Did you come here for a fight, or do you actually want to help people?" he asked. It wasn't the first time we'd had this argument. I grinned devilishly. Even he knew the real answer—to stick it to the Virin-leen, the ruling caste. Though I never did pass up a good fight. "Damnit Darynn. I'm calling this one."

"You know as well as I do we can't give up. Your sister won't make it to the next one."

His shoulders slumped and he sighed loudly. He had his thinking face on, where his eyes were slightly closed and his mouth was puffed out and twisted a bit. He knew his sister was wasting away a little bit more each day without the medicine.

"She won't be the only one who won't make it. Stick to the plan. No killing." He said those words every time, and I'm pretty sure our raids had never gone to plan. I'd only killed two officials—and both times I didn't have a choice. Well, maybe the second time I did, but I wasn't going to let us get caught.

"Not making any promises. If it comes down to Militia or your sister, I'm picking your sister. Besides, she's star hot. You know, maybe once she gets better I'll—"

"You'll what?" He glared at me. "You touch her, and I will break my killing rule."

"Sure." I smiled and focused on the shipment below.

The half-sphere-shaped cargo hovers formed an orderly line behind the Captain's speeder, and like metallic elephants, reached out their "trunks" and grabbed the hover in front of it. He rode with two Militia men, and each vehicle had a pilot and a guard. Each cargo hover had a huge, wire-frame box with several metallic boxes inside, each labeled in oversized text. The road that ran west from the dock was blocked from traffic and the hovers slogged their way down the street right below us, as we expected. Pavlar and I followed secretly on the rooftops.

"Last one's yours. I'll take the one before it. Clear?" I asked.

"You want *me* to follow *you* into the Dark Plaza? Do you—"

"I know my way around." *Or at least, I'm pretty sure I do.*

He nodded in agreement, though his jittery eyes and lip-chewing betrayed his nervousness.

We followed the convoy for about twenty blocks, well into the gloomy slums of Hargonla. Just to the south, I could see the mushroom-shaped buildings of the Dark Plaza. *Almost go-time.*

"Weapons check," Pavlar said.

I rolled my eyes. He did this every damn time at the last minute. He tapped the back of his wrist to relay that he was waiting on me. I sighed as I unholstered my Acid Pistol, loaded with ten casings and a superacid vial. Then I unsheathed my father's custom Plasma Edge, which resembled a sword riddled with bullet holes. I clicked a button just below the cross-guard, sheathing the sword in cobalt blue plasma until I released the button.

My father. Every time I looked at that sword, I saw his mint green eyes in the dull steel reflection. *Why did he—*

"Hey, you there?" Pavlar asked, presenting his slightly rusted Militia Cutlass and Electron Pistol, which had a barrel that resembled a garage for matchbox cars.

There were a lot of dings in the electricity-generating wheels that spun behind the barrel. "E-Pistol looks pretty beat up," I said.

"We're gonna need more than ten casings, unless you suddenly got your grandpa's skills."

"If you're such a good shot, why don't you take the Acip, and I'll take that thing?" I held out the Acid Pistol, but he shook his head. "Ready now?"

We slid down a mangled staircase to the street, and with our backs to the cold wall, we crept up to the last cargo hover. I was just about to leap into it when Pavlar reached out and pulled me back by the shoulder. That's when I heard the sudden commotion from the front of the caravan.

"Sssssstop! Get out of the vehiclesssss. We do not wisssssh for violencccccce," boomed a raspy, chilling voice that drew out every 's' like a snake.

I knelt to look through a gap between the shabby merchant tents and hovers. The Captain held a Double Plasma Edge, each blade curved like a circle from the central handle. In front of him stood five hooded villains, armed with short daggers and spears. More approached from behind and on the rooftops.

Only one group dresses like that.

"The Nama-Da," I whispered to Pavlar. He shuddered. I guess they thought it was their turn to steal a shipment after the other Hargonla gangs already had.

"I knew this was a bad idea," he said, and for once, I felt the same way.

The Captain and lead Nama-Da were having a conversation that didn't seem to be going too well. I couldn't quite hear it aside from the Captain stating his name as Salvak, and sinister hissing from the Nama-Da. Every time it spoke, the hair on my arms bristled.

The chatter stopped, and the lead Nama-Da raised one arm in front of him. His six long fingers were bent as if he were snatching a skull. He hissed, and from his hand streamed black smoke. The smoke began to take the shape of a figure about sword's length from Captain Salvak. A skull emerged, staring directly into the eyes of the Captain, floating menacingly in the air. The soldiers behind him shrieked in fear, but Salvak did not flinch. The smoke continued to work its way down the body, crafting all of the bones and the midnight black armor of the skeleton warrior.

I looked at Pavlar in disbelief; his eyes were like saucers and his mouth was gaping. My excitement morphed into fear. I'd heard the rumors about the Nama-Da being necromancers, but to actually see the dead walk chilled my heart.

Captain Salvak replied by slashing his Edge at the undead warrior, deftly slicing off its skull with a quick flash of orange plasma. While the skull rolled towards its master, the body still stood. Captain Salvak kicked the creature in the chest, crushing its ribs with a sickening series of cracks. It did not rise.

The Nama-Da leader hissed at the Captain and then screamed sharply in its native tongue. Random blaster fire rained on the caravan. The soldiers wildly returned fire, but it was clear this battle would be brief. The sadistic light show was mesmerizing on the backdrop of the shadowy slums. The absorption shields surrounding each hover were quickly depleted. Captain Salvak brushed aside the Nama-Da who guarded the leader, then clashed in combat with the leader himself. The leader fought back with a jagged dagger, dodging the spinning orange blades while striking out like a snake.

Half of the Militia was already dead or injured. The summoned creatures were not skilled fighters, but their near-immunity to death and sheer numbers were too much for the Militia to overcome. Then I noticed the chaos had created an opening...

I pointed to the only two Nama-Da standing between us and the nearest hovers, their backs turned to us.

Pavlar cleared his throat and whispered, "Now?"

"Yeah. The trunk's been severed between the two, so you'll need to drive." He nodded, and I crept toward the unsuspecting Nama-Da with Pavlar following closely.

Once I was within arm's reach, I pulled my Plasma Edge and

held down the plasma activation button. I sliced across the black robes of both Nama-Da, feeling as much resistance as a sharp blade through silk. As soon as the bodies hit the alley floor, the robes lost their volume; the bodies *vanished.*

"I said no killing!" Pavlar said in horror.

"Nama-Da don't count. They're monsters," I replied, though the look on his face—a mix of terror and disappointment—did make me feel guilty. I shook it off and pointed to his hover.

He held his glance just a moment longer before continuing on his mission. Then I skulked toward the second-to-last hover. The pilot and guards were already dead. I pushed the bodies out, doing my best to avoid thinking about it, and snuck into the driver's seat—a blinking red light here, some digital indicators with numbers there, half of a steering wheel, and a cerulean touchscreen grid.

I glanced at Pavlar; he was pinned next to his hover by gunshots from above. I ripped out my Acip and fired a wayward shot toward the roof. The blaster rain trained on Pavlar stopped; he took advantage and hopped into the driver's seat. I shot again, which gave him just enough time to back up and zip into the alley. One more shot, then I dropped my Pistol in the seat next to me and touched my fist to the hover's touchscreen grid. I gently motioned forward; the vehicle lurched and took off into the alley. The thrill of the theft coursing through my veins, I smiled widely—almost home free.

As I turned into the alley, I peeked over my shoulder at Captain Salvak. He had killed the lead Nama-Da and was heading toward his speeder. The adrenaline in my veins pumped ever harder. I slipped into the alley and quickly caught up to Pavlar.

"The Captain's right behind me!" I yelled. One more twist and a turn and we had reached the Dark Plaza.

I slowed and glanced from the alley to the street. The overpowering darkness created by the mushroom-like rooftops made every entry and exit look exactly the same. *Which one is the way back?* Aimlessly, I spun the hover in circles. Windoon's Star was completely hidden. Panic crept in.

Pavlar moved up alongside me. "What in Josar's name are you doing?"

"I don't remember the way!"

"Pick one!" he urged.

With that encouragement, I recklessly rocketed into the alleyway in front of me. It narrowed too quickly. *This isn't right.* A solid wall seemingly materialized in front of me; I slammed on the brakes and tried to spin the hover around.

The hover slid sideways into a pile of garbage. Pavlar, who must have heard my crash, was able to stop a few feet short of my hover. He managed to get turned around, but I couldn't dig out of the garbage heap.

I frantically searched for doors nearby, but the alleyway was like a mine tunnel. The little bit of light that marked the entrance grew smaller.

Maybe we could hide here, I thought as I jumped out of my hopelessly buried hover.

Then the humming of another craft drawing near became audible. The lithe speeder stopped right behind us, effectively blocking any chance of an exit.

"Did you really think a couple slum rats could steal from the Militia?" Captain Salvak asked. His shining ring lit up much of the alley and illuminated a new addition to the scar collection on his face.

Pavlar disembarked from his hover. "Until we stepped in, the weakest Olan-Har weren't getting their share," Pavlar replied with authority.

He doesn't care what you have to say, Pavlar. He's just like all of the other bastards at the top. I inconspicuously touched the handle of my Edge.

"Survival of the fittest, kid."

"They deserve it no less than you, Captain!" Pavlar yelled. A little bit of blasphemy from my strait-laced friend. I liked it.

Good fight coming.

"My piss is purer than your tears!" Salvak smirked proudly. His torn cheek twitched as he looked at me. "Let's see what you got, kid."

I unsheathed my Edge and pulsed the cobalt blue Plasma once. Pavlar glanced at me disapprovingly.

The Captain's thin, bushy eyebrows narrowed. "A Xenon Plasma Edge! How does a ratty bastard like you come across a weapon like that?"

I grinned with pride, but then remembered that really it was my father's Edge, and I only had it because he was dead.

Pavlar interjected, "We don't wanna fight, but we desperately need the food and medicine! The Iveleen themselves couldn't stop us."

"Your friend is itching for a fight." Salvak sniffed hard, and a bit of blood trickled from his nostrils. He twirled his Edge in his left hand and rushed at me.

I caught a look of horror on Pavlar's face. Brimming with confidence, I readied my Edge.

Salvak whirled the bottom of his Edge toward my head. I easily blocked it and swung back with my plasma activated. Scarlet lightning flashed with every clash of the magnetic fields and metal of the blades. Swing, clash, flash, again and again.

Then the Captain found another gear. He mercilessly swung his blade in a furious circle towards my shoulders. I blocked every blow, but I was flagging. Sweat slickened my arms. I stepped back until I could feel the cold brick wall right behind me. He grinned ruthlessly. Salt touched my lips.

Finally picked a fight you shouldn't have, Darynn.

A foreign squealing noise suddenly filled the air, like the screaming of a metallic banshee. The Captain backed off to investigate and I used the chance to regain my breath.

Pavlar was charging the E-Pistol, his thumb mashed on the back button, the wheel spinning rapidly, generating the dreadful squeal. The Captain turned away from me and advanced on Pavlar.

This is my chance. I raised the plasma-sheathed blade high above my head with two hands and sliced down on his shoulder with all of my strength.

He dodged it with a single step to his left. I flailed wildly, slamming the tip of my blade into the stone ground. It cut deep into the stone, sending a shockwave through my shoulders.

While I was stunned, he countered by slashing the tip of his blade across my right thigh. My body jolted as the plasma ripped through my skin. I howled in pain as the muscle turned to ash. Blood streamed into the black road below like a waterfall into an abyss.

He glowered over me with a cruel smile. "Fool boy! Now, as for you!" He turned back towards Pavlar, who grimaced as he held down the button on the back of the E-Pistol's wheel. It rapidly spun up, then with a crack, lightning zapped out of the gun in a crooked bolt.

Salvak's Edge flashed bright orange as it soaked the shot into the plasma around his blade. Pavlar's face melted into terror. He desperately fired a few more shots before the Captain charged at him. Just before the Captain reached him, the squealing of the gun intensified. My eardrums tried to vibrate out of my ears.

"Shut it off!" I yelled. I covered my head with my arms and curled on the ground, hoping to shield myself from the pain, but nothing worked. The ringing only hurt more and more, overpowering the painful screams from my thigh. I looked up to see what the hell he was doing.

Light bright as a star rushed from the cracks all over the gun. The wheel broke as it continued to spin frantically, hurling the terrible light in all directions.

Pavlar dropped the gun as he screeched in pain.

On impact, it exploded.

The explosion attacked my senses; light blinded my eyes, a rolling roar quaked my eardrums, the smell of burning flesh raced into my nostrils. Horrifying screams erupted from both Pavlar and Captain Salvak, overcoming the roar of the ongoing explosion. It was so bright that, even when I closed my eyes, the veins in my eyelids were visible. Waves of electricity rolled from my toes to my brain. For a moment, my heart stopped.

After several long seconds the light finally subsided, the incessant shocking finally ceased, and my heart continued to beat, but slowly.

Pavlar wasn't moving.

I killed him.

Plasma blades rely on the power of plasma to provide exceptional cutting power, resulting in what's considered the superior weapon in the P.A. Plasma blade varieties include: Plasma Edges, Lances, Daggers, and others.

While designs vary, all Plasma blades have these characteristics:

1. Reaction chamber built into the handle, beneath the blade

2. Magnetic field generator above the reaction chamber

3. Metal blade with vents to leak the plasma in a sheath around the blade

The density and color of the plasma are determined by the base element.

The plasma is activated by a button or switch usually located on the handle. On activation, the reaction chamber phase changes the element to plasma and passes it through the vents in the blade. The magnetic field, also activated by the button, holds the plasma in a shape generally matching that of the blade.

—From *Shard Training Manual, Plasma blades*

CHAPTER TWO

I scrambled to Pavlar's body, ignoring the painful vice my whole body was trapped in. I first stumbled over Salvak's body. His skin had fried to the armor, like egg residue on a frying pan. His body twitched like a dead cockroach. Even his ring had lost its luster. *Iveleen, let Pavlar look better,* I prayed. But I already knew it would be worse. Blood and tears mixed over my eyes.

His skin was pale, transparent, every vein in his face protruding from the skin of his cheeks. His skull bled through his pelt. His russet eyes showed no signs of life as blood dripped from their corners. His brown hair had turned black, singed as if roasted over an open fire. Electricity still traveled in waves from his feet to his head.

"Pavlar! Pavlar!" I shouted, shaking his body mercilessly. Some part of me was still searching for a shred of hope. "You have a lot more people to save." Tears rolled down my cheek, dripping onto his lifeless body.

"Iveleen, why? This is Your fault! What do You want from me?" I stared at the lightless, remorseless sky. Any faith I had left in the gods was slipping through my fingers like fine sand.

But what else do you do when someone dies? I prayed. "Iveleen, please take my friend into your arms. He had as good a heart as any Virin-leen. Have mercy!"

I had done my best to ignore the slice in my leg but now it

was becoming too much to bear. I hobbled to the hover and rummaged through one of the supply boxes. As I had hoped, I found yellow roots from a Malair bush and bandages. I squeezed the honey-like liquid from the roots and applied it to the wound. Within seconds I could already feel cool, soothing relief. I finished by wrapping it in the bandages.

There were other medicines and equipment in the box, but what was the point if it couldn't help Pavlar? *Never enough, or never what you need.* I scoured through my memories of soldier training, back before my family's fall, but the first aid training was limited.

Utter hopelessness expanded through the alleyway. *What do I do? Who can help me?* A shadow of uncertainty lingered on the horizon, feeding off of my fear. Pavlar would want me to deliver the shipment, but all I could think about was getting him out of there.

I tried to heave his body over my shoulder. It crackled with every movement, like bacon in a skillet. His arms and legs swung freely as if they weren't connected. After only a few steps, I tumbled over, nearly falling on him. His terrified expression had not changed.

Maybe I could use the hovers? I attempted to start one— nothing. The shock had ruined them, too.

I hugged Pavlar's body and pushed his eyes closed with two fingers on my right hand. I took his necklace—a small, worthless icon attached to a rope—and his cutlass. I sobbed uncontrollably while some part of me urged to get moving. *When was the last time I cried? When Mother died?*

Something shuffled in the distance—thieves. *Let them come.*

The faces of Pavlar's family floated into my mind, like phantoms drifting through walls. His poor, sweet mother, his hard-working father, his kind, wise sister...

Suddenly, I knew what I had to do. I fumbled through the supply box again. *What kind of herb did Pavlar say his sister needed? Maroon, star-shaped. Khalil tree leaves.* I tossed medicines out of the box carelessly until I finally found a clear plastic package filled with the maroon leaves. If I could not save Pavlar, I would at least save his sister.

I looked over my shoulder one more time at Pavlar. I mouthed "Good-bye," and then hobbled out of the alley. I limped to the center of the Dark Plaza and spun in a slow circle. I still didn't know my way out and it was even darker now. I picked an alley at random and started towards it.

The thieves circled like hyenas.

"Boy, drop them weapons now, and anythin' else ya got there," said a gruff voice creeping up behind me. I didn't respond and kept walking. "I'm not playin', boy," said the thief, pushing the barrel of a gun into my back.

Just shoot me! Do it! Instead, I mumbled, "Leave me alone."

He nudged me even harder between my shoulder blades. "Last chance."

Reluctantly, I dropped Pavlar's cutlass, hoping it would satisfy him. I had taken just one step when he said, "I want that one."

"Then have it!" I whirled around and plunged the plasma-activated Edge into his chest until it came out his back. His alien beady eyes changed from pitch black to white, his tubular mouth slumped, and his grass-green body slunk heavily to the ground. The other shadows shrunk back. I slid my bloody Edge out of his body and swung it wildly, flinging jade blood towards the shadows.

"Who's next?" I yelled.

The shadows trembled but didn't follow me as I wandered away. I felt almost disappointed.

"Sorry Pavlar," I whispered as I looked over the dead alien. *Not even an hour and I broke his rule.*

I sighed and continued my directionless trek until somehow I found my way back to neutral Hargonla, where Pavlar's family lived. I must have hobbled many miles, but I felt like Pavlar was still so close. Much to the surprise of his family, I barged into their house and plopped on their dilapidated couch.

Just me. No Pavlar. They knew that something happened to him. Their worried eyes begged me to tell them what it was.

I killed him. Then the world faded.

"Ouch!" Perspiration soaked through every pore, and I felt the sudden vulnerability of nakedness. A wrinkled face with half a pair of glasses was tending to the wound on my thigh. I jumped up from the bed but immediately crumpled to the ground—like my leg was disconnected from my brain.

"You're safe, kid. You're in the Solia house."

I took a good look around—a second mismatched bed, a shabby dresser missing drawers and drawer handles, a wobbly table between the beds, and endless newspaper scraps on the walls. I was in Pavlar's bed.

Imposter! A wave of sickness bubbled up from my stomach. If I'd had even an ounce of strength, I would've vaulted through the window.

Pavlar's father, Makaro, walked into the room and stared at me with his large, deeply set eyes. He stroked the rough stubble covering his neck and opened his overly large lips to speak, but said nothing. I'd never known him to be at a loss for words.

With one hand I rubbed both of my eyes, then tried to answer the unspoken question. "We...we were..." I choked.

"You were on another damned raid. Where is he?" His body, shaped like a barrel of ale, trembled violently. He was trying to hold it together, but I could plainly see the hopelessness on his face.

"He's dead, he's dead!" a voice shrieked from behind my ears. I stared at Makaro stupidly for too long. I choked out a few grunts, and tears flooded my eyes.

"He...he didn't make it," I stammered.

"Didn't make what?"

Please don't make me spell it out for you. "The E-Pistol. It exploded in his hand. I'm sorry."

Makaro erupted. "What was he shooting at? You and your damned schemes!" He grabbed the night table and effortlessly swung it across the room. It splintered against the wall. The doctor scurried out, and Pavlar's mother, Lia, came in, followed by Pavlar's sister, Fyra, who leaned heavily on the door frame.

"It was Pavlar's idea..." *Why did I say that?*

"You...you bastard! You killed him! This is your fault!" Lia ran wailing from the room, nearly knocking down Fyra on the way out. Makaro lifted me up by the shoulders and shook me violently. The stitches from my thigh ruptured; blood spewed onto Makaro's torn shirt and workman's pants. But I barely felt it.

"F-father!" Fyra cried weakly. Her pale face glistened with tears.

Makaro regained control and dropped me on the bed. I covered the spewing wound with my hands and pressed hard. Makaro's fists were still clenched tight, like he was holding a hatchet. Lia's cries filled the silence.

Fyra left the room and quickly the doctor reappeared. "Are you trying to kill the boy, Makaro?" He rushed over and set to work on the wound again. With every poke and prod, a sharp pain raced through my nerves.

"I should kill him! It should've been you! I told him you were cursed. I told him. Not my boy. Not my boy—" And with that, the anger subsided, and tears suddenly flowed over his oversized nose, mouth, and broad chin.

He was right. *It should've been me.* Wooziness set in from the blood loss.

"The Iveleen cursed me. It's Their fault, not mine!"

His eyes reflexively looked up to the ceiling, but quickly he turned back to me, and to anger. "You're the fighter. If he was gonna shoot someone, it was because of you!"

"I had to fight the Captain!"

"A Captain!" He slammed a fist on the wall. "You're trash! Fighting a Captain?"

My cheeks were hot with rage. "I almost beat him!"

"You killed Pavlar!"

It felt like a beehive dropped on my heart. Pavlar's shrill scream played over and over again, piercing my heart with the tiniest needles with each playback. I covered my ears desperately, but the screams kept playing. *I killed him. I killed him!*

Fyra reemerged in the doorway, leaning heavily against one side, her hand tightly grasping the frame. Then I remembered.

"I saved your daughter. Doctor, check my pockets."

The doctor found my pants crumpled on the floor and removed the maroon Khalil leaves from my pocket. He removed one from the package, rubbed it between his fingers, and sniffed.

"A potion made from these leaves will cure your daughter's sickness," he remarked matter-of-factly. Makaro was motionless again.

"We saved her. That was why we went on the raids. To save her, to save everyone." I looked at Fyra; she had always been slender, but the sickness had wasted her away.

The doctor walked to the doorway and helped Fyra back into the main room. I spotted my Plasma Edge on the floor and used it like a crutch to take the weight off my injured leg.

"He was my brother, Makaro. I'm sorry."

He said nothing and looked through the wreckage of the night table. He picked up a small pouch and handed it to me. "Just get out. Don't come back."

I put the pouch in my pocket, got dressed, and painfully hobbled out of the room.

In the main room, Lia sobbed uncontrollably on the threadbare couch, her tears soaking her cornflower blue dress, Fyra's head in her lap. She unconsciously stroked Fyra's straight, platinum white hair. The doctor was working the

Khalil leaves with a mortar and pestle.

"Where is my son, has anyone seen my son? Where has Pavlar gone?" Lia cried, over and over again. Her anguish is something that can never be forgotten, entirely indescribable; the words rang out in uneven tones, sometimes reaching unbearable pitches. It was like a torch held to my ears, the cinders leaping into my brain, searing every synapse.

I made my way to the front door and glanced over my shoulder. The doctor had finished grinding the medicine and was helping Fyra take it. Her small lips curled as she took the apparently vile potion, but the doctor forced it all down.

I hope it works. I reached my hand into my other pocket and left Pavlar's necklace on a three-legged console table, then stepped outside. A few rays of sunlight snuck through the cloudy gloom into the lifeless streets of Hargonla.

Where do I go? The apartment seemed unbearable. Maybe drown my sorrows at a bar? *No money.* I heard rustling inside— Makaro's eyes peered through the clear plastic window. Something compelled me to just start walking, and I found myself hobbling in the opposite direction of the apartment.

"Get off the streets," Pavlar's voice said in my head. Even dead, he was still taking care of me. But he was the person I went to for advice, and now I didn't know where to go without him. I'll take my chances on the streets.

I passed a starving family on the curb, a mother and two small children. Their emaciated bodies were laying on the sidewalk, looking up lifelessly at the sky. Pavlar would've helped them, but I have nothing. He was going to change the world someday, and he was only getting better at it. He had all of the ambition, the good intentions. Not me. Makaro's voice echoed in my head. *It should've been you!*

The glare of Windoon's Star reflected off a muddy puddle in the road. I looked directly into the star, challenging the god that it was named after, and all eleven others.

Nearby, I heard the chants of a wandering preacher,

encouraging everyone to find hope in the Iveleen. They've taken everything I have, and They expect me to still have faith? I kicked the puddle and continued on.

Even in the middle of the day, the streets of Hargonla were lifeless. It muffled the cries of the penniless vagrants; it snatched children from their families; it hid the ruthless brigands in the shadows of its bosom. Families huddled between the crumbling walls and crawled under the sunken roofs, anything to hide from wind and rain, anything to hide from the fury of night's fiends.

On the ground level sat boxes and crates and counters covered in old foods, rotting vegetables, and brown fruits. Some of the more skilled Olan-Har sold crafts or hand-woven clothing. There was one merchant I knew who sold handcrafted weapons nearby.

I reached the central intersection, where the main roads of Hargonla that run north to south and east to west meet. I stared listlessly in each direction but found none of them to be welcoming. *Nowhere for a cursed bastard like me.*

A young girl bumped into me from behind, knocking both of us off our feet. I winced as pain shot up my leg. I looked into the familiar face of the girl, about the age of nine, with hazel eyes, a pelt of unkempt blonde hair, and exceptionally large ears. She jumped back up to her feet and started to run again, but a large hand grabbed her from behind.

"Girl, that ain't yours!" yelled the burly man, his oversized hand still gripping her shoulder. His shoulders were broad enough to fit the little girl's waist twice, but he was so thin that he looked molded out of clay, smashed flat.

"I'm hungry," replied the girl, with sad eyes and pouty lips.

"That's one of the few good ones I got. You know what stealin' gets ya, girl!"

"Both my pinkies are already gone!" cried the young girl, holding up one hand for him to see. As she said, she was indeed missing the pinky on each hand.

"Middle finger then, eh? You'll learn!" He dragged her over to his counter despite her stiff-legged resistance. He pulled a rusty dagger from his belt and placed it on one of her middle fingers. She cried hysterically, but no one stopped to even look. The penalties for theft had been handed down for hundreds of years in the Hargonla slums.

That doesn't make it right. If only there was enough for everyone. What's the point in raiding shipments if little girls are going to grow up without most of their fingers? I could imagine Pavlar stepping between them, offering the man exactly what he needed in exchange for the apple. *But what can I do?*

Before the merchant could bring down the dagger upon the girl's finger, I called out, much to my surprise. "Give her a break!"

I pulled myself back onto my feet, leaning heavily on my Plasma Edge.

His head swiveled toward me, an angry eye sizing me up. "D'you know how much I'd lose every day if I let little thieves like this go? My family needs to eat too."

Pavlar's spirit acted through me. "You have your apple. Let the girl go." The words felt foreign coming out of my mouth; Pavlar was speaking for me. I stood, wobbly on my own two legs, angling the bright blue blade of my Edge towards the man.

"Ha! Can you use that fancy weapon, boy? And your leg! You limped the whole way up here. Is it worth it, for this wretch?"

I noticed he, too, was missing a pinky on his left hand. "You were once like her, but only lost one finger."

He hesitated with his dagger. "My kids don't steal. I learned my lesson. It's about my kids, not me."

I hobbled over to the man as he placed the edge of the dagger back on the girl's dirty hand. With my off-hand, I grabbed the merchant's wrist. "Let the girl go."

He looked again into my eyes, saw my resolve, then his gaze wandered to my Edge. He threw my hand off of his wrist and turned, his dagger menacingly pointed towards me. In tough times, evil had grabbed our people. This is an Olan-Har: murder, theft, sin ran in his veins according to the teachings of the Iveleen. I backed away and prepared to fight.

It only took one swipe—I dodged painfully to one side and then swung at the dagger. My Edge went straight through it, like a hot blade through cheese. He stumbled backwards, looked at the remaining stub of his dagger, and retreated into the dilapidated building behind him.

"I'm not done with you yet!" I yelled. But before I could take a step, the little girl grasped my empty hand.

"Follow me!" She took a bite of the apple and tugged me into a back alley. I followed her through into a dark room of a dark building on an ever-darkening day.

"Wait here!" she said, leading me to a chair before scampering off to the front of the building. Handcrafted swords of various materials and shapes hung on the cinder block walls, each with the same craftsman's insignia on the handle. Before he even walked into the room, I knew where I was.

Silently the man shuffled in, leaning on a swirling iron cane. The last time I had seen him he was a proud man, but now he looked old and broken, like so many who suffered from the embargo. He lit a torch inside, exposing the cut copper wires that dangled from the lights and walls.

"If she brought you here, that means you've managed to get yourself in trouble again. Eh?" He lifted a wispy gray eyebrow as he massaged his bony left hand with his gaunt right. The tone of his voice mirrored his body.

I tried to smile, but I think only half my mouth responded. "Your kid, Captain Madra?"

"It is," he whispered. She ran back into the room, nearly tripping over a bevy of leaning swords. Madra's face conveyed that he was going to tell her to be careful, but no words came out. Dozens of swords and spears and lances were lying around; he wasn't selling. "The officers aren't coming to buy anymore with the embargo. Damn P.A. Just jealous, you know, of our success and our pristine planet." That was what the royals told us, anyway. He coughed. "Soon, these weapons will be all that is left of me."

"They're beautiful." Another good man teetering on the edge of death. One of the most honorable in Hargonla, though the royals disagreed.

He coughed again. "Didn't imagine going out like this. A Captain I was, a damn good one. Until that night. One dark night and whole life goes up in dust."

I'd heard the story before. He was onto a killer in the Dark Plaza, but when he skewered that killer, it turned out to be an undercover Militia Captain. The Virin-leen stuck it in him up to the guard, showing him their boundless mercy by dropping his caste to Olan-Har.

Pavlar would have known what to do to save this man and his daughter. Me? Not so much.

It was hard for me to imagine him as my sparring partner, as he had been in the past, with his muscles shrunken and his skintight to his bones. He couldn't have more than a few days left.

"Can't believe it's come to this. My child, stealing in the streets!" He finally showed a sign of life. "I didn't teach my only child honor. I was so consumed by my own fall that I was lax in raising her."

"You're a good man, Captain Madra," I said.

"Maybe, but I've been an awful father." He settled down. "I feel as if I should reward you." He easily slipped a ring off his knobby finger and placed it on the table. "You know what this is, don't you?"

I looked over the silver ring, its emblem an eight-point star, called the Alerian Star. Each point was made of a sparkling, clear jewel, while the circular center was made of a jewel that reflected a different color on the slightest change of angle. The emblem was oversized, maybe the size of a small bullet.

"Yeah," I replied. "I'm surprised they let you keep your Captain's Ring." The dead face of Captain Salvak flashed through my mind, and my leg started to hurt.

"Let me? Oh no. I hid it in the folds of her babe's blanket. The Alerian Star is a symbol of glory, given to heroes as designed by the Iveleen." My saliva turned bitter. *What glory?* He continued, "You're the hero now. Saved my daughter, saved the Olan-Har. They whisper your name in the alleys. Take the ring. Let its glimmer in the darkness remind you of honor."

I polished the ring on my shirt and placed it on my left middle finger, admiring the Captain's Ring on my hand. "Thanks, Captain Madra." I stood up and placed a hand on the weakened man's shoulder, then looked at his daughter. "What about her?"

"My brother is going to take care of her." Madra smiled and removed my hand. His fingers felt like cold talons on my skin.

"Darynn, times are tough, and the people need you. Even humble beginnings can lead to great triumphs."

As soon as I walked out, I took a deep breath and the familiar, grungy stench hit my nose. *Time to go home. At least for a bit.* I crossed the main east-west road of Hargonla, then took the familiar route southeast along back streets and alleyways.

Henceforth, all Vastirians will be divided into five living castes: the Virin-leen, the Elite, the Middle Caste, the Poor, and the Olan-Har. My Iveleen brethren occupy a caste above the Virin-leen, while Haskar and his Demons inhabit a caste beneath the Olan-Har.

The Virin-leen shall rule Vastire in Our Name. The Elite, under the direction of the Virin-leen, will uphold and advance civilization. The Middle shall not be restricted, but are expected to act as righteous citizens. The Poor shall perform limited tasks as befit their rank. Olan-Har will be confined to the slums, forced to live amongst their evil brethren, with only the worst of tasks to perform.

At the clergy's behest, the wicked may fall from higher castes to lower and the virtuous may rise to higher castes, though never higher than Virin-leen and never lower than Olan-Har.

—From Pavlon's Decree on the Caste System, 43 ARI

CHAPTER THREE

After a while, I reached the apartment building, which was only two or three good Minotaur punches from tumbling into a heap of rubble. I leaned on the wall to hold myself up, and its aquamarine paint flaked off in my hand. The cheap materials of the twisted staircase creaked and cracked under my weight. I forced myself through the thin door.

My body seemed to double in weight every minute I stood in that room. My leg roared in pain—too much walking. I sat down on a box that doubled as a chair and swung my foot up on the pedestal dining table. I popped a pain pill from the pouch Makaro had given me.

Pavlar's standard-issue data pad that contained the Scriptures still sat on the table. Part of me yearned for the comfort in its digital pages, the words written directly by the goddess Cuiray. But mainly, I just wanted to smash it with my Edge.

My eyes always seemed to find their way to Pavlar's bed. Every time it felt like a bullet tearing through my heart. *What do I do now?*

I thought about what Captain Madra said. They don't need me—they need Pavlar. *So what would he do?* He would tell me I needed to rest up, and in the meantime probably work on a food drive or something. I closed my eyes and let my thoughts wander.

Captain Salvak's tanned, scarred face slipped into my vision, and I panicked. *They're going to be looking for his killer. If anything could be traced to me...Pavlar's body was still there. That'll lead them here!*

I scrambled to my footlocker, but it was basically empty. I switched my blood-soaked shirt out for a loose, forest green button-down. *It didn't used to be so loose.* I didn't have any other pants. I crawled up to the head of my bed and looked in a shoebox I kept there. There were only two things in it—a thumb-size hologram of my mother and father, and my mother's Golden Spiral. The hologram pictured them just before I was born, happy and carefree at home.

I stared at my father's face: short brown beard, strong cheekbones, deep-set, ocean green eyes, short, wavy brown hair. He looked so plain; no one would guess that he was basically a warrior spy that worked for the Shard, the intergalactic intelligence agency on Vastire—except for that Plasma Edge that hung at his side, and his muscular build. People always told me I looked a lot like him, but I never saw it as a round faced-kid with wavy hair below my ears. *Not so round-faced anymore.*

The Golden Spiral was the only thing I had left from my mother. She was plainly pretty, with black hair, blue eyes, and a warm smile. I seemed to have inherited nothing from her physically. I held the uncoiled spiral in my palm, then pushed it together into a sphere, and then uncoiled it again.

"The uncoiled spiral represents the chaos that existed before the descent of the Iveleen, whereas the sphere shows how the Iveleen used their divine power to organize us into a civilization," echoed the local priest's voice in my head.

I nearly crushed it in my hand. My mom encouraged me to always rely on Them, but that became so much harder after she died of a common illness in Hargonla. Neither she nor my father even had graves. I stuffed the Golden Spiral as deep into my pocket as I could, hoping it would bring good luck for once.

Next, I looked in Pavlar's footlocker. Empty, aside from his broken Acid Pistol.

My stomach rumbled. We didn't have a kitchen, but we did have a pantry next to the table. Most of the food packages were nothing but crumbs. A hollow smile slipped across my lips as I remembered Pavlar's annoying habit of leaving empty containers in the pantry instead of throwing them away.

Another growl from my stomach chased away the smile. I found a nearly empty package of crackers, along with some assorted nuts. Not much of a meal, but enough to keep me going. Ironic that we were the ones who always stole the food, but never had any ourselves. Pavlar never let us keep more than a day's worth, even though I did manage to sneak some extra every now and then.

I poured the nuts onto the table and laid out the crackers. I tried to make the meal last as long as possible and saved my favorite, the spicy Mulvorn nuts, for last. *Okay, gotta go.* I looked over my shoulder one more time as a depressing sense of finality came over me. The door clicked ominously behind me.

When I hit the ground, I turned my head left to right. *Which way?* Probably back to the docks. I could stow away on a ship, maybe to the southern countries, or maybe the wild land of Erodia to the east.

But when my head swiveled back deeper into Hargonla, I wondered if the medicine had worked for Fyra. The sun was starting to set, so it had been maybe twelve hours since she had taken a dose. The darkness spurred a new thought—*where am I going to sleep?* Not in the apartment, not at the Solias. Only one place left. Reluctantly, I headed west, toward the Hargonla Chapel. Just this one time, I would trade a lecture for a bed to sleep in.

I didn't bother going through the front doors of the chapel— the beds were in a separate building in the back. Maybe just this once, Father Ckoost wouldn't see me.

I slipped in through the transom window into the cold stone basement. Fresh citrus incense wafted from the main chamber above. Luckily the beds—really just mats of straw—weren't taken yet. I dropped down on the bed furthest from the door and fell asleep quickly.

"Darynn Mark, you know the procedure for getting a bed!"

I reluctantly opened my eyes—daylight streamed in, so Father Ckoost had actually let me sleep through the night. "I had to turn someone away because of you!"

"Sorry, Father."

"I distinctly remember telling you you couldn't sleep here anymore. Didn't you swindle your way into an apartment anyway?" I looked straight into his turquoise eyes, and he immediately sensed the pain. "What happened?"

"Pavlar's...gone," I choked.

"May the Iveleen take him up in their arms. I'm sorry my boy." He placed a wrinkled hand softly on my shoulder. "You were raiding the shipment, weren't you? Did you kill that Captain?"

"News travels fast. Technically, Pavlar did."

"They came by today, saying they were looking for an Olan-Har boy, about sixteen. Don't worry, I didn't say anything, though I knew you were the only one who could be mixed up in something like that. I told you to trust that the Iveleen would provide."

It wasn't the first time we'd had this argument. "They should probably get on it then."

"They will, in the right time." He had so much patience—for Them, for me.

"Pavlar and I saved hundreds of your congregation. You should be thankful."

He stroked his bald head. "Pride is reserved for the royal Virin-leen, who deserve to be prideful of their pure hearts and good works; for all others, it serves merely as a device for Haskar," he said, paraphrasing the Scriptures.

The demon Haskar, the Iveleens' nemesis, was far from being a concern right now. "Whatever." I realized the pillow was wet when I lifted my head from the bed. *Tears for Pavlar.* I brushed past Father Ckoost.

He grabbed my arm and said, "If you're going to sleep here tonight, follow the procedure. Otherwise, trust in the Iveleen. They'll show you the way."

Doubt it. I shook off his arm and exited the church without so much as a glance at the interior.

My leg still throbbed, but through the tatters of my pants I could see the wound was healing. I popped another pain pill and thought of Pavlar and Fyra again. *Did the medicine work?* Makaro said don't come back, but I had to know.

It didn't take long to reach the one-story fourplex, one of many identical units in a row. I sat down on the curb across from the unit and stared at the dirty white stucco as the smell of garbage wafted up from the sewers. Pavlar and Fyra's bedroom was on the right, with a single, broken window covered by some shabby beige curtains. On the inside, the whole house was mismatched, as almost every furnishing was gathered by their father, the garbage collector. The family was almost as mismatched—the angry-at-the-world father, the submissive, optimistic mother, the extroverted son, and the introverted daughter. But they always took care of each other. Hargonla had broken so many families. Their neighbor's father indentured himself to an Elite to keep the house, while everyone on the other side starved, despite Pavlar's best efforts. And my family...

I shook my head wildly as if I could shake the thought out of my ears. *Not going there.* I stared at the house again and saw Pavlar's specter leaning in the doorframe. He glared at me with a pale face and bleeding eyes, an uneasy smile on his face. He would want me to stay, to watch over them. *I can't.* I stood and hobbled over to the bedroom window. I thought I'd be able to see through the curtains, but no luck. Lightly, I pushed one of them just out of the way; Fyra was resting peacefully on her side, facing the window, her bangs just covering her eyes. Her milky skin looked a little brighter than it had yesterday, so the medicine must be working.

I lingered longer than I meant to, but it was nice to see that maybe our last raid wasn't completely a disaster.

Her eyes fluttered open.

I backed away from the window as quickly as I could and toppled onto the ground. I tried to get away, but Fyra already stood at the window.

Fully prepared for her to call me a creep and a pervert, I preemptively said, "I was just checking on you!" She looked at me dubiously. "I just wanted to make sure Pavlar's sacrifice was for something."

She pushed her bangs out of her sapphire eyes and then rested her bare, thin arms on the windowsill. "I-I-I don't blame you, like my father does." A single tear rolled down her cheek.

"I pushed him into it. He wanted to call it off, and I pushed him. I said I could beat the Captain. He trusted me. I was supposed to protect him!"

Another tear. "That's the way he would've wanted it. Protecting you. Protecting me."

Just then, I remembered Fyra's incredible power. "Did you...did you see it?"

Then the tears started flowing in earnest, dripping heavily onto her sky-blue tunic. "I thought it was a fever dream. But actually, I...I foresaw it weeks ago. It was gruesome."

"Weeks ago? Why didn't you tell us?" Then the tears started for me. "We would've called it off."

"These visions, Darynn...I never know when they'll occur." She paused for a breath, or really it was like three mini-breaths struggling on top of each other. "It may have been this raid, or the last one, or the next one. Pavlar wouldn't have stopped, especially with my illness." She shifted uneasily.

I wanted to argue, but she was right. "Pavlar only went through with it for you."

"I know. But maybe...I should've told you. But...I would've died. Was I just being s-s-selfish?" She was choking on tears and snot and I felt the uncontrollable urge to hug her. I took her hands in mine and rubbed them gently. She let me, but only for a minute, then quickly jerked her hands away.

"You know," she said, sniffing hard, "Pavlar was named for the Iveleen Pavlon, and it couldn't be more amiss. Pavlon divided people, while Pavlar united." Somehow, I'd always missed the connection to the god Pavlon, and she was right. Pavlon was the chief designer of the caste system.

Then I realized Makaro, Pavlar, and Fyra were all named after one of the dozen Iveleen that descended from the Heavens. "Fyrain is much more fitting for you."

She shook her head. "Fyrain was the Scholar of the Iveleen. She not only knew things; she understood the world and the people in it. I couldn't even withstand more than one year of University."

"You would've, if you hadn't gotten sick." Pavlar always told me how smart she was, and I would tease him about how she seemed like the complete package. He'd slapped me, hard, more than once over similar comments. I felt a small smile on my lip.

"I had already decided to come home." She gazed into the distance as silence lingered between us. I heard Makaro's voice inside.

"Makaro will kill me if he finds me out here."

"What are you going to do next?" she asked.

"You're Fyra the Farsight, you tell me."

Her eyes narrowed under her thin platinum eyebrows, and she brushed her hair from her eyes again. "I hate that name. And you know I can only see death anyway."

"You predicted the embargo."

"Only because I knew it would kill thousands. I guess you're not dying any time soon."

"Good to know," I snapped.

"I-I-I'm sorry. I just can't believe he's gone."

"I know." Then it seemed to really set in for the first time— I was never going to see him again. Never argue with him about the Iveleen or the royals; never squabble over food; never spar in the alley; never hear him laugh. The world seemed suddenly darker, my legs felt weaker. I wanted to portray strength for Fyra. He was her *brother*. But really, he was like my brother too, the closest thing I had to family left.

Fyra drew another deep breath. "You haven't answered my question."

"I don't know. The Militia is after me, and Pavlar's gone, and my mother's gone, and...I'm cursed. I think I just need to get away."

"Pavlar would've wanted you to continue his mission. Oh, that reminds me."

As she walked away from the window, I said, "I'm not Pavlar."

Returning, she said, "You're the closest thing the Olan-har have. Pavlar wanted you to have this." She pressed a small white stone, hardly larger than the last digit of my thumb, into my hand. I turned it over between my fingers and saw that it was sculpted into the shape of an animal. An eagle's head and wings, a lion's body—a Gryphon. Mostly extinct, I think.

"One of the Olan-Har families gave that to Pavlar after he saved their daughter from a disease, I think. He would hope for you to protect the Olan-Har, like a Gryphon protecting his pride."

I shook my head.

"It may not seem possible now, but I think the Iveleen have great things in store for you. I can help."

Humble beginnings can lead to great triumphs. "You're

wrong. Pavlar was the visionary. I'm just a dumb kid looking for a fight." She was at a loss for words. I stuffed the stone Gryphon in my pocket. "I'm glad you're feeling better. Goodbye, Fyra."

I turned away, though I still didn't know where to go. I let my legs lead me.

I glanced over my shoulder, viewing Fyra through my glassy eyes. Sad and yet beautiful. I turned back and kept going. Alone.

The Windoon system only contains five planets: Ignis, Vastire, Yindia, Yiptae, and Khaleri. But in a cosmic improbability, four of those planets are inhabited by sentient races.

Ignis, the largest planet in the system, is a hot, gaseous planet that cannot support life.

Vastire, by many standards, is considered a perfect planet, with an even climate, lush vegetation, and expansive oceans.

Yindia, the second-largest planet, is marred by large swaths of uninhabitable desert and ice.

Yiptae is hardly more substantial than a large moon, with below-freezing temperatures over its entire surface. Yet, the small planet left the Yiptaens yearning for more, and they were the first to interplanetary spaceflight.

Khaleri, though farther from the star than Yiptae, possesses an atmosphere that traps heat phenomenally well.

—Excerpt from *An Introduction to Planetary Alliance Planets: Windoon System*

Chapter Four

Fyra said she would help me. I had a chance to avoid this lonesome journey to nowhere, but it was just too dangerous. The Iveleen had forsaken me to a lonely life.

I pulled Pavlar's Gryphon out of my pocket. *Freedom.* I felt a new determination well up in me. They wanted to crush me by taking away all I love. *I will succeed, despite Them.* I will get away from the cruel gods and make something of myself yet.

Night was falling on the city. Everyone rushed into their makeshift homes; the unlit streets were not safe at night. Torches were extinguished, leaving the faint scent of burning candles in the air. At least I knew the Militia wouldn't be looking for me—they were too cowardly to patrol this den of shadowy thieves. As the night grew darker, the Alerian Star on the Captain's Ring grew brighter, giving me the slightest bit of confidence.

After a short while, I realized that I was moving aimlessly west, instead of east, toward the docks. *Why west?* I had that empty feeling that I'd felt only twice before—when my mother and I were first sent to Hargonla, and after she died. I used to have a purpose—become a Shard agent just like my father, then keep my mother alive, and more recently to protect Pavlar on the raids. Now those were all gone. The only things I knew how to do were steal and pick fights.

When I looked up, I found myself in the Courtyard of the Broken Statue, an empty place even in the day. The blood-stained charcoal bricks served as reminders of the terrible Barma Massacre that occurred nearly fifteen years ago. The whole place was supposedly haunted, but I wasn't afraid of ghosts when I had real dangers to worry about.

"Damnit!" I yelled as I strayed too far from the path into a bramble bush that had taken over the garden. I tore a thorn out of my arm and looked up to the Broken Statue in the middle of the courtyard. I felt like the statue was telling me the story of the massacre when the rival Diterian family had ambushed the Barmas. The Iveleen showed them no mercy, just like me, even though the Barmas tended to the weak and sick of the Olan-Har.

I guess the statue had been beautiful once, but now it was worn and withered. The head was really just a thin sliver of rock shooting up from the neck straight to the left eye. The hazel eye was lifelike, tinged with flecks of white. The statue was commemorated the day of the ambush, a memorial to Gond Barma, the great healer. Now it oversaw a lifeless courtyard that somehow still smelled like death.

Something howled from one of the buildings. The old soup kitchen on the corner? Was it a man, or an animal, or...

"Come out! I dare you!" I pulled out my Edge and flashed the blue plasma just once. No response. I stood completely still, itching to fight something, anything.

Soft footsteps echoed behind me. Inconspicuously, I took a few steps, then whipped around, brandishing my Plasma Edge.

A woman stood there, wearing a transparent veil over her face and a foreign red suit of armor, tight enough to reveal her slender yet muscular body. I examined the maroon framed armor closely—only three vulnerabilities: her hands, her arms under the shoulder pauldrons, and above the collarbone. *Not Vastirian armor.*

She was sizing me up too, but even though she approached

me, she seemed somehow surprised. Then, in a single fluid motion, she slipped two thin rapiers from the cuisses covering her thighs. They glowed with a faint white light suggesting untinted sunlight, not the familiar glow of a plasma weapon. *Definitely not a Vastirian weapon.*

I tried to get into my balanced stance, my Edge held at an angle directly above my right leg, but my left leg whimpered in pain. I couldn't let her see me favoring it, but I didn't have much choice. She bent her knees and pointed both rapiers at me.

"What do you want?"

"You," she said confidently.

"Not today." I didn't wait for her to respond. I charged and tried to knock the rapier out of her lower hand—no luck. I tried a backhanded swing into her chest, but she easily deflected it with the upper rapier.

I continued my aggressive attack, timing my plasma pulses with expected hits. But she blocked each one while barely moving her feet.

Then she swept my feet out from underneath me, and I landed on the hard cobblestone.

I took a wild swing at her feet, but she backflipped high into the air and landed gracefully on the shoulder of the Broken Statue.

"Your technique is wild," she said. "I expected more, with your father and all."

I jumped up to my feet. "You don't know me!"

She didn't respond, fueling my anger. I leapt onto a nearby stone post and propelled myself with my good leg up toward the statue. I swung at her head, but she ducked.

She grabbed me with a free hand (how did she have a free hand?) and tossed me to the ground on the other side. I rolled, then bounced up and spun. She was right there, waiting for me. I could feel sweat mixing with dirt on my cheeks, but she looked like she had exerted no effort at all.

Before I could plan another attack, I heard the low whir of

an approaching vehicle. *A spaceship?* Two spear-wielding men dropped from the disc-shaped ship, which was imperceptible until it was nearly upon me.

"We are not your enemy. Come with us," she insisted. Her voice plainly told me that she was foreign: she rolled her 'r's and stressed the last syllable of "enemy" more than a Vastirian would.

"I don't take orders well."

"So be it." She motioned the two men over.

They stabbed at me with their spears, like I was a cornered animal. Despite my fatigue, I could feel my adrenaline rush as the taste of the oncoming battle filled my mouth. They were nothing compared to the woman. I stole a glance at her to see her casually leaning on one of her rapiers, studying me.

I allowed the two men to attack me as my eyes darted from one to the other. Hard armor as black as night obscured them in the darkness, but their cropped blonde hair acted as beacons to track. Though they fought side-by-side in the narrow pathway, I slipped between them and landed a strong kick. He crashed through the open window of the building behind him, tossing up a cloud of dust.

The remaining one backed away quickly until he was under the center of the hovering ship. Sensing a trap, I stopped just short of the edge of the ship.

"That's enough. You will come with us," the woman reiterated. I didn't realize just how close she was until she spoke; I turned just in time to see a net of deep purple energy rush from her open hand. The heavy threads of light forced me to the ground; the more I struggled, the tighter the net enclosed around me.

"Rest for now; there is much to discuss." She motioned her gloved hands downward.

My eyelids followed the motion, and suddenly, I was asleep.

I opened my eyes and something just felt...off. I was...floating? I flailed my arms and legs as I tried to find my bearings. I grabbed onto the nearest thing—the side of a bed. I was bombarded by a monotony of dull silver. The walls, the doors, the ceiling, and even the bed of this chamber were colored with the same boring gray, only broken by a black line where two plates met. There was no smell.

Floating, nothing holding me down or pulling me to the ground—*I'm in space!* My joy was only tempered by my mysterious surroundings.

That woman. A mercenary, maybe? Collecting my bounty? But then they wouldn't have brought me onto a spaceship. *So who caught me?*

I pushed off the wall and glided to the door, which of course was locked. There was an intercom next to the door and I held the round button below it. "I didn't kill the Captain. It was an accident. Let me go!"

I turned away from the door and realized there was a window behind me. I tried to swim over to it, but just kind of waved around. I stretched out and pushed off the door. Through the heavily tinted window, the sparkling, mint-green ocean and moss-green land of Vastire dominated the view. *I'm in space.* I gazed longingly at the awesome, huge planet, and I felt the anxiety of capture wash away. I tried to pick out home, but it looked like we were over the west coast of the mountainous, jungle-covered Erodia. I pressed my face against the glass for a better look.

I heard the door behind me.

Through it came the same woman from before, still dressed in her red armor, but no veil. She wasn't much older than me, maybe mid-twenties, and she was ostensibly not as delicate as some women appeared. Though her features were hard and stern, she was still quite beautiful. Her feet were stuck firmly to the floor.

"Who are you?" I asked. "What do you want from me?"

"I am Kaylaa Reesae, an ambassador for Senator Shuka of the planet Yiptae." So her accent was now explained. *Yiptae? Fourth planet from Windoon's Star. What is she doing here?*

"I guess you already know who I am."

"Darynn Mark, son of Zilpohn Mark, Shard and traitor." She spoke as if giving a report. "You look exactly like him."

I'd heard that my entire life, every time I met someone for the first time. "So how'd you get through?"

"Good pilot, better ship." She paused. "You'll be our dinner guest tonight." The way she looked at me, like a soldier examining a new weapon, made me very uncomfortable.

"Dinner with a prisoner?"

"A prisoner wouldn't have his weapon." Without any further explanation, she walked away.

She was right—my Edge was strapped down next to the bed. I picked it up and allowed her to lead me into a slightly curved corridor, again composed of the same gray metal. "There are Magna Boots there on the floor, if you don't want to float." I looked at the boots, which looked like normal brown boots except for the thick, flat soles. *Much more fun to float.*

We took an immediate right out of my room, and then a left into a straight central corridor.

Directly in front of me was a dark mahogany door marked "Captain's Quarters." We passed it and a few other hatches, all closed, much to my dismay. I had loved spaceships ever since I was young, and for the first time, I was actually on one! Under different circumstances, this would've been the adventure of a lifetime.

We reached our destination within just a minute or two. Inside was a small metallic bar with a pair of wooden stools and a rectangular dining table covered with a velvet cloth—all bolted to the floor. Eight chairs, also covered with velvet, surrounded the table. The woman stood at one end of the table and motioned for me to stand to her right, behind another chair. Across from me stood the two men with spears, still in their armor. An older, fleshy man walked in and stood next to me, wearing an old-fashioned pair of goggles around his bulbous neck along with a pair of dog tags.

I started to position myself in the chair, but Kaylaa forcefully grabbed my wrist and pulled me back up. We must have been waiting on someone more important.

A blue-skinned man in a long gray robe swirled with deep purple strutted in. He stood at the head of the table and stared relentlessly at me with silver eyes, but no eyebrows. The oversized sleeves of his robe wiped the table as he motioned for everyone to sit with his meaty hands.

As I twisted myself into the chair, someone else came into the room—a metallic monster, covered in soot-colored armor from head to toe. That armor, that helmet, with the onyx, overlapping triangles making up the visor—a Slicer. I kept my hand on my Edge. *How do I fight without my feet on the ground?*

The blue-skinned man, who could only be Yiptaen based on his skin color, rapped his knuckles on the table. "Dumbfounded," he said in a booming voice. He let the word hang uncomfortably in the air, and when the time was ripe, he continued. "That would best describe how you're feeling?" His arrogance dripped from the sides of his mouth; I already didn't like him.

"What?"

"I will explain in due time. But first, introductions. I am Senator Shuka, the chief representative of the planet Yiptae in the Planetary Alliance Senate," he said. He carefully selected which syllables he stressed, while precisely enunciating each word in perfect P.A. Standard. "I know that you are Darynn Mark, sixteen-year-old son of Zilpohn, grandson of Gallant."

I shifted in my chair. He wasn't royalty, but he was close.

"You have met my first bodyguard, Kaylaa Reesae of Yiptae. My second stands behind me, Nova Karr of Wicetlin."

"Nova Karr? The serial killer who pretends to be a bounty

hunter?" My father had tried to arrest the bloodthirsty vampire more than once but just couldn't catch him. "Just what kind of business are you in, Shuka?"

"Senator Shuka, child. Allow me to finish. That is our pilot, Bolar." He sat back and rested his perfectly-shaven head against his obnoxiously tall purple collar. His gem-studded chain betrayed his hidden belly under his flowing robes.

"Can you get to the point?"

He clenched his angular jaw and said, "Patience. I merely have a proposition for you. But first, some background." I sighed audibly. "I voted against the embargo, and this trip has only proved that I was absolutely right. Your people are suffering, the very people we were trying to protect."

"Yeah—your embargo killed my mother and best friend."

"Not my embargo. You need to listen to me if we are going to come to an understanding." He rolled up his sleeves, revealing completely hairless arms.

"An understanding about what?"

"I know much about you, Darynn Mark. I know you have been helping the Olan-Har. Your father, and his untimely end, are also well known in the P.A."

"Will you stop bringing up my father? I'm not like him!" I said. For the first time, I saw Nova Karr shift—the light reflected off his visor like he had hyena eyes, hunting at night.

"You're lying to your heart," the Senator said. "Your father was a leader of men, and you can be too. You even look like him, save the hollowed cheeks and scrawny arms."

I shook my head. "He was a traitor and a madman. I am Olan-Har because of him! It's all his fault!" My hand instinctively covered my Olan-Har tattoo, a red disc with a black sliver on either side.

"Where is the justice in that? A man can pay for his father's, his grandfather's sins, and even further back. There is nothing differentiating a Poor from an Olan-Har, an Elite from a Middle."

"The Iveleen teach that good people will raise their caste, while wicked blood leads to wicked acts. Pavlon of the Iveleen said, 'The corruption flows freely through the generations until it is cleansed.'" *Why am I sticking up for the Iveleen?* Even Pavlar, a fierce believer in the Iveleen, thought the caste system as it stood today was wrong.

"But the Virin-leen and the clergy, the people in power, get to make that decision. Caste-raising ceremonies are exceedingly rare; I looked into it."

I slammed one hand on the table. "Stop acting like you know about Vastire. A search on the DataAxis and you think you're an expert. You're all just jealous!"

A reddish tint rushed into his cheeks. "Jealous? Vastirians think they're so great when all they've ever done is steal tech from the other Planets! Do you think I would be here, risking my life and career, if I didn't know what I was here for? Do you think me a fool?"

"You're the one who hired a bounty hunter and picked up street trash."

He glared at me, but before he could speak, someone else barged into the room. She nearly crashed into Nova Karr, her hands and arms precariously guiding floating, covered plates.

"Oh Deus, Nova, you almost made me turn over all this food!" she said, a navy blue bob bouncing up and down on her head.

She placed a plate in front of Senator Shuka and pushed on the edges to attach it to the table.

"Peylee, our cook," the Senator said with a sigh.

She bowed, swinging her hefty breasts nearly into her remaining plates. "Best ship cook in the P.A., if I do say so!" She smiled a huge, buck-toothed smile and set about putting the rest of the plates in front of us. "I whipped up some erlock etouffee over a bed of rice. Took me some time to get that erlock tender enough! Feels like I spent all day just beating it with a tenderizer! And the rice, whoo-eee, that took much longer to boil than usual. I hope it's not too gummee for you!"

I wondered what erlock and etouffee were, but didn't dare ask.

"That will be enough Peylee. Thank you," said Senator Shuka, apparently trying to cut her short.

"Well you all are going to be needing something to wash it down with, now aren't you? I figured water would do, but we have some wine back there and I thought maybe you might want to share some. This is an occasion, isn't it?" Every word she spoke that ended with an "e" sound made me cringe.

"Water will do, Peylee. Wine would likely upset our guest's empty stomach."

I wanted to object, but he was probably right.

"Water it is then! Don't start without mee." She barged back out into the hallway. I'm not sure I had ever seen a woman with so little grace.

"Don't mind Peylee. I think she feels like she has to talk a lot to justify such a large mouth," Shuka said. "You must be starving, so eat, and we'll continue our conversation later."

Eagerly I removed the lid from my food and let it float away. Steam rushed into my face as well as a variety of smells and spices that could easily clear up any sinuses. The etouffee looked like a kind of gravy, except in a reddish-orange color, with chunks of white meat spread throughout. The etouffee smothered a bed of white rice, and on the side was a piece of crisp white bread with yellow crust. All of it was floating a bit off the plate. My stomach growled so loud that the entire table could hear.

Peylee made her presence known as soon as she returned to the room, this time with a tray covered by eight plain, metallic cups, each with lids. "Water for all! Bolar, I got you no ice, just like you like it, hun. Oh Heavens, I didn't ask our guest. Mr. Mark, would you like ice?"

"Whatever you have for me is fine, thanks." I can't remember the last time I actually had ice and fresh water, so I sure hoped that was in my cup.

Peylee smiled widely. "Don't be so meek, dear! Peylee is here to serve."

"Then serve and shut your mouth," grumbled Bolar. "Can't you see the gov'ner is trying to have a conversation?"

Peylee *tsk-tsked*. "Oh, Bolar, don't be so grouchy! Don't mind me, just keep talking. And can't you ever remember? He's a senator, not a governor!"

Bolar shook his head and took a sip of his iceless water.

Peylee placed a cup in front of everyone and finally sat down at the empty spot.

The food tasted better than anything I had ever had in my life. The foreign spices awoke taste buds that had lain dormant for years. The warm etouffee slid down my throat and into my impatiently waiting belly. The erlock tasted like some sort of fish, but the thought of Peylee smashing fish to tenderize it didn't make sense.

I was so entranced by the food, I didn't even realize everyone was staring at me. I didn't really care—I couldn't remember my last proper meal. *Maybe from my mother?*

Kaylaa asked, "Do you think you're evil?"

It caught me off-guard. "I guess. I must be. No one thinks they're the bad guy, right? I killed more than a few people, and fought with all of the ruthless gangs of Hargonla."

"Blood or circumstances? Would you steal or kill if you were not hungry?" the Senator asked, before taking a bite of his dinner.

"My father killed plenty, and he was in the Elite Caste. We need the caste system to keep us together, or else we'd go back to the chaos from before the Rise of the Iveleen. You'd think, of all people, I would want to get rid of it, but—"

"Do you really believe that these Iveleen, these omnipotent deities, descended from heaven five hundred years ago? By the time your modern history began, Yiptaens had already conquered two planets!"

"What are you suggesting?"

"How can you be so naïve?" the Senator asked with a sneer.

Naïve! "You're just like all of the other royals! You think you're so damn smart with your big ideas but you know nothing of the real world!"

Bolar interjected in a voice akin to a tuba. "Sir, aren't you getting away from the point?"

Shuka took a deep breath. "You and I have the same goal. If the caste system were abolished, the embargo would be dismantled. Our troops could return home. I have relatives circling your planet in one of these ships. How we get there does not matter to me. I sought you because of your father, and I thought you may be of the same mind."

"You're wrong. My father left for a year and he came back." My mind struggled to find the right word. "Confused. Different. I'm like him before he left, not after."

"What turned your father? Where did he go?" Kaylaa asked.

"I..." I choked. "I never found out. I lost my father before he died."

"It is unfortunate, his reaction, his death. But consider the thin line between traitor and hero—had he succeeded that day, he would be revered as a hero, and you would not be considered corrupted. There is much truth to what he taught, and much honor in what he did," said the Senator. He now looked very tense, as if he were in the heat of a battle, but for a senator, a debate of words created his battle high.

"Honor? You're joking." I paused and let the sadness pass. "I'm done talking about him. Tell me why exactly you brought me here, and then let me go."

"Kaylaa found you, and lo and behold, it was you stealing from the Alliance shipments. Every action Kaylaa reported proved to me you are your father's son."

I slammed my fists on the table and pushed up out of my seat. "I am not! He was crazy, a traitor!" I shoved the last bite of dinner in my mouth and pushed for the door.

Nova Karr's imposing presence blocked the way. He unsheathed two electrically charged swords from his back— dangerous weapons, even to the wielder I held my Edge unsteadily and flashed the cobalt plasma to show I was serious. *But how the hell was I going to fight without my feet on the ground?*

Suddenly, a light started flashing and beeping obnoxiously on Bolar's uniform.

"Gotta jet, boss," Bolar said calmly, rising from the table and starting out the door. Nova Karr moved like a shadow.

"What's that mean?" I asked.

"Risk of detection. Come with me. Now," Kaylaa commanded. My heart jumped and obediently I followed her. The ship descended rapidly, forcing my body to the ceiling. I couldn't help wondering who was about to detect us...and what they would do with me if we were caught.

There are at least thirty bodies—men, women, and children. As far as we can account, every member of the Barma family is dead, though identification is difficult due to the degree of mutilation.

The Barma family was made up of a mixed heritage of Vastirian and Erodian blood, which gave them healing magic. They used it to keep the Olan-Har, including the suspected Diterians, relatively healthy. They were all gathered here, in the Courtyard, to celebrate the patriarch Gond Barma's 60th birthday. Gond especially was known as a good man, trying to overcome his grandfather's crimes of poisoning Virin-leen. He was also a hero of the Mondoon Conflict, saving hundreds if not thousands of lives.

The suspected Diterian Family mounted turrets on the rooftops surrounding the Courtyard and slaughtered the entire family with a rain of homebuilt Acid casings.

—From A Militia Report on the Barma Massacre, 485 ARI

CHAPTER FIVE

I pushed from wall to wall as fast as I could, following Kaylaa to the escape hatch. The ship didn't wait for us to disembark before it started its ascent. The last step was a long one, and I stumbled on the hard pavement of the Courtyard of the Broken Statue.

"Shouldn't you be going with them?" I asked as I dusted myself off.

"No." Kaylaa scanned our surroundings. "We are being watched. Follow me."

I looked around but didn't see anyone. "Why?"

She got so close to my face I felt the heat of her stale breath on my nose. "Are you always this difficult? You have nowhere else to go, right?"

I smirked, but I had no smart answer for her, so I reluctantly followed her into a shadowy alley adjacent to the Courtyard.

"We'll stay the night here," she said.

"It smells like garbage," I said.

"Your whole city smells like garbage," she replied, wrinkling her small nose.

"Shouldn't we keep going if we're being watched?"

"Precisely why we can't go to our destination."

"What if they attack in our sleep?"

"They'll never get a jump on me," she said, loud enough for our watcher to hear. "Besides, you slept enough on the ship."

Mockingly, I said, "Sure. I'll just stand guard tonight. Go on to sleep."

She nodded and leaned against a black stone building. She removed her gloves and fashioned a pillow out of them behind her head. Her bare hands lightly grasped her rapiers as she closed her eyes.

"I could kill you in your sleep," I quipped.

"No motive," she said without opening her eyes.

"To get rid of you."

She glared at me through the corners of her eyes. "More likely you'd run away, but I'd find you. Don't you want to know the Senator's plan?" *She's got me there.* "So just sit there like a good boy." It seemed like she fell asleep instantly, snoring faintly.

Am I a dog? I stared at her as she slept, my arms crossed. *Just what is going on here?* She seemed a lackey to that cocky Senator, but unlike the rest of the crew, she didn't completely defer to him. I felt my own eyes fighting sleep as I listened to her soft snoring.

"Hey, hey you! Hey, can you hear me?"

My eyes snapped open. *Dozed off.* In front of me knelt a small, frail man, maybe thirty years old. His face was shadowed with only the light of the Captain's Ring, but he held a yellow, electrically charged dagger in his right hand. I kept my hand near the grip of my Plasma Edge.

My eyes focused on the short, scarred blade as I slid my Edge out just enough for the blade to glint in the small light. "Back off, street beggar."

"A minute, a minute." He pulled the forest green hood off of his head. His face was thin, with a pointed chin, pointed nose, and hollow cheeks. His eyes looked eerily familiar. "I am Canfod Barma."

"The Barmas are all dead."

"So the Diterians believe. But I am the blood of Gond Barma, the war hero," he proclaimed. But the pride quickly dissipated. "I am still here, and I am...dying."

The proof of his heritage was in his eyes, almost exactly the same as the Broken Statue in shape, color, and eerie stare. He spoke with a strange, gruff accent.

"What do you want from me?"

"You can help. I cannot save myself, but I can help the Olan-Har." He gritted his teeth—or rather his gums, as most of his teeth were missing. "And somehow, I survived that...that..." He looked off like he was following a fly. "Since...I have wandered, hidden, like a roach. No one knows me, I know no one. And then I heard of you..." He smiled in such a way that the hair on the back of my neck stood up. "Darynn Mark, you, you are so strong. So powerful. And you are successful! I found a purpose, Darynn. Because of you! But the hour is late for me."

"Then let's get you to a doctor."

"Too late for me! I cannot believe this...now." He could barely stand still; his hooded cloak shivered in the darkness. "You bring joy to my heart where it did not exist, not for decades." He spoke with such admiration, it made me wonder if it went beyond just that. I smiled uneasily. "I came to give you a...shove in the right direction."

"What?" I rose to my feet and kept my hand on my Edge. Somehow, Kaylaa still slept soundly. I wished she did not.

"You were once Elite, Darynn, son of Zilpohn Mark, a great soldier. But you are not a great fighter, you have a different niche. Do you know what it is? Do you know what has protected you during the raids?"

I shook my head. *How does he know so much about me?* My heart hammered in my chest as if pounding a chisel into my ribs.

"Do you remember your Diterian raid?" He turned his head, revealing razor-sharp ears that could surely cut the straggly hair that hung precariously about them.

I covered my left pectoral with my hand, remembering the ugly scar, the Acid burn just beneath my shirt. "Yeah."

"How did you survive? How did your friend survive?"

"I...I don't know." *And he's dead now anyway.*

"I do, I do! You were not far, and I had to see you. The boy always in the Hargonla chatter." His downcast eyes suddenly lit up as he looked at my face. He started to motion like an excited curator showing great pieces of art. "When I look at you I see greatness, like my grandfather!"

I shifted my weight away from him. "What made your grandfather so great anyway? You were just as poor as the rest of us."

"We know ancient healing magic, from our Erodian ancestors." *Magic!* Even if it was taboo, it sounded fascinating. "Even the Virin-leen would come to us to be healed, when the situation was dire. 'The Olan-Har are worthless trash,' indeed!" He scratched at his Olan-Har tattoo, digging deep with his sharp fingernails.

Olan-Har literally translated to "worthless trash" in Old Vastirian, a fact we were constantly reminded of. Canfod turned to me, and his joviality turned serious. "This is my purpose...to pass it to you."

Me? I stood motionless. "Vastirians can't use magic, you know that." *But what if I could?* The ability to fling objects or set things on fire with a thought? *No, it's impossible.* Our enemies across the sea, the Erodians, can use magic. We can't.

"Ah, but you are *special*," he said. "In that raid, *your magic* saved you and your friend! You cannot control it, no, not yet, but the power is there, Darynn!"

Weakly, he took a step towards me and continued, "You were surrounded on the rooftops by the Diterians and their junkyard androids. Daringly, you jumped off the building, down four stories, into a giant trash heap. A glancing blow flashed across your chest."

That I remembered: the searing pain of the Acid casing, the fear of the fall, the cushion of the trash heap, and then the desperation when Pavlar and I were stuck. The gray-skinned, stout Diterians, in their flamboyant armor, congregated on the rooftops above us. They rained pipe bombs and Acid shots on us. I thought we were dead for sure, but Pavlar didn't lose hope. And then I blacked out.

I woke up next to two dead beggars, a bloodied Pavlar, and no Diterians. I remembered running my hands over my body to make sure I was intact and found myself soaking wet. Pavlar helped me out of the trash and we hobbled away.

"The Iveleen spared us that day, probably just to torment me later," I said.

"That wasn't it, not this time. You rose above the trash, and raised your hands high, your eyes rolled in the back of your head." He started moving erratically, talking wildly. "A sheath of fire suddenly formed above you, the bombs exploded on the sheath, and it started a chain reaction, until the bombs still in the Diterians' hands blew up in their faces!" He paused, licking his lips, savoring the moment like a juicy steak. "After the bombs stopped, the shield transformed to a disc of water; when the burning shrapnel hit the disc it changed to healing rain! I've never seen anything like it, not even from an Erodian...like Iveleen power."

Impossible! I tried to concentrate. What happened after I landed on the trash pile? But my thoughts were scattered, incomplete, like a half-finished jigsaw puzzle. Why were Pavlar and I able to walk out of there at all, while the two beggars were dead? Why weren't we followed? My scar burned painfully. "That...can't be what happened."

"That's *exactly* what happened. But that kind of release would be so chaotic, so...draining. I'm not surprised you don't remember." He coughed and doubled over. "My time grows short."

I rushed over to him and laid my hand on his bony back.

Both of his arms shot up from the ground, his fingers bolted to my shoulders. He looked at me with a crazed visage, his scraggly hair pushed forward, his eyes glowing menacingly. I frantically tried to free my shoulders, but Canfod Barma was strengthened by desperation. I tried to cry out, but no sound escaped my lips.

He began to chant something in the language the preachers use, Old Vastirian. Suddenly, a blue light appeared on his chest, over his heart, and flowed into his shoulders, through his arms, and finally into my body. It danced artfully through his body and mine; I felt like our souls were touching.

A soothing feeling swept through my body from head to toe, like cold milk over a burning tongue. The flames of pain that consumed my body, whether it was the old scar on my chest or the new one on my leg, were doused like rains falling directly from the Heavens. My mind and spirit were cleansed, every physical ache and pain faded. Even the weight of Pavlar's death lifted. My heart seemed to be mended ever so gently, deft hands sewing it together with strings of lotion. Then the blue light disappeared from Canfod's heart and surrounded mine. Canfod fell to one knee.

"You are awakened, Darynn Mark. Now, you can use it to save this world," he choked. "Darynn..." Then his body dropped to the ground like a mortar shell.

I shook him with strength I hadn't felt in years, but there was no life left in him. It dawned on me that I witnessed the end of the Barma family. I heaved his light body on my shoulder like a rolled blanket and carried him to the Broken Statue of his grandfather. I picked the best-looking of the four gardens and used my Plasma Edge to dig a hole just large enough for Canfod's body. I covered it with dirt and looked to the stars above. Mechanically, I said the last words said at any funeral: "May the Iveleen preserve his soul."

Something is different. Not just the newfound stamina, but something else...deeper inside, something stronger, but not altogether new. *Was he right?* I looked at the nearest bramble bush, held out my hand, and thought about the biggest, hottest flame I could imagine.

Nothing happened. *I guess he was just crazy after all.* But the healing was no joke. How did we survive the third raid? He did say it was like Iveleen power, so maybe it was Them?

I wandered back to the alleyway where Kaylaa still soundly slept. *She knows how to use magic.* Should I ask her about it? Can I trust her?

On this day, we announce the formation of the Shard, an elite agency whose purpose will be to protect the Virin-leen, the Clergy, and the People. The Shard will act under the direction of a Commander chosen by the Virin-leen Lords.

The Shard will use any means necessary to gather intelligence on other races of the Galactic Sector and the growing Erodian threat. Their primary focus is beyond the Western Continent of Vastire, but in extreme cases, Shard agents may be brought into local jurisdiction.

The Commander and his top Admirals' first charge will be to develop a Code of conduct, governing how the Shard will eliminate threats and maintain peace and justice with honor.

—From the Dedication of the Shard by King Warles, 216 ARI

CHAPTER SIX

Kaylaa awoke with a puzzled look and, even before she raised herself from the cold street, asked, "What happ—you...you're different."

"What do you mean?" I asked, though the smile on my face betrayed me.

"I can feel...a presence. It was a shadow yesterday, and today it is a lion. You don't know anything about magic." She said it more like a denouncement than a question.

"You're right. Magic is the tool of savages and demons." Those were the rote words of the Iveleen, since They insisted magic was reserved for Them. "I know you can use it."

"Naive to think of it as savage or demonic." Her eyes narrowed. "Have you never seen anyone wield it?"

"Not much. Nama-da necromancy, Barma healing, and whatever you did to capture me. My father was very powerful and he didn't need any mystic force." *But imagine if he could?*

"You shouldn't dismiss it—it's the one great, unexplainable power in this universe."

Just to be defiant, even if the words were empty, I retorted, "The one great power in this universe is the Iveleen."

"Bah! Vastirians are naïve." Even though her words suggested irritation, her stoic manner never changed. The way she said *Vastirian* was annoying, like "vost a rhian" than "vast ear ian."

"Maybe you're the naïve one," I suggested. *I guess that was childish.*

She shook her head. "Let's go back to your flat to figure out our next move. We're not safe out in the open."

"Where?"

"Where you live, your...what do you call it...apartment," she said.

"Oh. I don't want to go there. I think you know why."

"Other ideas?"

I nodded and started north. It seemed like everyone we passed had their eyes transfixed on Kaylaa. *How did she sneak around before?* One man was so brash to directly step in her way.

"Well, ain't you a beauty? Drop the kid and I'll show you a good time," said the man, reaching for Kaylaa's arm while flipping the hair out of his eyes with his other hand. He was actually quite handsome, especially for an Olan-har.

Kaylaa didn't even bother responding. She ripped the two rapiers from their sheaths and crossed them at his throat. His eyes bulged and his mouth was agape.

"Find a woman you can handle." She kicked him forcefully in the chest and he crashed into a merchant's stand of rotting fruit.

He leapt to his feet and dashed away, screaming. I chuckled. Everyone stared at Kaylaa, but when she returned the stare, they all pretended like they had something to do.

"Let's go," she said.

We continued along the road, weaving through empty alleys and broken roads until we burst into an open, sage-colored area with withered trees and red brick paths, blessed with the scent of crisp rosemary. Kaylaa followed me to a crook in a verdant green creek that snaked lazily around a circular patio, with sprigs of clover and weed growing through. I picked up one of the polyhedral seeds that fell from trees that only existed in this park, and tossed it in my hand. I sat on a twisted wrought iron bench and put up my feet on a pedestal table fashioned from a knotted tree stump. "If you need somewhere hidden to talk, there is a grove over there."

"What was this place?" Kaylaa asked, over the peaceful trickle of a small waterfall just upstream. She sat down uncomfortably close to me; she smelled like flowers after a light rain, but from a foreign garden.

"Somewhere we could all relax together. The royals built it to keep Olan-Har out of their parks. Adults would take these seeds and turn them into dice, and play games on these tables. I played with other kids over there in that clearing, and that creek is still the best water source for the Olan-Har." I found a plastic cup lying on the ground and filled it from the creek. One sip of the cool, clean water, and instantly I felt days of thirst quenched. I filled it again and handed it to Kaylaa. She initially refused it, but I forced her to take it.

"This actually...is really good. How can this water taste this good?" She drank the rest in a few big gulps.

I shrugged and said offhandedly, "Some say it's a magic spring."

She nodded. "Then where is everyone?"

"Most are dead. Not in the mood to hang out. People still come here for water." I could still imagine children running in the grass and old men quibbling over their last dice roll. This place used to be one of the few true sources of joy, but no longer. "Anyway, can you tell me what Shuka was thinking?"

"No." She pointed down the path, where a beautiful girl strolled idly with her eyes fixed on the ground—Fyra.

"It's okay." I strolled over to Fyra. "Hey, what are you doing here?"

"Darynn? I-I-I didn't see you there. P-P-Pavlar and I used to...we used to hang out here together. We'd observe the people and fabricate stories about them. Or at least I did, but he cheated. He didn't invent the stories—he knew them. Oh." Her

65

eyes wandered to Kaylaa for the first time.

"I actually met Pavlar here—I guess I was one of his stories, at first, then we became friends. We came here a lot and didn't play that game. He just told me their story and what they needed. Then we figured out how to get it." Reminiscing over Pavlar was somehow refreshing and depressing all at once. I thumbed the stone Gryphon in my pocket.

"It still doesn't seem real...I keep thinking I'm going to look around one of these trees and he's going to be there. We'll get to discuss his next half-baked scheme or the last family he helped. Then he'll run off to get you, and you'll help the next one."

"Just one wrong turn killed him. That's all it took..." *Why couldn't I remember the way out of the Dark Plaza?*

"Are you here with that w-w-woman?" she asked, stroking her platinum hair that hung down to her shoulder blades.

"Yeah. She's from Yiptae." Kaylaa still sat on the bench, hunched forward, examining us.

"Oh...yeah?" Fyra said.

"Yeah." I shifted my weight. "Well, Makaro would be madder than a Minotaur if he saw you with me. I'm glad the medicine is working. Can you make it home?"

"Yeah but...Father's become almost intolerable and Mother is drowning in her own tears. I don't blame them, but...that's why I had to get out, to come here. I had to think, think about what's next." She looked toward the creek but seemed to be fixed on something far beyond it.

"Actually, that's why I'm here, too. She and her boss have some grand plan for me that I'm not on board with."

Kaylaa jumped up and stomped over to us. "That's between you and me, Darynn. Don't involve her."

I smiled. "Jealous?"

She grimaced. "Too dangerous to involve anyone else."

"What's so dangerous?" Fyra asked, her interest piqued.

"Go home, girl," Kaylaa commanded.

"She's probably right, Fyra," I said. "I'm cursed anyway, and I wouldn't want anything to happen to you, like..."

Fyra took a deep breath. "No, I want to hear it. I'm not so frail as you seem to think I am."

Kaylaa glared at her and said, "Let's just get this over with." She went and sat back down on the bench and waited expectedly. I sat on the other end of the bench and Fyra modestly perched on the pedestal table, her oversized skirt covering her knees and calves.

"Shuka wants you to lead a revolution."

"Right to the point." I sighed. "No. We've seen how that story ends."

"Shuka will get you the backing you need. The Olan-Har already know you, and not just in Ziphyr. You're one of them. In fact, you don't even have to do much. You would have to be the face, and you would have to fight some. Shuka and I would do the rest."

I tried to push back the waves of horrifying memories of my father, but my brain seemed frozen like an overloaded computer. "What the hell do you and Shuka know about revolutions and Vastire and the Olan-Har? What makes you think I want to be part of your game?"

"I've been around Yiptaen immigrant rights groups almost my entire life. Shuka has operatives in every major Vastirian city. It's a long road, but you can save these people and end the embargo." She said it so seriously, so matter-of-factly, like it wasn't an insane, huge undertaking.

"I think I can name half a dozen uprisings of the Olan-Har and Poor over just the last century that have all failed," Fyra said. "That's enough reason to make what you're suggesting outlandish. But the Olan-Har are necessary. That's not to say changes aren't needed, but that's totally the wrong way."

"Diplomatic means alone won't work. You have to apply pressure." Kaylaa picked up one of the polyhedral seeds. "There is already external pressure from the P.A. Combined with internal pressure, the caste system would crumble." She pushed her thumb inside the seed, then crushed it in her palm.

"Things weren't so rough before the embargo," Fyra said. "I mean, it's not like we could go on off-world beach vacations, but we could eat. Now Vastirian industry can only support the upper castes, meaning we die from starvation and colds."

I tried to think back to those days before the embargo, but those memories were foggy. All I could remember was that I wanted to run away until I met Pavlar. *Now I want to run away again.*

Kaylaa went silent, her pupils scanning the near horizon.

I smirked. "We make some good points, huh?"

"Shh! We're not alone." Boots crunched on the grass nearby. Heavy boots. "We need to go."

Militia? They were after me. My heart started thumping as I looked around frantically. All of the color had drained from Fyra's face and her sapphire eyes had grown to the size of large gems.

Kaylaa said, "They're on this side of the creek. I don't see a bridge."

"Not anymore," I said.

"Then we're going to get wet." Without another word, Kaylaa gracefully dove into the creek.

"They're not after you, Fyra. You can stay."

Her wide eyes were fixed on the slow-moving stream, one hand attached to her cheek. "Darynn I...I can't swim."

"Then just stay, they won't hurt you."

The white and mint green uniforms were approaching fast, armed with a variety of SABs. Fyra was wrought with indecision. And then, so was I—I couldn't just leave her here to deal with the Militia on her own. I readied my Plasma Edge.

"Put down your weapon!" commanded one of them as they approached in a half-circle.

Just then, a wet hand grabbed my arm and threw me into the creek.

"We can't leave her!" I shouted, bobbing in the slow-moving water.

"Damnit!" Kaylaa yelled, turning back for Fyra. The Militia opened fire as she roughly threw Fyra in and jumped in after her. I swam upstream and tried to help Fyra keep her head afloat. She was flailing wildly and swallowing water.

"Fyra," I said between breaths, "You have to calm down."

"I...can't!" she gurgled.

Shots splashed in the water all around us.

"Darynn, you have to swim!" Kaylaa shouted.

I did my best to both swim and drag Fyra downstream, but it was working about as well as a turtle helping a cat swim. We were out of range of the Militia, but a few had jumped in the creek.

They were gaining on us.

Kaylaa drifted to the shore and pulled herself out. She rolled behind a tree and suddenly opened fire on the Militia behind us. *When did she get a gun?*

I struggled to help Fyra to the shore. She spat out a mouthful of water and huffed and puffed. I helped her to her feet and we floundered to the nearest tree.

Kaylaa fired another shot and then ducked behind the tree. "There's a safe place not too far from here. Get her ready to run!"

"Can you run?" I asked, between breaths.

"I...will," Fyra huffed.

"Kaylaa, let's go!" She shot three more times, then I noticed purple energy concentrating in her other hand. She threw the ball of energy like a grenade. With a flash, a wall of pulsing amethyst energy rose from the ground. Kaylaa took off, and we weaved through the creaking trees.

"Darynn, was that—?" Fyra asked.

"Yes!" I shouted.

Soon we were accompanied by stray shots tearing through the withering trunks and branches. I looked over my shoulder to see the Militia paused at the wall, looking puzzled as they fired through it.

"This way!" Kaylaa yelled, and we broke out of the park and back into the slums. She led us down a winding alley, then we burst across a main road and into another dark alley. She stopped abruptly at a large, iron door. Kaylaa quickly but precisely entered a code into a panel hidden in the wall, and the door clanked loudly. She pushed through, pulling us behind her. A putrid smell of alcohol, urine, and vomit filled our nostrils immediately.

Inside was an assortment of aliens, all with scowls upon their faces and anger in their eyes. They were of all shapes and sizes, hairy and hairless, colorful and colorless, angry and angrier. Scantily-clad women danced hypnotically on tables. When we entered, the women disappeared and the aliens stood, accompanied by the sound of chairs scooting on tile, and aimed a variety of weapons at us.

"Yer better hope yer belong here," boomed one of the aliens, a tall, muscular beast standing on a pair of long legs, with glowing red eyes and tiny spikes placed around his outline. He pointed a pistol that looked like a trumpet with his right hand and held a small, energized dagger in his left.

"It's just me," Kaylaa said, shoving to the middle of the room.

The alien—a Shravek, maybe—looked me over, grunted approval, and plopped back in his seat.

"Kaylaa, where are we?" I asked.

"The Kubahhn House," she replied, leading us through the crowd to a private booth. This was the kind of place where you had to put your hands on people's shoulders to wiggle through the aisles.

"Th-th-these people have b-b-b...torched churches, Kaylaa!" Fyra whispered. I remembered talking to Pavlar about this group—they had blown up a few Virin-leen and Iveleen buildings in Ziphyr. Pavlar loathed them.

"They're unorganized, reckless, and, frankly, stupid," Kaylaa said. "But they're muscle. You need muscle for a revolution."

I rolled my eyes. "There isn't going to be a revolution."

"So how are you going to get rid of the embargo?"

"Why is it my responsibility? Tell Shuka to get rid of it. Or maybe the Shard will blow it up."

Kaylaa sat back and crossed her arms. "Then what are you going to do?"

I sighed. "I...I don't know."

We sat in silence for a few minutes, and Kaylaa went to get a drink from the bar.

"I-I-I don't like this Darynn," Fyra said. Her eyes darted from one menacing presence to the next, much faster than her brain could possibly process them.

"I don't either, but this seems like a good place to hide out from the Militia for now."

Her eyes fixed on me. "Do you trust that woman?"

"Not really. But she did save us back there."

"She nearly killed me back there!"

I shrugged. "Fair point."

"And she...she used magic. That's heretical!"

"She doesn't believe in the Iveleen, so..."

"That doesn't mean it's acceptable."

Kaylaa returned to the booth, a hoppy, foaming drink in her hand. "Darynn and I already had that argument. That barrier bought us some time and disrupted their aim."

"But..." Fyra stammered.

"Besides, I'm not the only one. Both of you can use magic. I can feel it." Kaylaa took a sip of her drink and smacked her tongue.

Fyra huffed and crossed her arms. "That's preposterous. Vastirians can't use magic, even if it weren't a sin. 'Magic is folly for anyone beyond the gods,' said Josar."

"Even you have visions," I pointed out.

71

"I can't help it! They come to me, usually when I'm sleeping." Fyra slumped in her chair.

"That's rare." Kaylaa puzzled over that before taking another sip.

"I've tried to use magic before." I remembered my failed attempt in the Courtyard of the Broken Statue. "It didn't work."

"You imagined a fire and thought that would do it?"

"No, I really tried."

She raised one eyebrow. "It's much more complicated, intense, involved."

"Maybe you could teach us?" I asked.

Fyra looked at me with wide eyes, grinding her teeth. "Darynn, absolutely not." I didn't remember her ever speaking that confidently.

"It could come in handy. Maybe you can stop your visions."

Fyra took a deep breath and stared into the crowd.

Kaylaa took a swig of her drink, then a deep breath, and said, "It starts with—"

Suddenly, the side door erupted into a heap of splinters. Faint light streamed in from the alley, quickly blocked by two large figures. I felt a sudden wave of nostalgia as the two figures entered the dim light of the bar, both wearing the three-layered, black-as-void, characteristic Shard armor. *The Militia called in the big guns.*

"You are now enemies of the People. Put down your weapons and no harm will be done, as in the Code," announced one of the men, holding an oversized Split Rifle. The other, much younger than the first, was armed with a pair of thin Plasma Edges.

Immediately, the Kubahhn unloaded their lasers and Acid Pistols and whatever other weapons they held. But the lasers were absorbed and the acid casings dissipated on contact with the rare Vastirian moon metal of the Shard armor shell.

The two Shards overturned tables and started to advance. The Split Rifle lit up the entire room with amber power. The second Shard advanced quickly with his two blades and engaged the Shravek we met when we walked in.

"I can get out. Hold them off. I'll come for you," Kaylaa said.

Before I could respond, a third Shard walked through the door, but this one was different. He had no plates on his armor, and instead of black, the shell of his armor was bright white, like pure starlight. He surveyed the room with owlish eyes, then sprung into action, swinging his massive Plasma broadsword, which was also pearl white. He deftly ran his sword through the chest of the first alien he met, then neatly beheaded the next, all with a flawless, cunning smile on his face.

Commander Aseus, longtime leader of the Shard. My father's former boss.

Kaylaa had disappeared. *Hold them off.* She didn't know that Aseus was here. My mouth dried and I shuddered, but reluctantly I pulled my heavy legs from the booth and faced him, Edge ready.

He tossed aside a lifeless body and advanced toward me with recognition in his eyes. "Are you going to fight me, Darynn?" he asked with a half-grin.

He slashed downward with his broadsword. I feebly blocked it. Two more quick swings—*how can anyone swing a sword that size that fast?*—and I went down to one knee.

Sweat ran in rivers off my cheeks while Aseus's amber eyes glinted in the dim light. He attacked again and again with ferocious power.

Even though he was clearly holding back, I may as well have been fighting a Minotaur.

"You look like your father, but you are nothing like him with an Edge. I expected...more," he said in a strong yet raspy voice.

Weakly, I replied, "I expected honor." I gestured to the carnage around us.

"These aliens have broken many laws, not to mention they fired first." He turned his head from side to side, his chin cradled in his hand. "Speaking of, where is the alien you've been seen with?"

"I don't know." That was actually true.

He considered my words, then replied, "Drop Zil's Edge and let's go."

I gritted my teeth and considered a quick slice, maybe down low where his heavy sword wouldn't block it too fast.

As if he could read my thoughts, he slammed the tip of his broadsword into the floor, effectively blocking his entire lower half. *I'm no match for him.*

I looked to Fyra, she replied with an exaggerated nod. My Edge hit the floor with a metallic thud. The older Shard came and slapped magnetic shackles on me. "You look...exactly like Zil. Trained me, ya know." Then he spat on the floor. "Bastard." He inserted a pin into the shackles, which shocked me with a light jolt of electricity, and locked the handcuffs in place. He didn't bother cuffing Fyra; just grabbed her by the wrist and led us out.

He loaded us and a few of the living Kubahhn into a windowless cubed cruiser, and with a lurch, we were on our way to prison.

Olan-Har residence: may only live in the designated Hargonla areas of a city.

Olan-Har curfew: may only be outside of Hargonla between sunrise and sunset.

Olan-Har employment: may only take jobs sanctioned by the local Cardinal.

Olan-Har property: all property from previous caste, if applicable, must be forfeited upon Olan-Har designation. Other castes may not sell property other than basic necessities to Olan-Har. Donations to Olan-Har must be made through the local church.

Olan-Har tattoo: must be displayed at all times regardless of clothing or weather.

Olan-Har education: all formal education must be sanctioned by the local church. At the local priest's behest, certain Olan-Har may be allowed a limited University education as a means to raising their caste.

Olan-Har health: healthcare may only be provided by designated doctors.

Olan-Har transportation: may not use public transportation.

Olan-Har DataAxis access: may not access the DataAxis or own personal DataAxis Access Links.

—From the Vastirian Law Code

Chapter Seven

This is it. All of that sneaking around, stealing, and killing finally caught up to me. The penalty for killing an Elite like the Captain is death for an Olan-Har, and all it takes is a single judge to decide. No witnesses needed, just sent straight to the death chamber. Especially me, of all people, son of Zilpohn Mark. Time to end that bloodline.

The car stopped suddenly, slamming me into the beefy arm of a furry, sweaty Kubahhn alien. He half-growled, half-hissed at me, then said, "This is your fault, boy." He looked at me like he'd sooner eat me than kill me. I looked straight ahead instead, at the much easier sight of Fyra. She was breathing quickly, like a leopard panting in the heat.

"It's gonna be okay, Fyra," I lied.

"D-d-don't do it," she said quietly. But she wasn't looking at me; her eyes were transfixed on the alien next to me.

"What, Fyra?"

She shook her head.

"Can you believe these aliens?" said one of the Shards in the front, the younger one I think. "They think they own us, like we're children. They shouldn't even be here." The other grunted in response, and the first continued. "If I had it my way, they wouldn't be allowed to live in the cities at all, even Hargonla. And I'll tell you another thing—we would've blasted that Haskar-cursed embargo on day two."

"Don't talk like you know better than the Virin-leen," replied the elder.

"I don't," stuttered the younger. "I just...I'd like to go on a vacation. Somewhere nice, warm, tropical...off-world. Have you ever been off-world, for vacation?"

"Only work."

"Then you don't even know. A juicy minas steak." The younger whistled. "Ever had that? They come from Kiri. Best slab of meat you'll ever have."

The elder must have responded nonverbally, as the younger shut up after that.

Their conversation made me wonder why the Kubahhn were here, why they cared about a revolution on Vastire. So I asked.

Mostly, the response was grunts and grumbling, but the alien next to Fyra answered.

"My girl's up there, in one of them ships." His voice was high, and he pronounced *ships* more like "sheeps." His gullet inflated and deflated like a toad when he spoke, though he resembled a short-snout black bear. "Got here before the ships did, wanted to end it quickly, get her home to her ma. No luck."

"Is that why you're all here?" Fyra was listening intently; her interest helped contain her anxiety.

"Most of us. Some of them just like an excuse to kill." He shut his eyes and was so still it seemed he turned to stone. The four other Kubahhn in the cab were much more agitated, scowling and making fists and stamping their feet. The whole car smelled of dried blood and aged sweat.

Pavlar and I had talked about going to prison. If it was so bad when we were free, prison had to be miserable. He'd always said he needed to be the one caught, between the two of us, because I could get him out, but not vice versa. He never told me how he planned on me getting him out, but he had full confidence that I could. *So maybe I can?*

Once we were inside, there would be almost no way out. But the cab didn't seem any easier. The car was a solid block of metal, except for the door, which was sealed with electronic locks. Just a bit more time and Kaylaa would've explained how to use magic. Maybe that would've been the way out.

We came to a sudden stop, and hopelessness swept over me—we were going to prison.

The Shards opened the doors. The furry alien next to me rushed out the door at one of the Shards. With incredible agility and anticipation, the younger Shard ripped out a thin Plasma blade and the alien impaled himself on it. The body slumped, jiggling once like a plop of pudding upon hitting the ground. Fyra shrieked loudly and started sobbing.

"Anyone else want to take their chances?" With no responses, he said, "Everybody out!" My feet hit the rough gravel and kicked up reddish-gray dust. The whole area was filtered through this dust, and my eyes started to water.

We piled out in a somewhat orderly fashion, but the older Shard held Fyra and me back. "Not you. You're going to headquarters, Boss's orders." He roughly pushed us back into the cruiser, while the other aliens were taken by a group of prison guards. Fyra's tears were caked with the dust.

When we started moving again, I expected some of the tension would have left with the Kubahhn. But I was wrong—my mouth was drier, my legs were stiffer, and the dust was still in my eyes. *Shard Headquarters.* I hadn't been there since before my father died, before his last mission.

I had been sitting in his office, impatiently waiting to go home. There was nothing special about my father's office—some Shard kept trophies of their exploits, like unique weapons or artifacts, but not my father. There was nothing on the walls besides some maps and a calendar. He seemed normal that day, intently studying information on his computer for the next mission. He left a few days later, and when he came back, he was never the same.

Somehow, going to Shard Headquarters was worse than prison.

"Darynn!" whispered Fyra. "Do you have a plan?"

"Rushing out of the cruiser didn't seem to work."

"It's not funny! I saw him die. I tried to warn him."

So that's what 'Don't do it' meant. She'd had a vision. "I'm sorry, Fyra."

"Just...just get us out of this predicament." She laid down on the bench on her side and drew her knees up to her waist, carefully tugging her skirt down. She rocked back and forth.

She looked like she didn't belong in Hargonla—she was too clean, too pretty, too pure. She had managed to get out for just a little while, being one of the select few chosen by Father Ckoost to go to University. But Hargonla had reached out with its iron tentacles and dragged her back.

How can we get out of this? Every moment drew us closer to southwest Ziphyr, where the Shard Headquarters jutted out like a sword from the flat landscape. Once we entered that building, even Kaylaa wouldn't be able to get us out.

Logically, that meant we had to break away before then. But that Kubahhn alien had tried and died. Where were they going to take us—the glassy, sparkling main entrance to the building, or the dark, hidden back way? If it was through the front, there would probably be other Shards and officials around, and we'd never get away. But the back...maybe that would give us a chance.

The car stopped, and the Shards pulled us out. We were in the front.

A few people milled around, but luckily it was later in the day when most people would've gone home from work. My eyes followed the path to the building, then up the glittering black glass of Shard Headquarters. The building was anything but subtle, as it mimicked the Shard symbol—a broadsword, called the Fused Sword, broken into three pieces above the guard, each representing one group of people the Shard was supposed to dutifully protect: the clergy, the Virin-leen, and the people. Each piece was connected to the bottom with struts and an elevator shaft. At the sharp tip was Commander Aseus's office.

The point of a gun prodded me on, toward the front doors, toward the inescapable fortress. I took deep, measured breaths; every step seemed weighted down by lead. To my right, Fyra seemed to purposefully place each step, her eyes trained intently on the ground. Her whole body was shuddering. *She doesn't deserve this.* I belonged here, but she didn't. *How dare they drag her into this.* If I could just knock these two Shards down, we could run.

My whole body started to pulse. Beads of electricity seemed to zip through my veins. My eyes became hyperactive, darting from site to site: pillars on either side, a bush here, a woman there.

As if I'd been hit with the butt of a rifle, I dropped to one knee. I slammed my cuffed hands on the concrete. My veins glowed like neon lights. Black and white energy, like static on an old television, blurred the ground. The concrete cracked as it trembled, first in small spiderwebs, then in growing faults.

The nearby pillars broke and fell like sawed tree trunks. Fortuitously, they fell onto the two Shards, breaking their backs under the great weight. My shackles de-magnetized and fell to the ground. The quaking stopped; I seemed to regain control of my body.

Dazed, I helped Fyra to her feet. The two Shards sprawled on the ground helplessly, both unconscious. I took my Edge from the older and stared at it. A voice in my head screamed "Kill them! Kill them!" as I held the blade above one of their necks. I pulsed the plasma.

Fyra tugged on my arm, her eyes wide. "Let's go!"

We broke into a run. I knew exactly where to go.

I led us into a city park, my heart beating out of my chest. We burst through a hedge, scratching our hands and faces on its branches, and into a clearing. Pursuers shouted behind us, not very far—not nearly far enough.

I led Fyra to a specific tree, as big around as a space cruiser, and showed her a crack on the other side. It was just large enough for me to slide through, and Fyra followed me into the hollow tree trunk.

The only way both of us could fit was if I hugged her very closely. Her breath danced lightly on my neck, and she just felt right in my arms.

Voices outside called for us, but I knew they'd never find us in here. I remembered hiding from my father in this same tree, when I would visit him on lunch breaks. He never found me.

Our hearts pumped in unison as I held her closer. I don't know how long we stood there, but I could feel my legs weakening from standing so long. *Why so weak? What happened back there?* Whatever it was, it stole my stamina. There was no way to move or reposition ourselves in the tight space. I knew I was sweating, and surely she felt it. *I hope she doesn't smell it.*

It was dark outside when I finally felt like it was safe to speak. Part of me wanted to stay here in this moment, but I felt so weak.

"I think it's safe now—can you wiggle out?"

She looked up at me, relief in her sapphire eyes, and I felt the nerves dancing in my belly, and then the strongest urge to kiss her...

But I didn't. She slid through the crack and I followed her out. It was late enough that even the lights in the park were shut off. No one was around. I sat down on the ground to give my legs a well-deserved rest.

Fyra asked, "Wh-wh-what just happened?"

"I used to hide in that tree as a kid."

"I wasn't talking about that!" she snapped. "The energy...you used *magic*."

"I guess—I guess I did." I felt so...invincible, so powerful. I had just used magic to escape from the Shard, the best intelligence and fighting force in the Alliance. But we're not supposed to. "I just wanted to help y—us." I stopped myself short of saying *you*—that would've been weird. "I imagined knocking them down, and then suddenly something took over. Instinct?"

"That was incredible," she said breathlessly. Then her demeanor instantly changed. "But wrong. You're defying the Iveleen."

I crossed my arms. "You're going to lecture me on religion, now? I just saved our asses!"

"That's no excuse."

"You asked me to get us out of there, and I did. And, you know what? It felt good, too."

She stared at me with her mouth agape. "What is wrong with you? Father Ckoost taught you better than this. Maybe in the short term, you solved a problem, but in the long term, it's going to cause damage."

"I'll take that chance. Besides, your visions break the rules too!"

She shook her head and took a deep breath. "I don't have a choice. I don't enjoy them. You know that."

We sat in silence, refusing to look at each other, when we heard a loud vehicle drive by on the road.

"We need to get out of here," I said. "Two Olan-Har in the city at night, even if the Shard weren't looking for us..."

Her eyes pierced mine and she nodded reluctantly. I reached out to help her up, but she refused my hand. I just wanted to feel that soft skin again in my rough hands.

As we walked toward the entrance of the park opposite the Shard Headquarters, she said, "It's a long way back to Hargonla. We'll never make it without being reported."

"Maybe we could ride a bus," I replied.

"Our faces will be in the surveillance system by now, and they'll send out an alert on everyone's DAAL," she said. I imagined our holographic faces with bright red lettering on everyone's DataAxis-connected wristbands. "Too many people at a bus stop."

"Then what do we do?" I asked.

She looked ahead, then said, "We jump on at an intersection. Trailing cars will probably recognize us, but even if we could travel a few blocks it would help."

"Okay," I agreed. "We need to go generally that way." I pointed north along the road.

It didn't take long for my legs to tire. We had stood in that tree for hours, not to mention the magic. *Me, a Vastirian, using magic.* And not just any magic—I nearly killed those Shards. *Then I almost finished the job.* Where did that come from? Pavlar would've been so disappointed that it even crossed my mind. *But* did *it cross my mind?* It felt like it just happened.

I kept my eyes on the road, looking for a bus, but it must have been even later than I thought, and none were running. We kept as close to the buildings as we could, deep within their hulking shadows, and always turned our faces away from oncoming traffic when crossing streets.

We finally reached a bus stop, with four red benches and a tempered glass top held in place by four red girders. As my eyes followed the girders up, I noticed the small lens of a camera inset just below the canopy in one of the girders. I stopped Fyra short of where I thought the point of view would be.

"At least we know buses run through here, but we can't get any closer to that stop," I whispered. I pointed to the camera, and she nodded.

The sidewalk wasn't wide enough to completely avoid the camera, but jaywalking across the street, even with it not being too busy, was too dangerous. The longer we stood there, the more we attracted the attention of a few people at the stop. The worn condition of their clothes and tired looks on their faces indicated these people were no higher than Middle caste, and maybe even Poor. One tapped the bright screen of his DAAL on his wrist.

His gaze lingered on us. *Did he recognize us?* Or was he just bored, or not used to seeing Olan-Har? It was easy to tell us apart—we were required to display the red circle and black discs tattoo at all times.

I took Fyra's wrist and hugged close to the giant glass panes of the building behind the stop. I pretended like I was peering inside the building, though the glass was tinted and obscured anything on the inside. I hoped the camera could see no more than our scalps. But maybe that's all it needed?

After a few minutes, the low rumble of a bus approaching caught my ears—but it was going the wrong way. "Damn it," I said under my breath.

"Iveleen, show us the way," Fyra said in response.

I gritted my teeth but ignored her. Whatever gave her peace, I guess.

A low rumbling filled the air again, and this time, it was a bus heading north. "Come on!" I said to Fyra, and we hurried along the sidewalk to try to get to the next intersection before the bus. *I hope it stops.*

This time, we were in luck—the massive, two-story vehicle that looked like a pill capsule for a titan paused at the intersection. We dashed to catch up and climbed up the short ladder to the roughly-hewn Olan-Har seats on the outside. I gripped the arm bar and encouraged Fyra to do the same. I felt an instant of weightlessness as the bus rose off the ground, and I was nearly thrown from the bus as the AI pilot carelessly took off. I wouldn't be the first Olan-Har to die falling off a bus, not that the Virin-leen cared. As far as they were concerned, we weren't supposed to be on the bus at all, and these seats were a gift.

The bus continued north, and we were fortunate that the other sleek vehicles on the road didn't care to stay behind the frequently stopping bus. We had ridden several blocks when the city around us changed. It was the oldest part of town, the Local District, but unlike Hargonla, it had been kept fresh and new.

As we zipped by, the brown and red and orange and yellow bricks blurred together into an earthy canvas. Massive oak trees were given wide berths in the sidewalk, even forcing the roads to wind around them. The crowds grew and long lines, presumably out of popular clubs, turned into hives of buzzing activity themselves. Seems like the embargo wasn't affecting them much at all.

Fyra straightened up with a jolt and nearly fell off the bus. I grabbed her and gave her a puzzled look.

"I had a flash of a vision...a terrible death, but someone I don't know. All I remember is a Golden Spiral circlet, and his eyes—different colors, but in terrible pain. And also there was a purple light over him. Just another Olan-Har who's going to die in an awful way. Why do I have these visions, Darynn?"

"Maybe you could use them to help someone? Like maybe you could help this guy?"

"We'd never find him. Plus, that could be happening right now, or years from now. You can't imagine the stress. Not only of that vision, but you know another one is coming, another face with its eyes stuck open and mouth frozen in place." She paused and sighed.

I used to think her powers were a gift, but it sounded like she was just as cursed as me. Seeing death all the time? Never knowing if, when you close your eyes, you'll watch another person expire in some horrible way?

"You know, that's why I went to University?"

I shook my head.

She nodded. "I was hoping to learn about my visions. I either wanted to understand why the Iveleen would give me this gift, against their Teachings, or how to get rid of it. I studied psychology, neurology...I even looked into divination, fortune-telling, and gypsies. I found nothing."

As I listened, I felt more eyes watching us. We stopped at an intersection, and a Militia car was right behind us; the Militia woman inside was talking, presumably calling something in.

Us? I watched her intently, my heartbeat speeding up, but then she pulled around and kept going.

"So that's when you decided to come back home?" I asked.

"Yes. And then I got sick. While bedridden, I had many visions of you and Pavlar. Sometimes I felt like I was on your adventures with you. But now I know..."

Suddenly, gravity yanked Fyra into me and me off the seat to my left. The bus was turning east; I turned my head left to see the glittering, downtown skyline reaching irreverently into the night sky. I held Fyra tight again, I could feel her heart thumping—*for me?* Or because we were riding on a rollercoaster with no seatbelt? Her weight shifted back into her seat.

"We have to get off...we're going the wrong way."

Fyra nodded, and we waited impatiently for the next stop.

It took longer than we hoped, but another intersection came and we slid down the ladder into the street. There was hardly any cover here—fluorescent lights illuminated the entire area, completely swallowing the shadows of the trees. And surely, there were cameras. Lots of them.

I wanted to get off the main thoroughfare, but all of the surrounding roads were wide and busy main streets. I led us to a spot where two cars—one like a silver bullet and the other like a brown cardboard box—were parked closely together and squatted between them.

Fyra's head swung side-to-side. "I-I-I don't think this is a good hiding spot."

"I'm just trying to get my bearings. Downtown is there, which means we're only halfway to Hargonla. And the fastest way...is right through it."

"The Iveleen led us this far without being noticed, surely They'll guide us the rest of the way."

I smacked my lips. "Just got lucky."

"Randomness is in the fabric of the universe, but continued good fortune is only made by the gods," Fyra replied, quoting some line of Scripture.

"You have the whole book memorized?"

She smiled. "Just the best lines."

"If you say so. Then what are They telling you to do next? Lots of cameras, Militia, and Shards in downtown." I looked over at the beautiful buildings, which suddenly seemed more menacing, like glittering watchtowers full of armed guards.

She tilted her head upwards, lost in thought. "Are there any jobs that Olan-Har can do downtown?"

"Most everything Olan-Har could do has been automated to keep us away from there. Trash, sewers, janitors...can't think of anything left."

"How long would it take to go around?" she asked.

"Probably double the time? Way past morning."

People chattered next to the cardboard box car in front of us, and the car door clicked as it opened.

A stupid idea crept into my mind. I whipped out my Edge and jumped out from our hiding place.

"Darynn, stop!" Fyra yelled, but it was too late.

Amicrux was built by the eighteen Planetary Alliance planets 156 Amicrux Years (AY) after the founding of the P.A. It was built as a central hub in Galactic Sector 2.2 for the P.A. While its primary function was to facilitate physical meetings of the P.A., the more important function it serves is as a great data center.

The servers for the DataAxis, a central repository for P.A. and other GS 2.2 planets, make up the bulk of the "planet." Each planet in the P.A. also has its own copy of the DataAxis, but Amicrux holds the master data, and P.A. planets have the right to censor what information is held on the local copy.

P.A. citizens typically access the DataAxis through personal DataAxis Access Links, or DAALs. Information they want to access is retrieved from the planet local copy if available, or if not, downlinked from the central DataAxis, assuming the information has not been blocked.

—From *On Amicrux, a Server Planet*

CHAPTER EIGHT

I pointed my Edge at the couple dressed in club attire. Middle-class, I think. The car door was open, but neither of them had gotten in yet.

"Alright folks, I'm not going to hurt you, but you need to help us get to where we need to go."

The woman screamed, but cut it off quickly when I shoved my Edge in her face.

"Now look, buddy," said the man, trying to sound brave, his face flushed.

I swung my Edge toward him and flashed the plasma. "You're going to give us a ride." The woman's eyes were as large as headlights and her mouth was still wide open. "Scream again and I'll hollow out his insides." *I sound so...evil.*

The man's eyes wavered between my Edge and my tattoo. "Damn Olan-Har!"

"That's right, so you know I'll do it."

He stood there, considering it, his hand resting on the car door. He nodded reluctantly.

"Fyra, get in the car," I commanded.

"I-I-I can't believe you're doing this," she said but hurried into the car all the same.

"Okay, now you two." They didn't move at first, but another neon flash of blue plasma and they got in. I loaded in behind them and shut the door.

The four fake leather seats, clear from the plasticky smell, faced each other—two in the front and two in the back. The couple faced the rear while I held the point of my Plasma Edge toward them. Empty cups and food wrappers littered the floor. I felt a pang of hunger in my gut.

"Tell the computer to take us to..." My mind blanked as I tried to think of somewhere the car could even go in Hargonla. "Hargonla Prison," finished Fyra.

I looked at her incredulously.

"You...want to go to prison?" asked the man, as surprised as I was.

"That's where our friend will be looking for us," she replied with a sharp look.

I considered it—she was, once again, right. Kaylaa knew we were caught, and therefore she would've thought that we went to the prison with the Kubahhn.

"Do what the lady says," I said.

The man held a button on a side panel and said, "Destination—Hargonla Prison."

A robotic voice replied, "Arrival in twenty minutes, with light traffic in Downtown." The car smoothly rocked forward, and we were off.

"At least you won't have to go far when you get caught," the man said.

"I still can't believe you did this," Fyra said, shaking her head.

I shrugged. "Me neither. But you know, I was desperate to get home."

"You scare me sometimes."

Scare her? That's not what I wanted to hear. If she's afraid of me, then there couldn't be other feelings. *Right?*

The woman eyed her DAAL on her right arm; it sensed her looking at it and the screen lit up.

"Take their DAALs." Fyra reached over and unstrapped

their DAALs, the woman's held with a light red strap and the man's a dark gray. The woman's was still lit up and unlocked; Fyra swiped the screen a few times and found our pictures.

"They did circulate alerts," Fyra said. She continued to peruse the information on the DAAL. The color drained from the Middle-class couple's faces.

"So what happens when—" The man gulped. "When we get there?"

"Will you just shut up?" I held up my Edge again, a little bit closer to him. *What* does *happen when we get there?*

"Hey, not so close! If we stop hard, you're gonna impale me." He was right, and I would feel guilty killing this guy. Just for going out for a night together.

Despite the situation, it felt good to be moving again, and out of sight. I let my eyes wander to the window, where the shiny glass buildings zipped by. I couldn't see much from this vantage point, but I knew the buildings were looping all around us in shapes that didn't make much practical sense. The Virinleen and Elites preferred flair over function.

As the lights streaked by, my thoughts drifted. *What a day.* I looked at my free hand, my veins visible but not glowing. Did Canfod awaken this power in me? What am I supposed to do with it? He said I could help the Olan-Har. That's what Pavlar would've wanted. I pulled stone Gryphon out of my pocket and turned it in my hand. But a *revolution*, like Kaylaa and her boss wanted? People die in revolutions, lots of them. Pavlar wouldn't want that. My eyes flicked to Fyra. She wouldn't want it either, not only since she'd painfully see the deaths, but also because the goal was to get rid of the Iveleen's caste system. What should I do? *What do I want?*

The car lurched to a sudden stop just as we exited downtown. I swiveled my head around and saw a bunch of Militia cars behind us. *How did they find us?* The scream—it had to be when the woman screamed.

"Damnit! Fyra, we need to go—the central traffic computer

stopped the car!" I kicked at the door, but it refused to open. "And it locked the door!"

I looked at the couple, their faces mixed with fear and relief. *Hostage situation?* No, that's too far. I jammed my Edge into the crack between the door and the car, where I thought the lock would be. I held the button that activated the plasma, and the blue energy arced out of the blade. In seconds, the whole door turned red-hot.

The crack widened until, finally, the door sprung open. I reached for Fyra's wrist, pulled her out with me, and started running.

Voices behind us commanded us to stop. I looked up briefly to try to figure out where we were—definitely out of downtown, as the buildings were plain and huge, but still a long way from the prison. If we turned north, we could get into Hargonla pretty quickly. But which way was north?

"Darynn! Where are you going?" Fyra yelled.

"I don't know yet!" Just then, I caught sight of a road sign— "Road Ends, 1 mile." That would only end for one reason— Hargonla. I turned down the road and hoped it ended much sooner.

Some Militia were getting close on foot, others even closer in cars. We only had seconds before they caught us and blocked the path. On both sides of the road, the buildings changed to huge, blocky monstrosities with smokestacks and rusted metal. I veered into the nearest one.

These factories would've once been belching smoke and teeming with Olan-Har just happy to have jobs, but they had been abandoned even before the embargo.

I darted into the first open door and looked over my shoulder to check on Fyra. I ducked into the first room and slumped down next to the door.

"I...don't think I can run anymore," she gasped as she sat next to me. "I don't have my strength back."

"We can't stay here. I wish I had a gun. There are too many

to fight hand-to-hand."

Trails of flashlights shot through the doors and windows. I wiped the sweat from my brow. Soot covered my sleeves.

Fyra said, "I think they'll find the lights soon."

"Probably. Maybe they don't work?" As if on cue, the lights flashed a few times, then stayed steady on, accompanied by buzzing like worker bees. This place really was a disaster—twisted metal frames riddled with broken tiles made up the ceiling, and the floors were covered in soot and the remains of the ceiling tiles. Sinister vines twisted with copper wires and snaked through every visible crack.

I peeked out through the doorway. Two Militia, a man and a woman, stood nearby. Neither was physically imposing—I could beat both of them and get back through the door.

But they won't be the only ones.

"If the lights work, is it possible the rest of the factory still operates?" Fyra asked. I nodded. "If we can find the master switch, maybe we can distract the Militia long enough to slip away."

"That could be anywhere," I said.

Fyra's eyes scanned the building, tracing something. *The wires?*

She pointed to our right. "I think it's that way."

No door, but there was a hole in the wall large enough for us to crawl through. I let her go through first and followed closely behind. I found myself staring at her butt. *Focus!* No time for thoughts like that, especially now.

We emerged into the next room—a massive, open-air horror show. All around us were terrifying mechanical monsters, intended to mash and stretch and keep parts moving. I could still smell the smoke from the machines and the sweat on the floor.

Fyra was still following the wires, which appeared to be growing into bigger bundles, like we were getting closer to the trunk. So many lights were out that it was harder to follow them in here. Every footstep and creak of the machinery echoed through the empty space.

We stayed close to the wall as Fyra crawled toward the source of the wires. She pointed ahead.

Two Militia stood close to the wall, too close to be able to sneak by them. *Fight them?* No, that would draw too much attention.

A loud bang like hitting a baking sheet on a counter came from our right.

Fyra had thrown a small brick, and it worked! The Militia called it in, then went to investigate.

I took a deep breath and we scurried by, our hearts pounding loud enough to echo off the nearby wall. Then we hit a dead end—a yellow metal cage. But this was clearly where the wires were leading. The caged room was tiny and the door was locked by a rusted padlock.

"I'm going to have to use my Edge," I whispered.

"Please just be quick."

We moved around to the door of the cage. I took a quick look around. *No one here. Yet.* I flashed the plasma and sliced through the lock. It fell to the floor with a resounding *clank*. Fyra hurried in. I dropped to the floor, kicking up a small storm of dust.

A gruff voice called out, "What was that?"

Fyra pulled down a large lever with both hands, and the building roared to life. Old machines creaked and whined with treadmills and arms and turntables moving throughout the facility. Pieces of metal sheared and clattered about the entire room. Confused voices shouted over the din.

The owner of the gruff voice approached the cage. "Drop it!" he said. He pressed something on his DAAL.

I dashed toward him and slashed my Edge down across his shoulder. He blocked it with his SAB, but the Plasma sliced through it and nicked his armor. I swung a second strike across his ribs. He leapt backward, but the tip connected, slicing through his belly. Blood poured out over his silver armor. He doubled over in pain and yelled in agony.

"Leave him!" Fyra said.

What if he called it in? Then the distraction of the machinery was for nothing.

But she was right. *I hope I didn't kill him.* I could imagine Pavlar scolding me, and felt a sudden urge to cry. I shook it off.

We hurried to the nearest doorway, but there were two more Militia standing there, these armed with Militia Cutlasses, much newer than Pavlar's. I could probably beat them, but not quickly enough.

"Stop right there!" commanded a woman standing by the door, while the other approached me. She called it in on her DAAL before I could react. *Gotta end this quickly.*

I rushed up to the approaching officer. Just before reaching him, I swept my hand over the ground and tossed whatever I grasped in his face, the mixture of metal shavings and soot spraying into his eyes.

A mixture of metal shavings and soot went into his eyes. I whirled and slashed my Edge across his back. *Father would not have approved of that trick.* No choice.

The Militia woman looked at me, wide-eyed and slack-jawed. Her eyes darted from me to her partner. Surely she was thinking revenge—or aid?

She chose revenge. She dashed at me in a rage and attacked wildly, causing me to retreat a few steps. I backed up until I could feel the cool metal of one of the rattling machines behind me. She paused to take a breath and I checked my surroundings. Some mechanism twisted back and forth around the machine behind me. With my off-hand, I grabbed it.

My body swung off to the right with it. When it swung back, I used the extra momentum to jump into her, feet first. She crashed to the ground, stunned.

I thrust downward and buried my Edge in her chest with a flash of blue. I removed the Edge and dashed toward the doorway, where Fyra stood, her jaw clenched and her eyes huge.

"You...you did it again." Was that surprise? Disappointment? *Terror?*

I felt a pit in my stomach and the saliva in my mouth tasted like metal. "I know...I'm sorry. I really didn't want to. They're just doing their job...but they'd do the same to us." *Pavlar would be so disappointed.*

We stepped out of the factory and surveyed the situation. There was no road on this side, so no Militia cars, just another building that looked like the one we just left. But there were Militia soldiers on both sides of us, hopefully fewer thanks to the whirring machinery inside.

They saw us.

"We can't keep this up all night," Fyra said.

I replied, "If we can just get into Hargonla, maybe they won't follow." *Wishful thinking.*

We ran into the next factory. Bullets and acid casings pinged all around the doorway. We cut across the strewn machinery, broken chairs, and wobbly tables until we reached an exit on the other side. But the door wouldn't budge.

I cut the hinges and around the handle with my Edge, but still it wouldn't move. *Something must be behind it.* And by now, at least half a dozen Militia had entered the factory, closing in on us.

"M-m-maybe you should just...use magic," Fyra said with a panicked sigh.

"It's not that easy!"

"Why is this any different than before?"

"I don't know!" I pulled my Edge and readied for another fight, but these Militia were armed with blasters—if I attacked one, the others would light me up. My eyes frantically darted from one officer to another.

I took a deep breath and desperately tried to do whatever I had done earlier, but it just wasn't coming. I hesitated as the

Militia moved in closer, and I prepared for my last fight.

The door behind us flew inward with a loud metallic crash. Without a thought, we bolted through it. *Kaylaa!* With a Militia cruiser. Purple energy dissipated from her hand—she had used magic to clear whatever obstacle was blocking the door. As soon as we came through, she blocked the door again, her hand glowing as she moved in a flowing motion. Without a word, she hopped in the cruiser and motioned for us to get in. Within seconds, we were off; Fyra and I collectively let out a sigh of relief.

"How did you—"

"Went to the prison and bribed a guard," Kaylaa interrupted. "Then I went to Shard Headquarters, but the place was crawling with Shard agents. Figured you must've escaped. I came back to the slums and went to a Kubahhn's house. He'd tapped into Militia comms. I hurried down here, stole a car. I heard shots in that building and found you."

I looked out to try to figure out where she was taking us. *Does it matter?* We were getting away.

"Remember what I said about good fortune?" Fyra said.

"Yeah but...I mean...Kaylaa's not from around here."

"You think the Iveleen can only use believers? Have you read any of the Scriptures?"

"Some...I guess."

"It doesn't matter. I explained to you, logically, how I came to find you," Kaylaa said. "But I shouldn't have needed to find you at all—if you got away from Shard Headquarters, why were you stuck in a factory with Militia?"

I briefly explained to her how we escaped Shard Headquarters, the car hostage situation, and my failure with magic in the factory. "Something was...*off* when we were stuck there. It was nothing like at Headquarters."

"You weren't focused."

"It's been a long day, Kaylaa. And you haven't even told me about how it works. I think I did pretty good, all things considered."

The exhaustion hit me all at once and my eyes struggled to stay open.

"No point if you're just going to make excuses. If you fail, it's because of you."

Harsh, but not wrong, I guess. I wanted to change the subject. "Where are you taking us, anyway?" We should've been deep into Hargonla by now—at least as far as you can drive. The shabby buildings told me we were definitely in the slums, but it wasn't a familiar area.

"Senator Shuka has an operator on the west side of town." She turned abruptly into an alley and stopped the car.

"Are we here?" I asked. Both Fyra and Kaylaa looked at each other, then at me like I was an idiot.

"He's just tired," Fyra said in my defense.

"You explain it to him. Follow me." She quickly started off, and Fyra and I followed as closely as our tired bodies would allow.

"They're tracking the car, even though Kaylaa disabled the central traffic computer control."

Now I was caught up. "I hope it's not far, then."

"Me too."

We left the southern border of the slums, marked with a rusted iron fence, and walked through a field of dead grass, broken junk, and gnarled trees. I hadn't been here before, but I knew this was a buffer zone between Hargonla and a Middle-caste neighborhood. To the east, the stark, hulking presence of the Olan-Har prison loomed. My nerves danced anytime I looked that way, so I avoided it.

"The operative is a Middie?" I asked.

"A Yiptaen spy, even before the embargo."

After crossing the field, we came across rows of identical houses, except for color. Each had trimmed lawns and two groomed trees in the front.

Kaylaa was counting out loud as we walked along the street

until finally she came to the one she was looking for. Nothing distinguished this house from the others—a boxy three-story building with white wood panels all around the outside save for some spaces cut out for shaded windows.

Kaylaa knocked furiously on the dark wood front door until finally a very tall Vastirian man in pajamas that were too short for his legs and arms emerged, armed with a small Acid Pistol.

"What the hell do you want?"

Kaylaa didn't answer and pushed by. The Acip shook in his hands.

"I work for Senator Shuka. We need a place to stay for tonight."

"You're wanted, all three of you," he whined. "You can't be here! You'll blow my cover!"

"These two need sleep and we have nowhere else to go," Kaylaa protested. "They won't find us in one night."

"I've been here ten years! I'm not letting your haphazard operation jeopardize that!"

"We can make it look like a hostage situation. Second one tonight," I said, angling my Edge at him.

He considered that, looked at my blade and said, "Be out before dawn. Two Olan-Har and a foreigner...in this neighborhood."

Kaylaa nodded and Fyra politely introduced herself. He tersely gave his name as Caval.

Kaylaa led us to the most Middle-caste living room I'd ever seen. This guy was clearly an expert in blending—or had no personality of his own. A three-cushion couch and a two-cushion couch, each in an ugly paisley pattern, an oak coffee table and matching end tables, and a projector. Data pads on each surface displayed tabloid photos and headlines. Pictures of Caval fishing or hiking hung on the walls, along with some paintings of Vastirian landscapes—the majestic Vorn Mountain Range, the glittery Frozen Foothills, and the dangerous Dagger Isle. I'd never been to any of these places, but similar pictures could be found in houses and restaurants across Ziphyr.

I immediately sprawled across the larger couch; my head sunk—and this is where his butt goes. Fyra and Kaylaa sat on the smaller couch, while Caval leaned against a doorway. Fyra's eyes kept flicking to the data pads. When she noticed me watching her, she blushed and turned away.

"Do you read those things?" I asked.

"G-g-guilty pleasure," she admitted as her cheeks turned even redder. I chuckled as the irony hit me: this brilliant girl also liked the trashy papers. It was actually endearing. "Th-th-the Virin-leen have interesting lives!"

I snatched up the data pad and read the first headline: "Lady Chamalmat seduces Lord Balleen." *Not too crazy.* Next one: "Baron al-Lysta is an Android!" *Now we're getting there.* I laughed again as I choked out the last headline: "Lord Castamere's Newest Daughter is a Mermaid!"

Fyra smiled, then giggled. I swiped through the data pad and read a few more headlines. She snorted, then was embarrassed by that, but that made me laugh even harder. In turn, she completely broke up. Once the laughter finally died down, I realized how badly we both needed that. It had been a heavy few days for both of us.

Kaylaa was stone-faced the whole time, while Caval at least smiled.

"So why are you looking at these?" I asked.

Caval turned red. "It's a decent source of rumors to investigate. The headlines are almost always ridiculous, but the content sometimes contains nuggets of truth." He shrugged.

"I'm sure," I said.

"It's mostly celebrity gossip," Fyra said. "But sometimes it's just nice to liven things up. Our lives aren't too exciting, you know. Usually."

That was something I could sympathize with. So many Olan-Har sleepwalked through their meaningless lives: wake up, scrounge for food, stay out of danger, go to sleep, repeat.

They deserved better.

I laid back down and was starting to doze when Kaylaa said, "No sleep yet. We need a plan for the morning."

"You're supposed to be the one with the plan," I said.

"We thought you'd help us. We expected you to be more like your father."

I sat up and glared at her. "Everyone expects that. Guess what? I'm not." I took a deep breath. "You keep saying that like you knew him. But you didn't."

"Actually...I..."

"What?"

She hesitated. "I wasn't supposed to tell you. At least not yet. But..." She was always so direct, but this time, she couldn't spit it out. Her emotions—if she had any—were hidden behind a veil of blankness.

Does she know him? I jolted awake, feeling a direct injection of adrenaline to my heart.

The last days before my father left on his final mission flashed in my head. He was so distraught; completely disinterested in me. I was only eleven when he left, but that last day was burned into my mind. He was dressed in his dark Shard armor and wore a troubled expression. My mother begged him to stay, which was especially odd since he wouldn't have had much choice. He insisted that the mission chose him. He said he would only be gone for a season, but instead it was almost a full year later. And he was never the same.

Hargonla in Ziphyr is divided into four sectors.

The east sector is governed by the Maltans, a loose organization of drug runners and flesh peddlers. Unlike the other gangs, they recruit heavily in Hargonla.

The northern area is inhabited by the Nama-Da, and only the Nama-Da, a group of Kirilite necromancers who fled their home planet in 399 ARI.

The west sector is run by the Diterians, descendants of the Silopaskar shadow people from Ivendimm. The Diterians primarily sell home-built weapons and ammunition. Only Diterian family members may live in the compound, but others work for the family in the sector. Prior to the Diterians, the sector was controlled by the Barma family, a half-Erodian family blessed with remarkable healing power. The Diterians seized the region after the Barma Massacre in the Courtyard of the Broken Statue in 485 ARI.

The central area remains mostly neutral, managed by the church, a sort of truce zone between the gangs.

—From Report on Hargonla Gangs by Captain Madra,
489 ARI

CHAPTER NINE

Kaylaa leaned forward, her elbows on her knees, and licked her teeth. "Your father's last mission...was to Yiptae."

I jumped out of my seat. "Yiptae? But why? How do you know?"

Kaylaa shook her head. "He never said. He spent half an orbit in a Yiptaen prison, but never said."

"My father was never caught!"

Caval, suddenly very interested in our conversation, sat on the end of the couch opposite me.

Kaylaa continued. "He was this time. He was nicked at the Yiptaen Center for Interplanetary Affairs. Had to be spy work. But he insisted he was there on personal business." I heard what she was saying, but my brain seemed to be submerged in molasses; I couldn't process it. "My father was a guard at the prison. He and your father talked a lot."

"About what?"

"Religion, mostly. They swapped ideologies: your Iveleen, our god, Deus." She inhaled a deep breath. "Zilpohn said he learned more about his religion in the last few years than he had his entire life prior."

She spoke agonizingly slow, wearing out my already exhausted patience. "Is there more?" I asked.

"My father said he acted erratically. Had wild mood swings.

Sometimes he'd pray to the Iveleen, tears in his eyes, and other times curse them at the top of his lungs. My father asked why, but he would never say."

"How did he escape?"

She shrugged. "No one knows, but..."

"But what?"

"My father was found cold the same day Zilpohn escaped." Somehow, she said this completely devoid of emotion, not even watery eyes or flushed cheeks.

It felt like the muscles holding my heart in place failed. *What do I say?*

Fyra asked, "You're saying that Zilpohn Mark killed your father?"

Kaylaa blinked and seemed to try to answer, but no sound escaped her mouth.

Caval jumped in. "Yes, Zilpohn Mark started a prison break, and Rigel Reesae was killed in the fray." Our eyes shifted to him. "It's my job to know these things. Then Zilpohn Mark returned here and—" I gripped the handle of my Edge so hard my knuckles turned white and my veins popped bright red. Seeing that, he stopped talking.

"It never made sense to me," Kaylaa said. "Our fathers had become friends, at least the way my father described it in email. Zilpohn Mark was supposed to be an honorable man." Still not a shred of emotion.

"So then why are you here? Revenge?" I asked, my hand hovering over my Edge.

She shook her head. "I never met Zilpohn Mark, but, foolishly, I thought you could help me understand. Senator Shuka offered me this job, and I couldn't refuse."

My mind raced through every negative emotion I knew— anger because she withheld this information, grief because of my dead father, empathy because of Kaylaa's pain. Then—fear. "Kaylaa, we shouldn't travel together. The Iveleen teach that his wicked blood runs in my veins. Odds are I'd kill you just like my father killed yours."

She smirked. "No amount of luck could result in you killing me. Besides, I won't put the sins of the father on the son."

I looked out the window onto the tranquil street lit by solar streetlamps. Only one house on the block still had any lights on inside—it must have been really late. Dawn was approaching, and we hadn't slept at all. But how was I supposed to sleep now, with the adrenaline spreading like wildfire in my veins?

Fyra interrupted the tension by asking, "So you have no idea what Zilpohn was doing on Yiptae?"

Kaylaa answered. "Just one clue. I didn't talk to my father much then, but he said Zilpohn mentioned a Temple of Stria-Fate, over and over again. I did some research on the DataAxis, but there wasn't much. Mostly nonsensical things, like curses and monsters and crusades." She looked at me questioningly.

No idea what she's talking about. I shrugged.

Fyra jumped in. "The Iveleen Bekivala cursed the Temple to reflect his hatred of it. He is the grandson of Stria-Fate the Healer and Josar the Sorcerer. The curse is an echo of Josar's magnificent power: no electronic technology functions near the Temple and it transforms people into blood-drinking Vampires." She shrugged. "Or so it is written."

"Vampire myths are common in the P.A., mostly on Khaleri, but nothing credible," Kaylaa added. "Even so, I couldn't go alone—something real must have attacked the crusaders."

My brain desperately tried to make sense of the conversation, but couldn't overcome my exhaustion. "I'll always listen to a military history lesson, but what are you suggesting, Kaylaa?"

"My mission is clear: push you into a revolution that ends the caste system. This isn't it, but the only way I see to go forward is to go to the Temple. Find what your father did. We have to know that to understand what happened to your father. And why he killed mine if he did."

I looked at her dumbly, rubbing my face.

"I'll have to report this to Senator Shuka," Caval said.

Kaylaa glared at him. "Tell him it's a training opportunity. Tell him maybe it's the push Darynn needs. Darynn needs sword fighting lessons and leadership skills. We can't do it in the city."

Caval mulled it over and said, "I just report the information. It's up to the boss what he does with it."

"K-K-Kaylaa, we cannot succeed. Holy crusaders have tried, and failed, to conquer the Temple multiple times," Fyra said, her voice trembling.

"Zilpohn Mark did," Kaylaa countered.

"My father is the greatest warrior in P.A. history." I tried to conjure an image of my father, the unmatched champion, but all I could remember was the broken man, unwilling to train me in sword fighting. That would be him *after* Yiptae. "I want to know what he found there. More than anyone else. But us? We'll die."

Fyra narrowed her eyes and stared at me. "You're right, but that sure sounded like Pavlar."

She's right. The sweet syrup of adventure spread over my tongue; it was far too luscious for me to resist. A large smile crept across my face as the thought of heading into a largely unexplored and dangerous wilderness unfolded in my mind. It was the first time I felt joy—purpose—since Pavlar died. My fingers caressed the stone Gryphon in my pocket.

"I have nothing left to lose," I said. "Fyra, you should go back to your parents."

"I can't. The Shard and Militia are after me too," she said. "I want to know what Mr. Mark found. Whatever it was may enlighten us more on how the caste system was meant to be."

"It's settled," Kaylaa said. "Tomorrow we set out for the Temple. But we're going to need more equipment." She looked at Caval. "Any ideas?"

He crossed his arms. "I purely deal in information. You're on your own."

"I have an idea," I said.

"Save it for tomorrow. Get some rest," Kaylaa commanded. She and Fyra followed Caval up to some vacant bedrooms, while I made myself comfortable on the large couch.

As exhausted as I was, I just couldn't sleep. Thoughts zoomed through my head so fast I couldn't catch one and concentrate on it.

Someone shook me awake. Reluctantly I opened one eye; Kaylaa was fully dressed and standing over me.

I asked, "Are you a machine?"

She scowled. "Get up and you'll have time for breakfast."

I looked out the window and saw that the only light was the imitation sunlight from the streetlamps. "It's still dark," I whined. She ignored me and walked into another room. My stomach rumbled. I stretched and wandered into the bland dining room.

On the table was an assortment of bagels, ham, bacon, and sweet pastries. Fyra silently chewed on a bagel with a spread of butter, while Kaylaa inhaled a large piece of ham. I sat at the table and grabbed a bit of everything.

"The plan, Darynn?" Kaylaa asked, her mouth full.

"Can I just eat in peace? It's early."

"No."

I sighed and said, "The Diterians make weapons, not far from here."

"Are they reliable? Enough ammo?"

I shook my head. "Not most of them. But if a Diterian has it, then it works."

"Didn't the Diterians almost kill you?" Fyra asked.

I shrugged and scarfed down my breakfast. A few minutes later, we walked out into the still-dark morning. A woman was out jogging, but she didn't seem to pay much attention to us.

We crossed the junk field into Hargonla.

Daylight was just peeking over the rooftops when we reached a high, crumbling stone wall. From where we stood, we could see this wall was bookended by two turret-topped watchtowers. I knew there were three more, each at the point of a pentagon. Bright graffiti swirled all over the beige stone.

I had been inside the Diterian compound only once when I was considering joining the family gang. Building and selling weapons and robots seemed like a better job than running drugs and prostitutes like the Maltans. But, safe to say we didn't get along, and they never forgot it.

"How do we get in?" Kaylaa asked.

"Th-th-this seems like a bad idea," Fyra said.

I grinned. "Who said we were going in?"

I kept a hand along the rough wall as we crept around the facility. We moved around one of the towers and I motioned with my hand for the other two to stop. I peeked around and saw the front gate of the compound, which looked like a splintered wood drawbridge held together with dark iron.

"Now we wait." I leaned against the wall and slumped to the ground, waiting to hear the drawbridge open.

Fyra fidgeted, causing the ends of the white rope around her waist to swing. Her head swiveled, constantly scanning for danger. Kaylaa was so still, even her straight brunette hair didn't move. But her eyes were focused, alert. *They couldn't be more different.*

Finally, I heard rotating metal and creaking wood and knew the drawbridge was being lowered. I peeked around the corner and saw three people stroll out, all about the same height and size. Probably brothers. It's easy to spot a Diterian family member—gray skin, jet black hair, and obnoxiously bright clothes—lime green, tropical orange, rainbow indigo. One of them was wearing all of those colors, with a zany green cape flowing behind him. The other wore a pineapple yellow vest over a scarlet long sleeve shirt and sparkling white shorts. The

Diterians carelessly displayed their weapons as they strutted out of the friendly confines of their home. *Probably more weapons tucked away.*

Surely no one would challenge people walking with such bold and obvious weaponry. *No one but us.*

I let them get just out of sight before moving from my position. I scrambled along the side of the road, beyond the edge of their peripheral vision, Fyra and Kaylaa right behind me. Just when we left the field of view of the towers, I charged the nearest Diterian, the one with the amber vest and oversized machine gun strapped to his chest. With a quick horizontal slash, I cut the strap and the gun clattered to the ground.

Another Diterian, armed with a gun-sword, pulled his weapon and aimed the tip of the blade at me.

He was quickly disarmed by a vertical slash from Kaylaa.

I suddenly found a staff pointed right at my chest.

"Could burn a hole right through ya, kid," the staff wielder said in a raspy voice. The butt of the staff started to glow red like embers jumping off a fire.

My eyes fixed on the staff, I said, "Wouldn't end well for you."

"Jumpin' us in the shadow of the Compound ain't gonna end well for you."

"We'll see."

Kaylaa's strong hand grabbed the staff and ripped it out of his grip. His gray eyes opened wide in astonishment. "What the—"

Kaylaa tossed the staff to Fyra, who juggled it and dropped it to the ground, then picked it up. Kaylaa took up the machine gun and tied the strap around her. I picked up the gun-blade and pointed at the three Diterians.

"Got anything else?" They shook their heads in unison. "Liars. Empty your pockets." They didn't move. "I said empty them!" I shot the gun blade between their legs—a bullet slid down either side of the blade and hit in two places by their feet.

They produced some homebuilt Acid Pistols, cartridges for them, and small, charged daggers. Kaylaa picked up and holstered an Acip and a dagger, then handed one of each to me and Fyra. Fyra wasn't quite sure what to do with hers, and she held it awkwardly at a distance from her body, the staff still in her other hand.

"Let's go," Kaylaa commanded as she walked away.

As I turned my back, one of the Diterians let out a shrill whistle. Sirens blared from the Diterian Compound; instinctively, the three of us turned and ran.

The entire lightless neighborhood was woken up by the Diterian sirens; homeless people crawled out to the main street, blankets covering their thin and naked bodies.

We sprinted down the main street of the Diterian sector.

A deafening screech rang out overhead and two gleaming, silver birds soared high above the avenue, their gaze fixed on us.

"Sentry Eagles!" I grabbed my Acid Pistol and attempted to shoot the mechanical birds over my shoulder while still running. I missed badly without them even trying to evade. *Grandfather would've hit them.* "Kaylaa, you try!"

She stopped, turned on a dime, and opened fire with the light machine gun. Bullets sprayed into the air, but the Sentry Eagles just swooped and spun around them. It was almost graceful, except that these metal raptors' singular purpose was to tear out our eyeballs.

"Down!" screamed Kaylaa as she dropped flat to the ground. Fyra and I plunged to the pavement. The Sentry Eagles swooped down as low as they could, their razor-sharp talons extended menacingly towards us. They were forced to pull up at the last second to avoid crashing into the street.

We jumped back to our feet and continued our mad dash after turning down an alleyway. My heart beat so hard I felt like the walls were reverberating around us; a stone loosed and fell from the wall.

In front of us, a door opened. I grabbed Kaylaa's shoulder pauldron and Fyra's shirt sleeve and yanked them into the building with me. "They can't get us in here."

"Thieves! Thieves!" cried out a hysterical voice. A light switched on to reveal an older woman dressed in comfortable clothing, shakily holding a homebuilt pistol. "Out, out!"

I protested, but she interrupted, "I'll shoot!"

We rushed out of the building only to find the Sentry Eagles circling patiently overhead. Voices called out in the distance. "They've got to be over here somewhere!" Shadows crawled down the alley.

We sprinted in the other direction, the Sentry Eagles not far behind. We hurried on until we were in the Hargonla junkyard.

The open space of the junkyard was just about the worst place we could be with the Sentry Eagles overhead. We were surrounded by small mountains of rusted spaceship parts, twisted metal, and trash that smelled like old paint. They circled the clearing briefly, shrieking to report our location, then simultaneously descended.

Kaylaa stood still, her eyes fixed on the diving raptor. *Did she not see them?*

"Move!" I yelled.

But she just stood there, eyes trained on the glinting metal claws. Purple light quickly gathered around her feet and her hands, and when she opened her eyes again, they had mutated into eerie amethyst beacons.

"Kaylaa, watch out!" I cried in horror. The Eagles were moving too fast! I rushed towards her with my Plasma Edge drawn, but I wouldn't make it in time.

Just before the tips of their talons grazed her skin, Kaylaa glided out of the way, almost as if she was weightless, and spun her body in a circular motion, her Rapiers extended. Sparks flew as they sliced through the metallic bodies of the Eagles. The steel clanged to the ground as Kaylaa completed her pirouette. The glow in her eyes faded. I looked at Fyra to see if she had seen what I saw—she was just as awestruck as I was. Those birds had been diving faster than the speed of sound...and yet, Kaylaa was faster.

"Stop looking at me like I'm a ghost," she said nonchalantly. "You've seen magic before, stop being surprised by what it can do." *But not like that!* "And you're going to see a lot more of it." She tossed the machine gun to the side; out of ammo, I guess, and started out of the junkyard.

Before we could leave, I heard the clash of metal on metal; something fell off one of the nearby hills of rubbish, but I didn't see anything that made it fall. I listened intently—I thought I heard rustling, less than ten feet away, but when I looked, nothing was there. I held my breath and spun in a slow circle. The Diterian Sentry Eagles had alerted everyone to our location, but it didn't seem like anyone had picked up on it.

Another clang, this time softer, reported from my right. I looked to the spot, at a once-red pickup truck, but nothing there. My eyes climbed the hill of corrugated metal and trash bags, but everything was eerily still.

Out of the corner of my eye, I saw something. I jerked my head around and scrutinized the spot. Still nothing.

Kaylaa pulled out her Rapiers, which seemed to emit their own light. "You hear that, right?"

At least I'm not crazy. "I hear something."

I reflexively presented my Edge and flashed the blue plasma. Fyra stood a few steps to my left, looking at us curiously.

There were no sounds, no sights, for several minutes. *Must be nothing.* I needed more sleep. I sheathed my Edge and said, "I think you're just paranoid."

"Your senses are untrained. We're not alone." Kaylaa was deep in concentration.

Then I saw a shadow from the corner of my left eye. I looked, and a misty figure was advancing rapidly toward Fyra.

"Get back!" I yelled, rushing toward her.

A blade flashed and nearly severed her right arm from the rest of her body. Flesh hung loosely from her shoulder, white bone flashing through the lake of blood forming at her arm as her attacker disappeared. She wailed in pain hysterically as she dropped to her knees; I hadn't heard a sound so terrible since Pavlar's death. I dragged her limp body back into the light and laid her on the ground. I used my hand to support her head.

She hyperventilated feverishly. She looked at her wound then turned away in disgust and fear. Tears raced down her cheeks to the ground, mixing with the bright crimson blood.

Kaylaa seemed almost unaware of Fyra's gruesome injury. "Show yourself!"

"What's the matter? Can't see me?" growled a demonic voice.

I traced the source of the voice but saw only a long shadow from one of the junkyard trash mounds. Kaylaa advanced slowly, but I didn't think she could see the voice's owner either.

I held Fyra in my arms. She sobbed uncontrollably, her left hand covering the festering wound. We had no medicine, no bandages. *What do we do?*

"The girl will die," said the voice.

A painful wave of panic flooded over me. *Not again. It can't happen again.*

"No, she won't!" I cried.

"Only a Barma could save her now, and we killed them all," said the voice with a grotesque, wet smack.

A Barma?

Fyra convulsed. She seemed like she was having a seizure, but if I rolled her to her side, her arm might fall off.

"No no no no no," she said, feverishly.

"I can fix this, Fyra," I said, only half-believing it.

"You need to...protect...yourself," she replied.

She stopped sobbing, her tears dried. *Is she in shock?*

I thought of something Pavlar told me—that Fyra never cried when she was sick, or vomiting, or when she couldn't get out of bed from her sickness. She never drew attention to herself. She always focused on others in worse pain or closer to death.

I pressed both of my hands on the wound, trying to slow the bleeding while my mind raced for the answer. She screeched in pain but held it in as best as she could. The warm blood flowed over my fingers. *What do I do?*

The voice said only a Barma could save her. *Can I do it?*

I remembered the strange feeling that enveloped me, the weird light that filled the alleyway when Canfod did *something* to me. *I won't lose her.* Not like Pavlar. I had to save her.

A faint blue light began to emanate from my hands, first pulsing slowly but rapidly increasing in frequency. Surprised, I lost my concentration and the beryl light began to fade.

A loud sob of pain snapped me back into focus, and the light pulsed again. As it began to envelop Fyra's shoulder, her pain became my pain; I cried out in agony but closed my eyes and forced my mind to continue to focus. It felt like a Gryphon was tearing my arm from its socket. *Have to concentrate.*

When I opened my eyes, I watched as thin threads of flesh wove across each other as if manipulated by invisible knitting needles. As each thread of flesh crossed the wound, it integrated seamlessly with the rest of her skin. Rushing blood was choked back into the wound, unable to find a crack to seep through.

As her pain lessened, mine became more unbearable. Every nerve in my arm exploded, and even though some part of me knew my arm was uninjured, I was sure that it was being ripped away. Even visually reassuring that I had no injury did not lessen the pain.

Finally, Fyra's wound was completely closed, and my pain slowly dissipated. An ugly scar, like a patch sewn into fabric, still remained.

"H-h-how did you?" Fyra tried to raise up, but I lightly pressed her back to the ground. She rubbed her arm mercilessly, as if she could not believe it was still attached.

"I don't—I just knew I had to help you." I saw her mouth curl slightly into a smile. "I couldn't let Pavlar's sister die right after him." Her smile disappeared, replaced with disappointment. *Because I mentioned Pavlar?* "Kaylaa and I will handle this." I stood, keeping my feet near Fyra's body. "Come out, fiend!"

"Good show!" It chuckled, or I guess it was a chuckle, but it sounded like the spit of a pig roasting over a fire.

"Darynn, I think it's a Silopaskar!" Fyra said.

"A what?"

"Why can't I see him?" asked Kaylaa, now interested in what Fyra had to say.

"Silopaskars are shadow-people; they blend in seamlessly in the darkness," she replied. "They're supposed to be extinct."

"Not all. Arrogant Vastirians," it crackled, like a wildfire.

"Darynn, your eyes might betray you, but your magic never will," Kaylaa said. She closed her eyes and waited calmly.

I nodded, but I had no idea what the hell she meant.

Suddenly, her Rapiers and the monster's blade clashed; one, two, three bright flashes of light reflected off the old metal surrounding us. But I never saw the enemy, and the skirmish stopped. Something thumped behind me. I whirled around and swung my Edge wildly, but hit nothing and lodged it in hard rock beneath the pea gravel.

I flashed the plasma to quickly release it and searched my surroundings. My heart drummed arrhythmically and sweat dripped into my eyes. *How do you fight something you can't see?*

Another noise behind me.

I swung around, but with less conviction than before. I didn't want to get stuck again. I flailed wildly at open air, and then a terrible pain shot up my spine.

I reached around to my back with my off-hand and it came away covered in blood. I dropped to a knee and held my hand to the throbbing wound on my lower back.

"You are going to die here, Darynn Mark."

I managed to get back on my feet and balance myself. "I think it's time for the Silopaskars to go extinct," I replied. I concentrated fully on my surroundings, even as warm blood dripped down my back. I realized that I was standing in a shadow, giving it an advantage. I took a few steps to my left, positioning myself in full daylight. "Come and finish me off!"

I didn't hear it, but I felt the hairs on my right arm stand. *It's coming out of the shadows there.*

I crossed my blade to protect my body, and at the last second, saw the black blade slash at my neck. I blocked it and tried swinging horizontally.

I missed.

The blade flashed again, this time aiming for my belly. I parried and struck downward on where its arms should've been, but again hit nothing.

"How long can you keep this up?" it asked.

"Long enough." I swung where the crackling voice came from, but only hit air.

Then it struck at Kaylaa again, and a short exchange ended in a minor nick in Kaylaa's wrist. It disappeared.

"Even you are helpless against me. I expected more." Another quick skirmish, nothing more than a flash of sunlight and shadow. This time, Kaylaa avoided injury.

My breath quickened and my anxiety grew. *What is it waiting on?* I knew it was still around; I could feel its terrible presence lurking nearby.

"Darynn, to your right, now!" blurted out Fyra.

I swung to the right wildly and hit metal. I slid my blade up and flashed the plasma as I slashed the beast's skin. It roared in pain as the black sword clanged to the ground. Attached to it was its arm, which seemed to vary in shade with the light.

I slashed through the air in hopes of finishing it off, but it had already moved. A small puddle of silver blood replaced it.

"You...you...impossible!"

116

I could see the shadow totter a bit, growing long and short in the courtyard.

"You...Fyra...Fyra the Farsight!" It hesitated. "I will haunt you, Darynn." Then, like a fog lifting over a field, the sense of dread was gone.

Fyra jumped up and embraced me, but then released me before I could even react. "Oh, sorry," she said awkwardly. "Praise the Iveleen; I've never had a vision come to fruition that quickly. They saved you, Darynn."

"Fat chance," I muttered.

She didn't hear me and continued talking. "I think my powers are stronger. I knew exactly what he was going to do— I could clearly see the deadly gash in your throat."

"Did you change the future?"

"I-I-I'm not sure. But I sure hate that name, 'Fyra the Farsight.'" Her face soured as she said it. She rubbed her healed shoulder vigorously.

"It's hard to say whether it told you the future, or if it showed you what you feared in your heart," Kaylaa said. "Our alliance, our unity of purpose, has strengthened all of our magic. As the old cliché goes, it is our friends that make us stronger. Accept the bond, and accept the strength." She started down the nearest alley. "We need rest before heading to the Temple. But where is safe?"

"If we're going to be gone a long time, I should say good-bye to my parents," Fyra said.

Kaylaa shook her head. "Absolutely not. They'll be looking for us there."

"I can't just leave without saying good-bye. They just lost their son."

Kaylaa thought for a moment, then said, "We scope the flat out first. Then you two go in and see if they can spare any food for the journey. I'll keep watch outside."

We headed east, avoiding main roads and crowds. I watched Fyra closely as we walked, as if at any moment her shoulder would rupture. *I healed it.* I stared at my hands as if they belonged to someone else. *Our friends make us stronger*, Kaylaa had said. I guess that made us friends now—friends about to go on a dangerous journey following my father's footsteps to madness. *But at least I will know.* No more wondering about my father. Maybe, with that uncertainty gone, I could finally put him behind me. For good.

Current King is King Istar of the Plains.

Twenty-one Regions in Vastire ruled by Lords. By Vastirian Law, any House that has had a king may not again for one century. Hence Searon of Ziphyr, Lysta of the Soquok, and Castamere of the Lakes may not be the next King.

My analysis leads to either Lord Gaza of the Khellen, or Lord Delta of the Xalon becoming the next king. Both of them are extraordinarily wealthy and can likely buy support.

A wild card may be Lord Babajide of the Jinqir. No one from the four Southern Countries Houses has ever had a king, but he seems to have an outsized influence. Maybe due to the political maneuvering of his oldest daughter, Lady Chamalmet?

At this time, I would not recommend putting any resources toward favor with the other Houses.

—From Caval's Notes on the Houses of Vastire

CHAPTER TEN

"What is this thing?" Fyra asked, clutching the staff from the Diterians with both hands.

"Let me see," I said. I examined the staff as we walked—a knotty, white bark walking staff with two strange ends. One end looked like a blunt stalagmite, light blue in hue, while the other resembled a deep red glass flame. There were four grips in the middle, two gray, one blue, one red, each about the size of my hand. "It's an Erodian weapon, an Elenduil staff."

I spotted some loose garbage on the ground and pressed the flame end against it. Then I moved one of my hands to the red grip—the glass flame was engulfed in a real fire, and black smoke rose from the trash. "One side fire, the other freeze." I showed her the two grips that activated the ends and handed it to her.

"An enchanted weapon," Kaylaa said.

I nodded as we turned a corner. "Erodians enchant most of their technology. That's why the Erodian Conflicts all lasted so long." That made me think about my grandfather, the great war hero from the last Erodian Conflict, a big reason why we won. He was really old by the time I was born—my father was something of a miracle baby, born late in my grandmother's life. But he was always gentle, and his hands always still.

"Pay attention, we're here," Kaylaa announced.

We started our surveillance at the corner opposite the Solia unit, where an elderly couple still lived with young grandchildren. Every alley, every rooftop, was clear. We slowly circled the building, and even though we didn't find any suspicious onlookers, Fyra and I went into the abandoned unit adjacent to the Solia's. We passed through the unit, which was identical to the Solia's except for the thick layers of dust, like fine gray sand; then into the common courtyard.

Nature had reclaimed the courtyard, with overgrown fronds and spiky plants covering nearly every inch, except in the center. There was the shared outdoor kitchen, with a wood-burning grill, a stone preparing surface, and weathered cabinets covered with chipped red paint.

Fyra's mother, with her long, shining gray hair and pallid skin, stood at the grill, cooking. She whirled around when the door opened, but we were hidden from view thanks to the long, hanging vines.

"Mother, it's me."

"Oh, baby, I'm glad you're safe." Lia dropped a rusted spatula and rushed over to Fyra. "Don't scare me like that!"

Fyra embraced her and explained that we couldn't stay long. Lia shot me a suspicious look. Sweat dripped from my sideburns down my chin. Fyra asked about any food they could spare, and Lia led us into the house.

"Damnit Fyra, don't disappear..." Makaro said as soon as we walked in, but his relief quickly changed to anger. "I just knew it was your fault. I told ya, Lia, I told ya she'd run off with this damn kid!"

"Father, this is my path." Fyra must have repeated herself a hundred times, and each time Makaro's face grew redder and sweatier like he was holding a hot pepper under his tongue.

What does that mean, her path? I should ask her later.

Lia stepped out and brought back the chicken that she had been roasting on the wood grill. It was a meager bird, not nearly large enough for five of us, probably not even enough for

Makaro, but they shared it with us anyway. It was tasteless, odorless, and a little rubbery, but still felt good in my belly.

"Please, please stay," Lia begged.

"I have to go, Mother. I'm sorry."

I felt so awkward—surely they were thinking I was dragging off another one of their children to death.

Makaro dragged both of his hands down his face. "You're so damned smart...but you're gonna follow this fool. You act so dumb sometimes!"

Fyra's eyes went glassy and her lips parted as she looked at him in disbelief. But she didn't say anything.

He had no right to talk to her like that. But I knew why—Pavlar told me over and over again how guilty he felt because he knew he was Makaro's favorite, even though Fyra was the smart one, the pretty one. Even though she went to University, all he could say was that she didn't finish.

I almost said something to him, but I was too scared.

Fyra asked, "Can you please just pack up some non-perishables so we can go?"

Lia went to their cupboard with a rucksack while Makaro stewed. She loaded it as much as she could and handed the sack to me. "Some bread, nuts, potatoes, and dried meat. It's not much." Then she grabbed both of my wrists with her bony hands. "Please, please bring her back safe."

Makaro's obsidian eyes shot daggers from under the cover of his bushy eyebrows.

Fyra embraced Lia tightly again, then tried to hug Makaro but barely received more than a one-handed pat on the back. He might not see her again for a long time, and still he'd rather be mad. *Some father.*

I led Fyra through the back door, then through the unit we came through. Kaylaa found us and eyed the rucksack suspiciously. I held the bag while Fyra looked through it. "They shouldn't give us this much. I'm going back in," she said.

"We're going to need it," Kaylaa replied.

I added, "Pavlar still has enough goodwill—your parents will be taken care of."

She seemed satisfied with that response. "Where to now?"

We were at a loss, but Kaylaa at least guided us away from the house. We hadn't gone far when I heard the clicking of a cane on the pavement behind us. Looking over my shoulder, I saw an old man with a salt-and-pepper beard and chocolate-colored skin hobbling toward us.

"Darynn!" he called.

I turned around. "Do I know you?"

"You should."

I searched his features—protruding cheekbones, more hair on his sharp chin than on his head. His arms were too short and his legs were too long. His beard was twisted into two strands, each with a ribbon hanging near his chest. But it was his eyes I recognized—crystal blue, sharp like an eagle's.

"Master Makai," I said.

"Come with me," he said, and without acknowledgment, shuffled off.

"Can we trust him?" Kaylaa asked.

I shrugged. "He trained my father. But he left the Shard a long time ago."

Kaylaa didn't seem fond of the idea, her mouth twisting to one side. She sighed and said, "No better choice."

We caught up to the old man quickly.

"Where have you been?" I asked him.

"Think tactically, Darynn. Do you think it's a good idea to talk out in the open like this?" Master Makai asked.

He took two quick turns, and then led us into an unsuspecting building. It appeared to have once been a cafe, with a bar and wooden chairs and tables, as well as a few couches. There was a mural that was probably uplifting once but now was more depressing as it flecked off the wall. The smell of warm coffee still permeated the air.

"No coffee left, but it's a fine place anyway," Master Makai said.

"I haven't seen you in...eight years? At least?" I said. No specific memory came to mind—just generic images of him and my father sword fighting in blurs. Anytime my father even slightly missed his mark, Master Makai would whack him on the calf. My father credited Master Makai for making him a legendary swordsman.

"You haven't seen me, but I have seen you," Makai said. "I promised Zil I'd check on you from time to time. Lost track of you when your mother died, but heard about the raids and knew you had something to do with it. Came back when I heard the Shard were looking for you. You really stirred up the wasp nest, boy."

"Do they know you're here?" Kaylaa interrupted.

"No, got fired. I'm still too good for most of 'em."

"Mr. Makai, can we stay here?" Fyra asked politely. She sat down in one of the chairs, looking at him for permission.

"For a fee." I raised an eyebrow. "Want to know what the hell you're up to, armed like a Diterian and stocked on supplies."

Can we trust him? I knew my father did, but maybe that's not the best opinion.

"You can't stop us," Kaylaa said, placing her hand on her sword.

He stroked his beard. "Starlight Rapiers, eh? Yiptaen officer weapon. But you're too young for that. Kill someone for them?"

She ripped one out and swung it twice. "I earned them." Its thin blade was no wider than a finger, with a small handle that enclosed the hand and bright starlight emanating from the entire blade. *What was the source of its power?*

"Prove it." Makai picked up his cane and slid off the bottom of it, revealing a very thin Plasma Edge. *Awesome!*

"Yeah right," Kaylaa snorted.

Undeterred, Makai advanced slowly and swung his weapon at her. She deftly blocked it, but he struck again and again. He was not fast, but he was precise, and each blow forced Kaylaa to contort her arms into uncomfortable positions.

"Flat-footed. Otherwise, yes, you earned them." Makai sheathed his weapon.

Kaylaa glared at him and the seconds passed awkwardly.

"We're going to the Temple of Stria-Fate," Fyra blurted, cutting the tension.

Makai's eyes widened, then he swallowed as his gaze moved to the rotten wood floorboards.

"You knew my father went there," I said. "What did he find?"

"Never told me. Wasn't good. Think he failed it though, somehow. It changed him. He was a good man, an honorable man, until the day he died. Had conviction. Don't let anyone let you think otherwise. It's in your veins too, kid."

Good? Honorable? Hardly. "That's not a good thing," I said, fighting an oncoming wave of mixed sorrow and anger.

He whacked my calf with his cane. *Ouch!* "You're letting the narrative, the media, color your memories. He loved you, loved the Iveleen, and loved the people."

I rubbed my calf. "You don't know that! He left me! My mother died because of him!" I felt a single tear drop down my cheek.

Fyra came over and wrapped her arms around me. I held her closely and did my best to push away all thoughts of my mother and father.

"Sorry my boy, I miss them too," Makai said. "You can stay here tonight."

Kaylaa took a quick look around while Fyra seemed to be daydreaming at the coffee counter. Master Makai hobbled over and placed a small bottle of cream in my hand. "For your back."

"How'd you know?" I popped open the cap and applied a generous amount to the dagger wound in my back. "Got it fighting a Silopaskar, believe it or not."

"Heard rumors one lived here," he said. "So you beat him,

with Zil's weapon. Kept up your training, then? Glad you did. It clears your mind, gives you focus." He sighed. "Knew one day you would end up going to that Temple. Zil didn't tell me much but said the monsters are real—terrifying, bloodthirsty, deadly. Not going to say don't go, but..." He pleaded with his eyes. I felt a chill up my spine—the Vampires are real? *And that's where we're heading?*

He stroked one of the strands dangling from his beard. "Be good for you to get out of town. The Shard, Aseus, is more interested in you than you know. You are the viper, a powerful and dangerous hunter, but a shadow of a hawk slips along the ground beside you. You must avoid the hawk while hunting your quarry."

"Can you just speak plainly?"

He chuckled. "Habits of an old guide. It just means be careful, because a threat looms."

"Why would Aseus be so interested in me? I mean, they think I killed a Captain, but that's hardly a reason for his involvement."

"The truth can only be truly understood if you find it for yourself." He paused. "Your father was a great Shard. You should've been, too..." He lifted himself from the chair, his joints creaking like an oil-starved machine. "Lots of rest keeps old bones moving." Then he ambled back to a cot behind the counter.

I plopped down on one of the couches, and dust swirled like a storm. I covered the bright Captain's Ring with a torn pillow. Despite the lumps, it was reasonably comfortable, and the fabric was soft.

The hair on my neck stood on end and sweat dripped into my mouth. Warm breath kissed my neck, and hot blood ran down to my collarbone. My eyes fluttered open, but I was surrounded by total darkness. I sunk my fingers into the fabric. The smell of coffee brought back that I was still in the abandoned cafe. The boarded-up window didn't give me any clues on what time of night it was, but Makai snored loudly in the back, while Fyra curled up in an armchair like a housecat and Kaylaa sprawled out on another couch. They seemed to be sleeping peacefully enough, considering we were about to leave the city for the deadly wilderness.

I tried to rejoin them, but I couldn't escape that nightmare, the feeling of sharp teeth sinking into my flesh. *Was my father afraid?* No, probably not. He wasn't afraid of anything he could fight with a sword. He was full of exciting stories in exotic places with mysterious foes. When he told them, I wanted to go on these adventures. Dense jungles of the north, mouth-drying deserts of the south, and the shadowy alleys of Vastirian cities. Battles with notorious foes: the wicked murderer Lastar Xow, the slippery smuggler Bonn Trava, the deranged bounty hunter X. Occasionally, he would tell me about impossible battles that he won against all odds in the Mondoon Conflict. Sometimes, I thought he was exaggerating, and I'd look to my mother for confirmation; she reminded me he never exaggerated. It was all true—my father was heroic and powerful. Pride bubbled up within, but it faded quickly.

Now here I was, about to go on an adventure of my own, but it was still his adventure. It destroyed him. Why would we fare any better? What did he find? Was it something about the Iveleen? *Will I turn out just like him?*

I stood and crept over to the nearest window, peering through a sliver between two boards. Rain lightly pitter-pattered outside. Nothing to see but endless darkness. Then I thought I saw someone—auburn hair, strong jaw, slender frame...Pavlar?

"Can't sleep?" Fyra whispered. The phantom disappeared.

I shook my head. "Can't stop thinking about tomorrow. What if I go mad just like my father?"

"I doubt that it was something he found that turned him to...maybe it was just years of solo missions and constant danger? The pressure of the government? Or it could've been torture from the Yiptaen prison? There are so many things that lead to that condition...or a similar one, I guess."

She was right, of course. Being tortured in a prison for six months or longer could definitely cause that. Or maybe the visit to the Temple just took the finger off the pinhole in the grenade.

"Maybe we shouldn't go at all," I mused.

"But aren't you curious?" she asked, rising from the chair to stand next to me. "He went there for a reason."

"Risking our lives for some 'reason.'"

"What would you rather do?"

Good question...I shrugged my shoulders. "Just survive, I guess. Can't do much else in the slums."

"So then we get out of the slums. You told me before you were just looking for a fight—there will be plenty to fight out there." I felt a surge of excitement as she continued to talk. "To see the ruins of the Temple of Stria-Fate...a place that was supposed to be a gift to the gods, and instead, They cursed it. But why? It's supposed to be magnificent, especially for a place built with Vastirian hands." Her face glowed.

"A place surrounded by wild jungle and Vampires."

"I have prayed for the Iveleen to protect us. You should too. This is a great opportunity for us, to learn something about Them. Maybe your father just misunderstood Their message." She placed her left hand on her same-side shoulder, mirrored with her right hand, and bowed her head to pray.

I shook my head. "They don't care about me."

"Of course They care. Maybe They're giving you a shot at redemption."

Redemption? "More likely They're setting me up so you can die and Kaylaa can die, and torture me more."

She glared at me. "That's not how They operate, and you know it."

"That's easy for you to say! Your parents are alive! One of mine died in cold blood on television, and the other starved to death!"

Kaylaa stirred, but she didn't wake.

"My brother is dead, Darynn." The pain was clear in her eyes. "I see people die almost every day. Don't you think I feel tortured? Believing in Them is the only thing that keeps me going." She let a tear fall, then she curled up on the chair, facing away from me. *How does she keep her faith, despite all that?*

No chance I'd be able to sleep now. I couldn't stop thinking about the Iveleen. The Rise. Their immense power. Their caste system. Their watch over the world and the universe. Only one place to go.

I strapped on my Plasma Edge and quietly left the cafe. We were on familiar streets, even though I'd never noticed the cafe before. I walked southeast along the lightless roads, nearly slipping on Hargonla's wet cobblestones a few times.

The Hargonla Chapel truly was a marvel, like it had been carved out of a single block of wood. The wood wasn't weathered like you'd expect because it was built on sacred ground, which kept the lumber strong and lively as if newly hewn from a tree. There were countless arches over massive doors, leading to high vaulted ceilings. A golden spiral the size of a man hung just above the main door, coiling and uncoiling, flashing blindingly when lightning streaked across the sky. I took a deep breath and pushed past the heavy doors.

The smell of cedar pleasantly overcame me as soon as I walked in, and the warmth of oversized silver braziers invited me closer. There were only two wooden pews left in the church, near the back, as the rest had been converted into firewood. This place had electricity, but only enough to power the holograms that played endlessly in each side chapel.

I looked in the first side chapel, where a representation of the Rise of the Iveleen was displayed. The twelve original Iveleen descended upon the dark chaos of Vastire and cleansed it with Their immense power. Words flashed below the image: "The Iveleen came to force man to stop feeding on his own flesh."

I moved on a few rooms, to the hologram about Stria-Fate the Healer. It told the story of the Haskar Virus, which ravaged Vastire until She healed it, sacrificing Herself in the process. I watched the hologram a few times, but it wasn't clearing my restless thoughts. It told me nothing about the Temple, though I knew it was built to commemorate the event. Stria-Fate didn't curse it anyway—her grandson Bekivala did.

The last hologram, hidden in the back of the building, was supposed to bring hope to the Olan-Har. An Elite falls to Olan-Har, then his child rises to the Middle caste. Of course, that never seemed to happen anymore. I saw myself in the child, but could I really rise again? Maybe Fyra was right about redemption. But could conquering the Temple or ending the embargo really be the way?

"Darynn Mark, have you found solace in this sacred place?" a quiet, familiar voice asked from behind me.

"Is that what I was supposed to find?" I asked in reply without turning around.

There was a short pause where I could almost feel his head shaking. "I pray that your soul forces you in a different direction than your feet. I have heard very little that inspires promise from you lately."

"It seems that my soul is stuck in my body, Father Ckoost."

"Darynn...do remember the last of the Iveleen's, Silva's, dying wish. *Follow the road We have paved and thrive with Us in death.*"

The bitterness left me for a moment, but death could only remind me of those I have lost. Some part of me wanted to run into his arms like I had when Mother died. Without responding, I walked back into the street. The storm had passed, yet the dark clouds remained overhead.

I remembered the first time I had visited the slums. My

father brought me here as a lesson. I had seen someone die for the first time that day. I also saw a woman steal coins from a child. My father was trying to show me how blessed I was.

Now look at how blessed I am.

At least I was getting out of this damned place. Maybe forever this time.

12 Original Iveleen and their Artifacts:

Pavlon the Leader: Circlet of Pavlon
  user can persuade crowds
Makar the Warrior: Saber of Makar
  wielder is a great fighter with a sword
Deesa the Mother: Eyes of Deesa
  user can watch children from far away
Nebula the Mechanic: Tools of Nebula
  find any problem with machines
Stria-Fate the Healer: Chalice of Stria-Fate
  turns water into medicine
Josar the Sorcerer: Staff of Josar
  wielder can use magic
Rax-Kon the Builder: Hammer of Rax-Kon
  wielder can attach any two materials
Fyrain the Scholar: Tome of Fyrain
  reader learns to read and write
Lolan the Pilot: Compass of Lolan
  leads user to their heart's desire
Cuiray the Priestess: Amulet of Cuiray
  wearer can talk to the Iveleen
Windoon the Astronomer: Totem of Windoon
  user can control the weather
Qui-Tos the Shepherd: Lyre of Qui-Tos
  player can talk to animals

—From a child's church notes

CHAPTER ELEVEN

Master Makai scrounged up some bagels for breakfast. The four of us sat at the largest table in the café to eat. It was stale, but food in the slums always was.

"Zil said the monsters out there are immortal. No use wasting Acip casings on them," Master Makai said.

"So they're real?" Kaylaa asked.

"Zil wouldn't lie. Said all you could do was incapacitate them."

"You can't win the battles of the future if you lose the battles of the past, eh Master?" I said.

Makai smiled. "You remembered something."

"I remember you made me read more than I sparred."

"Glad it wasn't all for naught. Preparation is half the battle. You know how to get there?"

"North out of the city, then find the Old Crusader's Road. At least, according to the DataAxis," Kaylaa said. She clearly had thought about going to the Temple before.

"Sounds about right. You'll have to go on foot—the Road is no good for hovers, and the woods too thick for aircraft." He stroked his wiry beard, sighed, and fixed his gaze on me. "Be careful out there. The Shard are always watching."

We gathered our weapons and supplies and left the cafe, heading north.

After a few shadowy blocks, Fyra spoke up. "Kaylaa, you know the N-N-Nama-Da district is this way, right?"

"So?"

"The Nama-Da assault anyone who wanders into their district. They say the Nama-Da suck out the souls of those they kill, for their necromancy," Fyra said.

"I've seen it. The necromancy, at least." I shuddered as I imagined the wicked skeleton warrior that fought with Captain Salvak.

"It doesn't get easier after we leave the city. The forest is full of powerful and frightening creatures," Fyra added.

"We deal with whatever gets in our way." Kaylaa's confidence emboldened me as we continued onward. "Sure seems to be a lot of magic on your planet, considering it's illegal."

Fyra opened her mouth to respond but instead shook her head.

"They've all bonded to something—your religion is cutting off your bonds."

"What do you mean?" I asked.

"The bond is vital to magic. The other parts are the intent and the will, and a poorly understood genetic component," Kaylaa said. "Your necromancers are bonded to the land of the dead."

"So what's that mean for us?" I asked.

"I don't know. Neither of you makes much sense. Bonds are like a magnetic force—like being very attracted to something, or very repulsed by something. Both can work. Love or hate can cause a bond to draw power from. I'm not a teacher—my grandfather would be better."

"Your grandfather?"

She spat on the ground. "He's a wizard." *What does that mean?* She must have noticed my expression because she added, "Meaning he's proficient in many kinds of magic."

"Maybe we'll get to meet him someday," Fyra said.

For the first time, Kaylaa actually looked upset for a fleeting moment.

"We'll never get off this rock, Fyra."

Fyra frowned at me, then asked, "What about the intent and the will?"

Kaylaa thought for a second. "You have to know what you're going to do, that's intent. Will is being willing to sacrifice to do it. Intent requires focus; will requires resolve. Bonds can be with almost anything. I draw my power from alliance—as our alliance strengthens, so will my magic."

"Does that mean you like us?" I asked, trying to get a rise out of her.

She glared at me. "Allies unite for a common purpose, whether they like each other or not."

"That's not a no." I smiled, but my grin was quickly wiped away.

The stench of rotting corpses filled my nostrils, and the contents of my stomach tried to rise through my chest. Bones and skulls—mostly of people—lined the roads. Not a single light was on in a window, not a single person was on the street, and the whole place was as quiet as a cemetery. In a way, we were in one: the Nama-Da sector.

Fyra shrieked in horror and dropped to her knees.

"What's wrong?" I asked, rushing to her side.

She was sobbing. "Th-th-these skulls...I can see their faces. I can see how they died! The Nama-Da...they're monsters!"

"Quiet, or we're going to join them!" Kaylaa commanded.

But it was too late. A hooded figure emerged from the nearest alley. "Ccccelebritiessss in our ssssector," it hissed. Kaylaa and I presented our weapons. "I am alone, for now. Why have you come here?"

"Just checking out your bone collection," I said, trying to sound confident. *Not easy to do when facing a phantom.*

It glided closer to us, its black robes flowing around its thin body. "Our father Naman will have many of my brotherssss on you if you take this road. Follow me to ssssafety."

"We can't trust these monsters," Fyra said, standing on wobbly legs, her face still damp with tears.

"We are not monsterssss. Merely different."

"The bones say otherwise!"

"We did not kill mosssst of thesssse people. We merely collect the bonessss. If you do not follow me ssssoon, my offer will exxxxpire."

Shadows seemed to gather on the horizon of the main road. "I think he's right." I followed him into the nearest sidestreet. Kaylaa grunted unsatisfactorily and followed, with Fyra right behind.

At least there were no bones on this sidestreet, but the smell was just as bad. The road seemed frozen, with no movement whatsoever. And somehow darker.

"So uh...Nama-Da, why are you helping us?" I asked, partially just to break the eerie silence.

"Call me," it hissed, "Guide. While you would ssssurely die in a confrontatttion, sssso would many of my brotherssss. I'd rather avoid that."

The sidestreet was narrow but provided plenty of escape routes if we were ambushed. Something banged and clunked on the ground nearby. I swung my Plasma Edge, but it was just a brick that had fallen from the wall. Fyra jumped and gripped my right arm tightly, much to my pleasure. More than once, I thought I saw a flash of green eyes, but nothing was there.

"We're going too far east," Kaylaa said.

"We're here," Guide said. We had stopped at an intersection, and the building at the northern corner actually had flames flickering inside. "Darynn, you musssst come in here."

"Yeah, right."

Just then, three Nama-Da, all identical to Guide except in height, exited the building.

"My sssson was badly injured in the lasssst raid. Only you

can ssssave him."

I shot him a side-eyed look, with my focus remaining on the other Nama-Da. "Why do you think that?"

"A Nama-Da sssseer can ssssee when ssssomeone is clossse to death. The girl almost died a few dayssss ago, but you ssssaved her. Do the ssssame for my sssson and I will lead you out."

The Nama-Da that came out of the house advanced slowly. *If we go into that building, we'll be trapped for sure.* But if we stay out here...we'll have to fight. And there may be more of them.

"You should've told me up front."

"I wasssss about to come look for you. Fortuitousssss that you came here instead. Maybe a game of fate?" Guide said.

What does it mean?

Guide hurried into the building and pushed two other Nama-Da out. Then it motioned for me to follow. I looked over my shoulder before going in; Kaylaa's eyes shot from rooftop to alleyway, guarding against an ambush, while Fyra's eyes were fixed on me.

Guide led me to a bed.

I recoiled in disgust.

The creature was a shriveled brown mass of bones, complete with an oval head and a hooked snout. His bloodshot, lemon-yellow eyes were only partially open. The top of his head was bald but completely covered in a tribal pattern tattoo.

"I know that to your eyessss he is...hideousssss, henccccce the Nama-Da robessss. We did not alwaysssss look like thissssss." Guide pulled the covers down to the creature's waist.

From the middle of the chest down to the waist was a cavernous hole, revealing every internal organ. Blood ran freely through the surgically repaired veins, but several tubes punctured the lungs. Vomit crept up my throat, but I pushed it back down.

"Our doctorssss are not sssskilled. We only know

necromancccy. You're the only one who can sssssave him," begged Guide, holding its son's hand. It was strangely touching, despite their monstrous looks.

"This is pretty serious, but I bet I can do it." I placed my hand as near to the wound as I could without sickening myself and tried to imagine Canfod Barma's power, but nothing happened. I concentrated harder, remembering Kaylaa's words about the will and the intent and the bond. *But what bond do I have with this creature?* I remembered healing Fyra and felt the sudden urge to rub my shoulder, as if I was the one injured. *I must form a bond of pain.* I looked over the wound again: grotesque, wide-spread, and surely excruciating. But the only way to cure it was to feel it.

But still, nothing. *The intent, the will, and the bond...* "I intend to heal his wounds, and I want to heal his wounds so that we can continue on," I said aloud.

"You do not sssssound motivated enough," said Guide with a tinge of irritation. "You musssst heal my sssson." His polite manner was washing away to desperation; his last sentence sounded like a threat.

Sweat formed on my brow. I took a deep breath and raised my hands from the wound, then put them back down slowly. With my eyes closed, I tried to muster more intent or willpower to heal his son. But something about this place, something about Fyra and Kaylaa waiting outside, alone...something was blocking my focus.

I lifted my hands again and shook my head at Guide. It stood there motionless, soundless.

Swords clanged outside the window.

I hustled to the window. Two Nama-Da were attacking Kaylaa with sickle-like swords while Fyra stood trembling behind her. Kaylaa overmatched even the two of them together, but there were a third and a fourth standing behind the first two, raising their hands up and down—like they intended to raise the dead.

"Guide! Stop them!" I yelled, rushing toward the doorway.

Like an apparition, he moved in front of it, blocking my way.

"The only way to help them...isssss to help him!" it said, pointing a bony finger at its son.

I pulled my Edge from its sheath and threatened him, but from the corner of my eye I saw that Kaylaa was losing against the Nama-Da and the pair of undead warriors. I whipped my head back towards Guide's child and, without a second thought, raised my Edge above his head, ready to plunge it into his skull. "Guide, you will call them off, or I will crush his skull!" I flashed the plasma once to enhance the threat.

As quickly as he blocked the doorway, he banged on the window, attracting the attention of the Nama-Da. During the momentary distraction, Kaylaa managed to knock off the head of one of the undead creatures. While the four Nama-Da stopped their attack, more gathered outside, surrounding Fyra and Kaylaa.

Guide turned back toward me and said, "There isssss only one way out, and your time isssss running out. If you do not heal him before Naman arrrivesssss, your sssssskulllsssss will be added to our collectttttion."

I took a deep breath and placed my hands inside the gaping hole in the creature's body. The creature's organs squished sickeningly under my fingers.

I glanced out the window one more time—Kaylaa had her eyes closed, breathing deeply. Fyra's head whipped from foe to foe, her eyes fixed open wide.

With a flash, the power roared from my hands—silver strands of light slipped in and out of his organs like a needle and thread. My own insides began to howl with pain as if my intestines were being hollowed out by a great vulture with a slashing beak.

I almost doubled over with every new organ added to the mixture of pain, as I could feel my lungs, my stomach, my heart being mercilessly torn away.

But still, I stood steadfast. No amount of pain could prevent me from saving Fyra and Kaylaa.

Though it felt like it must have taken hours, within seconds the last bits of silver thread sewed up the wound and faded away. Copper lines marked the skin where the threads of flesh had been far apart, but no tears remained. The boy choked back to life with wide eyes. He grabbed my hand and squeezed it in a gesture of appreciation.

Guide sighed in relief. "I will lead you out. Hurry."

I could still feel the power pulsing through my veins, overwhelming the pain in my chest and stomach. I felt like one of the Iveleen—like Stria-Fate herself. *Blasphemy!* I flexed every muscle in my body. *So much power...*

"Darynn, I could teach you necromancccccy. With your extenssssssive power, I'm ssssssure you could masssssster the Netherworld."

Images of the Nama-Da who attacked the shipment days ago came to mind. I could still imagine the fear in the eyes of the Militia who fought them, fear brought on by the emergence of dead creatures walking once again. *Such great power.* I could almost feel my mouth watering. But... "No. The dead should be left to rest."

Guide nodded. "That issss wisssse. The plight of the Nama-da is the ressssult of our own foolhardinesssss when it came to the realm of the dead. There is always a consssssequenccce to usssssing magic. Ourssss is the sssslow transssssformatttion, over generattttionsssss from Kirilites to the very creaturessss we ssssummon." *Consequences to using magic?* Why hadn't Kaylaa mentioned this? "Tell your friendssss to come in. A back door will lead you to ssssafety."

I cracked open the window and called out, "Fyra, Kaylaa, come through here. It's safe now."

Fyra darted through the door while Kaylaa backed in, her gaze still fixed on the enemies. Once inside, their eyes locked on the gruesome-looking Nama-Da child. Fyra audibly gasped upon seeing him, but immediately covered her mouth and did everything she could to look away.

Guide ignored her and said, "Thisssss way, quickly." It led us into the main room of the Nama-Da household, which was scarcely decorated with tattered rugs, metal tables, and of course, bones.

Guide led us through a curtain into an empty alleyway. We rushed up the alleyway and I thought of how, despite the circumstances, it had shown us some mercy, and clearly loved its son.

"Thisssss isssss asssss far asssss I can take you," said Guide. "Three blocksssss north liesssss the outsssssskirtsssss."

"Guide, why not just give up necromancy so that your people can live peacefully?" I asked.

"It issss an addicttttttion; it isssss a part of usssss now. Sssssssometimesssss, we forget we are alive. Entire daysssss have passssssssed where I don't remember taking a breath. Many men can wield magic, but magic alsssso wieldssss many a man." With that, it bowed and slipped into the shadows.

Desperate to get out of town, we hustled north, until an explosion of color filled my sight.

Fyra gasped. "Wow."

Waist-high turquoise and verdant grasses covered the ground like a wild blanket. The sky above was clear and blue, Windoon's Star directly overhead tossing its rays onto the great field. In the east, the planet Ignis was faintly visible, reflecting its characteristic violet glow. From the grasses emerged sounds of wild creatures, their notes combining into the peaceful symphony of nature. Not far from us was a herd of Karkhar, massive creatures with long, twisted antlers emerging from their foreheads. A sweet smell of grass and honey filled the air. It was all such an amazing contrast to the dirty slums.

We stopped to catch our breath.

"What happened back there?" Kaylaa asked, looking up and

inhaling deeply.

I said, "At first, I couldn't heal the kid. I thought about the intent, the will, and the bond like you said, but nothing happened. Then, when I saw you in danger, it rushed out and healed him in minutes."

Kaylaa shook her head. "It is a classic problem when fools like you stumble across magic. You need to learn control."

"You need to teach me."

Kaylaa ignored me and started heading west. I couldn't keep my eyes off the sea of dancing grasses and the way the sun reflected off of them. I stumbled once or twice on the uneven ground.

"Have you ever seen anything so pretty?" Fyra asked me.

"Yeah—when I was a kid, I lived in a small town called Cax-Ark-Uhn. The whole village was surrounded by a prairie like this." Whenever my father was on a long mission, my mother and I remained in Cax-Ark-Uhn. When he returned, we'd move back to the city. Life was so much simpler there—the markets were local, cars used only to go back and forth to the city, and there was so much serene open space to play.

"I didn't know that." Fyra had lived in the slums her whole life, except for her brief time at University.

"Still a lot to learn about you. I mean, uh, me," I said. *Damnit Darynn! Get it together!* She smiled awkwardly. *Next thing to say...next thing to say...* But nothing came to mind. Instead, we got caught in the trap of an awkward silence. And the longer it grew, the worse it got—for me, at least.

"We're here," Kaylaa said finally, oblivious to the tension she just broke. A downtrodden dirt path broke like an ugly scar through the prairie, meandering north. It was not even wide enough for two cars side by side, and it seemed to rise and fall into small peaks and pits. I could see why it was unsuitable for vehicles, even hovering ones. "It's a half day's walk across this prairie, then five days or so through the forest."

"Well, we'll never reach the Temple at this pace!" I said,

feeling the enthrallment of adventure wash over me, like standing under a waterfall. Or maybe it was freedom from the city, liberty from the caste system. But even so, I remembered Master Makai's words about the Shard always watching, and I did feel like I was being watched. The watcher felt so close I thought I could even feel the tingling of breath on my neck. I glanced over my shoulder, but there was not a soul around. Pavlar's paranoia did really rub off on me. *I miss him.* I rubbed the stone Gryphon in my pocket.

We followed the road at an uneven pace between jogging and walking. I reached out to run my hands over the grasses, like a kid putting his arched hand outside the window of a car. They were light and fluffy like wool.

There was less than half a day's light left when Kaylaa froze in her tracks.

An enormous viper stretched across the road, entirely still, part of its body concealed in the high grass. Its angular head was larger than mine, its body thirty feet long or more. Two rows of sharp spikes began just above its nostrils, circled its eyes, and rippled down the body. Two jade green tails wobbled in the air behind it. Fortunately, something else had its full attention.

Kaylaa covered her mouth with her hand, shook her head, and backed away slowly.

The grass on our left rustled and I jumped into the air.

Knotted antlers poked out of the grass. The Karkhar was frantically pushing off its front legs, but its back legs did not work. The viper surrounded the Karkhar, and it bellowed a sorrowful sound.

"Aren't you going to do something? It's helpless!" Fyra whispered.

Kaylaa shook her head. "No. It's natural. More importantly, it's not trying to eat us."

Kaylaa was right, but I wanted to make Fyra feel better about it. I aimed my Acip at the head of the viper, but just before

I took the shot, Kaylaa disarmed me with a quick movement. She skirted around the viper on the path and encouraged us to do the same. I took Fyra's wrist and pulled her along. She covered her mouth with her other hand. Both of our hearts thumped loudly. I hoped the viper couldn't hear us over the moaning of the Karkhar.

Once we were sufficiently away, we sprinted until the viper was out of sight. I doubled over and tried to catch my breath. "Kaylaa...why did you...?"

"You just would've pissed it off. The Acip wouldn't break its thick scales." She handed me my pistol.

"I think that's the theory of Rapid Evolution," Fyra said. "Since the Iveleen and joining the P.A. resulted in Vastirians evolving technologically much faster than normal, animals have evolved at a quickened pace, almost like nature is arming itself against us."

Kaylaa nodded, and we continued along the road. For the first time, I noticed a wall of tree trunks and emerald leaves on the horizon—Soquok Forest. Before that, just to the side of the road, was a small, man-made building.

Kaylaa had noticed it too and was creeping along the road with both hands on her Acip. I followed suit.

The building was skillfully made from dead trees, and even though the logs were all different widths and lengths, the home fit together perfectly. It seemed like it was held together by living vines. The doors and windows were made of the hide of a Karkhar.

A twig broke behind us, and we whirled around, pointing our Acips. A tan-skinned man and woman aimed weapons right back at us.

The man was wearing rough leather armor and chains over his muscled chest, and a dark mane covered his head. The woman was hardly covered at all, with straps of soft brown leather covering her chest and legs. Both of them had blue and red feathers hanging from belts at their waists, and the woman had them strung around her neck too. A green vine (alive, maybe?) wrapped around one of her legs, up to her waist and down her left arm. Both looked strong enough to break a man's neck.

I tried to focus on aiming my gun, but the woman's body had me distracted, despite the fact that they were both holding long, curved sickles.

The man held out his other hand, ready to cast some horrible spell on us.

Erodians are divided into seven tribes that span the Eastern Continent. Six of these tribes are nomadic. Each tribe is led by a Chief and protected by a Champion.

While there have been hundreds of skirmishes between Vastire and Erodia, three main wars stand out:

The First Erodian Conflict in 83 ARI lasted three years. The Iveleen were trying to bring their light to Erodia, and the Erodians were not interested. The war fizzled after three years when Vastire recalled all troops.

The Second Erodian Conflict started in 220 ARI. The source of tension was Vastire's desire to join the Planetary Alliance, but a planet can only join when united. Erodians did not submit to Vastire's rule until they won the war after four years. The agreement allowed Vastirians to make decisions in the P.A. for the whole planet, and they did not gain any territory in Erodia.

The Third Erodian Conflict started in 420 ARI when the Erodians desired greater input to the P.A. This war lasted five years, and the Erodians may have won if their greatest weapon had not been turned against them when they landed at Ziphyr.

Distrust remains high between Vastirians and Erodians to this day.

—From a P.A. Brief on Vastirians and Erodians

Chapter Twelve

"This'a my house. Get outta he," said the Erodian man.

I felt equal parts fear and hate—my grandfather warned me many times about their brutality and power.

"Just let us through," Kaylaa said.

"Go on then."

Our eyes fixed on the couple, we backed away, still going north.

"You'a goin' the wrong way. Town's that way." He motioned to the south with his sickle sword. I felt sweat running down my cheeks as he twisted and turned the weapon.

"I-I-I think we all just need to calm down," Fyra said.

"Calm down? They're savages!" I replied.

"You'a one to talk. Pointed the gun at me first!"

"We're leaving," Kaylaa said, and we moved farther away from the Erodians. Once we were well out of range of their weapons, we turned and sprinted north. When the log house was out of view, we stopped to catch our breath again.

"Damn Erodians," I said.

Fyra hit my shoulder. "That wasn't necessary! They're just trying to make a living here."

"They're our enemies, Fyra! They kill Vastirians for the hell of it."

"That's not true. We were at war. We're not now. Can you

imagine how awful their lives must have been in Erodia for them to move here? Where they knew they would be hated and feared? They just needed a new start."

Kind of like I did.

"Was it because they're Erodians or because they presented a threat?" Kaylaa asked.

"Erodians *are* a threat," I said. Kaylaa looked at me disapprovingly. "Did you see them? They started three wars and keep on fighting! They're dangerous! And they know witchcraft!"

"Grow up," she said and started walking north. I looked to Fyra for approval, but she shook her head. *What's wrong with them?* I shook my head and followed them.

A wall of huge tree trunks twisted around each other, sprouting a canopy of leaves. Thin jade vines knotted around the branches and stretched across the gaps like spider webs. Newborn chicks squawked, monkeys hollered, and carnivores roared. All of the noises fit perfectly into the composition of the forest symphony.

Fyra dropped to one knee and prayed silently. Then she said, "The Iveleen Qui-Tos, the Shepherd, restored the harmony of nature after his work was done teaching farmland cultivation and animal domestication. This is His forest, where He laid His infant son Soquok to rest."

Kaylaa examined the overgrown road, littered with weeds and golden wildflowers, completely ignoring Fyra.

Listening to the song of the forest made it seem like a god was indeed conducting. Before I took that next step into the forest, I looked back on the city, now just a dirt mark in the painting of the prairie. My eyes moved up to the dark, cloudy sky, where a few objects glinted like stars in the daylight. Embargo ships. I felt a tinge of guilt for abandoning the Olan-Har to the careless royals and vicious gangs. *Is that from Pavlar?*

"You coming, Darynn?" Fyra asked. I nodded and stepped

into the forest.

It felt like a whole different world in the jungle. Now the sounds surrounded us, the light blocked by the leaves of hundreds of trees. The air was moist, and while it smelled fresh and minty, it felt heavy in my lungs.

Kaylaa dropped the rucksack on the ground and rummaged through it. She removed three potatoes and sat them on the ground. Methodically, she gathered some broken branches into a pile, just off to the side of the road, and instantly the bundle went up in flames.

"You made that look easy," I said, watching the flames dance on the branches.

"It *is* easy."

"But how do you do it?" Fyra asked.

"I told you—the intent, the will, and the bond." Both Fyra and I expected her to say more, but she didn't. Instead, she skewered a potato on a Starlight Rapier and held it over the fire. I shrugged and sharpened a lengthy stick with my Edge. I punctured a potato and handed it to Fyra, then made another one for myself.

I overcooked the potato, making it lumpy and uneven. Kaylaa had turned her back to us, I guess because she didn't want to talk, so I struck up a conversation with Fyra instead.

"I feel like a real explorer, like Sarka the Sailor or Itin the Traveler." I tried to remember if those were historical or fictional figures.

Fyra nodded. "Isn't it exciting?"

"Didn't Itin make it to the Stormlands?" She nodded. "My father told me about a Templar he knew that went there, and he swore there were settlements."

She shook her head with a slight smile. "Most of the Templars are half-mad now, even if they are the sworn protectors of the clergy. Your so-called settlements have been photographed from space, and even if they were once inhabited, they haven't changed in decades. Nothing can survive in that black soot wasteland."

Annoyed, I said, "The Templar said he used a sort of lightning rod to go out there. And he ran into some nightmarish electric creatures, like the gigantic Thunderbird."

"That's scientifically impossible—the lightning strikes are too strong and too constant."

"Not impossible, but unlikely," Kaylaa interjected. "Yiptaens have explored similar places." *Told ya so*, I thought as I looked at Fyra. "You need to get some rest. We should sleep in the trees tonight.

"Why?" I asked.

"Look around," Kaylaa replied.

All I saw were trees and bushes and green. I shook my head.

"There are large, deep prints on the road, all around us. Breaks in the bushes. Huge animals. Maybe dangerous. We'll be safer in the trees."

Now that she mentioned it, I did see faint impressions of paw prints in the road, as well as some larger depressions.

She was already climbing up the nearest, largest tree. The branches were spread out, but she fearlessly sprung from branch to branch and stopped about twenty feet up.

"Oh! I just remembered!" Fyra said. She whipped a writing pad and pencil out of her pocket and started scribbling fiercely. When she noticed me staring, she said, "I want to remember all of this. How it looks, how it smells." *Of course she does.*

I sized up the nearest tree and felt like a boy again, climbing a tree in the yard.

The branches of several trees came together at the place where I stopped. It was wide enough to hold my body, but even a jiggle to the right or left and I'd go tumbling down into the brush. I cut some nearby vines and wrapped them around my legs and waist.

I awoke to the whole world rumbling, like the tree was trying to throw me to the ground. The vines loosened around my legs and I clung to the branch.

Two monstrous creatures brawled on the ground below, like two small space cruisers mauling each other. Veiny muscles bulged from every part of their bodies as they punched with massive fists and stamped with onyx hooves. They tore at each other with sharp bull horns, opening new wounds next to old scars. *Minotaur!*

One of the Minotaur managed to lift the other, and tossed it against the tree next to mine; the tree broke in half and tumbled down on top of it. Dark blood washed all over its potato-colored skin, sticking in its brown fur. Even from here, I could smell the rotten blood. *Looks like we have a winner.*

But the Minotaur rose onto wobbly legs and shook its head violently, trying to regain consciousness. Blood streamed from its shoulders like tributaries into a flesh delta.

The winning Minotaur, distinguishable by a mane of hair around its collarbone, stamped and bellowed and grunted. The injured beast responded by bellowing and slamming its fists into the ground. The injured one charged but was rewarded with a powerful punch to the jaw. The two monsters continued their melee, furiously exchanging punches, splattering red blood upon every nearby tree.

After several minutes, they took another break, their chests heaving, and their mouths stealing air in the passing seconds. Then the injured Minotaur punched both fists deep into the ground, and starting another earthquake. Brown and orange energy surged around it. The maned monster charged, but before it could make contact, the injured one lifted a massive boulder from the earth, at least twice its size. It heaved the boulder, crushing the other beast under its incredible weight. The rock broke, and under the pieces, the Minotaur lay lifeless.

The victorious Minotaur roared thunderously. The sound rolled through the jungles for all creatures to hear; the news of the jungle was his victory. It stomped into the depths of the trees, crushing all the brush in its path.

My arms throbbed from holding onto the branches so tightly. I shimmied to the ground and admired the massive fist of the dead beast.

"I can't believe we just witnessed that," Fyra said. "They've probably been battling for weeks."

"Gladiators fighting over territory. One was bonded to the earth itself," Kaylaa said.

Fyra nodded. "They were fighting for the mantle of king of the jungle."

Then the earth shook slightly. *Maybe just a trick of my imagination?* But no, the broken rocks lifted up, and the bruised and bloodied Minotaur emerged from the rubble.

"How stupid...to come into...my forest," the monster said between deep breaths. *They can talk!* Its voice was somewhere between a lion's roar and an avalanche. It knelt on one knee, holding itself up with both arms on the ground.

I started to pull my Edge, sensing that the only way to beat this creature was while it was mortally wounded. But Fyra stopped me. "I'm sorry, my lord. We are just passing through."

The Minotaur gathered dirt from beneath its feet and rubbed it on its sore muscles. It said something, but some of the words were foreign. All I could gather was "Gawfaur went...spare you." Blood dripped off its body as it lifted from the ground.

We pointed in the direction the other Minotaur had gone. More foreign language, punctuated with "Kill you." It stumbled in the indicated direction, using trees to steady it as it walked.

"It nearly spoke P.A. Standard. How is that possible?" Kaylaa wondered aloud.

"Qui-Tos taught them language. He ordained them the lords of the forest," Fyra said.

Kaylaa lingered on that thought, then picked up the rucksack and started north along the road. "Lots of ground to cover."

Fyra and I followed.

"Can you believe they can use magic?" Fyra asked.

I shook my head. "Lots about them that's hard to believe."

"Bonded to the earth. I wonder how you go about that?"

I wondered too. The Barmas, the Nama-Da, the Erodians, the Minotaur...all this magic around us. *And me too.* Guide had explained the Nama-Da's consequence for using necromancy. What was it for all of these other peoples and creatures? *What about Kaylaa?*

"Kaylaa, Guide said something about magic having consequences. What did he mean?"

At first, she seemed to have not heard me, so I repeated the question.

She sighed. "It was right. You don't get to use magic for free. Many men can wield magic, but magic also wields many a man."

Same thing Guide said. A common saying in the P.A.?

Kaylaa hurried off, but Fyra pressed on, a touch of fear in her voice. "W-w-what does that mean?"

"It just means that there is a side effect. Healers feel the pain of the wounds they've healed. Necromancy is probably the most dangerous form of dark magic. The bodies are cold and should stay that way, and they steal back a little bit of warmth each time it's used," Kaylaa explained without looking at us. I felt anxiety creeping up my spine.

"What a waste—I healed that Nama-Da kid and I get to feel that the rest of my life?" I asked. "What is it for the Minotaur? For the Erodians? For you?"

"Consequences can be difficult to predict." She sighed. "For me...I'm unable to feel emotion."

That explains so much. "You mean no love, no hate?"

"Or anything in between."

"That's...horrible." Fyra said.

"It should be. But I can't feel it, anyway."

153

"How long have you been this way?" I asked.

"It doesn't matter."

"But I don't understand."

Kaylaa stopped to face us. "I use combat magic to overpower my enemies. It is common for soldiers to lose grip of their emotions and focus on survival. Love, compassion, morality—these things can get you killed. Now, they're gone entirely." Her eyes widened and narrowed almost into a glare, and she shifted her weight.

Fyra said, "You risked your life to protect me earlier, Kaylaa. You fought off those Nama-Da and protected me when it exposed you to more risk. That is a sign of compassion and caring."

Kaylaa shook her head. "It is a sign of alliance and common purpose. If you had died, I certainly would've lost Darynn. I don't have friends. My heart serves only to pump blood," she replied. Fyra vigorously rubbed her healed shoulder. Kaylaa did a mindless check of her equipment and then continued down the path.

For hours, we walked in silence. The light waned as the day continued; the trees seemed to twist to follow the light.

But all I could think about was Kaylaa and consequences. Magic had burned the emotion out of her. No wonder the Iveleen warned us about dabbling in magic.

What will happen to me if I continue?

As if on cue, I felt stiffness in my right shoulder, right where Fyra's arm had nearly been torn off. Just like Kaylaa said—aches of injuries that I had never had. The pain wasn't more than a distraction, but what if I healed many more wounds in the future?

I rubbed my arm and looked at Fyra. She didn't have a choice to stop using magic, not really. Kaylaa did, but she kept on using it, knowing the potential consequences. If I wanted to avoid the consequences, this was the time to stop.

But do I want to?

Something about using the magic felt so good, so...empowering. Healing Fyra was an obvious thing to do, but even healing the Nama-Da was worth it. It was like winning a battle against the greatest fighter in the world or demolishing an invading army with just your own hands. I could feel my mouth watering, and I looked at my hands like a newborn that had just discovered them. I closed them into tight fists, contracting the muscles in my forearms. I wanted to use the power again like I had at Shard Headquarters. I could level all of these trees around me if I wanted to.

Fyra was staring at me but turned away when I noticed. I must have looked like a fool, flexing my muscles. I shook off the thought of using my power and thought about Fyra's power instead. Hers was definitely the most potent—and the most dangerous. Changing even a tiny thing could drastically affect our futures. Even the negative things always have a purpose, learning through failure or falling through into something else. Could avoiding pain now cause more pain later?

How could the Iveleen do that to her? It's like she was just Their doll to play with, trying to see how she'll change her dollhouse if They give her glimpses of the future. *Are we all just Their toys?* I kicked a tall weed in disgust.

Windoon's star was setting, and it seemed like we were still in the same place we had been this morning—trees and branches and grasses and bushes. The monotony made me feel more tired than I felt I should be.

Kaylaa announced, "We'll sleep on the ground tonight."

"Seems like it was a good idea to sleep in the trees last night," I pointed out.

"Look at the branches carefully," she replied, pointing to the canopy.

I looked but noticed nothing out of the ordinary. "I don't see anything."

"Use your eyes! The branches have fresh, green scratches in them. Large raptors nest in these trees."

"What about the Minotaur?" Fyra asked.

"The birds are the immediate threat. The Minotaur have scattered the other predators, but not the birds." *She's so thorough.* "Now gather branches so that we can eat."

Fyra and I did as we were commanded, and then Kaylaa started a fire in the same manner as before. Then, strangely, she extinguished it. "One of you should learn how to do this."

Fyra and I stared at Kaylaa blankly.

"Not after what you told us earlier," Fyra said.

"I'll give it a shot," I said, feeling the desire to use my power again. Fyra looked at me incredulously. "It's just a little fire, Fyra," I assured her.

She looked at me disapprovingly, but Kaylaa ignored her and said, "You intend to light the branches, you have the will because of hunger. The bond is with us—we're all hungry."

Fyra crossed her arms.

I held my hands out over the bundle and thought about lighting them on fire. Nothing happened. I wanted to feel the power flow through my arms and into the fire.

"If you can heal that Nama-Da and Fyra, you can light a little fire!" Kaylaa said.

Frustrated, I started to lose my focus and all I could think about was how I couldn't light the fire.

Kaylaa shook her head. "No control."

"Well if you could teach me better, I'd be able to do it," I said.

"Don't blame me for your lack of control." She lit the fire herself and again we roasted our potatoes over the fire. I fixated on my failure as I mindlessly ate the mushy potato.

As soon as we finished eating, Kaylaa laid down on a patch of grass next to the road. "We should sleep close tonight. In case a predator comes along." She motioned for us to lie down next to her.

Fyra hesitated for a moment, and I felt like I could read her mind. She was probably thinking about what Kaylaa said earlier about protecting allies, and not being friends. She sighed and reluctantly settled down next to her.

So...sleep next to Fyra or Kaylaa? Not the first time I'd be sleeping next to a girl I didn't know very well...but this was awkward. Kaylaa probably wouldn't be any different than Pavlar—but Fyra? My stomach fluttered. But maybe this was a good way to show how I felt...*however that is.*

"Will you just lay down already?" Kaylaa asked, and I realized I had been shifting noisily in the grass.

It just seemed like the better idea to sleep on Kaylaa's side. *She can't feel emotions anyway, right?* I left a good amount of space between us and faced away from her.

But I couldn't stop thinking about Fyra. A low hum of insects filled the air, a bird occasionally cawing with no response. I rolled over and faced Kaylaa—she really was beautiful, despite her hardened features and never, ever smiling. Fyra was exactly the opposite, with her soft features and fleeting smiles. The kind of face you want to bury into your shoulder, the lips you want to kiss...

Kaylaa began to snore lightly. I made a mistake. I definitely should've laid down next to Fyra. I started to stand up to move but decided against it. *How weird would that be?*

I thought I heard something in the brush nearby. I looked in that direction, but couldn't see anything in the blackness. But it was silent, other than Kaylaa's snoring. Even the bugs had gone quiet. A shiver ran down my spine—I had the strongest urge to just ignore it and hope it went away. *It won't.*

I jumped up to my feet with my Edge in my hand and examined the area, but found nothing. Kaylaa and Fyra were still sleeping. I shook the bushes, trying to expose whatever had been there, but all I managed to do was kick up a cloud of dust. I smelled a faint whiff of cologne and baby power.

I laid back down—next to Fyra this time.

Even though Kaylaa was snoring louder, I felt much drowsier than before. I fell asleep almost instantly.

The Iveleen Qui-Tos approached the dark woods, even as they told Him to turn back. They warned him of the violent chaos in the forest. He was not deterred, and armed only with His Lyre, he stepped into the trees.

No light escaped from the mangled branches above, crawling things wriggled over his feet, moss and mold grew over every surface. Wolves and Minotaur and other beasts approached, bloodlust in their eyes.

Qui-Tos found a stump and wiped the mold away. He sat and plucked His Lyre, His eyes closed, His mouth singing a peaceful melody. Animals gathered around, prey and predator alike, and listened in awe as He played.

The music gave them instructions, told the wolves how to hunt, but to only eat their fill; charged the Minotaur with protecting the forest and making sure it endured; taught the birds how to sing the same melodies he played; and informed the trees how to grow to let the light in and stop the mold.

—From *The Tale of Qui-Tos*

CHAPTER THIRTEEN

"What do you make of these, Kaylaa?" I asked, examining the deep impressions in the ground from where I had heard the noise last night.

She inspected the prints, each paw was as big as my feet. Strangely, they just disappeared—no trail at all. There was some golden fur caught in the bushes, and a few white feathers flecked with gold. *Some sort of cougar that ate a bird?*

"Whatever it was," Kaylaa said, "it was huge and uninterested in us." She picked up one of the feathers, as long as her forearm, and twirled it between her fingers.

Fyra took the feather and studied it. She shrugged and tossed it on the ground.

"It's late, no time for breakfast. Let's go," Kaylaa said.

Why is she in such a hurry? She tossed me a piece of stale bread from the rucksack.

I caught it, broke off a piece for Fyra, and bit into it as we walked. We had walked on in silence for a while, and I listened to the harmonious songs and chirps and grunts of the forest. It still didn't seem like it had changed much—same road, same trees, same darkness.

"Darynn, I had another vision last night," Fyra said to me, not loud enough for Kaylaa to hear. "That same man as before, with the Golden Spiral circlet."

Who is this guy? "Why do you think you keep dreaming about him?"

"I don't know. Maybe he's going to die very soon? But that's not the point." She bit her lip. "I've been thinking. About my bond. I wonder if I could be bonded to...time? Or what if, I'm bonded to d-d-death, just like..." She swallowed. "Like the Nama-Da?"

"You're nothing like them." I started to reach out to reassure her with my hand on her shoulder but pulled back. "You actually care about those people."

"But...yeah...but, at least then, I might be able to figure out a consequence. But what if it is time? Isn't that dangerous?"

"What do you mean?"

"What if I can change the future? Even by accident? What if that's my consequence?"

I shrugged. "Not much you can do about it."

"If something happened that wasn't supposed to happen—or the other way around. That could be disastrous. I can't handle that. How would anyone make a decision, knowing that it could change the intended future?"

"What's that even mean? The only future is the future. Everyone makes decisions every day that set the future."

She considered what I was saying, but it clearly wasn't helping her anxiety. "But they don't see something else in the first place. I've seen what is supposed to happen. What happens if it doesn't?"

"I guess it doesn't happen then, and something else does."

Fyra sighed. "You're no help at all."

"I can't even start a fire. Ask Kaylaa."

She stumbled a bit but caught herself before she fell. "I guess. Kaylaa? Can I bother you?"

"What?" Kaylaa asked without breaking her pace.

"Can I be bonded to time?"

"Psychics, fortune-tellers, soothsayers are all bonded to time. A lot of fakers out there, but they do exist."

"What is their consequence?"

Kaylaa didn't respond for an overly long time. "Some isolate themselves to minimize what they can affect. Some anxiously overthink every decision, trying to drive toward a future. Most find that no matter what they do, what they see is what happens."

Fyra chewed her lip. "So what should I do?"

"I don't know. Magic partially controls our destiny, but it just sets the wheels in motion. Free will determines the future." She quickened her pace to get ahead of us.

"She sure does know how to end a conversation," I said. Fyra didn't respond, deep in thought. "What do you think my bond is? My consequence?"

She shrugged. "I don't know. Your powers seem to be on opposite ends of the spectrum. Healing or destruction. You probably feel the need to protect me with Pavlar gone." She sniffled.

Only because of Pavlar? "We're friends, right?"

"Yeah, of course, friends." She rubbed her shoulder. "Do you feel this too?"

I touched my shoulder. "Sometimes, like a small ache. Worth it, of course. I guess the healing consequence is easy, at least."

She nodded.

But what about the destruction? Shard Headquarters, the third raid? Would I end up like Kaylaa? Or worse?

The birds sang above our heads, a charming little song. Some vines that were hanging down into the path were covered with small pink and purple flowers that smelled like berries and lavender.

After a few hours, Fyra said, "Kaylaa, can we take a break? My legs are sore." I realized that my legs were starting to ache, too, and I was in pretty good shape for an Olan-Har. Fyra must have really been hurting, especially since she was still weak from her illness.

Kaylaa sighed. "A few minutes."

"Why are you in such a hurry?" I asked as I sat down next to a tree.

"I'm on the clock. If this turns out to be a waste of time, I'll lose my job. But there is a chance whatever your father found pushes you into the same course of action."

I studied her facial expressions closely, in light of what she'd told us, but they were generally blank. She should have been frustrated, but it wasn't in her tone of voice nor her face.

"Besides, people are dying every day in the slums," Fyra added. "That's reason enough for us to hurry."

"What if...we just never went back?" I asked sheepishly.

"Coward," Kaylaa sneered.

"We have to go back," Fyra replied.

"Why?" I asked. "We're being hunted there. We're in constant danger of being attacked or dying of starvation or getting sick. It's so much more peaceful here, even with Minotaurs and who knows what else."

Fyra said, "We have a responsibility to—"

"We don't have any responsibility! We're not better than them. We don't owe them anything."

I felt like the ghost of Pavlar was there, arguing right along with Fyra. Some of Pavlar's words echoed in my head; "We need to help them, Darynn. We're stronger than most of them. We should share our strength."

Fyra said, "I believe the ability to see the future was given to me for a reason—and that's to help the Olan-Har. "I don't know how, but that's what seems right to me. You have power too, and if you choose to use it, you should use it for them. We have to go back."

I sighed. "I guess. If you're going to go back and help the Olan-Har, you're going to need a bodyguard." *At least then I'd be close to her.*

She nodded. Then Kaylaa said, "Time to get going. Some daylight left."

We walked for a few more hours until the only light left was Kaylaa's Rapiers and my Captain's Ring. Kaylaa didn't bother to let me even try to start the campfire, but we did mix up the dinner by cooking a can of broth and dipping the potatoes and bread in it.

We didn't talk much over dinner—Kaylaa wasn't much of a conversationalist anyway, Fyra was shy, and I couldn't think of anything to say. The trip was getting a bit monotonous—potatoes and bread for every meal, surrounded by huge brown trees with high canopies and twisted branches, and a dirt road to follow.

"How much further to the Temple, Kaylaa?" I asked.

"Two more full days."

Two more days of this. But the Temple...that would be different. And it would come with a different kind of danger. I remembered what Kaylaa said: *Whatever your father found pushes you into the same course of action.* A revolution? No way. Madness seemed more likely.

"Trees tonight," Kaylaa said, clambering up the nearest tree. Fyra and I climbed up into two trees next to each other. The branches were flat and wide, with space to lay down. I could nearly reach Fyra, and part of me wanted to.

I woke up to the sound of hoarse breathing. I slowly slipped my arm to my side and gripped my Edge, then rose to face the onlookers.

There were two of them, and they were hideous—like a fluorescent green iguana crossed with a monkey, standing up on their back feet, no taller than the length of my arm.

"What the...?"

"Stick to ya spot, kid," said one of them in a raspy voice, pointing a primitive spear made of a sharpened stick at me. *Another creature in the forest that can talk!*

I flashed the plasma once, and both of them jumped back. Their legs were short, but their arms were long, and their claws seemed even longer. They used their arms and claws to steady themselves and pointed their spears at me again.

One of them, who had a shimmering rainbow crest on top of his angular head and wore yellowish fur in a vest and around his pelvis, lowered his comrade's spear.

"Where you goin'? Temple like dat utter guy?"

Fyra was awake too, watching intently. *What other guy?* It couldn't be my father—it had been more than five years. I nodded, but the lizard monkey didn't seem to understand the gesture. "Yeah."

"Strange tings happenin' dere. Always." He abruptly took a deep whiff of the air. I did the same, expecting to smell something, but just the same minty air. "Stay off da road."

"Why?"

He peered at me with yellow eyes and one eyebrow—eye arch— up. "We Libras know. Stay on da branches. Lots o' wolves. Dey kill anythin' up dat way." He motioned up the road.

"Then how do we get to the Temple?" I asked.

One of his eyes narrowed while the other widened. "Stay in da trees. Don't go all da way, but get ya mostly dere." He pointed a long, scaly finger. "Dis way. Count only tree trunks on da right. Can't touch it, don't count it. Left after nine trunks, then five and ninety trunks. Left again. Then eight and ten trunks. Then back to da old road."

I stared the way that he gestured, and incredibly, it looked like there was a road there, made of branches, covered in scratch marks. "Can you guide us?"

"No no. Must get to da village. New Minotaur lord. Vastirians in da forest. Big big news." And with that, he pushed past me, as did the other one, and they disappeared into the night.

"That was incredible!" Fyra whispered, her eyes sparkling. "I've read the myths, but they're real! We wouldn't have seen them if we hadn't been sleeping way up here."

Her enthusiasm was infectious, and I smiled. *What hadn't she read about before?* "Good luck getting Kaylaa to follow the branch road."

"I'll leave that to you."

I smirked. "Thanks."

"I wonder what else we'll run into in this forest?"

"No telling."

I tried to go back to sleep, but there was no way. I wondered how late it was as I stared up into the canopy—branches woven over one another in random patterns, with large, round leaves sprouting everywhere, blocking the sky. The branches shook back and forth rhythmically, seemingly more and more as time went by. I'd bet it was going to rain today.

Kaylaa called up from the ground, "Let's get going!"

Morning already? "Kaylaa, the branches up here are like a street—we should take them!"

"We should stay on the road."

"Come up here and I'll explain."

Reluctantly, she climbed up my tree and examined the flat branches. "What makes you think this goes anywhere?"

I explained the story of the Libras and the dangers on the road.

"I think you were dreaming."

"I saw them too," Fyra added.

Kaylaa sighed. "Lead the way."

The branches were wide enough for two Libras to walk side-by-side, so we were able to hike single file in a hunched-over sort of way. Ropes dug into the core of the branches: the Libras had forced the branches to grow this way. Anywhere one branch wasn't thick enough, another had been pulled and tied in. Thunder rumbled overhead; I hoped the branches wouldn't get slippery if it rained.

After twenty minutes or so we had passed the nine trees within reach, and as the Libra had described, there was a large road, three Libras wide, heading north on our left side.

"I think we should all count individually this time, in case one of us loses count. This is where we might get lost," Fyra said. "Ninety-five tree trunks, he said."

Just as the Libra had said, if we could not reach out and touch the tree trunk, we did not count it. Some of the trees were questionable, and we kept count of these separately, just in case it seemed like we had gone too far.

Discomfort grew within me with every step away from the road. Though it clearly ran north, with few twists or turns, I was afraid we could end up missing the Temple or never finding the Old Crusaders' Road again. The jungle looked the same, tree trunk after tree trunk.

This fear felt strange to me; it was always Pavlar's job to worry, not mine. If it sounded like a good idea, I went with it. But this time, there was a new apprehension foreign to me. It was like that soldier's mentality of *receive orders, execute orders*, was wearing off of me.

Did my father ever worry about stuff like this? He always seemed so sure of himself, at least until those final years of his life. He'd always preached that there was no sense in worrying because it just weakened you when you tried to do it. But he didn't always follow orders, either; he did things his way, as long as it accomplished the mission. *Maybe that's what doomed him in the end.*

"Thirty-three," Fyra said. "How much progress do you think we've made?"

"Difficult to tell," replied Kaylaa. "But I'm at thirty-four. Did you miss one?"

"Probably. I'm never sure when to count them. Darynn, how many did you count?"

I looked at her blankly. "I lost count at about twenty," I replied, embarrassed.

"Darynn, you need to pay attention," Kaylaa demanded. Their expressions, while different, both conveyed the same look of annoyance. I realized how difficult it was to travel with two women for so long, especially for a clueless guy like me.

"Yes, I know. I'm sorry. I'll start at thirty-three, and pay more attention."

I concentrated on the forest around us. "Thirty-four," I thought to myself, reaching out for a tree. After a few more steps, "Thirty-five." Then I heard growling from below.

Three massive gray and brown canine creatures were below us, clearly stalking something out of sight. Each one was probably as high as my waist at the shoulder, and three times my weight.

"The Libras were right, praise the Iveleen," whispered Fyra. *Maybe the Iveleen are watching us after all?*

"We could've fought three of them," I said.

"The rest of the pack is probably nearby," Kaylaa said.

"Can you see the prey?" Fyra asked.

"No, no...wait...I see something."

A pair of large, russet elk-like creatures became visible. One of them sported a gigantic set of horns of at least thirty points. The other was a bit smaller and lacked horns. The horned elk stood in front of the female, strutting and stomping confidently in hopes of scaring off the wolves. The elks were cornered against two trees close to each other, and the wolves circled.

"I don't want to watch this," said Fyra nervously, hurrying along the route.

"The male elk should move on. He can't stop three wolves," Kaylaa said.

"Would you?" I asked.

She thought for a second. "If there was no hope." I can't say she exactly surprised me with the answer, but I really thought we were becoming friends. *Guess not.* Just as the wolves were out of sight, we heard the sad bellowing of the elk.

The day continued on uneventfully in the trees until we reached the eightieth tree trunk, by Fyra's count. More growling beneath us. This time there were eight wolves in a circle and one wolf in the middle with five pups nursing.

"You see," whispered Fyra triumphantly, "there are more than just three. The Libras were right."

Kaylaa gritted her teeth. "But they led us over the den."

As if on cue, raindrops poured from the sky, making the branches ahead slippery. *Here is how the Iveleen even out our good fortune.* But the Libras did have one more clever design—there were small holes and channels in the branches to drain the water. Even so, they were still getting slick.

The wolves seemed to be having a conversation in growls. They all fell silent when another gigantic wolf, a head taller than the others, emerged from the woods. Its gray fur was drenched in blood and mud, and it dragged one leg behind him.

Kaylaa pulled on my sleeve to keep us going.

We had only passed four more tree trunks when the ground started to shake. I slipped from the branch but luckily grabbed it with both of my arms. I pulled myself up, but stayed down on my knees, grasping the branch. Smaller branches and leaves fell from above as the world violently quaked.

A Minotaur was just below us. Claw marks and bites covered its arms and legs. The air reeked of blood. He stopped and sniffed the air, seemingly aware of our presence but unable to find us. Why was he chasing a wolf? Didn't he have his brother to worry about?

After a few deep breaths, he stamped toward the wolves' den.

We waited a few more minutes until Kaylaa motioned for us to follow her. The next few tree trunks we passed silently, afraid of what dangers could be lurking nearby, but at about the eighty-fifth tree, we relaxed again. And the rain stopped.

The silence was quickly filled by the strange song of a small bird. It sounded like music composed on a piano, with a beautiful rhythm and harmony. It was so soothing, even Kaylaa was looking for the bird. Fyra finally spotted it, a tiny red-breasted bird that could fit in the palm of my hand. It danced back and forth on the branch as it sang.

"Qui-Tos Himself is giving us encouragement," Fyra said. I tried not to let the thought of the Iveleen ruin the song for me.

"It's almost dark," Kaylaa said, rudely interrupting the melody, but she was right. We definitely didn't want to still be in the trees when night fell.

Fyra counted the last few trees aloud, and we turned left on the ninety-fifth tree. "Eighteen to go. I hope I counted right."

My legs and back were sore—it wasn't quite like walking a tightrope, but we were high up and the path was narrow. This seemed to be some sort of side street compared to the main highway before.

After fifteen tree trunks, it was too dark to see anymore. Kaylaa said, "We should get down—should be close enough to the road to find it."

We murmured in agreement and slid back down to the ground. As we'd hoped, we stumbled upon the road quickly.

"We should still sleep in the trees," Kaylaa said.

"I'm tired of the trees," I muttered.

"Would you rather the Minotaur or wolves find us?" I shook my head, and Kaylaa opened the food pack. "Broth and bread tonight—it's all that is left."

"We could trap something," I suggested.

"Wolves and Minotaurs have scared all of the prey."

Kaylaa had a little trouble keeping the fire going with the wet branches, but she succeeded, and then she...she levitated the can over the fire, boiling the broth inside. She motioned the can back and held it, red-hot, just above her open hand. Fyra and I dipped our bread in the hot broth, softening the staleness.

"I really don't want to get back up in those trees," I said between bites.

"Why doesn't someone tell a story, then?" Fyra suggested. Kaylaa didn't respond; she just took the last bite of her bread and turned away.

"You're the smart one, you do it," I said.

Fyra shrugged. "I don't think you'll like my stories—probably about the Iveleen." I nodded in agreement. "Maybe a war story? You know your military history, right?"

"I guess I know one, but I'm not a storyteller."

Fyra gave me an encouraging smile.

"In the Third Century War with the Erodians, a Captain named Hurroc was leading a company in an Erodian forest, a lot like this one. His men made fun of him because he was insistent on protecting the trees—apparently, he had an ancestor who was a personal Templar protector to Qui-Tos. They called him Woodwall."

"I think I've heard of him," Fyra said. Even Kaylaa had turned back to the circle to listen.

I nodded. "I can't remember why they were in the forest, but it was between two strategic points. Their company of fifty was ambushed by at least twice as many Erodians. But under Woodwall's command, they formed a barricade that held off the ambush. They used the living trees as part of their wall, turning the terrain in their favor. They slew all of the Erodians, while only a dozen of their own died. They managed to move on and capture the strategic point and held it throughout the war.

"After that, Woodwall became a commendation instead of an insult, and he was later promoted, though he never went to war again. And that's the story of Captain Woodwall."

"I thought that was pretty good, though you could've been more animated," Fyra said.

"So what is the lesson? Protect the trees and they'll protect you? Maybe in an enchanted forest, but not this one," Kaylaa remarked.

Fyra sat up. "Why wouldn't this one count as enchanted? A god frequented this forest, and buried his Divine son here."

Kaylaa just grunted and shrugged. Without another word, she climbed up unto the nearest tree.

"She's just so...infuriating. She can't even stay and have a rational argument. She just makes her opinion known and runs off. Why can't you ever back me up?"

"What?"

"Back me up against Kaylaa," Fyra said, exasperated.

"How? I can't convince her of anything."

"You could at least try."

"Why?"

"Are you going to ask who and when next?"

"What?"

She threw her hands up. "I give up." She scoped out a tree and climbed it.

What was she even talking about? She seemed pretty upset, but why? Arguing with Kaylaa was like punching a wall. But I definitely didn't want Fyra mad at me. Would she be okay in the morning?

Yiptaen culture revolves around creating, spreading, and storing heat since the average temperature is -15 degrees. In some regions, it snows almost every day. Geothermal vents have historically been at the center of any large settlement.

The capital of Yiptae is the city Akuun Dey, which sits on the largest geothermal vent on the planet. However, most of the population lives in the Megalopolis, a collection of domed cities on the equator.

The Yiptaens charted their moons within a century of their first rocket launch. Then they were the first to interplanetary spaceflight in the Windoon system, leading to a large immigrant population (primarily Yindians and Khalerians) that outnumbers the native folk. The Yindians, mostly peaceful, willingly submitted to Yiptaen influence. Khaleri rejected Yiptaen influence, leading to the first interplanetary war in the system.

—From a P.A. brief on Yiptae

Chapter Fourteen

Lightning crashed above and rain plummeted from the skies, streaming off the canopy before splashing on the ground. The forest seemed cooler, but the darkness interrupted by short bursts of light was unsettling. To make matters worse, the road was covered in a thick layer of slippery mud.

"Can't let the rain slow us down. We are reaching the Temple today," asserted Kaylaa. She held out a Starlight Rapier to lead us on.

Fyra tried to wring rain from her hair, but found it impossible to do so, and gave up. Even now, drenched and worn down from the journey, she was still beautiful. And Kaylaa, the true soldier, looked completely unaffected by the long journey or the rain.

Mud covered all of us from the waist down, caking on in thick layers. Our legs became heavier as we dredged through the mush, but we continued on. No one seemed to be much in the mood to talk.

Everything seemed even more verdant than before, thanks to the rain. The branches, despite the increased weight, seemed to rise higher, as if they had found new strength.

"Does it rain on Yiptae?" Fyra asked.

"Rarely." *A place where it doesn't rain?* "Too cold."

"Do you live in an expansive city like Ziphyr?"

Kaylaa shook her head. "I grew up in the capital, Akuun Dey. Smaller, but more populated."

"I remember you saying something about being around Immigrant groups?" Fyra was showing a lot of patience considering Kaylaa's short answers.

"Immigrants are always campaigning for more rights in the capital. Hard to not be part of one of the groups when you're an Immigrant."

"Why do the Immigrants have fewer rights?" Now *this* was a subject I knew Fyra could sink her teeth into.

"Ask the Natives. They're the ones scared. Stupid, since they are the ones that conquered Yindia and went to war with Khaleri."

A short school poem to help us remember the planets popped in my head; *Five planets around Windoon's Star; Ignis, Vastire, Yindia, Yiptae, and Khaleri, they are.*

"How could the Khalerians stand up to the Yiptaen tech?" I asked.

"The Khalerians, particularly the chieftains, were extremely powerful in magic. And Yiptae was, and still is, best at designing and building vehicles, but not weapons. Not to mention, it's not like they had huge planet-faring warships."

"Did they ever try to conquer Vastire?"

"They wanted to. But their initial task force was brutally murdered. After the war with Khaleri, the Natives decided it wasn't worth it." Her accent seemed more pronounced as she talked about her homeworld.

"Guess that was before the Rise," I said. *Back when we were all savages.*

She stopped to think for a second. "I don't think so." Then she resumed her hurried pace.

"The Iveleen civilized us, so it must have been."

"The whole planet?" Kaylaa asked.

"No, it took the Iveleen about three decades to work through the Southern countries. And they were never successful in Erodia," Fyra said, stepping over a fallen tree branch.

"Where is your family from, Kaylaa?" I asked.

"Don't know. Immigrants have to throw away everything from heirlooms to religion to become Yiptaen citizens. Probably Khaleri, but could be Vastire. Maybe even a different system like Mildar or Arcta."

"How is that possible?" I wondered.

Kaylaa said, "There are theories, like the Common Form and the Ancient Ancestor, but don't ask me about them."

"That's something I'll have to look into," Fyra said.

We carried on a little past mid-day before we stopped for a snack. Even though Kaylaa encouraged us to gulp it down as we went, I sat on a nearby stump to rest, hidden under a particularly thick nest of branches.

"So Yiptae really isn't that different from Vastire then, huh?" Fyra asked. "I've been thinking about it, and it sounds like the Immigrants aren't treated much differently than the Olan-Har."

"No. That's why the Immigrants fight."

"Do you fight?" I asked.

Kaylaa sighed. "I have. But now look at me, working for a Native Senator. My allies didn't take well to that...but I couldn't pass on the opportunity to come here. To meet you. To learn about my father's suspected killer."

I was glad she said "suspected," but it still made me uneasy.

Fyra asked, "Then why is there an embargo around Vastire? "Why not Yiptae?"

Kaylaa shrugged. "Immigrants aren't starving to death, mostly."

"It's jealousy," I said. "The P.A. is jealous of how fast Vastire caught up. We skipped entire ages from other planets, thanks to the Iveleen. Our world isn't polluted or overcrowded like the rest of the P.A. planets."

Kaylaa cocked her head. "Doubt it. But it doesn't matter to

me."

"Isn't that the Virin-leen narrative?" Fyra asked. "I'm surprised you're listening to it, Darynn."

I gritted my teeth. "The royals should be right sometimes, with their perfect Virin-leen blood and all."

Fyra shook her head. "I'd like to believe it's about human rights."

Kaylaa didn't even ask if we were ready to go, she just started walking again. My legs were still sore from trudging through the mud, but I guess they weren't going to get any better after a short rest.

The rain continued until late in the day. When Windoon's Star finally tore through the clouds, it appeared as a red patch in the sky. The setting sun's light illuminated a fork in the road ahead: one larger, older road and the other a single file footpath. The small path was curiously well maintained and at its end, I could just make out a wooden, tent-shaped building.

"Kaylaa, what does that look like to you?" I asked.

"Nothing good."

"It looks...almost new, like someone lives there," Fyra added.

"I want to check it out," I said, beginning down the path.

"We're almost out of daylight and we're close to the Temple," Kaylaa said, annoyed.

"If someone lives there, they could know something useful," I insisted. Then I remembered the Libras talking about "dat utter one" in the forest. *Maybe he lives there?*

"Impossible," Kaylaa said.

"If no one does," Fyra said, "then it would be a good place to stay the night."

"I'm going to check it out," I said again and started down the well-worn path. As I moved closer to the building, I noticed stones piled in circles, none higher than my knee, overgrown by brush and moss. Foundations of old buildings? The building on the end started off just like these, as a stone circle, but with a wooden tent pitched on top. Just above the door was an inscription of a Golden Spiral, but half was worn away—or scratched out? When I came to the door, I realized the building was covered in religious symbols, and many had been scraped away.

My heartbeat sped up as I knocked on the newly-built wooden door, which was covered in scratches as if made by fingernails.

No response. I pounded on the door harder, but there was still no answer. I pushed on the door, but it didn't open—barred from the inside. I turned to Fyra and shrugged.

"Is...someone there?" called a voice from inside, weak and quiet.

"Yes! You live here?" I asked.

The door burst open and a blonde, tan-faced man burst out. "Guests! You must be very pious to venture here!" He had a slight Southern Countries accent.

"Hardly," I said.

Puzzled, he scratched his right temple with one finger. He wore a circlet bearing the Golden Spiral covering an ugly, tooth-shaped scar on his forehead. That, combined with his long pearl robe and swirling golden ropes draped over his shoulders, suggested he was a priest. But under the unbuttoned robes, he wore charcoal, scaly armor. "Then why come here?"

Before any of us could answer, he whipped his head back and forth as if he'd heard something. "Where are my manners? Please, come in!" He stepped to the side and motioned for us to enter, the oversized sleeves of his robe swaying.

I checked with Fyra, who nodded cautiously, before walking through. Kaylaa followed with her hands on her Rapier handles. It was dark inside, and even though the room was small, the Captain's Ring wasn't able to light the whole room. Two torches suddenly lit themselves in the back.

"Welcome to my shrine," said the priest. "I am Kirstoslaan-Shava, but my friends call me Kirstos...or they used to."

"I'm Darynn, this is Fyra, and that's Kaylaa." Fyra bowed politely while Kaylaa leaned next to the door without acknowledgment.

"You look...very familiar, Darynn. Hmm," Kirstos said. He closed his eyes tightly, and lightly knocked himself on the head a few times with a closed fist. His eyes opened wide, and I was surprised to see that they were different colors—one purple, almost red, and the other crystal blue. "Zilpohn Mark...you're a mirror image of him!"

"I need plastic surgery." I was so tired of people being unable to separate me from my father—especially people I didn't even know.

"So then...that makes even less sense to why you're here." He rushed up and grabbed me by the collar. "Did he tell you?"

"Let go of me!" I broke his surprisingly strong grip and pulled out my Plasma Edge. There was hardly enough room in the shrine to point it at him without actually touching him. "Tell me what?"

"The Great Secret, of course! But...if he did tell you, then why would you be here?" He paused and tapped his temple again. "He didn't tell you!" He slumped into a canvas chair next to a small dining table with a single place setting. "Why didn't he tell you?"

"What are you blabbering about?" I asked. But he ignored me. I put away my Edge, letting my hand linger on its handle. He sat there for a long time, not saying anything.

I scanned the shrine while waiting for an answer. More religious symbols, wooden shelves covered in bottles and supplies, and a Plasma Lance with a hooked blade. That didn't belong here—priests don't use weapons.

I was ready to leave when he said in a low voice, "Do you intend to go to the Temple?" I didn't feel like answering him, but Fyra nodded. "You'll never get in without me."

"Have you been inside?" Fyra asked.

"It's quite the pity. Only through the front door. But you

won't even get that far without me."

"We'll take our chances. I've had enough of this nutter. Let's go," Kaylaa said. She didn't wait for us to respond and went out the door.

"Enjoy the Vampires," Kirstos said, slamming the door behind me. I shuddered.

After a few steps, Fyra said, "I think I've seen him before, in my visions."

"Maybe we should've let him help us then," I said.

Kaylaa protested. "Absolutely not. "He's lost it."

"I'll admit he was odd, but are we tempting fate by not letting the priest help us?" Fyra asked.

"He wasn't much of a priest," I said. "He was wearing armor and had a Plasma Lance."

"That's the most sane thing I saw, if there are Vampires," Kaylaa said.

By this time, we'd reached the main road and started north along it. It was pitch black outside.

"Kaylaa, let's stop for the night," I suggested. "If there are Vampires, I'd rather not sleep in their den."

"Makes sense. No fire tonight—I don't want that priest to find us." She took a piece of bread from the sack and bit into it, then handed the sack to me.

I pulled out one of the last pieces of bread. "There won't be enough for the return journey."

"Maybe the priest can help us with that then." She climbed up a tree.

"I can't stop thinking about Kirstos," Fyra said. I felt a tinge of jealousy...but she didn't mean that—*right?* "I've seen him in my visions so many times...we're surely going to run into him again."

"He gave me the creeps. And so did his house."

"He claimed it was a shrine. But it didn't look like any shrine I'd ever seen. Some of those symbols were not Ivelenic symbols."

I tried to remember what any of them looked like, but they looked like wild scratching to me. "Maybe he found the shrine that way?"

"Maybe, but he'd met your father, meaning he'd been there at least six years, right?"

"It sounds like my father didn't let Kirstos come with him either, so maybe that means we did the right thing."

"Yeah, maybe," she replied unconvincingly.

"Let's get some sleep. Temple tomorrow."

She nodded, and we climbed up into the trees. I looked to my left, down the Old Crusader's Road, and it felt like something was looming on the horizon. The Temple was right there, just out of our grasp. *What was inside?* What had my father found?

Now, with it so close, I almost felt pain wondering what was in there. *You'll never get in without us*, Kirstos had said. He called it "The Great Secret." I guess that's why he's here, but is that why my father had come?

I shuddered. My father found it, and it turned him. He was a great father before he came to this very place, and then he was disinterested in me. What could change a man so dramatically in the course of a few days?

Something crackled on the ground—and it was moving closer. I strained my eyes to see, but it was too dark. I wiped the sweat from my brow. *Nothing will find us up here.* I thought I saw a shadow, but...no it was nothing. *Could Vampires live here?* I gulped.

I didn't hear anything for a while and relaxed a little bit. *Just Pavlar wearing off on me.* What would he think about all of this?

The weariness of my legs coursed through my body, and despite the rustling and cracking, my eyes closed.

Vastirian Militia are usually armed with Solid Arm Blasters (SABs) or Acid Pistols (Acip for short). SABs come in a variety of types: Rapid-Firing (RF-SAB), Zone (Z-SAB), Explosive (EX-SAB), and others. SABs mount to the arms of a soldier with a harness to allow them to carry and maneuver with just one arm. See Section 9 for details.

Acid Pistols use a combination of superacid vials and projectiles to harm their attackers. The acid works to counteract advanced armors, boring a hole for the following projectile to shoot through. See Section 11 for details.

Electron Pistols are uncommon now but may be used in the case of a SAB or Acip ammunition shortage. E-Pistols gather electrons from the air and accelerate them, imprecisely, at the target. See Appendix 2 for details.

Militia Cutlasses are also lined with the same superacid to help cut through advanced armor, though it requires frequent refills. See Section 15 for details.

Vastirian Militia armor is a woven Vibrine mesh that absorbs projectile impact and distributes it across the body. The Vibrine is woven too tightly to allow puncture, but it does not hold up well against laser or plasma weapons. Shards frequently wear a plate and shell to counteract those weapons. See Section 21 for Militia armor and Section 22 for Shard armor.

—From a Mondoon Enemy Armament Report

CHAPTER FIFTEEN

A shrill scream of mixed pain and terror woke me up.

My eyes flew open and instinctively I reached for my Plasma Edge. I scanned the area, but the darkness was overpowering. I shimmied to the ground.

Fyra knelt over Kaylaa, trembling. Kaylaa had a hand pressed to her neck, covered in rivulets of red. Both gawked at something in the direction of the Temple.

My eyes followed their line of sight, and my heart nearly leapt out of my chest.

Three ghastly creatures stood with transparent skin, glowing red eyes, and long, gleaming fangs. They were covered in dried blood. One of them had fresh red streams dripping down its chest.

"K-K-Kaylaa's hurt!" Fyra yelled.

I raced over to them and looked at Kaylaa's neck—blood streamed from two holes, surrounded by other small punctures. The color in her skin was fading—fast.

The creatures were sputtering and spitting and choking. One of them, wearing the same priestly vestments as Kirstos, advanced on us. It stumbled forward in a sort of hunched fashion, the pile of wrinkles on its bald head leading the way.

I shuddered as I stood to face the creature, my Edge unsheathed.

The priestly monster lunged, its white robes flowing behind it like a specter. It swung relentlessly with one strong arm, stretching out long claws to swipe at me. I blocked the blows with my blade, then flashed the plasma as I swung at the creature's neck. It jumped backwards before I could connect. It hissed and spat blood at me.

The other two advanced to meet the first one, but I stood my ground in front of Kaylaa. "Fyra, I'm going to need your help. Just hold out the burning end of your staff, and they'll stay back." *I hope.*

She took a quick, shuddering breath. "O-o-okay."

"Stay over Kaylaa."

"I'm scared."

"Me too." Leery, I advanced toward the creature that looked the most dangerous—an armored former crusader. I flashed my Plasma, and its eyes widened as it stared at my blade. A stab wound went cleanly through its dulled armor. Flesh hung sickenly in the hole, surrounded by scorch marks. *A Plasma Edge?*

I struck at the creature again and again, the plasma activated. But somehow its silver sword and shield, emblazoned with a gryphon, blocked my blows, like I was hacking at a tree with an axe. My heart pounded and sweat dripped down my cheeks. The crusader's armor seemed too heavy for the creature, weighing it down.

Finally, I managed to slice through its sword, the silver metal clanging to the ground. But before I could attack again, I noticed the priest and the third Vampire closing in on Fyra from both sides. Her staff glowed red with fire and blue with ice, but they were ready to pounce.

I dashed to her and took the third Vampire by surprise. She was the most terrifying of them all, with stringy black hair covering an angular face. Worst of all, her fangs pointed downward into where her jaw should be...but she had no jaw. Her chin was completely torn away, with strings of muscle hanging from her cheeks, her throat and spine exposed from the front. I felt my stomach turn, but I couldn't look away.

She gargled as I attacked and wildly swung with her talons on each hand. Her demented fury forced me back. Every swipe was so close I could feel the air whooshing by my skin. Her hot breath enveloped the air around me, reeking of corpses and rotting vegetables.

I struck out and my blade slipped through her shoulder socket, slicing off one of her arms. It flopped onto me like a cold, dead fish. There was no blood. She gargled and sputtered as she backed away quickly, gliding across the ground.

Fyra screamed. *Oh no!* I jerked my head towards her.

She had plunged the fiery side of her staff into the priest, and the priest immediately went up in flames. It leapt incredibly high in the air, a burning mass of robes and crackling skin flying through the air. *We might win this after all!*

The broken blade of the crusader Vampire swung at my head from the right. I jumped out of the way and sliced wildly at the monster, but my sword glanced off its shield. Fatigue started to set in, and my arms slowed with every swing. The crusader seemed to sense my exhaustion. It grinned a broken smile, brandishing rotting gums.

It swung and I was a tick too slow. The broken edge just barely sliced through the Vibrine mesh of my armor and into my ribs.

I backed up, my hand clutching my side, holding in the blood until I nearly stepped on Kaylaa. I heard Fyra behind me, hyperventilating.

The priest had returned, its skin ashy and cracked, its robe in burnt tatters. The Vampire with the missing jaw had also recovered despite missing an arm. They advanced on us.

"Darynn, what do we do?" Fyra asked, between gasps swinging the staff, desperately.

They're immortal, deadly, and blood-thirsty. *What can we do?* "They...can't keep fighting forever. I'll just hack off the rest of their arms!" I took another strong swing at the crusader.

I missed. My Edge buried itself in the ground, and my tired arms struggled to lift it.

"Focus, Darynn!" Kaylaa gasped from the ground. "Can't...beat them...this way...use...magic!" Then she passed out.

I took a deep breath and tried to concentrate. But the crusader swung at me, again and again. I feebly blocked the blows, but couldn't focus on anything but the monster. It seemed like its fangs grew longer as I became weaker, and my vision grew blurry. Drool mixed with dried blood dripped onto my chest. *Focus! Focus!* But on what? How do you hurt these creatures?

I fell to the ground next to Kaylaa.

"Darynn!" Fyra cried.

The crusader pounced on me and its hot breath covered my neck. I struggled, but the full weight of the crusader's body and armor was impossible to move.

*This is it...*I closed my eyes.

The breath stopped and a metal helmet crashed on my forehead and rolled to the ground. The crusader's body wasn't moving...and its head lolled on the ground next to me.

I shoved the body off. The priest and jawless Vampire were both headless on the ground. Dazed, I rose from the ground, blinking.

Kirstos stood there, Plasma Lance in hand, smiling. "The only way to stop them is to cut off the head!"

"Thanks," Fyra said, helping steady me.

"Help Kaylaa," I said. We couldn't let her die, not here. Or worse—become one of those things.

"I can help her at my shrine. Let's go, before more come!" Kirstos and I lifted Kaylaa off the ground, and we hobbled back to his home.

We rested Kaylaa's body on a table in the middle of the shrine. Kirstos rummaged through some boxes, tossing them carelessly until he found two small, grass-green capsules. He hurried back to Kaylaa and placed one capsule in each fang wound.

Kaylaa yelped in pain with each one but seemed powerless to resist.

"Wait, what is that?" Fyra asked.

"Who cares?" I asked. "Will it help?"

"Sirium. It'll help her regenerate blood and kill any disease from them."

Kaylaa's body convulsed and seemed to get paler every minute.

Kirstos turned back to his supplies and quickly mixed together some powder and a liquid, then drew it up into a syringe. The liquid turned black, the powder shining like spots of glitter.

"And that?"

"Starseed."

I'd heard of that before. The Maltans, one of the other gangs in Hargonla, ran drugs including Starseed. "Is that necessary?" I firmly grabbed his wrist.

"Do you want to save her life or not?" He had a twisted smile on his face and his eyes grew wide.

"How does getting her high help?"

"If you could've saved her life, you should have." Disappointment hit me like a sucker punch. *Someone else I couldn't protect.* "It will help with the pain, which I've heard is excruciating and...tingly. She'll also recover faster, so you can get into the Temple sooner. No one should waste time in this cursed forest."

I took my hand off, much to Fyra's dismay, and Kirstos injected the Starseed into Kaylaa's bicep. She recoiled and involuntarily slapped her bite wound.

"If you had just taken me with you in the first place, this wouldn't have happened, you know." He was right. We tempted fate, and it bit us. "You need to have your wounds looked at too."

I lifted up my shirt—it was worse than I thought. A gash stretched across my chest, dripping with blood. I doubled over like the sword had just sliced through me.

Kirstos clicked his tongue and shook his head, "Looks rough." He placed his hand on the wound and...pressed.

I cried out in pain. "What the hell?"

"Look, kid. I helped the woman for free. But you..." He pushed harder; blood streamed around his hand. I grabbed his arm, but my strength was draining quickly. "If you want my help, you have to swear to me I go with you into that Temple."

Is that worth it? He pressed harder—if he pushed anymore, I was pretty sure he'd graze my heart. "Fine."

"You heard that?" He looked to Fyra for confirmation.

"Yes, now help him!"

"And you?" He looked to Kaylaa. "Oh, you're worthless!" Then he giggled and said, "Let's get you stitched up!" He let off my chest, then pushed my shoulder down, forcing me to the ground. He was rough with the needle and thread, but efficient. He pulled the thread, cut it with a knife, and tied it off. I appreciated the blood flow had stopped, but every hole he had made felt like a small needle was still lodged in my skin. "Drugs?"

"I'll manage." Kirstos hummed as he put away his supplies. I wasn't quite sure, but it sounded like a song from church when I was young. "Why are you out here, Kirstos?"

"I'm here for the gods. They want to tell me the Great Secret, but I have to be patient."

"Did the Grand Cardinal send you here?" Fyra asked.

He laughed maniacally. "That old fool. He did not sanction this mission. He lacked the foresight to see the value, and he did not approve of my methods. Just wait until I show up on his doorstep with the Great Secret in hand!"

Fyra looked at the door. "It seems hardly worth it with those monsters outside."

"Merely part of the trial. The three you encountered, Stab, Old Baldy, and Jaw, they aren't even the worst of them." He looked amused with himself. "But they're all vicious and nearly immortal."

I started to lean forward, but pain held me back. "What is the Great Secret?"

He whirled around, his mouth agape. "Why would you be here, if not that?"

"I just want to know what my father found."

"Too bad he didn't just tell you. He would've saved us all a lot of trouble." Likely sensing my anger, he smiled. "You know the people built the Temple to commemorate Stria-Fate's cure for the Haskar Virus. But her grandson Bekivala was displeased, so he cursed the Temple and its grounds. Hence my blood-sucking friends."

I cocked my head. "So what's the Secret?"

"It's exactly that. Why was Bekivala so displeased? It's not a marvel like anything built by Rax-Kon's hands, but it's formidable. He was so angry he ensured no one could enter the building. Anyone who hung around too long transformed into one of those monsters. Seems like an overreaction, doesn't it?"

"The gods don't always share their motivations with us," Fyra said.

"Multiple crusades have failed, and even when they made it, all manners of traps and riddles block the entrance. Only your father has made it to the center in all these years." He beamed proudly. "He entered as a naïve man, but came out as an enlightened sage."

I gritted my teeth. "Hardly. He died leading a stupid rebellion just a few years later."

He raised an eyebrow, uncomfortably high. "Dead? A rebellion?" He licked his lips. "What did he find? I must find it! I must write in the missing pages of the Scriptures."

"Who's to say there are missing pages?" Fyra asked, scowling.

"You just sound like a fortune hunter to me," I said.

"How dare you!" Kirstos picked up his Plasma Lance and a rucksack and stomped out of the small shrine.

"I think he's nuts."

"I think you're right," Fyra agreed. "What should we do now? Kaylaa is asleep, and won't be ready to go until at least tomorrow."

Grimacing, I lifted myself off the floor and looked around the shrine. *Not much to do here.* Kaylaa snored loudly on the table. A scrap of paper marked with charcoal sat next to her.

"This is a map," I said, examining the paper. In the center was the Temple, and at the bottom of the page was a smaller circle marked "shrine." The Temple was made of three primary buildings and some smaller outcroppings. Just outside the shrine, not ten paces away, was a small circular body labeled "Pool." *A swim would be really refreshing.* "Let's go to this pool he has marked here."

She looked at me incredulously. "Vampires outside? Unconscious Kaylaa inside? What about that?"

"It's literally right outside the door. Kirstos sleeps here, so he must have found a way to ward off Vampires. I'll keep an eye out and we should be able to get back inside quickly." I reached for her hand and held it tightly. "I'll keep you safe. I promise."

She examined her hand in mine, seemingly entranced by it. Her muscles were tense. *Did she want me to let go?* "Okay. But not for long."

I smiled, putting my armor and shirt back on. With my Plasma Edge in hand, I peeked out the exit of the shrine. No Vampires in sight. I spotted the pool just on the other side of some ferns. "This way."

My heart fluttered, and I realized for the first time—*we were alone.* I looked back and smiled. Her beauty was plain to see, even after trekking through the forest. Behind her, the shrine loomed, and I found myself feeling guilty for leaving Kaylaa. "Maybe we shouldn't have left her," I said.

"Didn't I say that?" she asked. "You really care about her now, huh?" *A tinge of jealousy, perhaps?*

"We've been through a lot together. She seems so cold but...I think she really cares."

"She is very focused. And she...she protected me against the Nama-Da. Even though she didn't want me to come."

I nodded, and then we broke through into a clearing. The pool was shallow, with a sandy bottom and sparkling, seafoam-green water. The pool was fed by what seemed to be an impossible waterfall trickling down from the branches in the trees. It seemed all of the branches came together over the pond. Small, glowing sprites whizzed to and fro over the calm surface of the water. *We've walked into a magical painting.*

I looked over my shoulder to make sure I could still see the shrine. Satisfied, I peeled off my clothes, leaving just my undershorts, and leapt into the pool.

Icicles scrambled through my bloodstream, and I tried desperately to fly out of the freezing pool. Even though I was no more than waist-deep, I had committed too far. The water seeped through my bandages and shocked the slash across my chest and the healed wounds on my back and thigh. I feebly placed my hands on my shoulders and shivered. "Damn, it's so cold!"

"Pavlar always told me you'd jump in before testing the waters." She chuckled—only the second time I think she'd felt joy since Pavlar died.

"Seems I needed more lessons." I rubbed my shoulders and started to adjust to the water. "Getting in?" She kicked off her shoes and rolled up her pants a little. She gingerly put in her feet and sucked in a few fast breaths. "Is that it?"

"I can't swim, remember?" *Oh yeah.* The creek in Hargonla.

"It's shallow. As good a time as any to learn!" I grabbed one of her feet and started to pull her in, but her other foot connected with my jaw.

She jumped up away from the banks. "You can't solve every

problem by jumping into it!"

"I'm sorry. I wouldn't have let you drown." She crossed her arms and glared at me. "Will you come back to the edge?" I pleaded.

"Just promise not to touch me."

Damnit. "I promise." She slinked back to the water's edge, her shoulders slumped, staring at her feet. I leaned against the bank next to her. In silence, we stared at the carefree sprites zooming back and forth.

"I don't remember the last time I really enjoyed a swim," I said. "In my hometown, Cax-Ark-Uhn, I guess?"

"It must be strange for you, like you've lived two lives," she said. "One as the Elite-caste, wanting-for-nothing young boy. The other as an Olan-Har, scrounging for food and water."

"It's starting to feel like three, starting with the day Kaylaa landed." An awkward, swelling silence rose between us. I stole a glance at Fyra to see that she seemed unaware of it. *That makes it even worse.* To avoid it, I dunked my head and tousled my hair under the water.

When I came back up, Fyra's head was turned, fixed on something to the north. I shivered and hoped it wasn't a Vampire.

"Do you see something?" I asked, wading to the edge.

"No...it's just the Temple. I can feel it there, looming like a great shadow. What's inside? What is the Great Secret your father found? It's probably foolish but...I feel like whatever is in there may resolve an argument Pavlar and I always had."

I cocked my head. "What's that?"

"We agreed on most everything, but not the caste system. He was convinced it needed to go, that it was rotten to the core. I believe it's run by corrupt people, but the system is still good. Your father's actions seem to validate my view." She shrugged.

She was right. That was the best explanation that I'd ever heard for why my father would've acted like he did. The Great Secret is the linchpin. Find that and the questions will be answered. The familiar anger and hurt flashed, but faded quickly, overcome by determination.

She said Pavlar wanted to get rid of the caste system. I didn't remember him ever saying that plainly, though he always complained about it. *So would he support a revolution?*

I shook my head. No heavy thoughts, not in this moment. "What if we didn't think about that right now?"

She looked at me like a mother scolding her child. "If it was that easy to push out of my mind, I would. Just like my visions. But they're both just there, hovering in front of me all the time."

"Are you still having them, this far from the city?"

"They never go away. If I see less than a dozen deaths, that's a good night."

"You could've told me. I felt like we broke free from the slums, and I guess I thought your mind..."

"You thought wrong." She stared despondently in the pool. "I'm afraid all the time. What if I see my parents? What if the Temple holds something so earth-shattering...that it changes us forever? What if we don't even make it that far?"

"If you've been afraid this whole time, you sure have been brave." I didn't even notice, except of course when we were under attack by Nama-Da or Vampires.

Her expression softened. "You really think so?"

I smiled. "Of course! Besides, I've been afraid too. Even Kaylaa, though she wouldn't admit it, I bet she's been afraid one or two times. At least for a few seconds."

Her sapphire eyes sparkled, and she suddenly looked relaxed. She stared at the water. "Will you still teach me to swim?"

I nodded and she stood up on the side of the bank and gripped the bottom of her shirt. I didn't realize I was staring until she said, "Stop that! Turn around!"

"Oh, right." My cheeks warm, I turned and faced the other bank. My mind wandered, and I couldn't help thinking about what she looked like. Soft skin, slender body, beautiful...

"Stick out your left arm, but don't look!" I did as she commanded, and her soft hand grasped my arm. She splashed into the water and I turned to help her. She bent her knees to keep everything but her neck and head below water. I did my best to not look down. "It's shallow."

"Yep. Nothing to worry about!"

She took a deep breath.

"Okay. Let's go deeper." I held her tightly as we walked toward the center of the pool, the ground slowly slipping away beneath us. When we were at her neck's depth in the water, I faced her and held both of her hands.

"Okay, let your legs rise up and kick them slowly. See, you're doing just fine. Okay, I'm going to let go with one hand. When I do, you're going to start circling that arm around your shoulder, like a windmill. Cup your hand and twist it when you come around." I released one hand, and she started rowing with one arm. "I'm going to let go." I let go with my other hand.

But she panicked. She bobbed in the water and started hyperventilating. I reached out and pulled her close. She wrapped her arms around me and stared hatefully at the water. I felt her shoulder blades and spine as I moved my hand along her back. "You're okay," I said. "I've got you."

She gasped for breath, so I started to pull her back to shallower water. "N-n-o," she said between breaths. "I'm going to do this." She pushed away from me, this time staying calm as she bobbed up and down in the water. With more encouragement, she was soon swimming from bank to bank, not gracefully but functionally. I swam beside her, occasionally reaching out to touch the small of her back, letting her know I was there.

She stopped and huffed beside the bank. I leaned up against the shore next to her and we silently listened to the sounds of the forest. As before, the bugs and the birds hummed and tweeted in harmony as if directed by Qui-Tos's lyre. The sprites seemed brighter now with the sunlight dwindling.

I looked at her face, the slight pout to her lips, her slender cheeks. I desperately wanted to kiss her. She seemed unaware of my staring. Something fluttered in my stomach, the wings of insects fluttering against my insides. *Can I kiss her?* Should I? Did she want me to?

"Praise be to the Iveleen," she said softly.

The urge disappeared. "It is beautiful here but...the Iveleen took my father, my mother, and Pavlar."

"You know it hurts me, too, right? We cannot understand Their ways, but I know that happened for a reason. It's brought us here, together."

"Kaylaa brought us here, more than anything." I slid back into the water until only my head was above the surface.

"You don't see it, but They are working. You found the Khalil leaves that saved me, and somehow brought them to my house, thanks to Their help. We escaped the Shard, the Nama-Da, and even the Vampires thanks to Their intervention."

I cleared my throat. "As I recall, I was dead set on getting those Khalil leaves. We escaped the Shard and the Nama-da thanks to my magic, which according to Them I'm not even supposed to use. Escaping the Vampires was thanks to Kirstos, who claims to be a priest, but seems anything but with his weapon and drugs."

"You're discounting their influence!"

"You're giving them too much credit!"

"Fine." She lifted out of the water and I couldn't help but watch as the water droplets rolled down the curves of her body. Her hair flowed like a platinum stream down to the small of her back, and just below was her round butt. "Look away!" she yelled, her whole body tinted pink. I didn't apologize, just turned away.

"I'm dressed," she said shortly. I lifted out of the pool and quickly dressed. As soon as I was clothed, she surprised me with a hug. She rested her head on my shoulder. Any anger I had dripped off of me with the pool water. I felt like drumsticks rapped relentlessly on my heart. "Thank you for teaching me how to swim." She let go as suddenly as she had grabbed me and started back toward the shrine.

Was that more than a friendly hug? I chased after her, my heart beating loud enough to be a metronome for the singing creatures of the forest. My smile widened. *Could she have feelings for me?*

What I thought was just a fleeting crush was much more than that. *When did that happen?* And why not—she's gorgeous, intelligent, empathetic. And brave. My heart beat faster and I just wanted to catch her, to kiss her.

A wolf howling in the distance reminded me of the reality of our surroundings, and the reason for my desire to catch her changed. Danger lurked in every bush, and now, for sure, I would not let anything happen to her.

The Grand Cardinal is the head of the Ivelenian Clergy, with a direct line to the Iveleen. He makes all executive decisions for the Clergy. He preaches at the Grand Cathedral in Ziphyr.

Each region in Vastire is administered by a Cardinal, meaning there are twenty-one Cardinals in all. The Cardinals look to the Grand Cardinal for guidance, but otherwise have autonomy over the Church in his/her region. Each church or chapel in a region is managed by a local priest.

The clergy maintains absolute control over who is Lifted or who Falls between castes.

Ivelenian priests are generally taught at one of four seminary schools on Vastire: near White Cap, in Wavei City, in South Tip, and in Thunder Strike. Of these, the Vorn Seminary near White Cap is the most prestigious.

—From *Structure of the Ivelenian Clergy*

CHAPTER SIXTEEN

A purple glow, like wolf's bane, snuck through the cracks in the shrine door. The whole building rumbled, and I felt an onrush of dread. I cracked open the door and peeked in.

Every torch in the shrine was lit with a pillar of purple fire, wreathed in black energy. The markings on the wall looked more harrowing than before, like scribbles you see on the wall of the jail cell of a prisoner with a life sentence.

I heard Kirstos before I saw him, chanting unintelligible words mixed with guttural noises. His eyes were closed, his hands touching his shoulders like he was praying—but this was no prayer to the Iveleen. His eyes fluttered as if he were having a nightmare. The scar on his forehead seemed to be bleeding, a thin stream running down to his nose.

"We need to go," I whispered to Fyra. Her eyes were wide, fixed on the eerie purple glow.

"But Kaylaa..."

I looked for Kaylaa; she was still sleeping on the table. Kirstos continued his ritual as if she wasn't there. "I'll get her. I think he's in a trance."

The door creaked as it opened wide, and immediately Kirstos stopped his chanting. He glowered at me with pupil-less eyes, his eyelids impossibly wide open, his mouth curled into a wicked smile. I started breathing hard and fast, slowly reaching for my Plasma Edge.

His arms relaxed, his body slumped, and the fires returned to their normal red and orange. He closed his eyes tight, and when they opened, they were normal again.

"I didn't hear you come in," he said. "In fact...I hardly remember coming back." He saw the fear, the confusion in my eyes. "Oh don't worry. Sometimes the gods speak to me so clearly I become enchanted by their voices, and completely forget where I am." *Was that supposed to make me feel better?*

"Where am I?" Kaylaa asked woozily. We rushed to her side. Her hand moved instinctively to the wound on her neck and she rubbed it.

"The priest's shrine. How do you feel?" I asked.

"Wonderful!" she yelled with a sudden burst of energy. Instantly she hopped up on her feet. She brushed herself off with exaggerated motions. "I'm hungry!" She pushed Fyra out of the way and skipped out the door into the forest.

Fyra looked at me, confused. "Go get her!"

I darted out of the shrine, Kirstos cackling in the background. I grabbed Kaylaa's shoulder, but with seemingly no effort, she brushed my hand aside and kept walking. It took two hands to stop her.

"I'm hungry! What do you want?" She whirled around and looked me in the eyes.

"What are you doing?"

"Finding food!" She cocked her head. "You're actually quite handsome, you know. I think I might fancy you." Like a snake striking at its prey, she gave me a quick kiss on the cheek. My cheeks turned hot as I rubbed where her lips had set.

"What is your problem?" I asked, shrugging at Fyra, who had emerged from the shrine with Kirstos. Her arms were crossed and she frowned. *Real jealousy this time?*

Kirstos had a huge grin on his face. "It's the Starseed," he said. "It'll break any emotional inhibitions she has and give her an insatiable hunger." *Great.*

"You could've told us that *before* you gave it to her," I said. He shrugged and I turned back to Kaylaa. She pressed her lips against mine and tried to pry open my mouth with her tongue. Shocked, I backed away and wiped my lips.

"What, you don't like it?" she asked. "Am I not pretty?"

"Of...of course you are. But I..." I looked at Fyra. "I don't think of you like that."

"Like what? You don't have to think of me like anything, as long as you think I'm pretty." She approached again, a wolf on the prowl, fluttering her eyelashes.

"What about some food?" Fyra suggested.

"Oh yes, I'm starving!" *A temporary distraction, I'm sure.*

"Kirstos, what do you eat around here?" I asked.

"Nothing that will help," he said, still with a sly smile. "I live mostly off Ration Capsules, which get the job done quickly. She needs a snack to occupy her."

"Any ideas?"

"Tie her down. Or give her that other thing she wants." He smiled devilishly.

"No! Just get the RCs!" He sighed and went inside. "There's food inside, Kaylaa. Let's go." I grabbed her hand and dragged her in. "Fyra, can you block the door?"

"Like I can stop *her*," she said.

I rolled my eyes. By the time we entered the shrine, Kirstos had placed a shoebox on the table, about half-full of the peanut-colored Ration Capsules.

"Huh," he grunted, placing a handful on the table. I knew they were for soldiers on long journeys, meant to take the place of a meal with a single bite. That also meant it was dangerous to give her too many, or she could burst.

Before I could react, Kaylaa grabbed a handful and popped a few in her mouth. She had eaten three or four before I knocked the rest out of her hand.

She stuck her tongue out at me. "Why? I'm still hungry!"

"You'll regret it tomorrow."

"But I'm hungry *now!*" She stamped her feet.

"Kirstos, do you have any more drugs?"

"Darynn!" Fyra said.

"I can't deal with this all night," I replied.

Kaylaa said in a sing-songy voice, "I can hear you, you know!"

Fyra looked at her, then at me, and then said to Kirstos, "Sedative, please."

Kirstos rummaged around and found a clear yellow liquid that he drew into the syringe. He stabbed Kaylaa in the arm and released the liquid. She slapped him—hard—across the face, but almost immediately swooned. I caught her in my arms, and she looked at me lovingly.

"Good night, handsome," she said and nodded off.

I laid her down carefully on the floor and sighed in relief. "That was...weird."

"Best entertainment I've had in years!" Kirstos said. "About ten years, it seems. This is 500 ARI, right? Makes sense. I've felt...closer to the Iveleen lately. The Vampires have been more restless than ever."

"It's only 499 years after the Rise of the Iveleen. Next year is the Quincentennial," Fyra said. "The Grand Cardinal is planning the largest celebration in the history of Vastire!"

"A garish marvel, I'm sure." He yawned. "But it will be the perfect time for me to give everyone the Great Secret, to renew their faith. You will have to sleep on the floor. I only have one hammock." He undressed down to his undershorts, revealing tanned, heavily scarred skin, and climbed into his hammock. He swayed slightly as he covered himself with a thin sheet.

Kaylaa was passed out just in front of the supply cabinets, farthest from the door. There was probably just enough space for Fyra and me to lie down.

"I'll take the door," I said.

"Good. Then she can kick you when she tries to wander off again."

"Hey you know that...Kaylaa doing all that...doesn't mean anything?"

"What would it mean?" She sat down on a woven rug, running her hands along it. "I thought this rug would be better than the ground, but it's so rough."

"I'll take it."

She shook her head. "Good night, Darynn."

I settled down on the floor in front of the door, and as my nose came close to the ground I smelled something foul. For the first time, I noticed two small urns on either side of the door, wrapped in fur. I sniffed one of them and realized that the furs were soaked with dried blood, and I suspected there was more inside the pots. *Vampire-repellent, maybe?* Or leftovers for ritual sacrifice? A shudder ran down my spine.

Kaylaa was snoring again, while Kirstos swayed from side to side in his hammock. I didn't trust him, especially after his so-called worshipping, but he needed us to find the Great Secret. Or at least he thought he did, which gave me some security. Fyra laid on the rug, turned away from me. Memories of holding her in the pool floated through my head. *But did Kaylaa mess everything up?* Surely Fyra wouldn't hold it against me. It wasn't my fault.

But she was a good kisser. No, I don't care. She's so...cold. Beautiful, but cold. I fell asleep that way, batting away thoughts of Kaylaa's kiss while thinking about Fyra in the pool.

The Temple of Stria-Fate was completed in 100 ARI, built to commemorate Stria-Fate's sacrifice when She devised the cure to the Haskar Virus about ten years earlier. Over a million Vastirians died in less than a year due to the rapid spread of the sickness.

The Temple was built in Soquok Forest, close to His grave. The site was chosen because of Stria-Fate's affinity for the woods.

Bekivala's curse drove everyone away from the Temple less than a year after completion. Vastirians did not return until the First Crusade, led by Master Templar Osk Vito, in 138 ARI. The battle was hard-fought, but the Temple was reclaimed for less than a year before the crusaders were forced to leave.

In 256 ARI, the Second Crusade began, but it failed shortly after reaching the Temple. Few survived.

The Third Crusade in 435 ARI resulted in holding the Temple for eleven years. However, the small colony failed due to constant disappearances and an unstable supply line, given the dysfunction of technology near the Temple.

—From *A Brief History of Ivelenian Temples*

CHAPTER SEVENTEEN

Fyra had said she came on this journey in hopes of proving the Iveleen right, but maybe the Virin-leen—at least the current ones—were wrong. That would explain my father's actions, leading an assault against corrupt Virin-leen. That would be something worth fighting for. Maybe I've been unfair to my father all this time.

The morning was cool and welcoming as I sat on a stump outside Kirstos's shrine. It faced the pool, and I could just barely make out a deer-like animal drinking from it. The trees swayed in the light breeze, filling the air with the pleasant sound of rustling leaves.

The door behind me rattled on its hinges. Kaylaa stood in the doorway, fully armed and armored.

"You're not going anywhere."

"I'm going to the Temple. And so are you." She handed me an RC capsule from the rucksack. "Eat this."

"Thank the Iveleen you're back to normal." *Thank the Iveleen? Why?* I shook it off and asked, "How do you feel?"

"Very...healthy, actually. Some double vision, but otherwise fine. I don't remember anything after that monster bit me. It snuck up on me...nothing sneaks up on me." She touched the two holes on her neck, which had mostly healed and now just looked like blood-red moles. "Did you kill them?"

"Kirstos did, I think."

"Where is that freak?"

"I don't know; he somehow slipped by me before I woke up this morning. He's supposed to go to the Temple with us."

She crossed her arms. "Why?"

"Because *that freak* saved your life and he knows how to fight the Vampires."

She mulled it over. "I don't trust him."

"I don't either, but he didn't give us much choice." I stood, examined the RC, and popped it in my mouth. It tasted like a salt preservative in a bag and so much salt... I nearly spat it out but forced myself to swallow.

"Never had an RC before?" Kaylaa asked. I shook my head. "Seems like it would've been a good solution to starving Olan-Har."

Fyra had just come outside after Kaylaa, her staff in hand. "That's a trade of short-term problems for long ones. Studies show disturbing neurological effects of eating RCs for an extended period of time."

Kaylaa argued, "You have to solve today's problems before you can solve tomorrow's."

"I think that's remarkably short-sighted."

"Anyway," I said to break them up, "we need to go. It's his fault if he misses out."

We headed toward the Old Crusader's Road.

A crash in the trees shook us all to attention, and Kirstos dropped out of the branches and onto the path. He had a large burlap sack strapped to his back and a small leather pouch on his belt, along with his Plasma Lance and normal attire.

"Leaving without me?"

"I figured you'd catch up," I lied.

He grinned. "This way!" He stepped off the path and led us into the brush beside his shrine.

I looked at my companions, shrugged, and followed him.

The brush was thick and attacked us with every step, but

there was a small path that he had clearly worn in over the years. Kirstos rushed far ahead of us. The more distance he gained, the more worried I became about being attacked from behind.

"Slow down!" Kaylaa yelled, but Kirstos didn't listen and actually extended his lead. At one point, I thought the jungle man was skipping in the distance. *What is with this guy?*

It wasn't long before we broke into a massive clearing. Finally, we were here—the Temple of Stria Fate.

The building was huge but smaller than I had imagined, especially compared to the vastness of the clearing. The central structure was a three-story step pyramid, flanked in the back by two tall and narrow buildings, like giant slanted walls. The whole meadow was covered in multi-colored mushrooms. Kaylaa poked at them with one of her Rapiers. *Maybe no mushrooms on Yiptae?*

Kirstos fiddled with something on a bank of pillars to the left of the Temple—living trees that had been planted on each side to hold up a stone slab.

I was a little out of breath when we finally caught up to him. He had what looked like a leather hose in his hands, and was screwing it into a port at the base of the living pillars.

"What are you doing?" I asked.

"The entrance is controlled by hydraulics," he replied, struggling with the hose.

I followed the hose, as it snaked back toward Kirstos's shrine—probably to the pool. He managed to get the hose tight enough to his liking, then skipped back into the forest. Hidden in some bushes was a mechanism with a manual crank. He turned the crank a few times, and stones rumbled to my left. The granite doors to the entrance creaked open a little more with each turn of the crank. Just above the slab supported by trees on either side, on the second story of the pyramid, was a huge statue of Stria-Fate. She stood majestically in flowing robes with her Chalice in one hand and a scepter in her other.

The great Healer of the Iveleen.

"How could the Iveleen have been displeased by this marvel? It was a gift! Didn't Bekivala realize that?" Fyra asked, her head turning every which way to take in the beauty.

"Doesn't look like much to me," Kaylaa countered, heading toward the entrance.

Fyra opened her mouth to reply, but I put my hand on her shoulder. "She doesn't get it." She frowned and followed Kaylaa silently.

Kirstos stopped cranking and led us to the entrance. We passed the rubble of what appeared to be another statue and crept up the stairs of the portico. My heart pounded in my chest, a dull, slow thud like a blacksmith at work on an anvil.

"Your father was lucky I'd already built this pump for the door! And so are you!" Kirstos said, beaming.

"These doors are amazing," Fyra said, admiring the flawless white granite.

"Some say these doors, hewn from the perfect White Cliffs in the Forlorn Mountains, may have been what angered Bekivala so much. But I don't buy it!"

We walked into the overwhelming darkness of the Temple. *We're here.* I took one look back, feeling like someone was watching us. Vampires? The ghost of my father? The Iveleen? Anxiety overcame me as it seemed like every step landed in an impression created by my father's feet.

"No need to worry," Kirstos said. "Once I was chased by Vampires in here, but only one followed me in. Almost like the others were afraid."

I gulped. "What would they be afraid of?"

"No clue! This way! Hurry, hurry!"

I just shook my head and blindly followed him in the darkness. We didn't get far when an overwhelming stench overcame us. I held my nose. "What is that?"

"I...I don't know. It wasn't here last time. Maybe some light." Torches on the left and right burst into orange flames, thanks to Kaylaa, and revealed the swirling dust and stone of the inside of the Temple.

Fyra gasped. On the wall to our left, two ghastly corpses slumped against the wall. Both looked like they had been there a hundred years, with only bits of flesh left, but there was relatively fresh blood on the floor next to them.

"Where did those come from? Odd!" Kirstos remarked.

Kaylaa asked, "Are they dead Vampires?"

Kirstos moved closer, holding his nose, and said, "They are! This is Iron Boots and Righty! I must have locked them in here last time I was here."

It was clear why he named them that way; the one on the left had heavy, metal-bottomed boots, while the right one had no left hand. "I thought they didn't come in here," I said.

"Not usually!" He turned one palm up and shrugged.

"I thought they were immortal?" Fyra asked.

"*Nearly* immortal. They can only die of dehydration, and it takes decades. But...I don't think Iron Boots and Righty would've dehydrated that fast...odd!" He continued down the widening path.

"Only dark magic would explain this," Kaylaa said.

"I tried to learn—what spell could be more useful than dehydrating Vampires! But no luck," Kirstos volunteered from far ahead.

"A priest, wanting to learn dark magic?" Fyra whispered, louder than I think she intended. "I think he's closer to Haskar than Stria-Fate."

"Some sacrifices have to be made!" Kirstos called back.

I hurried to catch up to him but slowed down when I noticed the brick wall changed into an intricate relief carved into the wall. I looked around and noticed traces of others, mostly worn away.

Fyra walked up beside me. "It's splendid, huh? But I can't quite make out if it's supposed to represent something, or if it's just a design."

"Me neither."

"Come on, you three!" Kirstos yelled.

We hurried to find him stopped in the middle of the path, which had narrowed to where just one person could walk. On either side was a seemingly unending abyss. And no railing.

"This is the Chasm of Faith. All believers will pass without issue, but nonbelievers will fall to the side. Good luck, foreigner!" With reckless abandon, he dashed across to the other side.

Kaylaa smirked. "Nonsense. Unless the path is enchanted."

Fyra peered over the edge. "It wasn't uncommon for old Ivelenian buildings to have tests of faith...but this seems excessive. We should be permitted, right?"

"It's just a walkway," Kaylaa said, but even so, she took her first step carefully. Finding it secure, she took another, and then continued until she reached the other side.

"Seems to be more of a test of balance," I said.

"I-I-I'm clumsy, Darynn," Fyra said, shakily.

"Just hold my hand, I'll guide you."

I tested my left foot on the path. The stone bridge didn't react to a strong press, so I swung my other foot onto it. Over the edge to my right, a bead of sweat dropped off my forehead and disappeared into the darkness. I swallowed hard as my heart pumped.

I took another cautious step, and then extended my hand behind me. Fyra's soft, clammy hand took it, and slowly we made our way across the bridge.

"Do you feel that?" Fyra asked when we were about halfway across.

"What?"

"Like...invisible hands, guiding us."

"Uh...no?"

She let go of my hand. "It is a test of faith. The Iveleen won't let me fall."

I felt much more nervous now—if she did slip, would I catch

her in time? "I wish you'd just hold on."

"No need, focus on getting yourself to the other side."

I took a deep breath and watched my feet as I stepped across the bridge. *Without invisible god hands.*

I looked back to check on Fyra. She strolled across, relaxed, not even sweating. "You just have to believe, Darynn."

"I'm glad it worked for you. Looks like I made it Kaylaa's way."

She frowned and we continued on. *This doesn't seem so hard.* Surely others had made it deep into the Temple. *So the Great Secret is a myth after all.* I sighed in relief.

It couldn't have been more than a dozen steps when two paths veered off to our left and right. Kirstos ignored them, standing in front of a wall blocking the way forward.

I asked, "Where do these go, Kirstos?"

He turned. "You weren't very prepared to come here. Antechambers, both empty."

"So why haven't you learned the Great Secret?" Fyra asked. She looked smug. "You seem to be able to navigate the place."

He sneered at her like a wolf baring his teeth. "Because of this damned wall! There is only one way into the nave, and that is through this door."

"An Ivelenian Panel Door," Fyra said in admiration.

"Hmph. You know that much at least," Kirstos muttered. "Most of the Temple was built by Vastirian hands, but parts of the inside were remodeled by Bekivala. Including this door."

"I could just blow it up," Kaylaa said, holding out her hand.

"I've tried!" Kirstos whined. "Though with explosives."

"How could you? There are only a few of these doors, fashioned by the hands of the Iveleen, known in the world. The only other I can think of is at the Grand Cathedral," Fyra said. "You should've known it wouldn't work, anyway. The Ivelenian Panel Door creates a magic seal around the entire room that it's protecting."

"So then how do we get in?" I asked.

Fyra shrugged. "These doors were created so that the Iveleen could have private places to convene. I would think only the Grand Cardinal might know how to open it."

"And my father," I added.

Kaylaa struck the wall with the bottom of her fist. "Proof your Iveleen were hiding something."

Fyra puzzled for a minute. "It is peculiar. The door at the Grand Cathedral only seals a few private rooms. This one is blocking an entire place of worship."

Kirstos tapped his foot. "We'll only know if we get in! Now think, kids! Your father got in—how?"

"Shut up!" Kaylaa yelled. *Where'd that come from?* She readied her Starlight Rapiers as she warned, "There's something else here."

"Oh, that's impossible," Kirstos said.

"Not impossible, my dear," said a raspy voice from the shadows. A slender woman with impossibly pale skin, draped entirely in black, emerged into the torchlight.

Kirstos's eyes widened as he readied his Plasma Lance. "A Vampire? Here? Impossible!"

"You don't listen, do you dear? I am the Second Lady of the Temple." She bowed and her straight, jet black hair swung over her head.

"She doesn't look like a Vampire," I said. Her eyes were a deep amber and did not emit light like the other Vampires we had encountered.

She looked up and flipped her hair back. "Is that a compliment from the handsome man?" she asked, licking her lips and gleaming fangs. A shudder raced down my spine. Despite the fangs, she was actually quite beautiful, covered in skin-tight black leather with a popped collar.

"The last man I saw in here...you look exactly like him." As she pondered, she touched a nasty scar on her neck, partially obscured by her high collar.

"You fought my father five years ago. Be warned—I am

more powerful than him!" I boomed, trying to project confidence.

She placed her hands on her hips. "Now that was a *man*! But a man who nearly tore my heart asunder." She rubbed a cut on the left side of her chest, a deep wound that trailed all the way to her armpit. "Always the strong men that break my heart! You look scrawny, but can you do the same?" She snatched several flat knives from her belt, three fanned out in each hand.

"I'm warning you! I'll finish what my father started!" I flashed my Edge's plasma.

"Oh, I love a man who knows how to wield his sword!"

With incredible agility, she bounded across the room, her movements fluid, like a deadly dance. She slashed furiously. Hot blood ran down my arms and cheek.

Kaylaa rushed in to stop the onslaught. With a few precise strokes, she fought the woman off. The Vampire leapt across the room and held a knife up to her mouth. She licked the blade clean, staining her fangs red.

"That just will not do. Does your heart belong to another?"

"She's so...fast," I said, rubbing my cheek.

"You have to be faster. Your weapon is superior, don't let her get so close," Kaylaa instructed.

The Second Lady cocked her head upon hearing her speak.

"She is far more skilled than the other Vampires," Kirstos said.

"How many times have you been in here? How did you avoid her?" I asked.

Kirstos shrugged. "The Iveleen protected me."

"Do I look like a monster to you? Though I guess I did suck those other two dry..." She chuckled. "I'm just so thirsty, you see."

She threw three knives at Kaylaa, each at a different height. Kaylaa dodged, but by the time she stood up, the Second Lady was on top of her. She swiped at Kaylaa's neck, grazing her with a knife just before Kaylaa pushed her off. Both Kirstos and I swung our weapons. She seemed to bend impossibly at the waist, avoiding both blows, and simultaneously threw knives at both of us.

I just blocked the flying knife such that it tumbled and the butt hit me in the chest. She pounced again, but a flash of my plasma cut one of her knives in half. I managed to beat her back, and she leapt away again. My confidence grew as we continued to overmatch her, even with her blinding speed.

"This seems hardly fair." She seductively licked her lips again. "It's been hundreds of years since I've had to do this." She sliced one of her palms in an 'X' pattern, and her whole hand started to glow with black and blood-red energy, her eyes changing color to match.

She dashed again, somehow faster than before, but stopped in front of me. She slammed her hand out away from her body, and Kirstos, Kaylaa, and Fyra went sailing through the air. They slammed up against a wall. Kirstos and Kaylaa looked unconscious; Fyra was still awake but dazed.

The Second Lady placed her palm against her mouth and sucked in, covering her lips and pale cheeks in blood. Her hand stopped bleeding, and her eyes returned to normal. "That's better. Now it's just you and me, honey. Let's dance." She spun in a pirouette, moving so fast she was nothing more than a blur. Three knives flew out of the blur at me; I dodged two and knocked down the third.

I charged at the whirl of colors and swung at her waist. My blade connected, and she fell backward, blood spilling from her waist.

"How...dare you!" But then, like it was nothing, she ran her hand across her waist, and the cut closed.

"Impossible..."

"You don't listen either, do you dear? I am immortal. I am not like the other Vampires. Bekivala granted me a special curse, much stronger than the others."

"Why?" I huffed.

"Because we were in love."

"Blasphemy," Fyra said, still against the wall, rubbing her head.

"Oh, but he did love me. Many times he told me to move on, but I was the most exquisite woman alive. Only a god could satisfy me. And he obliged. He always came back to me. I don't look my age, do I?" She fluttered her long eyelashes, flecked with blood.

I ignored her. "Then why curse you?"

I thought I saw tears forming at the corners of her eyes. "Our love was forbidden, and that wretched bitch Silva found out. She made him get rid of me. Instead of killing me, he gave me immortality and bound me to this Temple. His love was so strong for me that the curse was doubly powerful."

"Is *that* the Great Secret? I've wasted ten years of my life because of Bekivala's lust for a whore?" Kirstos demanded, conscious but woozy.

The Second Lady tossed a knife at him, and it would've hit him in the chest, except that he had one leg up, so instead it burrowed into his calf. He yelped in pain and stared at the knife. He started to remove it, but Kaylaa, who had also woken up, held it in. He whimpered.

"You'll bleed out. Wait," Kaylaa said. She stood up and dusted herself off.

"There were other reasons to seal the Temple. I'm outside that door, you see." The Second Lady pointed at the panel wall. "But I don't know them, even though I begged Bek to tell me. One secret he wouldn't tell me. It was killing him." She licked her lips again and slurped blood. "Excuse me. My wounds have made me thirstier."

She feinted like she was going to attack me again, but instead bounded toward Fyra with two graceful steps.

I tried desperately to reach her in time, but it was too far.

The Second Lady opened her mouth wide to bite into Fyra's

wrist. One of her own knives suddenly whizzed by her ear.

Kirstos had pulled out the knife—against Kaylaa's advice—and thrown it to protect Fyra. He rolled onto his side and tried to keep pressure on the wound.

Both Kaylaa and I bore down on the Second Lady now. Even Fyra brandished her Elenduil staff, one side burning hot like fire.

"You are tiring me, though I have enjoyed it. But now, it must end." The Second Lady slashed both of her palms, then thrust them toward us.

This time all of us but Kaylaa went flying—she somehow blocked it. My back slammed against the wall and I slumped to the ground.

The Second Lady and Kaylaa engaged, and it seemed like the Vampire had gained the edge. She kicked and bashed Kaylaa against a wall.

I tried charging in, but was still disoriented, and staggered towards her. Like a blur, she slipped by me and attacked from behind. She slashed along my ribs on both sides as I turned toward her. I swung wildly and missed. I crumpled to the ground, the nerves in my body screaming in pain.

She was on top of me in an instant and licked my ear before whispering in it, "Your body has given up. Let your mind go."

I closed my eyes and rolled my head back. When I opened them, I was somewhere else.

The shadowy darkness of the Temple was replaced with the blinding light of too many halogen lights. The dusty stone walls transformed into gleaming metal, the smell of corpses changed to the biting smell of disinfectant. I blinked rapidly as I tried to figure out where I was, but the light was staggering.

Then an unfamiliar voice said, "Let it out, Darynn! Let your mind go!"

Blood dripped into my eyes as I looked for the source of the voice, but I couldn't see anything through the crimson light.

A figure started to materialize in front of me, but it wasn't the Second Lady...it was a bearded man in gray clothes...I think. And he was dangerous. I sensed a knife in his hand, already covered in my blood. If I didn't do something, he'd kill me. He raised the knife above his head, ready to plunge it into my chest. Unconsciously, my hands flew out to my sides. Something pulsed inside of me, starting in my wrists and leading all the way to my chest, like I'd stuck both hands in electrical sockets. The already blinding light was overwhelmed by a new bright white and luminescent black. Stars burned brightly in my hands, and I couldn't even look at them.

Fyra screamed.

The lights faded, and the scene flipped to the dark, musty Temple. The Second Lady of the Temple was on top of me, her hot breath on my neck.

I threw her off and jumped to my feet. *Wasn't I bleeding?* Thoughtlessly, I slammed my wrists together, and the two stars launched from my hands, swirling like a double helix of DNA, zipping toward the Vampire...or towards the bearded man.

The scene changed again and again, like two movies spliced together frame by frame, but I was in the same exact position.

"What devilry is this?" I heard the Lady shriek, then simultaneously a blood-curdling scream erupted from both she and the man. The wailing echoed off the walls and reverberated in my ears.

A flare, like the explosion from a bomb, rolled through the room and hid every feature. The scintillating screams of agony overpowered my ears and paralyzed my lungs. I panicked as I tried to breathe again, but I couldn't remember how to move my diaphragm.

I dropped desperately to one knee and beat on my chest, and the air started flowing again.

I scanned the room, but it was completely dark, like the torches had been blown out, or the light bulbs were destroyed. *Where am I?* I could smell death, but where—or when—was that from? I rubbed my hand on the ground—it was rough and covered in dust. *Okay, I'm in the Temple.* But what was that? A memory I don't remember?

I traveled northwest across the Great Plains of Qui-Tos and came across a collection of lakes. They seemed to fit together perfectly, as if they were once a great lake but shattered by the hand of a god. Silver sand with sprouts of healthy grass spanned the distance between lakes.

I followed a river north from the shattered lakes but knew my heading would soon have to change. A great jagged mountain range, with one peak dominating the others, blocked my path. The rocks were sharp, the cliffs were sheer, and thus I turned to the west.

The gap between the jagged peaks and an earthy mountain range to the southwest was not wide. I felt like I was walking through a demilitarized zone between warring mountains. I continued northwest until I hit an ocean, then turned my heading north again.

When the mountains were no longer on my right, the temperature dropped like I'd stepped into an icebox. Following the ocean led me to another narrow pass between it and a much smaller range of mountains. This sierra seemed to have lightning dancing on it all the time, a constant squall coming from the northwest.

I went through the pass and found that all the land here was covered in such a storm, and dared not go further. Even if I could survive the lightning strikes, the ground was dead and dry, rent open in long meandering cracks. No one could survive these stormlands.

—From *The Travels of Itin the Traveler*

Chapter Eighteen

My whole body shook violently. I slowly opened my eyes, but it was too dark to see. I blinked and squinted until finally, my eyes adjusted to the darkness. Fyra's pale face was the first thing I could make out, looking at me as if she'd seen a ghost.

"What...happened?"

Fyra smiled and hugged me tightly. "You're alright!"

"Yeah...where's the Second Lady?" I asked.

The others came into focus but just stared at me with wide eyes and tight lips.

"You obliterated her," Kaylaa finally said.

"It was the power of the Iveleen! There's no doubt about it!" Kirstos said. His calf was heavily bandaged, and he was clearly favoring his other leg.

"What do you mean?"

"Whatever magic you used completely annihilated her. All that is left of her are her weapons," Kaylaa said, as she motioned to the pile of knives, still covered in dried blood.

Fyra let go of me and said, "I don't approve but...I guess there wasn't much choice."

"You don't approve?" asked Kirstos, his head cocked. "The Iveleen used him as a conduit. They have blessed our journey."

A conduit? No way. The Iveleen wouldn't have put me through so much to just use me. *Or would They?* But I did feel...powerful. Invincible. I tightened my fingers into a fist. *And it felt good.*

With one eyebrow raised, Fyra asked, "They blessed our journey to break into their forbidden Temple?"

"The time is NOW! We have been ordained by the gods. They want US to know THEIR secret! It's destiny!"

Destiny? I guess a lot had to fall into place to bring me to this spot. Kaylaa had to find me, which meant the embargo had to happen. Fyra had to push me into coming. Kirstos had to have prepped the Temple. And most of all, my father had to betray the world and die.

Do you still love him? That was a thought that had lurked in my mind for years, and I'd always held it back, like I was holding a door closed with an avalanche on the other side. But it finally broke through, here in this place where his whole life—and mine—changed. So what is the answer?

My eyes wandered down, and I saw the bandages over my ribs blooming with fresh blood. The pain came screaming back to me. I doubled over, and blood dripped onto the stone floor.

"Darynn, are you alright?" Fyra asked, one hand on my back.

Kirstos unzipped his small pouch and took out a pinch of white powder. He shoved it under my nose, but Fyra knocked it away, spraying the powder across the floor.

"What are you doing?" she asked.

"We can't waste this opportunity! He's in pain. I was just trying to get him back on his feet so we can go on!"

"I'm not taking your drugs, Kirstos," I said, though every part of my body wanted the relief.

Kirstos sighed loudly, then licked his hand to preserve his powder. He returned to the panel wall while Kaylaa bandaged me up and helped me back to my feet.

I staggered forward but stopped when I saw a shadow on the floor. Slender, like Fyra, but taller. "The Vampire is behind me!"

I whirled, tearing my bandages.

Nothing. "Huh?"

"She's gone, Darynn," Fyra said, gingerly rewrapping the bandages on my back. "That's just an image of where she last was when you..."

"Darynn, that kind of power...I've never seen it before," Kaylaa said. "Did you know you could do that?"

I shook my head. *Should I tell them about the memory?* No, that would just bring up more questions. I hobbled over to the panel wall and leaned next to it.

"Now at least we know why no one except your father was able to get this far," Fyra said. "The Second Lady killed them. He must have hurt her deeply enough to give him time to get through the wall."

"I think he may have literally broken her heart," I said, remembering the scar that trailed from the left side of her chest to her armpit.

I examined the panel wall closely—a six-by-six grid of stone panels, each appearing to recess into the wall at least a finger length if pressed. Each one had a symbol on it, but they just looked like random strokes to me.

"They have to be pressed in a certain order," Kirstos noted. "But I have studied the wall for years and come up empty."

"I'm guessing the math isn't in our favor to just try random combinations," I said.

"Of course not," Fyra replied with a chuckle.

"Besides, one wrong press locks up the whole panel for quite some time. I left once and came back the next day and still none of the panels could be pressed," Kirstos added. *How did my father figure this out?* "I've figured out the first four just by systemically pushing them— Three dash one, one dash two, three dash three, and one dash two. I have no idea how long the sequence is, and apparently, numbers repeat." He pointed to each stone as he explained.

Fyra carefully examined each symbol, getting so close her

nose nearly touched them. Kirstos watched her with a slight grin while Kaylaa sat against the wall with her eyes fixed behind us.

Every ounce of me just wanted to push random panels—Kirstos already knew four, how many more could there be? Fyra gave up looking at the panels and sat cross-legged on the ground, her eyes shut.

My mind wandered away from the door and back to the memory. *Did that actually happen?* It felt so real—the sights, the smells, the feelings...and the scream. Canfod Barma said he awakened the power in me, but that memory suggests it was already there, long before.

It made no sense for me to have magic power. My father won with the sword. My mother was mostly an ordinary woman, aside from her heroic work ethic. My grandfather was a sharpshooter.

Maybe I have it for a reason. I pulled the stone Gryphon out of my pocket. If Pavlar didn't disapprove of the power, like his sister, then he would want me to use it to protect the Olan-Har. He'd told me before that it sucked for me to fall to Olan-Har, but it was literally a godsend for the people in the slums. If I kept using my power, opposed to the gods, then there would be consequences, according to Kaylaa. I could just let it go, once we got back to Hargonla. *No, it feels too good.*

"I think I've got it," Fyra exclaimed. Dust swirled as she jumped up.

Kirstos quivered with excitement. "You do?"

"The four you mentioned, then the last on the second row, and then the last one."

"How do you know?" Kaylaa asked.

Fyra blushed. "I had a vision. Darynn's father pushed those panels."

"Since when can you see the past?" I asked.

"Well, this...is the first time."

Kaylaa nodded. "Your powers are stronger. Allies and

common purpose."

Kirstos's head swiveled between them. "You *all* know magic?"

I shrugged. "Well, you do, too."

"Hardly!" He pushed the panels as described by Fyra. Each one sunk in with a low rumble at the lightest touch. Kirstos waited impatiently for each stone to slide all the way back out before pressing the next. He held his breath as he pushed the fifth one, then squealed excitedly when it didn't lock up the wall. "Praise be to the Iveleen! Share your secret with your most devout follower—me!"

Very delicately, he pushed the last one, and the whole Temple shook. Pebbles fell from the ceiling, cracks like boulders breaking off a cliff-face resounded through the hallway.

The chaos ceased.

"Wait, what? It's never done that before. It has to be right! It has to be!" He slammed his fists against the wall in a tantrum, but the panels did not budge.

"Could it be broken?" I asked.

Fyra shook her head. "It's Iveleen magic—it can't break!"

A dead end? Nama-Da, Minotaurs, wolves, Vampires, the Second Lady...and we get beat by a wall?

A tremor, stronger than the last, shook the Temple. The wall slowly slid up into the ceiling. Light streamed in from the cavernous room. I exhaled in relief, while Kirstos dashed in, kicking up hundreds of years of dirt into swirling dust devils.

As I stepped into the room, I noticed a second set of bootprints overlaid with a thin layer of dust. *My father's boots.* I didn't even bother to look over the rest of the room—I traced the prints to see where he went, adrenaline coursing through my veins.

They led me first around the outside of the ovular chamber, so close like he ran his hand along the rough stone wall while he walked. The hair on my arms and neck stood on end. *He was here. Right here.* I carefully stepped beside his path to avoid disturbing the prints, but Kirstos was making a ruckus in seemingly every part of the room as it echoed off the walls.

After passing through about a quarter of the circle, my father turned to the right, toward the center of the room. He walked between two sets of white wood benches, now broken down and rotten. At the center he stopped, facing a bronze pedestal with a hazy, crystal dome.

I used my sleeve to wipe the dust off the dome, and squinted to see what was inside; a vessel of some sort, crafted from gold and rimmed with shining indigo metal. *Could that be?*

"The Chalice of Stria-Fate!" I blurted.

Kirstos apparated next to me while Fyra hurried over.

"It...it cannot be! It *is* still here!" Kirstos frantically rubbed off more of the dust.

Fyra prayed silently, touching her hands to her shoulders and bowing her head. "An Artifact of the Iveleen...I never thought I'd see one!"

"Because the Grand Cardinal selfishly hides away the ones he has!" Kirstos said. "He doesn't realize the impact their magnificence could have on the common people!"

Fyra snorted. "You think you know better than the Grand Cardinal?"

"The old man is a fool." He bared his teeth. "He doubted my piousness, told me my quest was a fool's errand. But he is so wrong!" Kirstos slammed the edge of his Plasma Lance into the crystal, shattering it into a million reflective pieces.

I covered my eyes with my arm. "What the hell, Kirstos?"

Before any of us could react, he grabbed the Chalice of Stria-Fate and held it up to the sky with both hands. It glinted brightly in the sunlight streaming from above.

"I deserve this!" he yelled. "Ten years in this hellish jungle!"

"It belongs to the Church," Fyra countered.

"Never!" Kirstos scampered into a chamber in the back of the room.

Fyra started after him, but I grabbed her arm. "Let him go.

We'll get it from him later."

"How could he be so careless?" She took a deep breath. "So many of the Artifacts are already missing—seven now, I think. Can you imagine all of the good that could be done with that? A cup that turns water into medicine?"

I nodded inattentively as my focus turned back to my father's impressions in the dust. Unfortunately, Kirstos had disturbed many of them, but I could still see clearly that they returned to the wall we had come through. I followed them to the front of the chamber, but drowsiness was setting in, my steps becoming heavy. A small stage was set up there, with three granite podiums—likely where the priests would stand. The stage was made of white wood, but the area surrounding it seemed to have been chiseled from a single massive rock.

Two passageways led diagonally away from the stage, and my father's footprints went both directions. It was clear that he had walked back and forth down the two passageways multiple times. While I was still debating which way to go, Kirstos shrieked from the end of the left passage, shocking me back to attention. I hobbled that way, into a long, dark hallway, led by the light of my Captain's Ring.

At the end I came upon a small, domed room, lined with lit gold candlesticks. In the center was a large, circular pedestal, and on top of that, a stone sarcophagus. Kirstos desperately pushed on the lid of the sarcophagus, but it didn't budge.

"Help me with this!" he pleaded.

"Uh, no," I said. "You want to disturb the body of a god?"

"I want to look upon Her face with my own eyes! Can't you feel Her radiance?"

I didn't feel anything. *What does a dead god look like?*

I stepped up onto a carpet woven with golden and purple fibers, much like the Chalice itself. The lid of the sarcophagus was crafted into the general shape of a person, made entirely of granite dyed with the royal purple symbolizing the Iveleen. In the center, a Golden Spiral was inlaid into the stone. "You should leave it alone, Kirstos."

By this time, Fyra and Kaylaa had joined us in the burial chamber. Kaylaa still hadn't said a word since we entered the nave, while Fyra seemed to be overwhelmed by the significance of the chamber.

"Help me!" Kirstos said again, but neither of them moved from the entrance. "Fine!" He took off his backpack and removed two small devices, which he set a short distance apart on the lid.

I narrowed my eyes. "Are you going to..."

He armed the devices, and yelled, "Clear!"

I stumbled off the pedestal and back into the hallway, and a huge boom echoed through the chamber, followed by an eerie lime flash. A haze of smoke and dust wafted into the hallway. Kirstos, coughing, dashed back into the chamber.

"I can't believe he just...what kind of priest is he?" Fyra asked.

"Not a good one." Curiosity tugged at me, and I went to look inside.

Kirstos wept next to the sarcophagus, his tears stained with dark dust. He luckily only blew up the lid, like he'd hoped, but he was still disappointed. My fingers curled over the edge of the coffin as I peered in.

Empty.

"But how?" I asked.

Kirstos moaned in response.

"There is something else in here..." I reached down to grab what looked like pieces of old parchment. But a strong hand on my wrist stopped me.

Fyra shook her head. "Your touch will destroy it, and then we'll never know what happened to her body."

"How will we read it, then?" I asked, pulling my hand back.

"A more delicate touch," Kaylaa said, pointing her open hand toward the parchment. A single piece started to levitate, illuminating some scribbled letters on the page. Not P.A.

Standard.

"It's in Old Vastirian," Kirstos announced. "I can read it. 'To the Seeker: I have moved my grandmother's body to somewhere she can be truly revered.'" Kirstos's face lit up with excitement. "Bekivala wrote this!" *One mystery solved.*

He continued reading: "'In its place, I leave only my guilty legacy. I have no doubt now that the disease my grandmother cured actually came from us—the Vastirian bodies were not meant to harbor such a sickness. Maybe Silva was indeed correct about relations with the people.'"

"Th-th-the disease transmitted from the gods?" Fyra asked, covering her mouth with her hand.

"Relations? Like what the Second Lady talked about?" Is *this* the Great Secret? I suddenly felt like a soldier in muddy trenches before a battle, but I had no weapon.

Kirstos's eyes were wide, his pupils heavily dilated as he continued. "'But that is not all. I also know now that General Haskar did not act alone in his rebellion. He did not steal my grandfather's staff—my grandfather gave it to him willingly. Haskar was the tree, but Josar planted the seed and nurtured it.'"

Fyra and I both gasped, and she nearly swooned but used the side of the coffin to steady herself. Kirstos's whole body shook violently.

My mind thumbed rapidly through the Scriptures, through the history books, but it didn't make sense. Why would Josar stage a rebellion against his own divine brethren? The first of the enemy soldiers, with sharpened bayonets, had dropped into my trench, and I could feel blood in my palms from squeezing my fists so tight.

"'I hope the Seeker is both powerful and wise. Use great discretion with this information, lest you destroy the world.'" Kirstos took a deep breath. "Sealed by Bekivala himself." The bayonets dug deep into my heart, my hands bleeding as I desperately tried to pull them out. Why would the Iveleen turn on themselves? And why would Bekivala tell us?

I looked to Fyra for the answers; she was way smarter than me—surely she would have them. "What...does it mean?" I asked. My legs felt like they were ready to give out, so I allowed myself to collapse onto the rough carpet.

"If Bekivala wrote this...then..." she choked.

"That is his seal...and the Second Lady said he was torn," Kirstos said, staggering across the room, back to the entrance. "It can only be the truth. The Great Secret...I never...imagined." He disappeared into the hallway, his Plasma Lance clattering against the walls and floors.

Fyra's whole body trembled. "We don't know it's true. We don't know...but..."

"But what?"

"Josar didn't fight in the Fall of Haskar. He was arguably the most powerful of the Iveleen, despite his off-kilter nature. But...why? Is this...?" She trailed off.

My mind raced so fast I couldn't pause to catch any of my thoughts.

"This still doesn't tell us why Zilpohn went to Yiptae," said Kaylaa coldly.

Astonished, I glared at her. I tried to rebuke her, to say anything, but nothing came out of my gaping mouth. Tears streamed down Fyra's face.

Kaylaa said, "In fact, I doubt he even saw this."

"What?" I swallowed bitter saliva. "But this is it. This is the Secret he found that drove him to madness."

She shook her head. "Use your brain. The lid was too heavy for one man, even as strong as your father was. I had to use magic to lift and set down the parchment."

"He...he would have been respectful of Stria-Fate's tomb," Fyra said. *She's right.*

"Then...what did he find? What if...what if it wasn't here?" *What if this was all for nothing?* What did my father find that drove him to madness?

Could there be something even worse?

My anger at the Iveleen swelled until it erupted. "How dare they? They killed us with a disease that came from *them*?" I slammed my fist on the coffin. "And before that, they started a rebellion and killed tens of thousands of us? Why? *Why*?"

Fyra looked at me, wide-eyed, and more tears flowed. She sniffed and said, "That doesn't make what Stria-Fate did any less incredible. She used every ounce of her strength to heal the disease. They cared for us, Darynn."

"How can you say that? It was their own damn fault in the first place! And the Fall of Haskar...that led to the caste system. Haskar's son, Olan, was the first Olan-Har. His punishment for his father's sins. That led to all of this! All because of Josar!"

"You...you don't know." Fyra collapsed against the tomb. "Maybe Josar was truly mad? We shouldn't hold his shortcomings against the rest. The others risked their lives to protect us against Haskar and his troops!"

"All my life I've—" I was cut off by loud, labored breathing echoing from the main chamber. A harrowing cackle echoed off the walls and sent waves of shudders down my spine. The three of us looked at each other, simultaneously realizing Kirstos must be in danger. We gathered ourselves and dashed down the hallway.

Haskar's Rebellion will end today.
He has won many battles with his cunning, and strength,
and stolen power. He has killed Makar by his own hand,
wielding the Staff of Josar. His people killed Lolan in an accident
of pure chance. But today, he will die.
Thousands have died thanks to his bloodlust, his thirst for
power and domination. I don't recognize him anymore. He has
aged decades in a mere three years, trading his youth for
incredible power. His movements are governed by madness, his
thoughts held captive by demons.
He was my friend, my leader, and Makar's general. Now he
will die the greatest traitor, a slayer of gods, a chief of demons.
His sins will never be forgotten, and his child and ancestors will
be forever tainted by evil blood.

—From an account written by Haskar's former first
Lieutenant in 43 ARI

Chapter Nineteen

A twisted smile like a hyena's had conquered Kirstos's face. His eyes glowed red, the color drained from his cheeks, and his hair spiked chaotically. His arms were wrapped around his knees in a fetal position, and he rocked rapidly back and forth. His cackling grew louder and wilder; the echoes made it seem like there was a whole choir smothering me.

"Can't you see?" His head twisted awkwardly, farther than seemed possible, so that he could stare directly into my eyes. I tried desperately to turn away but he held my gaze as if his hand were fixed to my chin.

"You fools!" he roared, rocking to his feet in one slow, smooth transition. "The tricksters have been revealed!"

What is he saying? My heart sunk into my stomach.

"Kirstos, you're a priest!" Fyra said, her arms open. "The Iveleen have spoken to you. Don't throw it away!"

He swallowed hard. "Are you so blind? The pieces fit together now. Can't you see?" He circled us slowly like a predator waiting for the right time to strike. I stared at him blankly. "Your father was no fool, Darynn. Not like you. Not like you."

"You don't know! He didn't see that letter!"

He stopped and crept toward me until I could feel his hot breath scratching my face. "He knew this Secret. Josar whispered the truth to Haskar...so devastating that Haskar turned on his gods."

"What is this truth?" Fyra asked.

He threw his head back and laughed heartily. It echoed off the walls and hit us from every angle. "I see now...I see." He turned and walked away.

I took a cautious step toward him. "You see what?"

"General Haskar was well-respected and a formidable fighter. Josar spoke to him, and he started a rebellion. Your father learns the same thing, and he starts a rebellion. Your father is Haskar! Do you not see?"

I felt like a wasp nest had been implanted in my heart. Sting after sting, until the pustules grew large and burst. I fell to one knee, the weakness after the fight with the Second Lady overwhelming me. Fyra rested a hand on my back but didn't take her eyes off Kirstos.

"It is time...past time...to set things right. The whole system...is built on lies. Josar knew it. Haskar knew it. Zilpohn Mark knew it. Can't you see? You are Olan-Har—you know your place in life. Worthless scum. All because of Haskar's Rebellion. It is time to set things right."

"It was about order, Kirstos. You know that!" Tears streamed down Fyra's cheeks.

"It was about control. It was, and is, about domination. We cowered to them. Worshipped them."

"You're making an assumption," Kaylaa said. *She's right—a lot of assumptions.* I never thought it possible, but Kaylaa made me feel better. I struggled back to my feet.

He hissed. "Stay out of this, foreigner. You don't know the meaningless oppression."

"Those letters could be a forgery. Haskar's final trick!" Fyra suggested.

His eyes widened and he sneered. "Fools. You're all fools." He kicked the nearest pew, and it splintered into a hundred pieces. His whole body was enveloped in a purple glow. He ran both hands through his wild hair, threw back his head, and laughed menacingly. "I will save them. I will show the Grand Cardinal the error of his ways. He will grovel! And then, he will die!"

Fyra turned to us. "He can't tell anyone. We don't know enough. It will be another Betrayal of the Hero situation, and thousands, tens of thousands could die." She nearly fell, staggering forward. "I can...I can see it. So many corpses..." She screamed, desperately trying to keep her eyes open, even using her fingers to pry her eyelids apart. But to no avail; when her eyes shut, she screamed again.

"Fyra, it's alright," I said. I hugged her tightly. "He won't tell anyone." Her breathing was shallow but steady.

"Yes, Master. I hear you now," Kirstos said, only barely loud enough for us to hear. "I will spread your light. I will spread your truth." He threw down his circlet bearing the Golden Spiral and crushed it under his boot.

Who is he talking to? "What?"

He turned to me. The purple glow grew and streaked with black energy. "The Gospel of Haskar must be spread. The Iveleen must fall. Will you help me? Or will you meekly accept your fate, like Olan?" He reached out a bony hand, beckoning for me to grab it.

"Never."

Kirstos's eyes rolled back as his head jerked up. He chanted something unintelligibly. Black flames swirled around him.

"He's possessed!" Kaylaa yelled, her Rapiers in hand.

His feet left the ground as he started to float like a phantom. His Plasma Lance suddenly landed in his hands, like two magnets drawn toward each other. The power looked like the flames in the shrine when we'd interrupted his worship.

He'd been speaking to demons for a long time now.

"I don't want to fight you, Kirstos," I said as I unsheathed my Edge.

He clicked his tongue. "If only your father had brought me,

instead of you. He knew what he had to do, and he tried. You lack the conviction, the will, to do what is necessary. Even as your people die. Pathetic."

The wasps buzzed around my heart again. *Is this what a heart attack feels like?*

"He went mad. Now so have you. Who is really the weak one?" Kaylaa asked. *Yeah!*

"It's time for you to meet your master," I said with a flash of my Plasma Edge.

He floated gracefully down to the ground, not even kicking up any dust, and angled his curved Plasma Lance at me. He flashed the black plasma once on the hooked blade and charged.

I dragged my Edge as I took two steps towards him, but he was quicker. I blocked several of his blows, but I had no chance to hit him—his Lance kept him out of reach of my Edge. Every time I'd gain a step, he'd float backward. Then he'd lash out like a cobra, screaming like a banshee with every thrust. The dust swirled around us like a tornado, stinging my eyes, drying my throat.

Worst of all, my strength was failing.

He sensed it and swung his Lance across my knees.

I jumped, but the pole crashed into my ankle and I fell on my butt. Dust billowed around me like a mushroom cloud, so thick I lost sight of him.

He struck downward at me, but the first strike missed just to the side.

I parried each blow to the side. *How was I going to beat him?* He seemed invincible, buoyed by demonic power.

Like the Second Lady. That's the only way.

But I used it all up. My muscles felt like rags that had been wrung out of all water.

He stood back and leaned on his lance like a cane. "You are merely a shadow of your father. I will complete his work, like you never could."

Boiling anger pushed me to my feet and I swung at him

wildly. Still, I could not touch him. He kicked me in the chest and sent me sailing across the pews. I recovered on one knee, panting.

He flew at me, the plasma blazing on the tip of his lance like a flaming arrow. I covered my head with my hands. *Iveleen, if you're there, help me now.*

A sharp clang exploded over my head. Kirstos's Plasma Lance tumbled across the chamber.

Kaylaa stood next to me, her Rapiers in hand. "This freak is mine."

"Take him." I huffed loudly and Fyra came to my side.

Kirstos cackled maniacally and held his arm out. The Lance dutifully flew into his hands and he crouched, ready to strike. He licked his dusty lips. "I will enjoy this."

A deep purple ring, like the Iveleen's favored color, circled Kaylaa's heart and pulsed out to her hands and feet. The energy emerged from her skin, tracing a purple outline of her veins and muscles on the outside. Her eyes blazed the same color, and suddenly she seemed larger. She dashed at Kirstos at breakneck speed. As she moved, the corded muscles of energy flexed.

Fyra gasped audibly. *She's been holding back, this whole time.* This was her true power, and it was magnificent...and terrifying.

Dust obscured much of their battle, but even with Kirstos's advantage in reach, Kaylaa was too fast, too strong for him. More dark energy flowed from the corners and into Kirstos's body. When it did, somehow Kaylaa managed to get even stronger. The whole chamber rumbled as they stepped, kicking off the walls and the pews and the columns.

Kirstos floated away from her and hung suspended in the middle of the chamber. His chest heaved, his breathing hoarse but deep. He was caked in dust and sweat. "My Master will protect me," he said.

Every torch in the chamber extinguished as if blown out by the exhale of a demon.

Kaylaa snickered. "A cheap trick will not save you."

The torches lit again, but now with the eerie glow of the shrine. Smoke trailed from each one and flowed into his body. He pounced on Kaylaa, more viciously than before. His Lance was an extension of his arm, a gigantic claw tearing through the air.

Kaylaa lost her balance, but only for a moment. Using one Rapier to block the lance, she swung the other at his body repeatedly.

A surprise kick knocked Kirstos to the ground. She disarmed him and held a Rapier to his throat. "Yield."

Kirstos's chest heaved, and he inhaled deeply. "Never." The lights went out again—Kaylaa stabbed forward, but there was no yell, no agony.

Kaylaa screamed. The torches relit.

Kirstos sat in the nearest pew while Kaylaa rubbed her eyes vigorously.

"The bastard threw sand in my eyes!"

Like a wraith, Kirstos floated towards her and grabbed her throat. "My master wants your breath."

Weakly, Kaylaa clawed at his arms. His clothes were shredded, but his ashen skin seemed impervious.

I jumped to my feet and tried to get to her. Wooziness overtook me and I merely stumbled forward.

Kaylaa choked and gulped as her face turned purple. Kirstos lifted her into the air, his eyes glowing slits of red.

Fyra dashed in and stabbed him in the back with the icy end of her Elenduil Staff. The subzero stone shocked him and Kaylaa plummeted to the ground. She gasped hoarsely from her knees.

But Kirstos was still unharmed.

"Stupid girl." He backhanded her with a jaw-crushing blow, spinning Fyra all the way around.

I stumbled towards him, ready to slice him in half.

His head swiveled toward me, his mouth twisted into a sickly grin. He howled with laughter, a demon loosed from hell.

Suddenly, silver light emerged from Kirstos's mouth. His knees slammed into the ground. A silver blade skewered him through the base of his neck, keeping his body from falling. Blood poured over the blade and down his chest. He coughed and vile sucking sounds escaped his throat.

Kaylaa stood behind him, still wheezing, a slight smile on her face. The power subsided from her as she shuddered down to her normal size. She slipped the Rapier out of his mouth, and he fell.

"This was not...how it was to end..." he choked.

"I don't believe in your Iveleen or your demons. I believe in determination, justice, and free will. I am just a woman, and I defeated your demon." Even with her magical power fading, Kaylaa exuded a different kind of strength; the strength of self-reliance and training and unwavering determination.

"Darynn...you must give people...the Great Secret." Blood burbled behind Kirstos's every word. "Save them...let them decide...if you don't reveal the truth, who will?" He drew one more breath, exhaled blood, and his power faded. He was with his Master now, in the Nether—if there is such a place.

Don't meekly accept your fate like Olan, he had said. It echoed over and over again in my head. *Your father is Haskar.*

Fyra rejoined us, rubbing her cheek.

"Are you alright?" I asked.

She nodded. "Are you?"

"Just some bruises...and weakness. Kaylaa?"

There were deep bruises where his fingers had gripped her throat. "Fine." She loosed a deep breath. "That was brave, Fyra."

Fyra's eyes grew wide. "Th-th-thank you." I could read the expression on her face. *A compliment, from Kaylaa?*

When Fyra regained her composure, she turned back to me. "I didn't mean physically, Darynn."

I took a shuddering breath. "I don't know. Do you think he was right? Any of it?"

"No, of course not. He's lived in the jungle all of these years, with Vampires and other dangers. Almost no human interaction. Drugs. He probably wasn't even possessed. Just crazy."

She was probably right. *But where did his power come from, then?*

I stared at Kirstos's body, blood still seeping from the base of his neck. I didn't feel any attachment to him, but he had saved Kaylaa's life...and then she killed him. My eyes flicked up to Kaylaa, who was massaging her neck. That power was terrifying, and she felt no remorse, had no issue with killing a man. She even said she'd enjoy it. I wonder if that was the consequence of her magic, or if she'd always been that way.

I picked up Kirstos's trampled circlet and examined it. A priest, turned to Haskar. I guess even priests can fall, and he'd broken nearly every rule. I tried to push the Golden Spiral on the circlet into a circle, but it was too mangled. I was starting to feel just as unraveled as this symbol, unable to be put back together again. If any of Bekivala's letter was true, if Josar had aided Haskar in his rebellion, if the Haskar Virus was actually from the Iveleen...

No, can't think like that now. Kaylaa called it an assumption. Fyra remained steadfast in her belief. I was going to trust that.

"So what now?" I asked.

"Your father found something here that led him to Yiptae. We have to find it," Kaylaa said. It was as if the fight with Kirstos hadn't rattled her at all. It was hard for me to look at her the same way—she always looked tough, sure, but now I knew what kind of terrifying power she harbored.

Fyra asked, "How long was it between this trip and going to Yiptae, Darynn?"

I tried to think back, but the memories were so painful. "Six months, maybe," I replied, spitting out the first reasonable thing that came to mind. "He could've gone somewhere else, Kaylaa. Maybe he just came here to retrieve the Chalice for the

Shard."

"Then why didn't he get it?" Kaylaa inquired. "My father said this Temple was stuck in his mind. It has to mean something." I thought I detected the tiniest bit of desperation in her voice.

"He went that way, too," I said, pointing to the hallway opposite the one to the sarcophagus. Kaylaa led us down the path, but it felt like I was walking through a deep swamp. It wasn't only physical—more and more, it was sinking in that we weren't going to find out anything about my father here. We would leave empty-handed, and then we'd have to make the long, useless journey back to the slums, where I'd just die in rotting monotony. And I'd never even know why.

Making my way slowly down the hall, I noticed hundreds of glass ornaments reflecting the light of my Captain's Ring, hanging just a hand's width above my head. Each was the shape of the Golden Spiral, but at a different state of compression and in a different color.

"They're called animonilium. They were in the other hallway too, and they symbolize the path to enlightenment. But..." Fyra paused and examined them closely. "Why would they be in this hallway?"

"Why not?"

"Traditionally, these are hung only on the path to an Iveleen's grave or a holy site. But we're walking away from the sarcophagus, and the Spirals are tightening." Her pace quickened, and I struggled to keep up.

This hallway was shorter than the one to the coffin, leading to a huge room with smooth, off-white walls. There was no natural light, but Kaylaa had already lit the torches. Towering glass bookcases lined the wall, nearly reaching the ceiling at least four stories above us and painted a creamy color. If there wasn't a bookshelf, a dusty mirror could be found in its place instead.

"Just a storage room," Kaylaa remarked.

"So, nothing."

"But the animonilium has to mean something. Doesn't it?" Fyra pressed. Then, weaker, "*Doesn't* it?"

I slumped against the nearest wall, not caring if I cracked the mirror behind me. "It was all for nothing."

"Not...nothing," Fyra replied, examining some object from off a bookshelf. "The letters from Bekivala...if they are from Bekivala, mean something. Somehow, we need to verify the truth about them."

"But how?"

She looked at me with wide eyes and shrugged. "I don't know. If there's any truth at all, the people deserve to know. And if there's not, then the documents should be destroyed. The words on those pages are dangerous...the kind of words that could lead to..." She stopped short, I guess to spare my feelings.

"A rebellion," I finished. "But those words didn't. Something else did." It made no sense.

Kaylaa had completed a circle of the room but looked defeated. She ripped out a Rapier and smashed the nearest bookshelf, sending shards of wood across the room. "It has to be here!" *Where was this emotion coming from?* She seemed to notice Fyra and me staring at her in disbelief.

She recollected herself. "The fight with Kirstos, the uselessness of this whole journey, and...the uncertainty you feel...it got to me. You think you came a long way to get here, but I traveled millions of miles...for nothing. I feel like I've been tricked."

She had come so far, but it was worse for us. The whole reason the Olan-Har existed was because of that rebellion 460 years ago, started by Haskar...or was it Josar? Haskar's son, Olan, was the first one with "evil blood," and from then the children suffered for the parents' sins. What if that hadn't happened? *Don't meekly accept your fate, like Olan.*

"Maybe that's it..." Fyra wondered aloud. "A trick." She walked to the opposite edge of the room and back. Then she did it again, and again. "This room...it's not as big as it appears. It's an illusion."

I looked a little closer, and she did seem to be able to cross the room faster than she should've. "So?"

"I think this room isn't big enough. The coffin room was further back." She walked to the back of the room and started examining it closer.

"Are you saying...there's another room?" I lifted slowly to my feet.

"Either that...or a lot of wasted stone." She carelessly tossed objects off the bookshelves and felt the walls behind them. When she found nothing, she moved onto the next one. I reached the back of the room when she had finished every bookshelf, and she collapsed amongst the mess. "But why? Why make this room this way?"

I looked at the mess and my eyes wandered to the walls. There were only three mirrors there, each taller than me, dispersed between the bookshelves. I looked in one of them and saw my father. Exactly my height, green eyes like the ocean, but with a short beard. *What did you find here?*

Then I noticed smudges around the edges of the mirror, breaking up the thin sheen of dust. Is this...it? I pulled out my Edge and smashed his image. Fyra shrieked, startled.

"What the hell?" Kaylaa asked.

"I found...guess not." There was just a stone wall behind the mirror. Fyra and Kaylaa were saying something, but I was too focused on the next mirror to hear them. It also had smudges around the edge. I smashed it, leading to more yelling, but still nothing.

There was just one more smudged mirror on the wall. *I hope this is it.* I rammed my Edge into it and held my breath.

This time, when the mirror shattered, it revealed a small wooden door—so small I would have to crawl into it. My heart picked itself up and started racing.

"You found it, Darynn. Amazing!" Fyra exclaimed,

approaching to examine the door.

I suddenly felt a huge weight on my shoulders, like a Minotaur was perched on my back. *What is behind this door?* Whatever drove my father to madness, took him away from me, destroyed my life, was behind this door. Sweat dripped off of me like I'd walked into a sauna.

Slowly, I reached out trembling fingers and pushed on the door. There was no trick here.

The door swung open.

I felt an uncomfortable power emanating from the dark tunnel, and I thought Fyra felt it too; we stood there, gawking. Something we wanted to know, but also didn't want to know, both drawing us in and pushing us out.

Kaylaa gave us a quizzical look and said, "I'll go first." She didn't feel it, whatever it was, and she disappeared into the gloom.

My mouth was dry. "I'll be right behind you."

Fyra didn't react at first, still entranced by the fear of the unknown, then she nodded. "Whatever it is Darynn, we can't lose faith, or we could fall into the same pit as your father and Kirstos. It's just evidence—not truth."

I stared at her blankly. Evidence...not truth. Realizing she wasn't getting a response, she dropped to her knees and crawled into the tunnel. I took a deep breath and followed her in.

The tunnel was carved from the same stone as the walls, but it was, oddly, smooth as glass. No machine or tool could've made a tunnel like this, at least not four hundred years ago. Bekivala used his power to carve this tunnel, no doubt about it. I half-slid, half-crawled to the end and stood up in the hidden chamber.

This room was still submerged in darkness, the only light coming from Kaylaa's Starlight Rapiers and my Captain's Ring. But even so, I could feel the presence of something large looming in front of us. Whatever it was, it was made of some kind of curved metal, as our small sources of light reflected off of it. I thought I smelled a faint whiff of jet fuel.

Kaylaa lit the room with a small ball of flame in her open palm. The light spread across the room like sunlight over a shadowed hill.

The flickering blaze revealed the massive object—a spaceship.

As if the sun itself had descended on the horizon, blinding light filled the sky. From the light emerged twelve figures, each even more brilliant than the surrounding light.

The people shielded their eyes and fell on their faces as They approached.

The first of the Iveleen stepped forward and said, "I am Josar, first of the Iveleen." He tapped His Staff on the earth three times, and each time thunder boomed across the entire world. The blinding light faded, and darkness would have overcome the people except for the radiant glow of the Iveleen.

One person dared speak, and lightning flashed from the Staff of Josar. He transformed into a beast, a small wildcat with mangy fur and broken teeth. "Do not speak, for We are here to tame your tongues."

All were silent, in awe of Their sublime Power.

—From the Scriptures, the Rise of the Iveleen

CHAPTER TWENTY

Fyra reached for my hand, her eyes fixed on the spacecraft, and I gladly took it. Kaylaa tossed the ball of flame ahead of her. It floated like a balloon as it led us around the ship.

The nose of the ship was blunt, black on the bottom and graphite-colored on top. It smoothly widened from the nose out into a triangular shape with small, metallic jade wings and a huge, vertical tail. Struts and tires put the bottom of the ship at my eye level.

With my other hand, I reached out to the hull—completely smooth, as if it had been machined from a single piece of metal, aside from the landing gear and control surfaces. It was cool to the touch, even colder than the room. A chill snuck down my spine.

Silence loomed as we circled. I craned my neck to see the ship's underbelly. It was clear the ship had flown before—there were flaws in the material, especially at the nose, presumably from atmosphere reentry. From the outside, the ship appeared to still be in working order, down to the huge boosters that would propel it through space.

But...what is it doing here? In a Vastirian Temple? It didn't look like a Vastirian ship—not even an old one.

Kaylaa pointed to a rounded, rectangular door near the front. "There's a door there." Her voice echoed in the small chamber. She looked around as if trying to find a way to get to it. *Is she sweating?* The room was too cool to sweat. Maybe she was too close to the floating flame. "I can jump to it, but I don't see a way to open it. Look around for a controller."

Using my ring for light, I searched the ground around and under the ship, but didn't find anything—the room was completely empty, except for the hulking spaceship and years of dust.

"We have to get in," Kaylaa said. "We have to know where this ship came from."

"And why it's here," Fyra added. "Why would Bekivala hide a spaceship?"

I don't know. It made no sense at all. The letters were clear in their intent, but what could we possibly learn from an old spaceship? My mind kept drawing blanks.

"Could you pry the door open?" I asked.

"No. But...stand right here," Kaylaa said. I complied. "Be still." She put her hands on my shoulders and vaulted up to stand on them. I wavered a bit, already feeling weak, but she leaned against the ship to take some of the burden off me. "Fyra, hand me his Edge."

Fyra took my Edge out of its sheath and handed it to her. A cobalt blue streak reflected off the surface, then a metallic clang echoed in the room.

"I think I got it," Kaylaa said, and the hinges whined as the door came open. Her weight mercifully dropped off my shoulders as she climbed into the ship. She let down a rope ladder.

I motioned for Fyra to go up first, then weakly climbed up after her. As my foot hit the floor, I had the strangest feeling of being watched. I glanced over my shoulder, but of course no one was there in the gloom. *The Iveleen, maybe?* Maybe, just once, I was giving them something to worry about, instead of the other way around. I grinned.

The inside of the ship was like being inside a can—a round,

metallic tube, narrow near the nose and wider in the back. Every surface on the wall was actually a door to a compartment, or a fold-out table, or some other mechanism that popped out. But there was nothing loose in any of the compartments. There was only one other room, a closet with a tube for using the bathroom. Even the cockpit was hidden inside pop-out compartments toward the front, which held brightly-colored buttons, meters, and gauges, all in a foreign language.

Kaylaa plopped down into a seat that folded out from one of the sides of the cockpit. She examined the buttons, tracing the words with her index finger.

I scratched my head. "I don't get it, Kaylaa."

"I do."

My heart skipped a beat or two, then thumped harder to make up for it. "What do you mean?" Fyra came up beside me and we waited impatiently for the answer.

She took a deep breath and ran her hands along the dials. "This ship is from Yiptae."

"Yiptae!" Fyra and I exclaimed in unison.

"It's a very old ship," she said. "But all of the lettering here is in Old Yiptaen. I can't read it, but I recognize it."

My lungs pumped rapidly. I caught my breath long enough to say, "So that's why he went to Yiptae."

"Undeniably. This is the reason."

"But this explains nothing!" Fyra cried, frustrated. "It's just an old Yiptaen ship!"

Kaylaa started pressing buttons and pulling levers while I moved back to the main section of the ship. I opened every compartment and came across a long, narrow one. With a light push, the compartment popped open, revealing a bed with a thin cushion and straps to hold in a sleeper. Six more identical compartments were spaced evenly through the cabin. "The ship held seven passengers."

"Could this be the ship the Yiptaens came on, the exploratory mission you talked about, Kaylaa?" Fyra asked.

"It...it could be," Kaylaa replied. "That would make this ship something like five hundred years old."

"Why would the Iveleen hide it?" I asked.

"Fear, maybe? No, that's not right." Fyra rubbed her shoulder. "By the time this Temple was built, we already knew there were aliens—even hostile ones—in the galaxy. Nurka's Sacrifice in 76 ARI."

I nodded as I remembered the hologram from the Hargonla Chapel—one god, Nurka, in space, sacrificing his body to destroy an entire battalion of invading alien spaceships. He wasn't one of the original dozen Iveleen but was probably the most beloved for his sacrifice.

The whir of fans and beeps pulled my attention to the cockpit. One monitor lit up, dark black with foreign white lettering.

"Can you read any of it?"

"All Old Yiptaen. But the numbers...they look like dates. But I can't..."

Sparks flew from the computer and darkness cascaded down the screen. The fans slowed to a creaking halt. "Damnit!" Kaylaa slammed the panel.

Disappointed, I wandered to the back of the cabin and mindlessly opened a few more compartments. Empty. Empty. Empty. *Never enough information.* Always more questions.

One popped open with something in it. It looked like a coat: rough, shaggy black fur with fierce orange stripes. I showed it to Kaylaa.

"That is not Yiptaen. Way too bright. Almost all creatures on Yiptae are white or gray to blend in with the snow."

"I don't think it's Vastirian, either," Fyra said.

"We came here for answers, not more questions!" I shouted. "Damn Iveleen and Their Secrets!"

"Darynn! You can't talk like that in a holy place!" Fyra said, wide-eyed. Then she shook her head demonstrably.

"A holy place? Hardly." I kicked the floor. "This is the gods' hidden stash! And we can't even figure out why they needed to hide it from us!"

Fyra put her hands on her hips. "Obviously the gods are going to know much, much more than mortals will ever know, or even need to know. I am sure they were just protecting us from something."

I moved toward her, my nose nearly touching hers, my cheeks hot. "Are you so sure? You're sure that they started a revolution—against themselves—for our protection too?"

"We don't know that the letter was genuine! You're jumping to conclusions, just like Kirstos did, and you saw what happened to him!" She turned away and stared at an open, empty compartment.

"Maybe he was right. If they're truly gods, why did they have to hide anything at all from us?"

She looked back at me with her eyes narrowed. "It's about faith, Darynn. The gods told us what we need to know, not just what we want to know. And They left the rest for us to discover, to learn on our own, so that we can grow."

"What are we learning, Fyra, other than they lied to us! There wasn't anything wrong with this Temple, it was just a convenient place to hide something this big, especially if you curse it."

"I can see how your father—" She stopped short.

"How my father what? Went mad? Is that what you were going to say? You think my father was just like Kirstos, huh? Some madman needing just a little push over the edge?"

"No, it's not like that."

"And now you think I'm just like him. You think you're more devout than him? You're so damn smart, but you don't do anything with it! You just pity yourself at home and trust that the Iveleen will make things better! And all they do is make things worse!"

Tears flowed freely down her face. I opened my mouth to say more, but Kaylaa stood between us. "That's enough."

"You don't get to tell me that! You think you're the boss, but you're not. I can do whatever I damn well want," I said.

"Right now, that's acting like a child." I ripped my Plasma Edge out of its sheath and angled it at her. "You need to cool off!"

She jerked her hand in front of her, palm open, and a violet net of magic energy sailed at me. I covered my head with my hands, but the momentum of the net swept me out of the door. I landed on the stone floor on the base of my spine.

My adrenaline let me hop right back up to my feet. The rage swelled like a stockpot boiling over in my belly. The pain and anger concentrated into black energy in my hands. Steam rushed off my body into the cool darkness of the room. The whole room was illuminated by the light in my hands, bright enough to show my reflection in the metallic body of the ship.

Who is that? What am I doing? I closed my eyes and took a deep breath, and the energy dissipated from my hands. I slumped to the ground, my arms around my knees. Pain emanated from my back from slamming into the floor. The cuts across my ribs seemed to have reopened. I tried to stretch, but it wasn't helping.

This power is dangerous. I had been so eager to use it before...but one argument and suddenly it overcame me, wanting to hurt them, the only two people in the world I cared about. I'd only used it before to protect people, but there, that was me just protecting myself. My ego. My father.

This is the ship that drove him mad, eventually. He probably wouldn't have known this was a Yiptaen ship at the time. Just an old one, and not Vastirian. He must have come back and researched it on the DataAxis. Then he decided to go to Yiptae when that wasn't enough. Then something there confirmed the ship's origin.

Kaylaa jumped down from the ship and offered me a hand. I took it and she said, "Fyra is really hurting in there. I think you hit a weak spot. You should apologize."

"I didn't mean it. She must know I was just mad, and tired, and frustrated."

"That doesn't make it hurt less."

What does Kaylaa know about it? But she was right. I dusted myself off and started toward the ship. I grabbed the ladder and looked to see if Kaylaa was following.

She shook her head. "I'm going to look at the outside some more."

Fyra was laying down on one of the beds in the back. Her face and clothes were soaked with tears. I pulled out a bed across from her, uncomfortably far, but the other beds all popped out of the ceiling.

"Fyra, I'm...sorry. That was hurtful, and I didn't mean it."

When she turned to look at me, it wasn't pain or sadness in her eyes—it was fear. She should be afraid. She'd just seen me raise my Edge to Kaylaa, and after that, summon my destructive power. She looked at me like I was a demon. I wanted to get closer to her, but maybe that wasn't a good idea.

Death always came to those close to me, as if my touch etched a target for the gods. The Iveleen had made it clear I was meant to be alone. It was probably better for everyone that way.

She wiped her cheeks. "I wanted to do more, Darynn. I always have. But my power crippled me. I'm afraid, Darynn. I have always trusted the Iveleen to pull me through. How else could I stand a chance against so much death?"

"You've done really well with it."

The fear in her eyes started to fade, and she sat up and faced me. "Maybe. But it's only because of Them. These things in the Temple—the curse, the Vampires, the letter, the ship, they make your thoughts wander, if only for a moment. But we can't give into that. We have to know the nature of the gods is good, or it all falls apart. I'll fall apart." Fresh tears ran down her cheeks. I sat down next to her and put an arm around her.

"I won't let you fall apart."

We were silent for a while, her warm tears wetting my

shoulder. I really wanted to kiss her, but the timing didn't seem right.

Then she said, "I'm sorry about what I said about you and your father. This journey has been tough on me, and I can only imagine how it's been for you, knowing that your father went through this too."

"It's okay."

"I just don't want you to fall in the same pit he did. I...it..." She trailed off.

"You two need to come out here!" Kaylaa yelled from outside the ship.

I helped Fyra to her feet and gave her a hug. I felt my heart flutter and the strong urge to kiss her, again, but her head was buried in my chest. She broke off the hug and started toward the door.

Once outside, we saw that Kaylaa had lit another flame, this one was much larger than the other, and a few feet in front of her.

"What is it?"

"I... recognize this ship," she said. "I've seen it before...in a museum on Yiptae."

"This same ship? That's impossible."

"Not the exact same one." She held two fingers to her forehead with her eyes closed. "This is an early Yiptaen interplanetary ship, same series as the one in the museum."

Fyra asked, "So how old is it?"

Kaylaa seemed to be reasoning things out in her head. "This is a second-generation or third-generation interplanetary ship, putting it at around 250 Yiptaen years old." She paused to concentrate again. "Yiptae is about twice as far as Vastire, so double it. About 500 Vastirian years ago."

Five hundred years. "But that's when...the Iveleen came here." An odd thought popped into my head, a question that I'd never thought before. *Came here from...?* From? *From* was not a question you asked. They came from the Heavens. The answer wriggled into my brain like a corpse worm: from Yiptae. I sank to my knees and pounded on the hard stone of the floor, so hard I could feel my bones on the edges of my hands.

"They came from Yiptae! The Iveleen! They're...aliens!"

Kaylaa's head whipped around, her mouth agape.

"They're not blue, Darynn!" Fyra said. "Use your head."

I pointed at Kaylaa. "She's an immigrant! Maybe they're like her!"

"Not many immigrants back then," Kaylaa said. "Like I said, early interplanetary ship."

Fyra, still calm, said, "Besides, Darynn, the ship only holds seven, you said so yourself."

She was making sense, but the thoughts in my head were a runaway train. "It all lines up, Fyra! They took this ship from Yiptae, barely made it here, couldn't leave. Then they used their magic to dazzle the wild Vastirians! They tricked us, Fyra!"

She slapped me, and though it didn't hurt, it shocked me. "You're making so many assumptions, Darynn! It's more likely to believe in the Iveleen than your wild conjecture."

"How can you say that?"

"Because we have hundreds of years of evidence of the Iveleen, and you're trying to throw it away with incomplete theories."

"I agree with Fyra," Kaylaa said. "I don't believe in your Iveleen, but this isn't much to go on."

"It's *everything* to go on." I rubbed my temples. "They left Yiptae, they came here, and they took over our society. They invented a religion. They created the caste system to keep us under control. How can you just overlook that?"

"You're focusing on the negative! They gave us civilization. They taught us how to farm, united the tribes under Them. They cured a virus. One of Them sacrificed himself to save us from invaders. We can't understand all of Their designs, but They came here in the flesh to nurture us to adulthood. You think twelve aliens could do all of that?"

Maybe she's right. There were a lot of gaps in my line of thinking, and They had done a lot of good. Besides, if They weren't gods...then whose fault was it that everyone I loved was dead? The mere flicker of that thought made my head want to burst.

I took a deep breath. "So what now, then?"

"We rest," Kaylaa said. "Tomorrow, we go back."

"Then what?"

"We worry about that then."

Silently, we climbed back into the ship and clambered into the beds.

But I couldn't sleep. Today was, probably, the longest day of my life. How could so much happen in a single day? It had to be deep into the night, maybe even the morning. No light in here to be able to tell. Kirstos helped us into the Temple, and now he was dead. Bekivala's four-hundred-year-old mistress had tried to kill us, and I had obliterated her with some power I didn't know I had. We found a letter written by a god (or was he?) saying that his grandfather started the rebellion against the other gods, which then led to the caste system. And so much more. My head pounded as if all the knowledge was literally overfilling my brain.

Pure exhaustion took over, and I finally shut my eyes for the night.

I woke up stiff all over, but all I could remember were good dreams. Most of them were pleasant memories of my mother and father—camping in the serene Shattered Lakes, going to the soft black sand beaches on the Xalon Peninsula, even playing in the park in my hometown Cax-Ark-Uhn. The three of us, the perfect family.

Until this Temple ruined everything.

The reflective surfaces and musty smell of the ship's

interior quickly wiped out those memories. The pain came flooding back. I sat up and tried to stretch out the muscle aches, but that only seemed to make them worse. Fyra still slept, her cheeks damp from crying. Kaylaa was up in the cockpit, fiddling with buttons and levers.

I hobbled up to her, each step causing jolting pain through my whole body. "Find anything?"

She shook her head. "It's shot."

"What do we do about it?"

She looked at me very seriously. "That's not my decision. Your people, not mine."

"You must have an opinion."

"No. The only thing I'll say is don't rush into anything like you normally do. Look at the evidence. Weigh the consequences either way. And be damn sure you can deal with them."

"But...even waiting means people die every day." The reality of the embargo and the people it was killing flooded back to me—an embargo based on a caste system that maybe shouldn't exist.

She shrugged. "More people may die depending on what you do."

"Wouldn't Shuka want me to tell everyone?" I took a deep breath. "Start a revolution, like my father?"

"He would. But it's not his decision, either."

Fyra came up beside me. "Your father didn't tell everyone about the ship either, even after going to Yiptae. He blamed the Virin-leen."

"So what does that mean? He found something else, pointing the problem at the Virin-leen, or he just decided he liked that solution better?"

"The Scriptures are clear in that Pavlon designed the caste system, which created the Virin-leen caste right below the Iveleen," Fyra said. "But it was easy to point the finger at the Virin-leen—their government gives them more wealth and takes food off the table for the Olan-Har. Their corruption runs deep. The end probably justified the means."

I felt the memory of my father's last day creeping into my mind, but I brushed it away. "What if Kirstos is right? It's up to us to reveal the truth?"

"I don't think you can believe anything he said. His brain was addled with drugs; he had lived by himself in a cursed jungle and he was entranced by Haskar's power."

She was right. But his last words, seemingly in a moment of clarity, kept gnawing at me—*if we don't reveal the truth, who will?*

Kaylaa banged on the cockpit panels again, then stood up. "Nothing else to learn here. Eat an RC and let's get out of here."

We did just that. I checked the supply bag to find that there were only enough RCs for another day. The Chalice of Stria-Fate was also in the bag. "We're going to need to stop by Kirstos's again for the return trip. It's not like he'll need them anymore," I said. Kaylaa ignored me while Fyra just gave me a look that said, *did you really just say that?*

I shrugged, and we left the ship chamber. "Guess we can't really cover it back up like my father," I said, looking back on the door to the tunnel.

Kaylaa said, "With Kirstos cold, there isn't much to worry about."

"Still..." I tried to push one of the immense bookshelves in front of it, but it didn't budge. "I guess it wouldn't be well hidden anyway, with broken mirrors everywhere."

"Let's go," Kaylaa said.

We wandered back into the main chamber, where the sunlight suggested that it was evening. Kirstos's blood was splattered on the walls and pews, now dry. The panel door, incredibly, closed itself as soon as we went through.

Fyra shrugged. "Ivelenian power."

We passed where we fought the Second Lady of the Temple and slowly crossed the Chasm of Faith. I had a brief moment of fear due to my misgivings about Their origins, but Kaylaa's brisk crossing helped urge me on.

Finally, we emerged into the fresh-smelling clearing in the forest, surrounded by dimming sunlight and swaying trees. Fyra spun in a circle with her eyes closed. I took several deep breaths, trying to exhale the dust and lies.

"I think we should close the door," Fyra suggested.

Kaylaa nodded and unscrewed the hose from the pillar. The three of us followed the hose back to the pump in the bushes.

Fyra stared at the pump. "Should we destroy it?"

This was one of those decisions that Kaylaa had warned me about. I would have to live with the consequences. Destroy the pump, and we guarantee that no one else went into the Temple for a long time. And then, the Great Secret would be entirely our responsibility. Leave it, and it's still a puzzle without Kirstos, but the equipment is there. Maybe someone else would figure it out in our lifetime, and then it would be their problem.

I'd rather control the narrative.

I smashed my Edge into the pump and, for good measure, cut the hose. Fyra smiled while Kaylaa remained expressionless.

We used the hose on the other side of the pump as a trail to follow back to the pool near Kirstos's shrine. Even just that short walk pushed my body to the limit.

We came to the pool, and I glanced in the direction of the shrine. It was gone.

Primary Objective: Capture or kill Zacto Filch – Complete
Secondary Objective: Capture or kill other Ebonhearts – Incomplete
Tertiary Objective: Recover stolen Iveleen Artifact(s) – Incomplete

The Ebonhearts are 75-80% Olan-Har who have deserted the slums for a free life in the forest. Led by Zacto Filch and his lieutenant, Stefan Noreus. They live in the Soquok Forest, though I only found two abandoned settlements. Unsure of current whereabouts.

I have successfully apprehended Zacto Filch in the Docks district of Ziphyr, near Pier 27. He and eleven other Ebonhearts were raiding a shipping container of advanced weapons. Once they were aware of my presence, the Ebonhearts attacked while Filch fled. The Ebonhearts are not particularly good fighters in open spaces, unlike in the forest, so I killed two before abandoning the others to pursue Filch.

I caught up to him in North Docks Park. It seems unrealistic, but I could've sworn the trees were giving away my movements. Filch managed to score one surprise hit on my neck with his dagger, but I quickly dispatched him and brought him back to Shard Headquarters.

I was unsuccessful in capturing other Ebonhearts or retrieving any Artifacts of the Iveleen. Interrogations have been unsuccessful so far.

—From Report on the Ebonhearts for mission ZM061
by Zilpohn Mark, 490 ARI

CHAPTER TWENTY-ONE

All that was left of the shrine was a smoldering pile of ash.

"But who? Why?" I asked.

"The Iveleen," Fyra whispered. "This place was dark. Unholy. They rid the land of it."

I raised an eyebrow. *That's a scary thought, if true.*

"It's much more mundane," Kaylaa said, crouching to the ground. "Bootprints."

She was right—bootprints circled the foundation.

"Vampires don't use fire," I said. Kaylaa and Fyra both looked at me like I was an idiot. "Well, who else lives out here?"

"Maybe the band of thieves?" Fyra suggested.

"We have a bigger problem," Kaylaa said. "Only three RCs left."

"Even if we had food, I don't think I could make it all the way back," I said. "Everything hurts...and I'm so tired." I plopped onto the ground and the desperation of our situation hit me. Almost no food. No medical supplies. Four days away from civilization, and that was at a brisk pace. Vampires and other creatures living in the woods.

"Maybe the Iveleen don't want us to reveal their Secret after all," I pondered. They were just toying with us, puppets on a string. Now that we'd overcome so much, we just get to die slowly while They laugh at us in the Heavens. But if They're not gods...then I guess it was just our own damn faults.

Fyra crossed her arms over her chest and prayed quietly to herself. Kaylaa paced back and forth, completely lost in her thoughts.

I needed rest. Lots of it. None of my injuries were that serious on their own, but all together, it was like a larger army fighting a smaller one on all fronts.

"We rest here tonight, and hope it's enough to give us the energy to make it back," Kaylaa said.

We found a spot next to the pool where the fern fronds almost completely hid us from sight. Kaylaa removed the remaining three RCs and gave one to each of us. Then she put the bag next to the nearest tree.

After eating, we laid down to rest.

The next day, I felt worse. Fresh blood had seeped into the bandages around my ribs. *Not good.*

Kaylaa saw the new blood and shook her head.

Fyra asked, "What's wrong?"

"He's worse," Kaylaa said before I could respond.

The food bag, which now only had the Chalice of Stria-Fate in it, caught my eye. "Wait a minute. Fyra, doesn't the Chalice turn water into medicine?"

Her eyes lit up. "It does! I'll get it." She went to retrieve it, but when she picked it up, the bag fell flat. Her head swiveled from side to side. "It's...gone!"

She reached her whole arm into the bag and retrieved a piece of parchment.

"What's that?" I asked.

"It's a...note," she said, then started reading:

"'Thanks friends for the Chalice. Master Filch will be very excited that we've added this Artifact to our collection. Though I wish you hadn't closed the door to the Temple. We'll find the

Great Secret one day!

Thanks loves,

Stefan Noreus.'"

It was sealed with a symbol that looked like an arrow with tree roots growing out of it.

"I can't believe we were so careless," Fyra lamented.

"Even worse, that was our ticket out of here," I said.

Kaylaa shook her head. "How did he sneak up on us? He must have been silent as the wind."

While Kaylaa looked for footprints, Fyra and I stood in silence. Finding nothing, she joined us. "Nothing to be done about it except to just go."

We started down the small footpath back to the Old Crusader's Road. My ribs protested with every step. Just as bad, I couldn't imagine making the monotonous journey back home—and that was if we were lucky and not attacked by wolves or Vampires or Minotaur.

When we came to the road, Fyra swooned and dropped to the ground. I staggered over to her and took her wrist; it was like picking up a twitching icicle. "What's wrong?"

Her whole body shuddered as she craned her neck to look at me. "A death is near." She pointed a shaky finger to the northeast, off the path that went to the Temple.

"Whose?"

She closed her eyes tight and shook her head. "I don't know, but it's in agony. I think...I think we should go look."

Kaylaa tapped her foot. "No. We can't afford to waste any energy."

Fyra lifted herself to lay on her hip, using her arms to hold her up. "It's important."

"We're going," I said, helping Fyra to her feet. Without Kaylaa's approval, we hiked through the bushes in the direction Fyra had indicated. Behind us, I heard Kaylaa sigh, then break through the brush.

Within one hundred paces, we came to a small clearing.

Like the pool, small sprites like neon lights whizzed around the meadow. Great blue and yellow flowers, half the size of a man, formed a wall that secluded the small area. The flowers emitted a smell of honey, apple, and pumpkin spice. At one end, a small tree with a green trunk and large purple leaves like elephant ears sprung from a piece of gray slate in the ground. In front of the tree knelt a Minotaur.

He labored to breathe. Slashes of dried and fresh blood crossed every muscle, two bloodied holes piercing all the way through his body and large, raw burns enveloping his arms. His eyes were bloodshot, his mouth dripping crimson. His head nodded heavily, like his neck couldn't support the weight.

"This was the death you saw?" I whispered.

Fyra turned and stared at me, but didn't answer.

The Minotaur lifted his head and sniffed the air. "Know you're there," he said between gasps. He didn't waste the energy to turn.

None of us answered. Kaylaa grabbed my shoulder and beckoned for us to go. That was probably the smart move, but I was rooted to the spot.

The creature continued, with growls and unintelligible words interspersed in his speech, "Came here. Soquok's grave. Guidance...Qui-Tos."

I remembered what Fyra had explained earlier, that Qui-Tos had buried his infant son in this forest. Under that purple-leaved tree, under the slate; that must be the place.

"This is the natural order of the forest," Fyra said. "The one Qui-Tos put into motion. The strong survive and preserve the balance."

"Brother Torvaur...destroy balance. Crash, burn, kill." So it was Torvaur we had spoken to before; this must be Gawfaur. He had not moved from the spot, but his whole body shook, like chills from a sickness. "Must be stopped. I...peace with the wolves and others. Not he."

I felt the seed of a crazy idea sprout in my head, but I

couldn't quite piece it together. *How can we help the Minotaur? Should we?*

"Leave him," Kaylaa said. "We can't do anything for him anyway."

The idea bore fruit. "I can."

Kaylaa knitted her eyebrows as she looked at me, then her eyes widened. "No, not that."

"Gawfaur," I said. The Minotaur perked his ears upon hearing his name. "I'll make you a deal. I will heal your wounds. But you have to take us to the southern edge of the forest."

Kaylaa snatched my wrist. "Darynn, you can't. His wounds are as big as your whole body. That pain will kill you."

I pulled my hand away. "I'll never make it to Ziphyr, not like this."

She gritted her teeth and shook her head. "If you feel your consciousness slip, let go."

"D-D-Darynn, no!" Fyra pleaded. "You can't...we'll find another way."

"No food, no medicine. This is the only way," I said.

My feet dragged as I approached the beast. *Fear? Or exhaustion?* When I was close, his musk invaded my nostrils, nearly gagging me. I stretched out my hands and delicately placed them on his back. His muscles felt like a fuzzy rock, and there was absolutely no give in it as I pressed. His whole body was as hot as a rock in a lava flow. I closed my eyes.

The intent: to heal this creature's wounds. *The will:* I'll do anything to make sure we get home. *The bond:* Kaylaa and Fyra, and the pain we've gone through on this journey, both physical and mental. This creature was our way home.

The pain swelled, like an angry squall gathering strength to crash into the unassuming shoreline. Muscles that I did not have began to ache, wailing ferociously in my spinal cord, begging my brain to end the torture. My veins bulged from my arms, only a hair's length from breaking the skin. Pressure built in my eyes until they felt like they would leap from my skull.

Threads of new sinew crossed his wounds, cross-stitch after cross-stitch.

But it was taking too long. My brain was roasting in a furnace, so close to passing out. Kaylaa yelled at me to pull away...but no. My mind began to retreat to unconsciousness, my eyes rolling back into my head, but willfully I pushed back into the light, like prodding cattle towards a hungry Gryphon.

Through the haze that had covered my vision, I could see the job was almost done. The relief caused me to let my mind go for just a split second. And then...darkness.

I felt as if I was swinging from a bungee cord. My muscles refused to obey commands from my brain, and when my head rolled, I realized I was strapped down to a boulder.

But it wasn't a boulder. Another head roll and I could just make out the end of a horn swinging in and out of my vision. The tree branches zoomed by overhead, every step the length of a man's running leap.

I couldn't open my mouth to speak, so I tried to enjoy the fast-moving scenery above. Did we pass a songbird? Was that branch flat like a Libra road? But soon, that became dizzying, and I had to close my eyes to keep from getting sick.

Finally, we stopped. *Thank the Iveleen.* Or not. That made my head hurt. *Best to ignore it for now.*

Kaylaa and Fyra undid the straps and helped me to the ground. The Minotaur said some words of farewell, but my whole head spun and I couldn't make them out. He dashed off into the trees, presumably seeking his brother for the last battle.

Fyra knelt at my side while Kaylaa disappeared. I could hear her humming but couldn't make out the tune. The bright lights in the sky, no longer blocked by branches, seemed to change to the darkness of night.

I woke up as Kaylaa forced water down my throat. I spat

out the first gulp, but then realized I was thirsty and greedily drank the rest. My arms shook as I propped myself up.

"I guess it worked," I said.

"Stupid," Kaylaa replied. "I told you to let go."

I squinted and grinned. "We covered some ground, right?"

"Still a day to go, and now you're in even worse shape."

"Give him a break, Kaylaa," Fyra said, offering me another drink of water. "He's right, you know."

Kaylaa grunted. "How do we make it the rest of the way?"

Fyra thought for a second, and said, "We could ask the Erodian couple for help."

I spat on the ground. "Never."

"After we drew weapons on them?" Kaylaa shook her head. "That'll just be another fight."

"Let's just see how far we get tonight," I said.

Fyra rolled her eyes while Kaylaa murmured agreement. Using my Edge as a crutch, I hobbled down the Old Crusader's Road. The wind was harsh, bending the tall grasses in half, causing me to favor the east side of the road. It seemed like the Iveleen didn't want us to get back at all.

Darkness was fully upon us when my knees gave out. I howled as I hit the ground. It felt like I had been bedridden for months, my muscles atrophied and my mind hazy. The Erodian hut was nearby, and firelight danced in a window. Better out here with the snakes than in there.

"Fyra's right. We need their help," Kaylaa motioned for us to stay where we were—as if I was going anywhere. Her shadowy figure crept toward the cottage and out of sight.

"You should follow her. Call out if she gets in trouble," I said.

"Your blind hatred is clouding your judgment. If Kaylaa can handle Kirstos, she can handle an Erodian couple. But I don't think she's going to have any problems."

She was probably right about Kaylaa, but I couldn't believe her naivete. "You don't know what you're talking about.

They're dangerous and bloodthirsty. They think they're better than us."

"I'm sure they feel like we started those wars, or they had to fight, just like we did. Besides, we're not at war. We're just travelers on the road."

I shook my head, lacking the strength to argue with her. She sure seemed dumb on this subject.

Minutes passed and I started to worry. I tried to lift to my feet, and after a few attempts, got up, leaning heavily on my Edge. "I'm going to check on her."

"She's on her way back now."

A few minutes later, Kaylaa returned and said, "They'll help, but you need to keep your mouth shut."

"I'd rather—"

"I'm sure you would, but I don't care," she interrupted. "They have food, medicine, and a place for you to rest." She forced one of my arms around her and we hobbled to the wooden cottage. *I hope they don't poison us.*

The Erodian man glared at me as Kaylaa pushed us past the Karkhar skin door covering. I held his gaze until Kaylaa placed me on a furry mat on the floor. I plopped my head down into an incredibly soft feather pillow and sighed loudly. When I breathed in, the smell of fresh cinnamon tingled my nostrils.

The Erodian woman, dressed in a robe of stitched furs, was hard at work at the table with a mortar and pestle, the vine still wrapped around her arm. The cottage was just one room, with the bed high above the floor and a small shrine beneath it. The shrine was adorned with fresh blood. The Erodian man sat in a single-person hammock, his feet firmly on the floor and his curved blade on a small table next to him. Realizing how weak I was, some of the tension in his body released.

"Th-th-thank you so much for having us," Fyra said with a bow. She sat cross-legged on a mat next to me.

"Mean no harm. Just want to live in peace." The man struggled with his P.A. Standard, which made me remember it wasn't as common in Erodia.

"What are you mixing there?"

"Herbs for wounds." The Erodian woman seemed even less comfortable with the language and it sounded wrong coming from her lips. It seemed like the vine on her arm pulsed, and her wrist and hand glowed green.

"Thank you. My friend is in a lot of pain."

"Forest is...scary. Strong beasts there," the man said, making large sweeping gestures with his arms.

"We saw a lot of them. What are your names?" Fyra's fascination seemed to have overcome her social anxiety.

"Ragh'ark. Ragh'eena."

Fyra introduced the three of us and then started talking about where we were from. I felt uncomfortable with her giving them our personal information, but what were they going to do with it in a hut way out here?

The Erodians said they grew up around a place called the Lake of Fire in Erodia, but when Fyra pressed on why they were in Vastire, they refused to answer.

Ragh'eena chanted in her native tongue before applying the strong-smelling ointment directly to my ribs. She pressed gently on the wounds with her weathered hands, which seemed much older than she was. Every time she touched me, my skin crawled, but instantly I felt relief. It was like she was doing my healing magic on me, except using the ointment instead. The vine continuously slithered on her arm like a snake.

When she finished, I took off my shirt to show her the wounds on my chest and back. She sighed and went back to the table to make more ointment.

"How you get so bad?" Ragh'ark asked.

"Too many fights," I said.

"Should be dead."

"Yeah, probably," I admitted.

Ragh'eena came back and applied the ointment to my back and chest. After she finished, I settled down on the mat, feeling relaxed. Fyra interrupted my bliss by tapping on my shoulder.

"Say something," she whispered.

"Thanks, I guess," I said.

Ragh'eena smiled briefly, then climbed up into their bed.

"Do you have any food?" Kaylaa asked Ragh'ark.

He nodded and pulled down some long, dried strips that I hadn't noticed hanging from the ceiling. "Dried meat." He chanted something over them before handing a strip to each of us.

I tore into the rubbery, dried meat. It was salty and chewy, but it didn't taste bad. I devoured the whole thing and was tempted to grab another. But before I could even ask, it felt like the meat expanded in my stomach. *Maybe that was what the chant was for?*

Ragh'ark unrolled two more mats next to mine, and then said, "Tomorrow," before climbing into his bed.

"Good night," Fyra said, then turned back to me. "See, aren't you glad we stopped now?"

"I do feel better. But that doesn't mean that it wasn't risky coming here."

"Did you consider that maybe not all Erodians are the same? How many Erodians have you met?"

"Two now. But my grandfather..."

"Fought in the Conflict. I know," she said. "You realize that war ended almost seventy-five years ago, right? Things are different now."

"Whatever." I turned toward the wall. I heard the other two lay down, but quickly fell asleep after that.

Bright fluorescent lights burning through my eyelids woke me up. I could feel the presence of two men, and the mat under me had transformed into a solid metal bed. The overpowering smell of formaldehyde made me want to gag. My head pounded with a terrible migraine.

I heard a door open and another man came through it. "...operation successful?" he asked in a deep, gruff voice. All I could see was the shadow of a bear when I looked in that direction. "Then prepare him for his exit." He disappeared.

One of the other two men leaned over the table and seemed to notice that I was awake. "Go back to sleep, child." He touched his fingers above my eyelids and forced them to close.

I awoke again as the sunlight tickled my face and the smell of cinnamon wafted into my nose. *What was that dream?* It seemed like the same place from before. But why? And when?

The cottage was empty. I got up and stretched, finding that the pain had mostly subsided to a dull ache. Except for one of my ribs, where the skin was now purple and black. *When did I crack a rib?* I took a few steps around the cottage and looked over some of their possessions. Odd-looking charms were everywhere, made of sticks and strings and fur. I picked up some small toy animals, but they weren't toys...they were real. But they had to be miniaturized, definitely with magic. One was leathery with strong legs and huge tusks, another with teeth as long as its whole jaw, and a third was long, slimy, and spiky.

I put them down when Kaylaa walked in. "Playing with toys?"

"Just looking around."

"Grab one of those jerky strands and let's go." She glanced at the purple bruising but ignored it. "And put a shirt on."

I did as she said and met them outside. The Erodian couple and Fyra sat at a table in the shade, seemingly getting along really well. *Funny how likable she is when she actually talks to people.*

She got up from the table and we prepared to leave. She thanked them for their hospitality, then nudged me in the back.

"Thanks..." I mumbled.

They bowed, and we started back down the Old Crusader's Road in the sunshine.

As I chewed on the jerky, Fyra went on about how I was disrespectful, and I just nodded along with my mouth full. I guess Ragh'eena had been nice enough to heal me and they gave us food, but still. My grandfather told me all about them.

"You know, my grandfather practically ended that war," I said.

Fyra rolled her eyes. "Everyone knows that story, Darynn."

"It was the Psychic Trick operation. He and another soldier, Commander Aseus's father, actually, snuck into a top-secret Erodian facility and found their secret weapon—the SPHINX. Some kind of giant psychic machine the Erodians were building. They managed to inject a virus that would turn the SPHINX against the Erodian troops. The Erodians even landed on Vastirian shores, and when they released the weapon, it turned on them and decimated their troops. Then my grandfather and Graze Aseus climbed out, hungry, but unharmed."

"Sounds like a tale," Kaylaa said.

"It's actually true," Fyra said. "It was devastating for both sides. The Erodians lost most of an entire generation, and the Vastirians were only a little bit better off."

"My grandfather was a hero," I added. "Then he retired to take care of his baby son, who also became a hero. Then look at me..."

Fyra patted me on the back. "You just learned the Great Secret. I think that counts for something."

I smiled. "Yeah, I guess so."

Her encouragement just made my mind wander back to the Temple, the letter, and the ship. I did my best to reel it in. I knew I wouldn't get any further, just looping in my thoughts back and forth between how the gods betrayed us and how they weren't even gods at all, so whose fault was it really?

When we reached the edge of the prairie, we had another dilemma. Pass through the Nama-Da sector, or go all the way around? Fyra argued for going around, while I wanted to push through. Kaylaa thought either way was equally as risky.

"I don't generally believe in leaving things to chance, but I know a trick." She opened the palm of her hand, and two small balls of energy appeared, one red, one green. She closed her fist and shook it a few times. "Red or green?" she asked Fyra.

"Um...green?"

She threw her hand up in the air, but only the red ball arced upwards and exploded, showering glittery red sparks onto the ground. "We're going Darynn's way."

"That's not fair! You chose that one!" Fyra said.

"It's completely random." Kaylaa turned to look at the road ahead. Even in broad daylight, the whole area was shadowed and ominous. This road wasn't a main road either, so we would have to snake our way across the labyrinthian Nama-Da sector. "Maybe this section is abandoned. We move quickly."

The hard stone was rough on my weak joints, and the buildings felt too crowded together. We would go south for as long as we could, then turn west if we needed to, then back south again as soon as we had the chance. More than once, we ran into a dead end, usually punctuated by a pile of skeletons. The cawing of crows and ravens seemed to multiply as we moved closer to the center.

But then our luck ran out.

We hit a major road, in the middle of which stood a single Nama-Da. It was freakishly tall, wearing a crimson robe of what looked like stitched-together flesh and a cape of bones held together with hair.

"You crossed my sector once without paying the tax." He didn't hiss like the other Nama-Da but instead spoke like a Minotaur with a smoking habit. "Twice is unacceptable."

This must be their leader. "What do you want, Naman?"

His gaunt hands pulled the hood off his head and onto his shoulders. He looked like Guide's child, except stronger, with pearl white eyes with a black mist that floated through them at will. "There is only one tax I accept. A life."

"We will kill you if you try to take it." I felt a stirring in my chest like I finally had some of my strength back after killing the Vampire and healing the Minotaur.

"I have died and returned from the Netherworld many times. I have taken some and brought others back with me. I do not fear death. But I do crave souls. And you..." He eyed me suspiciously, his eyelids closing from inside to outside. "You will pay my tax...but not now. Certainly not now."

He whipped his cape around him and disappeared. His disembodied voice said, "You will pay soon, Darynn Mark." The crows disappeared with him.

"What does he mean by that?"

"I-I-I think he felt your destructive power," Fyra said shakily. "He's counting on you killing others."

"I'm not his puppet."

"You don't need to be. Your innate power is strong and dangerous," Kaylaa said. "It just blasts out of you uncontrollably. You don't know what you're bonded with."

"So? It's saved us a couple times."

"We've pushed our luck so far. Poor planning on my part. We need to use reliable skills or there are going to be consequences."

"Are you jealous?"

She glared at me. "No, but you're a fool with a big gun and a hot head. It's only a matter of time before there is collateral damage." She started along the nearest southbound road.

I looked at Fyra, but she just shook her head, a hint of fear in her eyes, before following Kaylaa.

It wasn't like it was my fault. No one taught me how to do this. I didn't ask for it. As long as I was using it to save our lives, I didn't see any crime in it.

We soon entered Hargonla and were instantly reminded of the situation. A dirty little girl knelt next to her mother, lifeless in the street. I went over to her and broke off a piece of dried jerky for her. Her mother coughed and ate the jerky. She slowly opened her eyes and mouthed her thanks.

"The caste system must go," I said to Fyra and Kaylaa.

Kaylaa nodded. "My mission is a success then. Senator Shuka will be pleased." She furrowed her brow. Her boss's goal, accomplished. Her own goal to understand her father's killer? Maybe a little closer, but still too many unanswered questions.

"I can't allow this to go on anymore," I said. Fyra gave me a reassuring smile.

No more orphans because their parents starved. No more mothers whoring themselves for shelter for their children. No more little girls with missing fingers. No more gang shootings. It all ends, somehow. *Was this how my father felt when he returned to the city?*

That ended with his death. I looked at the frail bodies around me, struggling to even stand. *I'll take my chances.*

Ziphyr, the capital, is the largest and most populous city on Vastire. It is in the district of Lord Searon, overlooking the Esowaith Ocean to the east. The Avingian Palace, where the King of Vastire resides, is found in Ziphyr.

The oldest part of Vastire is the Local District, just south of Downtown. The Grand Cathedral, seat of the Ivelenian Church, can be found here, amongst many other historical buildings.

The noble families live in the Virin-leen district in the southeast, looking over the ocean in grand mansions. A private Spaceport exists solely for Virin-leen use in this district. Off-world business is performed in the Merchant's Quarter, next to the Virin-leen district.

The Elite neighborhoods lie between the Merchant Quarter and Downtown, while the Middle-caste and Poor neighborhoods are west of the Local District, north of the public Spaceport.

Most Vastirian business is conducted either Downtown, in the center of the city, or in the Docks, which line the eastern seaboard.

Hargonla in Ziphyr is north of Downtown, separated from the rest of the city by a stretch of factories and barren fields.

—From *The Geography of Vastire*

Chapter Twenty-Two

The Solia house was dark and empty when we arrived at dusk. There wasn't anywhere else better to go. Fyra frantically searched the house and the courtyard, but her parents were gone. I wanted to help look, but my eyelids drooped and my feet dragged.

"Th-th-they're not here. Where would they go?" She rubbed her healed shoulder vigorously.

"Relatives? Friends?"

"Not in the city, and not at night."

Kaylaa was meticulously investigating the house. She stopped by the dining room table. "Blood," she said matter-of-factly. "A few days old." Fyra shrieked and rushed to look. "It's not much. There was a struggle here."

Fyra's eyes watered. "But who? Why?"

"It's a good place. Without Pavlar around, maybe a thug took it?" I suggested. *This bastard is going to pay.* "We'll just have to take it back."

"The thug would be here," Kaylaa said. "There's something else at work."

Tap tap tap. It came from the courtyard door.

Kaylaa bounded across the room with her weapon drawn, while I stood sluggishly by the couch. She tore open the door and threw the person standing there to the ground, her rapier at their neck.

"Who are you? Are you alone?" she yelled at the small, frail woman with a bruised face and greasy hair.

Fyra pushed Kaylaa's shoulder but wasn't strong enough to move her. "Get off her! That's just the neighbor, Mrs. Pyka." Kaylaa moved aside and Fyra helped Mrs. Pyka to sit on the couch. "What happened?"

"Few days ago was just mindin' my own self and some big men in armor bust open my door!" Her breath was overpowering; it was clear something was rotting away in there. "They say 'Where are they?' and I say 'Who?' and they hit me right across my face!" She sloshed some saliva in her mouth and spit it out on the floor. "So then they say 'the girl and the boy.' And I say the boy's dead. Then they hit me again! And I spit right on his boot, and then he kicked me right in the gut."

"Who was it?" Kaylaa asked.

"I'm gettin' there! They say 'Not that boy, the Mark boy' and I say 'I don't know nothin' 'bout no Mark boy, but the girl left few days ago with a boy and a woman.'" She sized up Kaylaa, one rust-colored eye a little larger than the other, and then continued, "And they say 'Which way?' and I say 'I don't know' and they hit me a few more times but my answer didn't change. Then they left and went to the next house. Then they left in a fancy car, and they took your parents with 'em! I didn't care too much about that, but why'd they hit me?"

"Who took them?" Fyra asked.

She stared at me long and hard; I shifted in my chair. "*His* daddy's people."

I wrinkled my brow and looked at her, confused. *My daddy's people?*

"You mean the Shard?" Fyra inquired.

"Yeah, dem." She spat again. "Oh yeah! They told me to tell you if you came back, if you wanna see 'em again, then you, and you, and you—" she pointed at each of us as she spoke, "—go see the Shard. They trade you for them. Fine by me if you don't do it. I got a sister that could move in here. Nice place."

"This is still my parent's house, so you keep your nasty sister out of it!" Fyra yelled, her face red. Mrs. Pyka spat again, right by Fyra's feet. "And you can get out too!"

"I get nothin' for tellin' you what happened? Fine by me, I'll go tell the Shard you're back. Then I get the house anyway!" She scrambled out the back door, slamming it on her way out.

Fyra sat on the couch and buried her face in her hands. I was wide awake and angry, now. "Who do they think they are? Makaro and Lia have nothing to do with this!"

"They're too interested in us. Do they know about the Great Secret?" Kaylaa asked.

I didn't answer her. I was too focused on this situation—the one I had created. "It's my fault, Fyra. Sorry. If I turn myself in, they'll let your parents go."

She looked up, her cheeks wet with tears. "We're not giving in to them. It isn't right." Her eyes narrowed. "You're strong enough to ransom a Shard, right? We should do that!"

Kaylaa shook her head. "You're smarter than that."

"Then what do we do, Kaylaa?" Fyra demanded. "You always have a plan."

Kaylaa paced. "Not for this situation. We can't just break them out of a Shard prison."

Fyra nestled her face in her hands.

I nodded. "Right. So if I turn myself in, then everything is okay. Your parents come home. Kaylaa, you found out what you wanted to know, right? You can go back to Yiptae."

"We all have to go to Yiptae," Kaylaa said. "We have most of the story, but we're missing the critical piece."

Fyra blinked out a few tears. "We can't go until my parents are free."

An uncomfortable silence clouded the room. My eyes fixed on the drops of blood on the dining room table. *Lia's or Makaro's?* Had to be Makaro's. Lia wouldn't argue with the

Shard.

Kaylaa broke the silence. "Don't the Shard have better things to do? It's one thing for the Militia to chase you after you killed one of their own, but the Shard? They have bigger fires to extinguish."

She's right. My father wouldn't have chased after an Olan-Har rat unless he was terrorizing the royals.

"We need some time to process this," Kaylaa insisted. "But not here. Let's go to the Shard swordmaster." Without waiting for a reply, she cracked open the door to the courtyard. After a short scan, she led us through another house. We snaked through the alleys to Master Makai's cafe. I felt like eyes followed us the whole time, but Kaylaa surely would've picked up on that. *Right?*

Before my father's fall, all I wanted to do was be a Shard, like him and my grandfather. My mother and father seemed reluctant, but my grandfather pushed me to chase my dream. Of course, that dream was shattered long ago, but still—the Shard weren't supposed to act like this. Honor, justice, protection. Ransoming an innocent girl's parents didn't show any of those values. This wasn't the organization I grew up fantasizing about, the one my father and grandfather gave their lives to.

We snuck into the cafe without knocking.

Makai rubbed his eyes as we walked in as if he'd been sleeping. "Thought you'd be back. Don't look so good though."

"They took my parents," Fyra said with a sob.

He raised one eyebrow. "Did they now? Not surprised. Every day Aseus leads the Shard, their honor crumbles a bit more. His father was a great man too." He clicked his tongue. "So what are you doing here?"

"Nowhere else to go, until we figure out what to do about Fyra's parents," I said.

"I see. You look beat. Get some rest and we'll make a plan in the morning." The old wood floor creaked as he hobbled to a cabinet behind the bar and pulled out some small packets. He dipped them in water and poured three mugs. "This'll help you sleep."

I sipped on the cold liquid, which tasted like a combination of peppermint and wood. The tea did the trick, and we all fell asleep.

In the morning, the four of us sat around a wobbly table and explained to Master Makai what had happened. We left out Bekivala's letter and the Yiptaen ship but told him everything else.

At the end of our story, he slammed his cane on the table. "You have done everything they wanted. I don't know how they do it—they manage to play the pawns that are not even on their board, and they play them flawlessly! A puppet without strings."

I squinted. "I don't understand."

He looked at me sternly, his face betraying no emotion. "The hook is set, they're ready to reel you in. But you can't go in. You're more than just a thief, kid. You can't even imagine..."

I bit my lip as my heartbeat quickened. "You're as bad as a royal. Stop dancing around it and just tell me!"

He twisted one of the strands of his beard. "Can't tell you. Have to see it for yourself. At Shard Headquarters. Save the girl's parents while you're there."

I shook my head. "The only way I'll get there is in the back of a cruiser."

He sighed. "There is another way. I know the weaknesses of that building, even after all these years. Know where you need to go." He went back behind the bar again and pulled out a small, silver disc. He placed the disc on the table and pressed a square blue button. A hologram of a building shaped like a segmented sword sprouted from it—Shard Headquarters. He pushed another, smaller button and the hologram changed to a wire frame of the structure.

"How did you get this?" Kaylaa asked as she examined the hologram.

"Still have friends. A little outdated, but mostly complete." While most of the floors had rooms of various sizes, the top floors were nothing more than boxes.

"What's up here?" I asked.

"Don't know, other than Aseus's office."

"Where are my parents?" Fyra asked.

"Floor nine." He zoomed in on the hologram, which he controlled with a small ball set in a socket. The whole floor was composed of tiny rooms and winding hallways. "Shard prisoners are held here."

"You expect us to climb to the ninth floor, break out her parents, and then escape?" Kaylaa huffed.

"More than that. Why did Zil go to the Temple in the first place? More importantly, why do the Shard want you?"

"You *could* just tell me," I said.

"If someone had told you the Great Secret, would you have believed it?" I shook my head. "I don't really know, anyway. But I know where you'll find out." He zoomed in on another floor in the building, this one almost at the top. Like many of the higher floors, there wasn't any detail to the layout. But there was one oddity—the center of this level was domed, going up into the next floor. "Floor twenty-four. Might be the hardest to get into. Don't know what the security is like, but I know you'll need a key."

Kaylaa crossed her arms. "You happen to have one of those too?"

He rolled his eyes. "No, but you can get it from the Mission Archive, on floor eight." He rotated the hologram and zoomed into the eighth level. This one was taller than the other floors and was mostly just one huge room. "Access to the files and evidentiary objects is strictly relegated to androids. All you need is the mission number and password. The key you'll need will be in the file KM149, and the password is *'unsolved genetics.'*"

"Why would the key be in an evidence file?" Fyra asked.

"It was one of my cases. Zil helped me when I couldn't solve it. The key belonged to Dr. Werus Capp, a researcher on floor twenty-four, who was murdered. Never did solve it, but the Shard conveniently pinned it on your father after he died. It's a shape memory alloy key, so you'll need a way to heat it."

"Easy enough," Kaylaa said.

Makai continued. "There will also be a retinal scanner, but Darynn, you'll pass just fine."

"Uh, how?" I asked.

"You've always heard you have your father's eyes, right?"

"That's just a generalization."

"Trust me, you'll pass." He sighed. *That doesn't make any sense.* Makai *was* a Shard. Was this an elaborate trap?

He continued. "While on floor nine, you should check out the Temple mission file. Don't know the number or password, but I bet you can find it in Zil's office."

He moved the hologram up to a familiar floor, the nineteenth. I still remembered walking down the hallway to my father's office on the east side, looking down over the courtyard and the city below. He wouldn't take me much. The visits were exciting at first, but like most office spaces, a kid gets bored pretty quick.

Fyra asked, "Don't you think they would have removed Mr. Mark's stuff?"

"Know for a fact they haven't. Old war buddy of mine still works on the floor. Says the new kids mostly think the room is bad luck. Hogwash, of course."

"Let me get this straight," Kaylaa said, rapping her knuckles on the table. "You want us to go to the lobby, the ninth floor, the eighth floor, the twenty-fourth floor, and the nineteenth floor? All without being captured?"

Master Makai smacked his lips and said, "Guess so. If you

get in and out once, you'll never get in again."

"What kind of security are we facing?" Kaylaa asked.

"The usual: badges with micro-locators, cameras, gas analyzers, motion detectors, scale tiles, armed guards, assault androids...probably a few other things."

"And you expect one trained operative and two kids to get by all of it?"

"You have a few advantages. The Shard are cocky and they're not expecting it. They're not well prepared to deal with magic. And you have one of the best mission planners of all time on your side." He smiled widely.

"We don't stand a chance."

"The unbeliever achieves nothing," Makai replied.

Kaylaa grunted and went to peer through a crack between boards over a window.

"My old buddy will help you get into Zil's office, and maybe the Mission Archive, but to do that, you'll need visitor badges. Obviously, *you* can't get them."

"If we're just going to be sneaking around, why visitor badges?" I asked.

"It will make your life easier on those floors. Scale tiles will give you away if you're not badged, and the badges will let the gas analyzer system know how many people are on that floor. But how to get you in the building..." He stroked his chin as he leaned back his chair perilously on two legs.

Kaylaa came back to the table. "Are all of the security devices on all the floors?"

"Cameras are. Scale tiles won't be in the lobby or the prison. Too many people coming and going. Elevators have cameras and gas analyzers, but the gas analyzers are known to be unreliable in them."

"What order do we need to go in? Nine, nineteen, eight, twenty-four, right?" I asked, feeling excitement beating in my veins. We may not stand a chance, but it would be fun to make Commander Aseus sweat.

"If we let them capture us, they'll take us to the ninth floor, right?" Fyra asked.

"Only if Aseus isn't in the building. So we make sure that's the case," Makai warned.

"But if we're captured, then we're no better off than your parents," I said.

"You can break out. I know a bounty hunter who can bring you in. He won't know how to deal with magic."

"So we let him take us in, and then we get to the ninth floor, break out of our bindings, and let your parents go...but then what?" I scratched my head.

"You can't just let them go. They'll be unauthorized. Recaptured and thrown back in," Kaylaa said, leaning on the table.

"Not if they have visitor badges," Makai said. "Your parents are nobodies. With some careful choreography and the Iveleen's blessing, you can pull this off. I think I've figured it out."

We spent the rest of the day going through Master Makai's plan, with Fyra occasionally adding a brilliant tidbit while Kaylaa added dashes of pessimism and strategy. I found myself drifting in and out of their conversation, frequently staring at the twenty-fourth floor. *What was in that big, domed, empty space?* I reached back into my memories, but I never remembered going above the twenty-third level, and not in the tip, but to the two sides of the blade, where the Admirals' offices were. My father never talked about any of those floors either, other than the Commander's quarters at the top.

"You got it, Darynn?" Kaylaa asked.

I nodded mindlessly. "Get captured, break out, use the elevator, get visitor badges, check out my father's office and the Mission Archive, then up to the twenty-fourth floor. Use the key, look around, jump out the window."

"You missed a lot of detail."

I shrugged. "You know what to do."

"What if I get captured or die?"

"Then we're screwed anyway."

She shook her head. "You never know."

That spurred a different thought. "Fyra doesn't need to go. Two will be easier than three."

"How dare you?" Fyra snapped.

"He *is* right," Kaylaa told her.

"Those are my parents. And I am just as invested in the rest of it as you are. Besides, are you psychic?" I stared at her blankly. "Of course not."

"I'll contact my friend, Polek Viln, tonight. If he's comfortable, you go tomorrow. Drink some more of my tea, and get some rest."

"Master, one more thing," I said.

"Told you, I can't and won't tell you."

"Not that. Why do all this?" I asked.

"The Shard's honor has long been deteriorating, even before Commander Aseus. Your father knew it too. Aseus hastened it. They're still a skilled fighting force, but now they've lost sight of the mission. Protect the people. Protect the Virinleen. Protect the clergy. They're dangerous, ruthless, and self-serving. It all starts at the head. You know Zil threatened to kill Aseus once?"

"Really?"

Makai stroked his beard. "It would've been a hell of a fight."

"My father was the best."

"He was—but don't underestimate Aseus. Not only is he powerful and quick, but he's devious. He should've been a fantastic leader. Too power-hungry to fulfill his purpose." Then Makai left. Dust swirled behind the slammed door.

The hologram still glowed on the table, looming over us like a bright shadow.

"You think we can pull it off, Kaylaa?" I wasn't sure why I asked—I knew what she was going to say.

Her expression was blank. "Absence of choice overcomes the impossible, so says a Yiptaen philosopher. It would be better if you had some training."

"You could give me a little more credit. I had Shard training until I was twelve, and my grandfather gave me my first gun, a Mark 19 Revolver, when I was only nine. I loved that gun."

"What happened to it?" Fyra asked.

"What do you think?" I snapped. "I threw it in a fire after my father went mad..."

Fyra scooted her chair close to mine and held my hand. "Darynn, I've never really heard the other side of the story. Would...you mind telling it?"

I wanted to say no. It was the most painful day of my life, and there were many days to choose from. I knew I'd cry. But even Kaylaa looked interested.

"I guess he's the whole reason for all of this." I took a deep breath and relocated to one of the couches.

The Mondoons began their surprise assault on Vastire in 480 ARI. They assembled a war fleet in Vastirian orbit and launched bombs at the major Vastirian cities. The cities were prepared with orbital shields, but many outlying areas were left to burn. The heaviest Vastirian losses occurred on the first day of the war.

The Mondoons lost their home planet to a rogue war Artificial Intelligence. They tried, unsuccessfully, to terraform two worlds. When that didn't work, they decided to seize a habitable planet by force.

Vastire, being the newest planet in the P.A., and still split into two distinct races, was a prime target. Though overtures to the Erodians failed, they launched their assault anyway.

Zilpohn Mark infiltrated the Mondoon command ship and killed the Mondoon War Commander in single combat. With the losses piling, and private citizens dying in the fleet, the Mondoons retreated to an unknown sector of P.A. space less than a year after their initial assault.

From then on, Zilpohn Mark was a world-famous hero.

—From *The History of Vastire*, on the Mondoon Conflict

CHAPTER TWENTY-THREE

I rested my father's Plasma Edge across my lap and clenched it with my right hand. "Imagine if he'd actually taught me how to use this like he promised. Instead, he was always giving speeches, riling up the people. He'd be gone all day. No time left for me."

"My father said he heard one of those speeches," Fyra said. "He said he almost went with Mr. Mark too, but my mother won that argument. Maybe the only one she ever has."

"Good thing she did. That morning, Stria-Fate's birthday, in fact, he gathered the Traitor's Army together. They were a ragtag bunch of Olan-Har and Poor, with some Maltans, Diterians, and even Nama-Da. I heard that even Pavlon had never given a better speech. My father said the Iveleen didn't write the Scriptures, but the corrupt Virin-leen did, and they filled them with lies and the caste system. He promised them new lives, democracy, and freedom, and they believed him. He became their Hero.

"The Hero marched his army southeast and ransacked the royals' homes. They slaughtered every Duke and Count and Baron and their families. The Vastirian Militia didn't have time to react until they marched on the Avingian Palace. The Traitor's Army was winning. My father didn't even have his Plasma Edge, and still they were winning."

"Why didn't he?" Kaylaa interrupted.

"He left it to me that morning. I was only half awake, and he said some things to me. The first words I remember are 'I'm sorry,' and then it gets fuzzy. Damnit, if I'd only woken up!" Tears amassed at my tear ducts, but I held them back. I gripped my Edge tighter. "He said I'd find out the truth one day, and he hoped I could love him again when I did. He said the strangest thing to me—that one day, I would be greater than he."

"Greater than he," Fyra echoed. "I just remembered something. Remind me to tell you when you're finished."

I looked at her quizzically but continued. "The Shard met them at the Avingian Palace. Hundreds deserted when the Shard slaughtered the front line. This part was televised—blood splattered all over the television cameras as the Shard sliced through them like soft bread.

"Then my father comes on scene. He was magnificent."

"Even I've seen this part," Kaylaa said. "The entire P.A. shows this clip to their soldiers. It was clinical, the way he carved up dozens even while getting nicked over and over again."

I nodded. "You probably didn't notice the pain in his eyes. He trained many of the ones he killed. When the dust settled, the whole Traitor's army was dead or gone, except for his broken, bloody body. Fifty Shards surrounded him. I remember he...he dropped to one knee..." The floodgates opened up, my lungs pushed and pulled in breaths laboriously, my nose started to drip. Fyra tried to comfort me, but I waved her off. "My mother desperately tried to pull me away from the television, but I was stronger than her. He took his common Plasma Edge...and he plunged it into his heart. And still, he didn't fall." I sniffled and rubbed my nose. "So he twisted it, completely obliterating his heart. Then he fell, flat on his back; his hands slid off the handle of the Edge and dropped next to his body. Then...then..." My voice cracked as the sadness overwhelmed me. I dropped my head in my hands, and they submerged in a salty sea. *He just left me.* What was more important than me?

"Then King Istar came out of his palace," Fyra said, choking on the words. "He declared your father a traitor, and said any remaining followers would be convicted of treason."

"You forgot the best part!" I said fiercely. "The fat bastard claimed the victory over my father as his own, and he burned the body with a lighter from his own pocket. He said there could be nothing left of this demon brother of Haskar. He let the fire spread to the other bodies; the Shard retrieved their fallen men but left all others to burn. To this day, that field is still charred, and you can see exactly where the fire started." I had only been to the field once, seeking a foolish confirmation that my father was, indeed, dead. Bones still littered the field, covered with ash. A stubborn, pungent odor lingered.

My eyes refused to stay open, and in my shame I couldn't look at Fyra or Kaylaa. I think Fyra kissed my damp eyelids, but I was somewhere else entirely. I had moved on to what I deemed my father's gravesite, a crude mound of dirt I built in the darkest corner of Hargonla. I don't even know why I bothered to build it.

I pushed aside my sadness for only a second to see that Fyra was sobbing, and even Kaylaa stared at the ground, rubbing her eyes.

I retreated back to my dark place as I rolled my head. It was so hard to remember the good memories of my father...as if his death had burned them all out of my mind with his body. But it was *his* choice. It was his choice to leave me. Either that...or the Iveleen had written it into his fate. *Damn Them!* Maybe they had used Haskar over four hundred years ago...and then they used my father in the exact same way. A striking echo of the past, a reminder of what could occur if the caste system was eliminated. *Were they using me now?*

"But why did your father go after the Virin-leen?" Kaylaa asked. She winced as if in pain. "The priesthood would have made more sense."

"The Grand Cardinal at least pretends to care about the Olan-Har. The royals don't even know we exist, unless they need a garbage man or whore. Even so, some of the royals he killed were his friends."

"That's been vexing me since we found the ship," Fyra admitted. "I honestly thought we would unearth proof of Virinleen corruption, but no. The Virin-leen *adored* him."

I looked off into space, trying to remember where I was in the story but struggling to grasp it.

Fyra took over for me. "I remember the next day so well; everyone was devastated. The Grand Cardinal gathered all to him and delivered a masterful speech, praising the greatness of the Iveleen and begging us to remember how They had united us. The things he said about your father..."

"A demon, Haskar's own brother, an Angel of Death. I was forced to watch the speech, in captivity." Bitterly I remembered the dark cell, its only source of light a television. Grimacing men swarmed the cell, muttering to each other, enjoying my pain. I tried desperately to keep my eyes closed, but the words forced them open.

"The Shards interrogated me, but now that I think about it, they didn't ask much about the rebellion itself. They asked about his activities before the rebellion. They released me to the Caste Management Bureau, and everything that identified me as *me* was cast into a fire. They removed the Elite tattoo, which felt like sawing out chunks of my arm. It was replaced with this ugly red circle with black surrounding it. My mother's screams were harrowing; I didn't even cry. I was completely numb."

"What pulled you through it?" Fyra asked.

I stood and looked out the boarded window at nothing in particular. "Mother, at first. She tried to do the impossible—replace our old life. But that really meant she worked during the day, then took care of me in the evening, and snuck out to work again when she thought I was asleep. To this day, I'm not sure if it was for the money or for an escape.

"My escape was the Plasma Edge, not because I wanted to be a soldier, not because I wanted to be him, but because it was all I had. Father Ckoost replaced my father, preaching the ways of the Iveleen and trying to make me a believer again. The Church became my other home. Fear was his main motivator. Over and over again, he said I would become my father unless I read the Scriptures and obeyed them.

"About six months later, I met a boy my age in the park. He was the first kid willing to talk to me. Even the Olan-Har were terrified of me. Pavlar wasn't. He became my fencing partner, and we would find a new adventure every day."

"I remember when Pavlar brought you home the first time," Fyra interjected. "You were depressed still. My father told Pavlar to stay away from you, but Pavlar never really listened to him. On that matter, or any other. I remember you tearing through the window late at night on more than one occasion."

"Yeah...I went on like that until...Mother died. Only one month after the embargo. Work was scarce, pay was worse, and she hid it from me. The doctors never found a cause, and just said she worked herself to death. If I hadn't met Pavlar by then, I would have killed myself. I even...tried once."

Kaylaa raised an eyebrow at that, and Fyra's mouth fell open.

"I tried to drown myself, but Pavlar swam out to me and convinced me to live. He saved me. And then he became my brother too. I owed him my life and knew I had to protect his. I couldn't kill myself for as long as he was around." I held my breath as I realized that I'd failed in that, too. Tears welled in Fyra's eyes as she contemplated the greatness of her brother. I found the stone Gryphon in my pocket and closed my fingers around it.

Darkness had fully engulfed the world outside by now and deathly silence had fallen upon the streets of Hargonla. We sat there drowning in our memories, remembering our sorrows, fighting to escape our pasts.

Kaylaa chewed on her lip, her eyes strangely watery? She was the first to speak. "Remember how I said that magic is strengthened by bonds, not just bonds of alignment, but bonds of friendship and love? Tonight, our friendship has grown our power. Tomorrow, when we take on the greatest challenge of our lives, this power will surround us and protect us. We will be stronger, as we have felt each other's joy, we have felt each other's pain, we have all claimed a stake in each other's hearts," she said, a tear appearing under one of her eyes.

"Kaylaa...are you...crying?" Fyra asked, her smile holding up the tears on her cheek.

Kaylaa raised one hand to her face and wiped the tear from her eye, then stared at the dampness on her finger. "For the first time in a very long time, I felt emotion. I felt pity when Darynn told us of the downfall of his father, I felt sadness when I heard of the death of his mother, and I felt joy when I learned of how he pulled through it, with the help of your brother. I am glad to have shared this moment with you."

Fyra threw her arms around her, and Kaylaa awkwardly held her. "It's time for bed." She got up and shrugged Fyra off. She made three cups of Master Makai's tea and handed us each a mug before she went to her bed.

Fyra sipped her tea. "Thank you for telling us, Darynn. I know it was hard but I feel like I know you so much better now."

I managed half a grin. "You said to remind you of something..."

"Right." She set down her tea. "I had a vision last night. You were standing on the edge of the world, a painful look on your face. There was a huge flash, and the whole world was on fire. Seconds later the fire went out, and everything was dark. That's all I remember." She rubbed her shoulder.

"I wonder what it means."

"I don't know, but it was nice to not dream of death for one night." She sipped her tea again. I drank mine down in just a few gulps and gazed at the front door. Master Makai hadn't returned. *I hope he's okay.*

Fyra ambushed me with a hug. "We're going to make it tomorrow. I just know it." I held her closely and listened to her heart. Her hair felt soft against my cheek. I kissed her on the crown of her head, then let her go. I went back to the couch and stared at the ceiling.

My head swam between thoughts of Fyra, my father, and tomorrow's daunting task. It would be so much better to just stay here, with her. But my father pushed me on; the Olan-Har pushed me on. We had to save her parents—and then, maybe, everyone. But not until we knew whatever he knew. The missing piece. Maybe it was at Shard Headquarters, though it seemed unlikely. And then...Master Makai's mysterious secret. The thing that made the Shard so interested in me. How does it all fit together?

The Vastirian Militia is a mess. They're like twenty-one separate armies, expected to be able to fight together like a unit. Each Lord has a ground unit (simply Militia), a Cosmic Fleet (VCF), and a Sea and Air Force (V-SAF). The Lord chooses how large each of these units are.

The Virin-leen know they fight terribly when combined. So they usually just send a single Lord's companies as opposed to mixed regiments.

The King selects the Commander General, usually from his own lordship, to command all Militia. Each Lord selects a General to lead their forces. The General chooses his Lieutenant Generals, who control each wing of that Militia's force. From there, the ranks differ between branches.

The Militia is led by Colonels, who control regions, and Captains, who lead smaller, local units. When a Militia man reaches Captain, they are given a Captain's Ring, jeweled with the Alerian Star. That tradition has been passed down since the Fall of Haskar when several Captains were key in turning the war. The Alerian Star is the brightest star in the Vastirian sky and represents the glory of the Iveleen.

—From Caval's notes on Vastirian Militia

Chapter Twenty-Four

In the morning, I joined Master Makai and Kaylaa in the middle of an argument at the dining table. The Shard Headquarters hologram glowed in the center.

"Everything set?" I asked.

"As it's going to be," Master Makai replied.

Kaylaa shook her head. "Not good enough."

"The Shard know you're back in the city. The window will close quickly. Has to be today."

"Besides," I said. "Fyra's parents are in there. We can't just let them rot while we wait for perfect weather."

Kaylaa grunted in agreement. "Get your gear. I packed a backpack for each of you."

Something crackled behind the main counter. I smelled eggs...and sizzling bacon.

"Figured you needed a decent breakfast," Makai said as he went back to tend to the food.

Fyra yawned as she sat at the table. She asked Makai if he needed any help, and after he responded negatively, she asked, "Can I pray?"

I swallowed my half-chewed bite of the salty, runny eggs. "I guess so." Kaylaa stared at her, seeming to say "get on with it" with her eyes.

Fyra crossed her chest with her arms, and Master Makai did

the same, while I bowed my head. "Deesa, we are all your children; watch over us today as we go to rescue my parents. Makar, lend us your strength to tackle the inevitable combat. Pavlon, grace our tongues with witty words to avoid conflict. Fyrain, please embrace our pursuit of knowledge. To all Iveleen, I ask for your wisdom, your guidance, and your blessing."

I dug into breakfast, quickly slurping up the still-hot eggs and crunching through the cooling bacon. My mouth watered for more when I was finished, but my stomach was full.

We each grabbed our fraying black backpacks and headed for the front door. My heart pounded so loud it seemed to echo throughout the cafe.

"You know the plan. I know you can pull this off. Don't let Aseus get his hands on you. Your father's greatness is in you." Makai placed his hand on my shoulder reassuringly, then gave me a little push out the door.

Was that supposed to make me feel better? As we walked south, toward Fyra's house, all I could think about was what he said. My father's greatness disappeared when he was faced with this same problem. Instead, he had turned to "madness, murder, and mutiny." That's what the Grand Cardinal said, anyway. But he could have been doing the right thing after all. Doesn't the bad guy always think he's the good guy? There had to have been a better way.

We reached Fyra's house and went straight in through the front door. Then we waited.

I knew it wasn't long, but it felt like the day wasted away in those minutes; critical time we would need to complete the mission.

The door cracked open, and a Vastirian man and woman walked through, with oversized weapons and undersized heads. The man huffed through his brown beard. "That ol' boy was right! Best score we ever had, dear!"

The strong, wiry woman replied, "Damn right hun! We bring 'em in and our huntin' days are done!" We raised our weapons to prepare to fight. "Now don't do nothing stupid, ya hear? These big ol' guns will tear your guts out in a flash!"

I looked to Fyra and Kaylaa and slowly, we put down our weapons. "Alright dear, you cuff 'em. Get the alien first. These other two are scrawny." The bounty hunter woman put down her gun and snapped some binders on Kaylaa, then did the same to me and Fyra. They didn't even bother taking off our backpacks.

"Alright now, these three go straight down to the Shard." They forced us outside, nearly causing Fyra to trip on the threshold. Then they stuffed us into the back of a shabby hover van with no lights and the overpowering smell of sweat.

"These two are just dumb enough to pull this off," I whispered.

"Too dumb," Kaylaa said. "It's not believable."

The van lurched forward, nearly throwing us into the back door. "Will you be able to get out of those binders?"

"Too easily. Not believable," Kaylaa repeated.

"Too late now."

Kaylaa shook her head. "Not yet. I could break out now and we give it another shot, another day, with a better plan."

"I won't let my parents be stuck in there even one more day," Fyra said.

Kaylaa sighed. "We'll all be stuck in there. We're walking on the sharp edge of a knife."

We rode in silence as we sped toward our target. I wondered if this was how my father felt on the day of his revolution. It had to be worse. He probably knew that the most likely scenario was his death. I guess that's real courage. *But is it courageous if you're wrong?*

The van stopped suddenly, and the blinding lights of the day filled the dank cargo hold. The bounty hunters jerked us out of the van and led us through the front door of Shard Headquarters. *We're here.*

A smile stretched across my lips when I saw the two broken

pillars. It was still hard to believe that I did that. I felt like I understood more now, but only barely.

Cameras hummed above us in every corner, and people walked in every direction inside the circular lobby that took up the entire floor. The bounty hunters' boots echoed softly on the gigantic, shiny tiles. They pushed us up to the half-moon-shaped front desk right in the middle of the lobby.

"Identify," said a tubular android at the front desk with a camera on top of its head.

"Merrow and Kly Fammuck. We got Darynn Mark and the other two on that bounty!" the bounty hunter announced.

All activity around us ceased. Everyone's cold, dark eyes focused on me, and the entire room was silent save for the buzzing of electronics. I swallowed hard but didn't have any saliva to swallow.

The android scanned us and recorded video of our faces. "Confirmed." It produced two badges, which it handed to the bounty hunters with hands that looked like oversized pliers. "Authorized for ninth floor. Prison level. Nowhere else."

The bounty hunters snatched the badges, but the woman, Kly, asked, "How do we get our reward?"

"Your reward will be prepared when you return to the front desk. Badges expire in thirty minutes," the android responded without looking up from its terminal.

The bounty hunters pushed us toward the elevator in the back right-hand corner of the lofty room. People mostly went about their business again, but when the five of us got onto the elevator, no one else did. I didn't mind—I was tired of being stared at.

"What should we do with all that money, dear?" Merrow asked.

"Go off-world. What about Garstacea? The red sand beaches are s'posed to be pretty."

"We can't leave, 'member? Damn P.A. embargo."

"Damn embargo."

The elevator doors opened to a dingy floor with low ceilings and cold metal. Immediately in front of us was a low desk with a blocky android, this one armed with tasers attached to each wrist. The android crouched behind a layer of thick glass.

"Follow the lights. Three cells. One each," the android said without waiting for the bounty hunters to speak. "Leave their effects here." A panel slid into the ceiling. The bounty hunters unstrapped our backpacks and handed them to the android. A door on the left slid into the wall, revealing a red pathway between the tiles. We followed the lights. *Almost time.*

Most of the cells were empty, but there was a good chance that two we passed in the winding hallways were occupied— Fyra's parents. They didn't see us—both were completely entranced by the featureless ceilings above their heads. *Maybe the Iveleen are watching after all.*

It was eerily silent inside, unlike any prison I'd ever heard of. Where were the wailing prisoners, or the catcallers? The red lights ended in front of us, with arrows pointing into the three cells on the right.

I nodded to Kaylaa and rammed Merrow into the wall with my shoulder. With a yell, he hit his head against the metal and glass matrix of a cell. He shoved me off and pointed his gun at me. He didn't know it was already too late for him.

Kaylaa was free, and she kicked the gun out of his hands. With a few quick hand movements, she stole the other hunter's gun and had it turned on her.

I pounced on Merrow's gun, and even though I couldn't pick it up with the binders on, I made sure he couldn't get it.

"Into the cells, now," Kaylaa commanded.

"What the hell do ya think you're up to? They'll be on you like vultures on a carcass!"

"Shut up and go."

Kly whimpered as she went into the first cell. Merrow tried to fight back but didn't stand a chance. Kaylaa smacked him on the back of his head with the butt of the gun, rendering him unconscious. The cell doors closed immediately, but the third remained open.

Kaylaa undid the binders on my wrists and then started back down the hallway.

"What about this door?" I asked.

"Just wave your hand inside the cell."

I wiggled my fingers just inside the door. No change. Then I stuck a foot in and pulled it right back out. That did the trick. The door shut and I followed the other two back down the snaking hallways.

When we reached Makaro's cell, Kaylaa cursed. "These have some sort of anti-magic field on the walls. The old man said they didn't have anti-magic protection."

"Guess they upgraded."

"Our weapons might be able to go through this. Come with me."

Makaro stood and pounded on the wall. Even though his mouth was moving, we couldn't hear him. No wonder it was so quiet in here. I followed Kaylaa back to the front desk, where the door was still open. The android was in his own locked room, with our stuff. There was also a camera above the door, but that was nothing to worry about. Master Makai had given us each a wristband that sent out a frequency that scrambled the nearby cameras. Or at least we hoped they did.

"I'm going to have to blow open the door."

"Doesn't it have the anti-magic seal too?"

She shook her head, then placed her hand in the center of the door. She concentrated, and purple energy gathered around her hand; she thrust her open palm at the door, and the energy streamed out to its edges, illuminating us in an indigo glow. The door flew backward, destroying its locking mechanisms and knocking the android to the ground.

Before it could get up (it wasn't designed for mobility), Kaylaa cut the android's visible wires with her Starlight Rapiers, which had been stowed in her backpack. I removed my

Edge, flashed the cobalt blue plasma once for good luck, and put the backpack over my shoulders. With Fyra's backpack in hand, we returned to the cells.

Kaylaa was right—our weapons plunged right through the wall to the cells like a cutting torch through metal. We fashioned openings for Lia and Makaro to crawl through, but one glance at the watch on my wristband told me we were behind on time.

Fyra and her parents gathered in a tight group hug. Tears streamed down both Lia's and Fyra's faces, while Makaro rested his head on Fyra's with his eyes closed.

Kaylaa broke them up. "Tight schedule."

As we walked back to the front desk, Fyra explained what they had to do—wait here until Master Makai's old war buddy came for them with visitor badges. When we reached the front, an old Shard with a rugged face and a long white beard stood there.

"You're late," he mumbled. "I'm Polek. I know who you are. Let's go."

Kaylaa quickly amended the original plan and had Fyra's parents hide inside the room with the broken android.

"You both need to breathe extra hard," Fyra explained. "The security will expect five prisoners after the bounty hunters leave, but when we leave, there will only be four. Take rapid, deep breaths to try to fool the system. Just wait for Mr. Viln to come back." It wasn't the best plan, but it was better than nothing.

Kaylaa had Makaro hold the door in place as best as he could, and we went back to the elevator. Polek handed us each a visitor badge, and up we went to the nineteenth floor. *One down.*

"You've lost about ten minutes. Zil was never late for anything. Maybe Kawto's faith was misplaced."

"We'll make up for it," I said through gritted teeth.

"Give us the situation on nineteen," Kaylaa said.

"Bossy, but direct, just like Kawto said." Polek's voice

shifted a bit like he was giving a formal report. "Everything's normal. We go to my office first, then to Zil's. His office will be empty. You'll have fourteen minutes once we arrive. I already ensured the door was unlocked." His voice returned to normal. "Fourteen minutes is too long. They're going to know it's odd that I went into his office with visitors. Faster you're out, the better."

The elevator came to a stop, and a wave of nostalgia nearly knocked me off my feet when the doors opened. I felt like a little kid again as I followed Polek's fatherly frame down the white-tiled hallway with swirly blue walls. It smelled like disinfectant mixed with slightly burnt toast.

A low chatter floated over the walls to our right, which didn't quite extend to the ceiling. Polek's office was only four doors from the elevator. When we turned the corner, I saw that the Planetary Alliance News channel streaming on the wall—odd, since all communications except those with the royals were blocked with the embargo. I guess the Shard found a way through.

We ducked into his office, which was far from the futuristic lair of a spy warrior. In fact, it didn't look much different than a classroom in Cax-Ark-Uhn—plain walls, detailed maps, a computer, a holo-projector, and ink stains everywhere. "Mill around for a few minutes and then we'll go down to Zil's."

"Were you a good friend of his, Mr. Viln?" Fyra asked.

"If Kawto wasn't around, he'd come to me for advice or to rant. We worked together on a few missions, too. He was a rare man—both skilled and disciplined. It's hard to find men like that."

I'm neither of those things. At least, according to Kaylaa. She was probably right though. But was that my fault? Maybe I should have inherited those traits. Or maybe he would've taught them to me, had he been around longer.

"Let's go," Kaylaa said.

"It's early," Polek protested.

"We need more time," she insisted and opened the door for him. He grunted and led us back out into the hallway. My father's office was only two doors down, and he had just opened the door when another Shard exited the opposite office. I tried to inconspicuously hide behind Polek's ample frame.

"Who are you showing around, Polek?" the Shard asked nervously.

"Just some family friends."

"And you're going to take them in Mad Mark's office?"

"They were interested in who Zil was before he went daft as a Dison."

"Watch out for flying books!" the man said with a chuckle. He strolled off in the opposite direction. I let out a breath that I realized I'd held in since he appeared.

"Get inside," Polek commanded.

The following account is from Polek Viln, who accompanied Zilpohn Mark on this mission. Mark was reassigned before his report could be made.

Primary Objective: Capture or kill Nova Karr – Incomplete
Nova Karr hails from Wicetlin, that war-torn hell hole. He stayed on Wicetlin long enough to become a Slicer, an elite, ruthless soldier for the Wicetari people. He escaped Wicetlin and used the vicious Slicer techniques to become one of the most effective bounty hunters in the P.A.
We tracked Karr to a swampy cave on Makadewa. Somehow, he knew we were coming, and he actually ambushed us. Little did we know that he had an elaborate network of tunnels around the main cave. He nicked me twice, but Zilpohn finally caught up to him. Karr's electric swords clashed with Zilpohn's Edge, lighting up the whole dark cave with an eerie glow. I don't know how Karr did it. He didn't beat Zilpohn, but somehow he knocked him back enough to sneak into a tunnel.
That tunnel must've led out because he launched from his ship before we left the cave. We had put a tracker on his ship, but somehow he disabled it.
The man is dangerous. I recommend assigning more Shards to eliminate the threat.

—From Report on Nova Karr for mission ZM073
by Polek Viln, 492 ARI

Chapter Twenty-Five

The room was dark and lined with metal, office building filing cabinets of different heights. I knew they were sorted by planet and filled with objects from his travels. A map was attached to the front of each drawer, indicating the origins of the contents. The office was dominated by a solid cherrywood U-shaped desk in the middle, but there were no chairs. Even my small pop-up chair I used as a kid was gone.

"Spread out," I said. "Someone check the files on Vastire for anything on the Temple and Yiptae for anything from there. I'll check the desk." I ran my hand along the top of the desk as I walked around it, and I thought I could feel it vibrating like a heartbeat—like *his* heartbeat. Standing behind the desk, I felt like an invader in his space, and his presence nearly overwhelmed me.

"Ten minutes," Polek said, snapping me back to the mission. Fyra and Kaylaa frantically searched through the files, examining all of the odd objects within.

On either side of the desk, there was a screen that could pop up in a wedge integrated seamlessly into the flat top. But every button I pressed and switch I clicked did nothing. I rummaged through a few papers on his desk, but nothing seemed interesting at first glance. Then I noticed an old photo taped to the desk—my father, my mother, and I when I was about five, a wooden sword in hand. I felt a tear welling up, but fought it off and opened the first drawer.

Nothing, just pens and pencils and styluses. Next drawer. This one was deeper, with a stack of papers and a data pad on top. I placed the data pad on the table and was just about to close the door when I noticed something small jammed into the corner. I pulled on it and examined the small card. It was a paper business card for Dr. Werus Capp, complete with a picture and a company name: *Helix Industries*.

Makai said this guy was murdered, but not by my father. He looked like any other scientist, with oversized glasses, sharp wrinkles, and thin eyebrows. *Why would my father have this?* I stuffed it in my pocket.

I turned on the data pad and clicked on a few random icons, but nothing would come up without a password. I found something with my picture as the icon, and I pressed it. A message started playing—a message from my father.

"Give this to my son if I don't make it," he started in a deep voice. A wave of emotions overwhelmed my senses. Everyone in the room stopped moving, maybe stopped breathing, to listen.

"This was the only way, and trust me, kid, I thought it through. You're going to be mad, you're going to hurt, but you deserved a better world, and I was the only one who could make it happen. It was past time for action. Maybe that's arrogant." He trailed off, and sadness overtook my anger. "I made a mistake, a long time ago. Ask Aseus about it. Tell him you know about *Fatalia di genalia fateria*. I always loved your mother, and I love you. To the end."

He knew he was going to die. And he was at peace with it— mostly, at least. He said he did it for me...but wouldn't it have been better to have been there to show me that better world? Anger swelled inside and I slammed the data pad on the desk.

Panic set in. *Did I just destroy my father's last words?*

I scrambled to turn it back on, and fortunately it lit back up, even with the screen cracked.

Fyra placed her hand on mine for comfort, but I snatched it away. Even his last words left me with more questions than answers. And Commander Aseus seemed like one of the last people I'd want to talk to.

"Time to go," Polek said, cracking the door to see if anyone was watching.

"Find anything?" Kaylaa asked.

"Lots of interesting things, nothing useful," Fyra replied. I shook my head. I clutched the data pad tight, wanting to bring it with me, but knew there was no room, and returned it to the desk drawer.

We followed Polek out into the empty hallway. Adrenaline coursed through my veins as we waited for the elevator. My thoughts rushed through my brain and back out.

He made a mistake? Fatalia di something-or-other and Aseus knew something about it. But he did love me—he did it *for me.* But maybe that was arrogant. He should've talked to a priest about it, maybe gotten more help if it was so right. He could've told someone else about the ship. *Maybe I should tell someone else about the ship?*

The elevator finally arrived and we hopped on. A middle-aged woman with short brown hair was already aboard, but she was completely engrossed in the DataAxis on her arm. We rode down to the eighth floor without stopping.

Much like on the prison floor, there was a desk manned by an android. An active hologram projected over the desk, showing thousands of tall shelves and rectangular gray-green boxes. A waiting room sat on either side, with chairs, a table, and flatscreens integrated into the table.

"What missions?" Polek asked.

"ZM079 and KM149."

Polek slipped his badge into the computer on the desk and typed in the two mission numbers. As soon as he finished typing in 'ZM079,' the android started to explain the mission.

"Operative: Zilpohn Mark. Destination: Temple of Stria-

Fate. Commanding Officer: Commander Aseus. Purposes: Discover the Great Secret of the Temple of Stria-Fate. Test the abilities of the enhanced subject, Zilpohn Mark." While the android spoke, the hologram zoomed in to show a small, flat robot winding through the shelves. The robot stopped at its destination and lifted high into the air.

"Enhanced subject?" I asked. Kaylaa only answered with a shrug.

The computer started explaining the history of the Temple, but I interrupted it, "Tell me the results of the mission." By now the robot had loaded a box onto its flat surface and was retreating to the ground.

The android stopped mid-sentence and stated, "Result: The operative was successful in infiltrating the Temple and discovering the Great Secret. The operative did not disclose the Great Secret. The operative described impressive swordsmanship but did not display any enhanced abilities. Overall result: failure."

Enhanced abilities? *What is it talking about?* Before I could think about it further, a drawer jumped out of the desk on our side. Inside was one of the gray-green containers from the shelf, clearly marked "ZM079." I ripped open the box with anticipation, but it was completely empty.

"Why even have a box?" I yelled.

"Quiet!" Polek said.

The elevator doors slid open and two Shards emerged, an older woman and a young man dressed in plain clothing. They were talking amongst themselves as they walked up behind us, seemingly unaware of our presence other than standing a respectable distance back.

"We're going to have to do something about them," Kaylaa whispered. She slowly swung her backpack around to her chest and pulled out her weapons. I did the same with my Edge, and on her signal, we pounced on the Shards.

We caught them completely by surprise, and each of us held

our blades to their throats.

"You know how this goes," Kaylaa said.

"Do you know where you are?" the Shard asked in a higher voice than one would expect. I snickered. "Your friend thinks this is funny?"

"Don't hurt them," Polek said.

"Polek?" the woman asked. "What is going on?"

"Sorry," he said. He strolled over to her and slammed her head into the ground, knocking her unconscious.

"You're a Shard! What are you doing?" gasped the man, but Polek deftly knocked him unconscious as well. Kaylaa smirked.

As Polek strode back to the computer, he said, "Seems our time is running out."

"Been lucky so far," Kaylaa replied.

"Blessed," corrected Fyra.

Polek typed in 'KM149.' Again the hologram showed the robot's path as it found its way to the relevant box.

"Operative: Kawto Makai. Victim: Dr. Werus Capp. Place of Death: Outside his home, 1212 Sheire Avenue. Occurrence: Dr. Capp was stabbed through the back on the ninth day of Windoon's Solstice in the year 495 ARI. Zilpohn Mark was charged with murder posthumously," said the android. A second hologram popped up from the desk, showing the murder scene with various annotations.

The drawer popped out again, and I knew as soon as I lifted this box that it wasn't empty. When I opened it, there wasn't much inside: another business card, some documents, some doctor's instruments, and, just as Makai said, the shape memory alloy key. I snatched it up and tried not to think about Dr. Capp's business card in my father's drawer. My father was a lot of things, but not a murderer who would stab a scientist in the back.

"Into the drawer, Fyra," Kaylaa commanded, and Fyra jumped into the drawer. The drawer closed, and Fyra popped out on the other side.

"Oh, my badge!" she said, and she placed the visitor badge in the drawer before it came back to our side.

"We're just about out of time," Polek said. The drawer popped out again, and we gave him all three visitor badges. "I'll do my part, hurry up." He hurried back to the elevator.

"Thanks, Polek," I said. He gave me a quick Shard salute just before the doors closed. His career was over. He did it for my father—for me.

"In, Darynn," Kaylaa said, and I stuffed myself into the drawer. It whooshed me into the towering archives room, which smelled of must and hot electronics. Kaylaa punched in the mission number again, then tucked herself into the drawer and joined us.

Using my Captain's Ring for light, we made our way to the center of the room, then turned right. We did our best to hold our breath, as the gas analyzers would quickly pick up on three more people than expected. The shelves soared above us, rows and rows filled with boxes. Only a robot would know where to go, though every location was labeled and theoretically could be scanned by hand. When we reached the edge of the building, we found another waiting room, but no android—just a computer. I assumed this was Aseus's private access to the Mission Archive since this was his express elevator to the upper floors.

Kaylaa and I slid our weapons into the crack between the elevator doors and tried to wedge it open. Even with a lot of straining and effort, we couldn't get the doors open. Kaylaa concentrated and drew in wisps of purple magic energy, and the door finally thrust open.

But the elevator was nowhere in sight. I peered over the edge, my hands clamped to the wall. A gust of wind, like the breath from a metallic giant, flew up the shaft. Not far behind was the capsule-shaped elevator. I snapped my head back, but just as we expected, the elevator stopped at the floor below.

"Polek did his part. Everybody on," Kaylaa directed,

jumping onto the top of the elevator. The nose of the capsule was blunt, though not large enough for us to step on. She stabbed her two Rapiers about shoulder's width apart into the elevator, then I jumped onto the capsule, using the Rapiers to steady myself. The elevator shook as its doors closed underneath.

"Fyra, come on!" I yelled, but the fear was plain in her eyes. The elevator climbed at faster than one floor per second—and we were going to sit on top of it, held by only our grips to the Rapiers and my Edge. I activated the plasma and thrust my Edge into the capsule, holding my hand out for Fyra. "I won't let you fall." The elevator lurched—she only had seconds. "Now!" Just as I felt the elevator shift beneath me, she jumped and grabbed my hand.

The elevator rushed up, and Fyra's body swung around the smooth edges of the capsule. I held fast. Even though she was light, gravity worked against us. Her feet couldn't get a grip on the elevator, and I couldn't pull her to the middle.

I felt my fingers slipping.

Violet energy rushed around the elevator and concentrated on Kaylaa's arm. With augmented strength, she reached out and snatched Fyra's arm. With Fyra secured, the pulsing energy dissipated.

My heart started again as the elevator gained speed in the near-complete darkness. It would've been exhilarating if Fyra hadn't nearly died. Any color that Fyra had in her pale skin was drained, her eyes were clamped shut, and even in the dim light, I could tell she was shivering.

Rationally, I knew we had been on the elevator less than a minute, but it was hard to gain a breath at these speeds. It felt so much longer when it finally started to slow down. If everything had gone right, the elevator should have stopped at the twenty-third floor, meaning the closed doors in front of us led to the twenty-fourth floor. Those two metallic doors, with a thin bead of light between them, hid something that Master

Makai would not share.

I took a deep breath and wedged my Edge into the gap between the doors. I steadied myself on the blunt nose of the elevator. Kaylaa did the same with a Rapier, and we pulled on opposite sides. The doors slid open, and we helped Fyra onto the landing.

The elevator lurched again; Kaylaa and I glanced at each other, then positioned our elbows on the floor inside the opening. She swung herself up, but when I tried, my left foot slipped. With a sudden *whoosh*, the elevator dropped out from below me, and I dangled over the chasm left behind. *Good thing it wasn't going up.*

My breathing quickened and my heartbeat raced, but fortunately, Kaylaa and Fyra were able to pull me up.

I didn't even have the chance to catch my breath.

"Authorization?" boomed a huge android with a barrel chest, four arms, and four legs.

When none of us spoke, a second identical android activated, and said, "Authorization, or you're under arrest." They gripped two red and two green Plasma Edges. Kaylaa and I prepared to fight.

"Combat mode engaged," they said in unison. Their middle arms, with red Plasma Edges, could spin around their central axis, while the upper arms attached like shoulders. They swung each of them in perfect—if mechanical—harmony.

Kaylaa and I moved in opposite directions away from the still-open elevator doors. I fought defensively—how the hell was I supposed to land an attack with four swords swinging at me?

Then it got worse.

They turned on two yellow lasers positioned on their shoulders. The lasers boxed me into a lane to fight. I couldn't dodge to the left or right. It knew that and switched to vertical strikes.

Then it got worse again.

The lasers turned inward. In seconds I was going to be

sliced in half. The heat radiated off the beams, slickening my whole body with sweat.

I lashed out at the waist of the android. It easily blocked my strike with one arm and knocked my Edge away with another.

Fyra yelled and tried to plunge the freezing end of her Elenduil Staff into the android's body. It anticipated her movement, blocked the staff, and threw her toward the open elevator shaft.

"Fyra!"

Her Staff went flying into the elevator shaft, clanking on the walls the long way down. *Did she fall?*

My blood boiled. I punched the android in the waist. A surge of black and white energy swirled down my arm and launched into its body.

The android flew backward and slammed into its companion. The second android instinctively swung its Edges at the flying mechanical monster. Two arms and a leg were hacked off in the scrum.

I rushed to the elevator shaft.

Her fingers, bone-white, gripped the edge. I grabbed her arm with both hands and tried to swing her up onto the floor. But my hands were damp with sweat, and I struggled to get a grip. *Come on, Darynn!*

"One...two...three." I finally swung her up onto the floor. Her whole body trembled as I wrapped my arms around her. "You're okay," I whispered.

Her backpack was gone, which meant we only had the means for two of us to escape. A problem for later.

"A little help here!" Kaylaa called, backing away from the flurry of colorful plasma.

Even though both androids were missing limbs, they were still effective. Especially now that both turned on her.

Her movements were so fluid, so precise. She somehow dodged all of the swords and lasers, but her time was running out.

I took up my Edge and dashed toward the weaker of the two androids. I leapt into the air and plunged my Edge into its chest. The blue plasma rushed out of my blade and into its circuits—the smell of burnt electronics overtook the landing. I wrenched my Edge free and approached the other. It fought me briefly with one Edge, two still trained on Kaylaa. It was an adaptable machine, but it didn't stand a chance now.

Kaylaa quickly hacked off an arm and a leg. It could still stand on three legs, but its mobility was compromised. She drove one Rapier through its body, then chopped off its head with the other. It tumbled to the ground, still spinning one Edge fruitlessly in the air.

I helped Fyra to her feet and tried to steady her trembling. We walked over to the panel by the main entrance to the rest of the floor. I pulled the shape memory alloy key out of my pocket and handed it to Kaylaa.

"I hope this works," she said. She held the key out in her open hand. In its present state, it looked like a plain block of metal. As she heated it with magic, it turned into a key with a loop and three teeth. She stuffed it into the keyhole next to the door.

A small, metal hole opened up next to the door at about eye height. "Retinal scan required."

"Ten P.A. Credits say this doesn't work," I said as I put my eye up to the scanner.

"Y-y-you don't have ten P.A. Credits," Fyra stuttered. *A joke?*

A laser flashed into my eye, and a few anxious seconds passed while I blinked out a tear.

"Identity confirmed. Welcome, Zilpohn Mark."

The three of us looked at each other, puzzled, but there was no time to process the result. The doors opened and a greenish glow flooded the landing. The dread drew all of the air out of my lungs like a vacuum. I had only felt like that once in my life.

My father had been out on a mission longer than expected,

and a Shard spokesman had come by. That always meant only one thing. When he stood at our doorway in Cax-Ark-Uhn, I felt the sudden mixture of fear, sadness, and longing each battling for supremacy in my mind.

I felt that now.

Lord Gling: "Why not just blast the damned ships out of the sky?"

Lord Lysta: "Any full-scale attack on the embargo would lead to war. A war we could not win."

Lord Xianl: "What about more subtle methods? Sabotage the ships?"

Lord Lysta: "Most likely, that would result in new ships. Maybe additional ships."

Lord Castamere: "If there even was such a way, undetected."

Lord Babajide: "We could acquiesce to their request, or negotiate some rights for Olan-Har in exchange for the removal of the embargo. Even their appetite for the blockade is waning."

Lord Searon: "No. We will not compromise. Our best course of action is to scare them such that they will not retaliate. Nearly half the P.A. voted against the embargo in the first place. A small push tilts the number in our favor. We must wait until the time is ripe."

—From a Virin-Leen Council Meeting, 497 ARI

CHAPTER TWENTY-SIX

We entered a circular hallway of shining silver metal that reminded me of a spaceship corridor. I took a deep breath and smelled disinfectant. Something tugged at the edges of my memory, like a child pulling at my shirttail, but I couldn't drag it forward.

The domed room from the holographic plans loomed ahead.

"We're out of time, Darynn," Kaylaa said. "I'll check out the side hallways while you go there. Stay out of sight and I'll meet you there." She crept down the hallway to the right and snuck into the first room.

I crouched down, but as soon as Fyra and I stepped into the dome, a scientist, head down in papers, bumped into me.

"Oh, I'm sorry...wait...Darynn?"

I grabbed him by the shoulders of his sea-green coat and slammed him against the wall. "How do you know me?"

"Well...uh...you're not supposed to be here...is Commander Aseus with you?" He babbled a few more words that didn't quite fit together and I knocked him on the head with the butt of my Edge. *Not much time left.*

Fyra and I stuck to the nearest wall, but I was confused by the contents of the room. A number of huge cylinders sat in the middle, filled with bubbling fluid and a large mass I couldn't quite make out. The walls were lined with screens and buttons and panels. Cords and hoses and flexible tubes connected the screens to the central vessels. Scientists were so engrossed in the screens, swapping between displays and scribbling on notepads, that they had no idea we were there. Everything seemed connected to the tubes in the center.

The lights were purposely angled away from the tubes, making it hard to see them. Fyra held my arm in a vice as we approached. With her other hand, she pointed to what looked like a light switch. I reached out and pressed it, and bright fluorescent light poured down from the ceiling directly onto the tubes.

The glass did not reflect the light. and now it was clear that bodies floated inside the bubbling green fluid. At first glance, they didn't appear to be moving. *Corpses?* What kind of research were they doing here?

I examined the face of one of the corpses, and it looked very familiar. I pressed my face up against the warm glass. *It's not dead.* Its chest rose and fell as oxygen pumped through a face mask. It was a young boy, maybe twelve. He looked so familiar—like a kid I knew from the slums, maybe. Were they experimenting on Olan-Har?

Fyra screamed, so shrill I felt my blood turn to ice. I blinked as I looked at my arm—*when did she let go of me?* A dozen lenses turned to us, each displaying information that blocked their eyes.

Fyra stared at the boy in one of the tubes, her mouth agape, one of her hands shakily pointing. I squinted to study the boy's face.

It was *me.*

My knees jolted like I'd torn a ligament. My eyes shot to the next tube...also me. Frantically, I dashed from tube to tube, leaving sweaty palm prints on each one.

All me.

Different ages, but all me. Each tube was marked with a

year, each a year apart, all the way down to an infant born this year. An infant *me*.

My heart pumped, but it felt like all the blood had been drained by a Vampire. I tripped and fell on a cord, and couldn't find the strength to lift myself to my feet.

The puzzle seemed like it should be coming together, but I still couldn't make the pieces fit. Oxygen seemed to be hard to come by, like someone sucker punched me again and again. I pressed my hand against one of the tubes, labeled 493 ARI, and tried to steady myself. The face of my ten-year-old self hung there, lifeless, his eyes closed, his body barely moving. At ten, I had been happy and careless. I still had both my parents. I still had a life. I didn't know if I could say that now. I could just be a vessel, like these poor souls. *Do they* have *souls?*

Fyra helped me to my feet and my vision blurred even though the movement wasn't sudden. Scientists watched in awe and silence. One even had the audacity to scribble down notes.

I staggered out of the central dome and into the nearest adjacent room. This room was square with metal walls, a metal bed, and three bright lights. This room I remembered—*but why?*

I staggered into the hallway and slumped against the nearest wall. Fyra found me but was speechless. There was nothing she could say right now anyway.

Kaylaa walked down the hallway. "Darynn, what are you doing? You won't believe this data I—" She stopped. I barely even raised my eyes to look at her. "What's wrong? We need to go."

"Darynn," boomed a familiar voice from the central dome—Commander Aseus. We were caught. *Too late.*

I rubbed my eyes and picked myself up off the ground. I took two steps toward the dome.

Kaylaa grabbed my shoulder. "Not that way! We can still get out of here!"

I brushed off her hand. "It's over." I let my backpack slip off my shoulders, but clutched my Edge, an object of safety, stability.

Aseus stood with both hands on the handle of his broad Plasma Edge, the tip dug into the ground. He stood next to the tube labeled 484 ARI, just one year younger than me.

"One day, I knew you'd be back. But in some ways, you've never left, eh?" He knocked on the glass of the tube, half a smile on his face.

"You...bastard," I forced out. My strength was gone. An image of me stupidly attacking him flashed through my head.

Kaylaa entered and her eyes went wide. "Cloning is illegal in the P.A."

"Indeed," Aseus replied nonchalantly. "But you won't tell. Your friend, Darynn; he too is a clone."

My heart plummeted. My knees weakened and I had to steady myself on Fyra's shoulder. *Now the retinal scan makes sense.* Now people telling me I looked exactly like Zilpohn Mark made sense.

I'm a clone of my father.

"You know your grandmother had Zilpohn at an advanced age. Helix Industries offered the ability to extend the fertility age for women, but only Virin-leen could afford it." *Helix Industries...*that was on Dr. Werus Capp's business card.

"The Shard made a deal with Gallant: allow us to continue our genetic experiments, and he could have a son. The birth of your father started the Storm stage of the project." *Storm.* That was my father's code name.

"Of course, there was a catch." Aseus grinned, cruelty in his eyes. "Helix inserted the magic gene, a modified version of the Mist stage, into your father."

I gulped again, but there was no saliva left in my mouth. The fog was clearing, but the destination was still fuzzy.

"Show Zil's training," Aseus snapped at the scientist, and a video played on the screens. It showed my father, around eighteen, fighting gracefully against Shards in training, far better than I ever could. "Gallant and Kawto trained him...Kawto helped you in here, right?" I tried not to betray him, but I think my expression did anyway. "We'll deal with him later."

"We tried to coax magic out of your father. But all we had was an incredible swordsman and hero, maybe the best since the god Makar. *Fatalia di generia fateria* was officially a failure."

That was what my father talked about in his recording.

"What does that mean?" Fyra asked.

Aseus looked to one of the scientists, who replied, "Children of Genetic Fate."

Aseus continued. "Your father came back from the Mondoon Conflict and wanted to have a child. He sought out Dr. Werus Capp to see how his genes would affect that. They decided that a child born naturally would suffer ill effects. Instead, the project would continue on a clone of Zil." I felt like a Vampire was attached to my neck, slowly draining my life force. Fyra held me up with both hands, while Kaylaa stood still as a statue.

"They knew how to inject, or awaken, the magic gene in a clone of Zil. And in 483 ARI, the new perfect magic soldier was born." He started into the hallway and beckoned for us to follow. My legs wobbled as we did, and he took us into a small viewing room that looked into a square chamber. I pressed my face against the glass. This was the room I saw when I fought the Second Lady. But with one key difference: dry blood splattered the walls. "You practically lived here until you were twelve."

"That's impossible!" I yelled. I would *surely* remember that.

Aseus clicked his teeth. "This was the first place I saw it. Saw that finally, all that genetic crap was successful. A vagrant held a knife to your throat, and suddenly, you exploded with power, and all that was left of him was blood." The memory came to completion—the smell of sweat and blood and bad breath, the cold hard steel against my neck, the greasy long hair swiping across my forehead. And then he was gone, and I wiped the blood off my face. "We repeated the experiment a few times, and while you were a bit emotional like Mist, you were more malleable. Especially with someone like me to wield you." He chuckled. I felt like he was driving needles with puppet strings into my arms.

"Then Zil's Haskar-cursed rebellion ruined everything." My father stabbing himself through the heart played in my mind—Aseus didn't know half of what it had ruined. "Helix used repression techniques to clear your memory of all of this. Then we sent you to the CMB."

Reflexively, my eyes fell on the disc and slivers of the Olan-Har tattoo. "This is...all...your fault," I growled. I flashed the plasma on my Edge, scoring a slice in the floor—but I couldn't lift it. It felt like someone stood on the blade.

"The rebellion was all his damned idea. I didn't even know why at the time."

"Meaning you know now?" Kaylaa asked.

Aseus produced a small, purple crystal ball with what looked like a white iris from his pocket. "Fyra, my dear, will you explain what this is?"

"That's..." She choked. "The Eye of Deesa. It's an Artifact that allows a mother to watch her children over great distances."

"One minor correction—anyone with a strong connection can be watched. I've watched you for years, Darynn Mark. I had to make sure our weapon was being taken care of, exercised properly."

"You...bastard..." I stared at his hard, hateful face and felt absolutely powerless. All of the times I had felt like I was being watched—it was him. Always him. *The Shard are always watching*, Makai said. Even he probably didn't know how right he was.

"I won't tell anyone about the letter or the ship. I leave that to you. The point was, Zil still didn't use magic, even against unholy threats like Vampires and the Second Lady of the Temple."

"So that's why you sent him to the Temple," Fyra said.

A cruel smile crossed his face. "Of course. We wanted to test his power. Just like we continued to test yours." I looked at him stupidly. "Just because you were out of our hands didn't mean we couldn't keep studying you. Then the embargo, the shipments, and your brother came along." *Pavlar?* What does Pavlar have to do with all of this? "We sent a young recruit to a bar in Hargonla and fed your brother the idea of raiding the shipments. He was reluctant at first, timid mouse he was, but he presented the idea to you, and you pushed him into it." Now strings were sewed into my legs, and Aseus was starting to pull on them.

"How dare you! That was my brother's idea!" Fyra cried out with a sudden burst of courage.

"Just you wait, my dear. You are all just cards in our deck." *What does that mean?* Fyra...Kaylaa?

I whirled and pointed my finger at Kaylaa. "Do you work for him, too? Are you just another card for him to play?" Around every corner was another betrayal, another player of the game. All of the so-called decisions I made—I was led to them. Even Kaylaa was just another agent, pulling my strings so the Shard could enjoy the show.

Kaylaa's eyes turned glassy and she blinked rapidly. "Of course not! I am Kaylaa Reesae, Senator Shuka's bodyguard."

Aseus snickered. "I would like to say I set that one up. We only saw your power once in the raids, when you killed those Diterians. You didn't even use it to save your friend on the last raid." He had found a dagger and pushed straight into my heart. *Why didn't it come then?* If it had...I would've saved Pavlar, and none of this would've happened.

"We would've brought you in when he died, another Olan-Har disappearance, but we had to let the Temple plan play out."

He turned his attention to Kaylaa. "Did you really think we didn't know why you were here? We would've shot you down, but you went straight to him.

"Then you demonstrated your power against the Second Lady, and the healing of the Minotaur. In between, I finally knew the Great Secret."

"Why haven't you told anyone?" I asked.

"It's all about leverage, my boy. When you have that kind of leverage, you can't waste it hastily." He chuckled again. "Then you came here. Did you really think your infiltration plan had worked out so well? We knew you were here the second you stepped into the building."

Another harrowing thought. "Is Master Makai working for you?"

He laughed heartily. "No, that idealistic fool. You see, my boy, it's always more advantageous when they don't work for you. You just bend events a certain way until you get what you want naturally. And sometimes, you get lucky."

A group of Shards appeared at the door to the small room. "Let's go up to my office and finish this discussion. I hope the boys aren't necessary." He motioned for us to drop our weapons.

I held my Edge up, the blade in front of my nose. I flashed the plasma, viewing Aseus through its cobalt light. He didn't flinch. My hands shook and the specter of doubt took over. Involuntarily, my Edge clattered to the floor.

Kaylaa's eyes shifted from my Edge, to me, to Aseus. Her grip on her Rapiers tightened as if she was going to grind them into dust. But she swallowed and let them fall to the floor.

The Shards took our weapons and escorted us to the elevator. But they didn't get on with us—only Aseus, who held his Edge to Kaylaa's neck. "I know what you can do, even without your weapon. Be calm and there will be no blood."

We rode the elevator silently, and I felt like my brain was on fire, like a computer with its fans blocked. I leaned heavily against the wall, as my legs had turned to jelly.

Aseus's office was the shape of a pyramid, with one-way glass around all sides. I was sure I would get a breathtaking view of the city, but I didn't have any breath to spare. He motioned for us to sit in leather chairs across an austere wooden desk from him.

"So you see what brought you here. What brought our whole race to this tipping point. Sometimes all it would take is a single question, one extra click on the DataAxis. But you don't question where you came from. You don't question your religion. People always question themselves, but they do it with bias, where they already think they know the answer. I don't know what to think of the letter from Bekivala and the ship, but I do know that we should have questioned the Iveleen all along. Not just followed the Grand Cardinal and the Scriptures. Validate them, then believe. Hell, I've seen Erodian Champions with power that may have bested an Iveleen."

"Faith doesn't require validation," Fyra protested.

"You're brilliant, my dear, but blind. Blind faith is dangerous—in friends, in leaders, in gods. Didn't that research lab seem familiar to you?"

She shook her head meekly. "No...why would it?"

"They've gotten better! You've been there, too. When we heard of Fyra the Farsight, we just had to know what she could do. You dated a boy at University, didn't you? He was one of ours. He validated your power and we brought you in. We studied it, tried to find the root of it, but found nothing. So we turned you loose, my dear." My blood boiled—how dare he speak to her like that? I reached for my Edge, but the sheath was empty. I sunk deeper into my chair. I couldn't protect her.

"The only boy I ever loved...was a setup?" she asked, her eyes fixed on the ground. *Only boy?*

"Everything is a setup, my dear. Everyone plays the role they're meant to play. Even Zil understood that—he would always question orders, which made him a difficult soldier. His way was usually better, so I let him get away with it. But the Great Secret shook him to the core." He paused and looked at the ceiling, pressing his fingers together. "If he had told me...maybe the Shard would've been at his side." I considered the thought, only for a moment—if the Shard hadn't fought him, he would've survived, for sure. History would consider him differently. I would view him differently.

"So what now?" Kaylaa asked.

"I have a proposal."

"Another setup?" I asked.

He laughed heartily. "Fair! You could call it that if you like. The embargo must be lifted. Kaylaa—your employer hired you to do that. Darynn—you were reluctant three weeks ago, but I feel sure that has changed. I need you to end it, and you have two options."

"You can't manipulate me anymore, Aseus."

"Finally some spunk. I was afraid it was all gone, and I would have had no choice but to use a clone."

"So they are clones of my father, like me," I said.

"More correct would be they're clones of you, post-experimentation. We're in the Hurricane phase of the project now." Mist, Rains, Storms, Hurricane. I should've been the eye of the storm, but I felt like I was getting torn apart. "Each one has been perfected just a little bit more, with one more year of research. But they're only for use in case of emergency."

"Option one: denounce the Iveleen. Reveal the Great Secret. Destroy the caste system from the inside out. Start your war with the Virin-leen and the priests."

I shook my head. "No...we're not ready...we don't know for sure."

"The Shard will not intervene, should you choose that path. If the Shard hadn't fought that day...your father would have won. And you have a power he couldn't fathom."

"No. We go to Yiptae first."

"Just like your father." A devilish smile crossed his lips.

"Option two: punch a hole in the embargo so big the P.A. never crosses us again." I swallowed hard. Kaylaa looked stunned. "Once they realize that all it took was one soldier, any remaining ships will flee. Vastire becomes the dominant power in the P.A. And you can do whatever the hell you want with the Great Secret. The Shard will even help, if you desire."

"My comrades are in those ships," Kaylaa said.

"Like you give a damn. I know what you are."

"They're still people," I said.

Aseus grinned. "So are the Olan-Har. A few thousand foreign lives could save tens of thousands domestic ones."

"Your eyes betray you," Fyra said. "Either way, you know what happens. Chaos ensues. Law and order will be required. Only one body will be strong enough to fill the void. The Shard."

"I overthrow the church and royals, and you rule the world," I said as I slowly understood Fyra's revelation.

"You need me to fight the Militia and Templars and maybe the P.A. You'll be the hero, the Savior. But you can't enforce order alone," Aseus said.

"What if the P.A. fights back?"

"They're cowards. A gaggle of politicians, not warriors. They surprised me when they actually agreed to a semi-military force imposing the embargo. But they won't start an all-out war. They won't risk their own people for people's rights on another planet. Not after they've already lost hundreds to a single warrior." Aseus leaned back in his chair.

I looked to my right and saw Windoon's Star setting over the horizon. "We go to Yiptae first, then we choose an option."

"No. Choose now, or you go into a prison cell until you do." That's when I realized—he had me. Just like Master Makai had warned against. The bones in my body disappeared. Maybe if he'd told me what I would run into, I could've been prepared. But I wouldn't have believed him. I couldn't even believe that my father and I had the same retinas. If he had told me we were, genetically, literally the same person, I would've laughed.

Aseus continued. "Think of all the people that will die if you're on Yiptae for six months. For a year? You can't wait that long."

A wave of faces flooded my mind's eye. The first time my father took me to Hargonla. My starving mother. Captain Madra and his thieving daughter. Pavlar's corpse. Even Fyra had nearly died. Tens of thousands had died locally, just in the last three years. It could be half a million if you added up all the Olan-Har slums. In their current state, there was no way we could stage a rebellion...which left only one choice.

I swallowed. "The embargo...I'll attack it."

"D-D-Darynn...are you sure?" Fyra asked.

"You can't just do that," Kaylaa said. "They're a peace-keeping force."

"I'll trade a million of our lives for a thousand of theirs."

"This isn't an equation, Darynn," Fyra said. "It doesn't balance like that. You will live with their deaths for the rest of your life. How would Pavlar feel?"

"I'm not Pavlar! Maybe he would have another way, but he's gone."

"What makes you think he can even do it? You are taking a big risk putting all of your faith in him," Kaylaa said to Aseus.

"He has only scratched the surface of his full potential," Aseus said. "You saw that video of the Mist kid. Darynn is far beyond that."

"Damnit, I said I'll do it."

"Excellent!" Aseus said. "You will be trained tomorrow, for a launch early the next morning. Sleep at home tonight. There's no use trying to escape—you'd only delay the inevitable. I'd recommend a sedative." He shooed us out into the elevator.

Before I knew it, we were on the first floor, Shards handing us our weapons. A Shard car waited outside, and it took us as close to Fyra's house as it could manage. My head swam in circles the whole way, but I'm not sure I had a single coherent thought. I leaned back with my eyes absolutely fixed on a small scratch in the ceiling.

Lia and Makaro, home safe, peppered us with questions, but none of us would answer—not that we had any answers. Everything we had learned was so unbelievable, we'd almost have to be mad to think it true. No wonder my father went mad.

Why didn't he tell me? Why didn't my mother?

I have no genetic link to my mother.

That was a hard pill to swallow. But I guess it didn't really matter—she always loved me, no matter what. Maybe that explains why they never had any other children. But, in a way, they had sixteen more children in a lab at Shard Headquarters. My father had to know about the clones if I visited that facility all the time, but I couldn't imagine him agreeing to that. His children—his brothers?—stuck in a tube their entire lives, unaware of their existence. And if they were anything like me, they were dangerous.

Can't worry about that now. All that mattered was the embargo. One step at a time.

Helix Industries entered an agreement with the Shard in 394 ARI to build genetically modified soldiers in exchange for funding.

The subject Mist was born in 402 ARI in our labs after extensive genetic modification. The Mist Affair in 420 ARI proved that the modifications were a success; however, it also showed the instability of the subject. Mist killed seven Shard agents, displaying magical abilities and fighting prowess before being killed.

The Rains stage of the project started after Mists's death. While these soldiers were potent, they displayed no magical abilities.

The Storm stage began with the birth of the subject in 460 ARI. Storm grew up to be the most capable fighter on Vastire, if not in Vastirian history, however even the most improbable of trials did not result in the use of magic. The stability of this subject is also in question due to the manner in which he died in 495 ARI.

The Hurricane project started on the son of Storm...

—From Helix Industries Project Report: Hurricane, Background

CHAPTER TWENTY-SEVEN

I spent the whole next day in a haze, like the head-spinning moments directly after a severe concussion. Lia served breakfast, the kind that was hard to come by in Hargonla, but it had no taste. Fyra's parents found it hard to believe they had been apprehended for no reason and blamed Kaylaa, which spurred an argument. The whole time, I felt Makaro's distrustful eyes on me.

The same car that dropped us off the night before took us back to Shard Headquarters, albeit with a different, chattier driver. I felt like I saw every person in Hargonla as we rode. *Would they approve of the trade I was making?* Surely they would; it's pretty easy to be in favor of anything that keeps you from starving.

We strolled into Shard Headquarters, every eye fixed on us, and up to the twenty-second floor using the express elevator. This time, we had proper badges.

Aseus met us there, in an entirely too gleeful mood, and escorted us to a conference room towards the opposite end of the floor. Every wall on this floor was painted black, and it was difficult to discern where the walls ended and doors began. We slipped into a large rectangular room with a multitude of tables covered in equipment and hologram projectors. The walls were all screens, displaying different views of the ships in orbit around the planet.

There, we met one-armed Colonel Meer, the leader of this particular mission, and Dr. Kole Shagod, the developer of the required technology. Meer was polite and charismatic, while Dr. Shagod was blunt and too smart for his own good. While Meer looked like your exemplary soldier, with neat clothes, trimmed hair, and shiny boots, Dr. Shagod looked nothing like your typical scientist—tree trunk legs and strong branch arms, mostly denim clothes, and some sort of electronic monocle, constantly flashing with data.

Between the two of them, they briefed mission number DM001 and introduced me to the Solo Atmospheric Fighting Armor, or SAFA. The mission was relatively simple from an objectives perspective—launch me into orbit and let me use my magic to obliterate most of the hundred-plus-ship embargo.

The SAFA, however, was anything but simple. It was a dark suit of metallic armor, tailored exactly to my body (which made me wonder how long they'd planned this). The tech was designed for the Mondoon conflict as a way to counter the ships in orbit with a small, hard-to-track soldier. Supposedly, I'd have nearly perfect mobility, while also being able to propel myself through space with gas thrusters located behind my calves and shoulders. They had removed all weapons, saying it was too classified for me, and insisted I didn't need them anyway.

The suit did have some drawbacks—small needles were going to be injected into my skin on every finger to help with tactile feel. It was going to be very tight to my chest, to help monitor my vital signs from the ground. Finally, they were going to inject some sort of nano machine into my spinal cord so that my brain could somehow communicate with the suit. That sounded terrifying. They said that eventually, the batteries would run out, so the nano machines would become useless.

They described everything that would display on the visor in front of my eyes—targets, debris, distances, etc. Everything I saw would be transmitted to the ground. They had me try on a simulated visor for a while to get me used to it.

Despite my general interest in weapons, I struggled to stay awake. It was too much for my brain to handle, even if I hadn't had a hole put through it yesterday by a bullet of secrets.

Before wrapping up after the long day of lectures, we had to have one more discussion: willpower. They seemed to doubt my ability to pull off the mission since I wasn't actually a soldier. A researcher from the twenty-fourth floor showed up for this part, trying to explain how my magic worked; as if he could tell me, since he had none of his own. It'd be like a textbook publisher explaining quantum physics.

When we returned to the Solia house, once again the Solias had tons of questions, but at least now we could use the simple denial: "Classified." As opposed to fighting them, Kaylaa went out for a stroll in the dark.

That night, while I tried to fall asleep in Pavlar's bed, much to my surprise, Fyra curled up beside me. The warmth of her slender body had a calming effect on me, which was sorely needed after the excitement of the day before and the tense briefings today.

"Thank you," I whispered, low enough that I thought she couldn't hear me.

"I still can't believe it," she said. "Everything Aseus said. It was hard enough for me. How are you getting through it?"

"Honestly, I'm trying not to think about it. When I do...all I can think is how the Shard basically commissioned a weapon—me. And then I get a migraine."

"You know that you're more than that." She turned to face me. "Weapons don't feel. They don't think. They don't...love."

Did she know how I felt? "All the same, they're going to load me into a gun tomorrow and shoot me at the enemy, and hope I blow it up. Maybe I should just...run away." Even though I knew Shards were outside, even with Aseus watching, I felt like I could still get away. *I should've done that at the beginning before Kaylaa caught me.*

"You need to do whatever you believe in, Darynn."

I rubbed my eyes. "What do I believe in? What *should* I believe in?"

"The Iveleen, but I know that's hard for you. Believe in Kaylaa and me. Believe in Pavlar. Believe that the people of Hargonla deserve to be saved."

She spoke with such resolution, I felt compelled to trust her. "You know, you've been through a lot of the same things as me. And you've stayed strong in the face of it. Sometimes you were scared when you were in physical danger, but mentally, you're just as tough as Pavlar."

She smiled. "It's because of my faith, Darynn. I believe the Iveleen have given me the tools to get through it, and I believe They want me to get through it. Without that...who knows where I would be? Even though it seems contrary to what you would think, I think They brought us to this juncture, and They want us to save their people."

"So do you think I should go through with it?"

"I...I don't know." We took a deep breath in unison. "But I do know you're fighting for these people, like Pavlar would. Selfishly, I know if you can end the embargo, then the Olan-Har will suffer less, and I will see fewer deaths. But I'm also afraid, Darynn. I'm afraid of what you may become if you go through with it." Fear rippled in her eyes, like when we fought on the Yiptaen spaceship.

"Have you tried to look ahead? To see what will happen?" I asked.

She gazed deep into my eyes. "I tried. I promise, I really did. But there was nothing. I hope...I hope that means you won't die. But I don't know what else it means. I'm sorry." She sat up on the side of the bed and touched her hand to my shoulder. She managed a smile and went over to her own bed.

Every part of me wanted to join her, but she had left me. *Because she was afraid of me.* What can you do when the girl you love is actually afraid of you?

Love. Yes, I loved her. She'd seen me at my worst, and at my best. She knew all of the best and worst parts about me. I trusted her. I almost didn't care what I thought I should do—I just wanted to follow whatever she thought was the best path.

As I went to sleep that night, all I could think about was her. That was a blessing, compared to the alternative.

Commander Aseus himself came to the Solia house to wake me up before dawn. Even Makaro looked small compared to him, though they had to be nearly the same height.

He didn't say much, just let his eyes command me to move faster. I scarfed down breakfast.

Fyra, Kaylaa, and I went for the door, but Aseus blocked it. "No need for them to come."

"Encouragement," I said. One of his eyes narrowed. He didn't move. "They come or I don't do it."

He grunted, opened the door, and motioned us through. I was met with a raucous cheer.

A large crowd had gathered outside, kept at a distance by a few Shards with their Plasma Edges drawn and riot shields out. In the center of the street was a gyrocopter, metallic blue with four silently whirling blades and a center passenger hold that looked like a shark. *I've never been on a gyrocopter before.* Most of the people around had probably never even seen one.

I took a good look at the surrounding people, their bones seemingly held together by the torn rags they wore. But there was a key difference from a regular day—they looked excited, hopeful. The embargo had stolen that hope from them, but something about the gyrocopter, about Commander Aseus in Hargonla, maybe even about me...had brought them joy. I felt my resolve strengthening with every bright, dirty face I saw.

Before we loaded onto the gyrocopter, Aseus grabbed my shoulder and turned me toward the crowd. He waved and proclaimed, "This day the embargo ends! The Virin-leen, the church, have sat on their hands for too long. Darynn Mark, the Savior of Vastire, is going to release you from your suffering today!" My face was hot with embarrassment and I felt the color drain into my neck. *I guess I don't have a choice anymore.*

He pushed me into the gyrocopter and helped Fyra up. Kaylaa hopped in without any assistance. Aseus tapped on the pilot and away we went, slowly at first, but with increasing speed. I wanted to berate Aseus for the stunt he had pulled, but I was distracted by the air rushing through my hair and exhilaration filling my lungs.

The sword-shaped Shard Headquarters loomed in the distance, but we veered west, over some Poor homes, and landed in an abandoned asphalt parking lot.

But it wasn't completely abandoned. There was a single shabby building in the middle, and two Shards standing at the door. *A secret base?* We disembarked from the gyrocopter and started toward that door, the heat of the asphalt baking my boots, but before we reached it, we were interrupted by a swarm of gold and purple helicopters.

As they set down on the ground, heavily armored troopers clad in white and purple jumped out. They were armed with spears and shields, each shield adorned with a familiar symbol—a shield with the Golden Spiral on it and two crossed spears underneath. The Templars of Makar, which could mean only one thing...

A larger, tandem rotor helicopter set down in the middle of the other helicopters, and from it emerged the oldest Vastirian alive: the Grand Cardinal. He was so old, his legs were too weak to carry him anymore, so he sped toward us in a small personal hover vehicle. At a distance, it was hard to see anything other than what appeared to be a mass of pearly white and wet gold blankets. But upon drawing closer, a pink man with scant hair and an impossible number of wrinkles emerged from the pile.

"What is the meaning of this, Commander Aseus?" the

GraCar called out as he came upon us. He had the look of a hawk searching for prey.

Fyra quickly knelt and crossed her chest with her arms. My instinct was to do the same, but visions of the Temple held me steadfast on my feet. But when Aseus knelt, albeit briefly, I did the same.

"This is a Shard operation, my lord," Aseus replied.

"But with him?" the Cardinal asked, vitriol laced in his words.

"He is well-suited for this suicide mission." *Suicide mission?*

"You put our fates in the dirty, blood-soaked hands of a Haskar's son?"

"I do not need to clear our missions with you. This is the path to carry out the Shard's sworn duty."

"Do not think me a fool, Aseus. I know you've long had an interest in this whelp."

"His father was talented, for all his faults. The boy is talented."

"Talented!" he spat. "He killed Templars and Shards alike that day!"

"Which requires immense talent. We are on a schedule, my lord, so we are going to carry on." Aseus grabbed me by the elbow and dragged me toward the door. The GraCar hovered out in front of him. "You did not bring enough men for a confrontation."

"I will supplant you, Commander. I have that power yet." He pointed a long, bony finger in Aseus's face, just off the tip of his nose.

"Feel free." Aseus stepped around the hover, placing one strong hand on it to keep it from moving. I saw the Templars flinch, but they did not dare attack. Even if it was just Aseus and two Shards against a dozen Templars, they knew they'd lose.

I glanced over my shoulder to see that Fyra still had not risen from her knee; she hadn't even lifted her face. But Kaylaa hauled her up to her feet and dragged her to us.

"I'm sorry, my lord," Fyra said as she passed the Cardinal. Amazingly, she found the strength to resist Kaylaa, if only for a moment, and stood directly in front of the GraCar. His eyes lingered on her, like he recognized her good faith, before Kaylaa carried her in.

The GraCar's words had bitten me like wasps, but somehow, the bites weren't irritating me as badly. *If the Iveleen aren't gods, then the Grand Cardinal is the impostor in chief.* Calling my father a Traitor? He didn't have much of a leg to stand on with that accusation. I smiled.

I exhaled as we went through the doors into the shabby metal building. All that was present here was a single elevator. Aseus scanned his badge to activate it. We went down three or four floors and emerged into a cavernous room, well lit by an overpowering array of white lights. There was a flurry of activity in the room, with Shards and scientists scurrying from one place to another like a hive of ants. The main features of the room were the rockets.

Sleek rockets, most only two or three times the height of a man, were spread out throughout the room, all in the vertical position as if ready to launch through the ground. My inner child wanted to geek out with the rockets, check out their details, but the embargo loomed over everything.

We stopped at the first rocket, a sharp, space-black one only slightly taller than Aseus. Dr. Shagod and Colonel Meer stood nearby, next to a SAFA suit. My *SAFA suit.*

Dr. Shagod motioned for me to sit, and he didn't hesitate to stab a large needle into my neck as soon as I did. I winced and swallowed as the cool fluid flooded my veins—that must have been the nano machine injection.

"Could've warned me," I said.

"You wouldn't have liked it anymore," Dr. Shagod countered. *Probably right.* "You won't like this, either." He stuffed a spoonful of green liquid into my mouth. It tasted like gritty sunscreen and I barely managed to swallow. "Anti-nausea medicine. Nowhere for you to puke."

Colonel Meer and a Shard technician brought the torso of the SAFA over and slipped it over my head like I was a little kid. I felt the pressure on my chest, just as they had warned, like I was being slowly crushed. Then the Shard tech brought over the gauntlets. I slid off the Captain's Ring and handed it to Fyra. The tech slid the gauntlets over my hands, and I felt a slight tingling sensation with each finger. I put on the stiff pants myself, and then, with a bit of assistance from Colonel Meer's good arm, put on the boots with the thrusters. Even with all of the equipment on, it was no heavier than medium-weight Militia armor.

"Once you put the helmet on, there's no taking it off," Colonel Meer said, motioning to Fyra and Kaylaa.

Kaylaa came over and clasped my wrist. I thought there might have been the slightest trace of a tear in her eye, but it didn't drop. "Sure you want to do this?" I nodded. "Don't get blown up. We still need to go to Yiptae." *Was that a joke?* I smiled weakly.

She let go and Fyra rushed in for a full-body hug. Even through the suit, I could feel her warmth. "Come back safe," she said amidst a few tears. "Don't lose yourself."

I felt a strong urge to tell her how I felt—what if I never saw her again? *I guess it doesn't matter how I feel, in that case.* I released her. "I'll come back."

She wiped away a tear and clutched the Captain's Ring to her breast. I turned back toward the hard faces of the Shard scientist and Colonel. I nodded and Dr. Shagod placed the helmet over my head and tightened it.

"Calibration check," he said. The visors came on, and I was flooded with text and symbols and colors.

"All systems nominal," said the tech through the speaker in my helmet.

"Remember," Dr. Shagod said. "Movement is no different than walking. Think it, and the systems will fire. Focus, don't panic."

"Let's go, soldier," Colonel Meer said, and a door into the core of the rocket opened. An opening appeared in the ground above us, giving the rocket wide berth to pass through. I backed into the rocket and faced my friends, my love.

"I love you," I whispered, but I knew Fyra couldn't hear me. She had dropped down to both knees, her eyes closed, her mouth moving quickly in what was certainly a fervent prayer.

The door swung closed, and I was enveloped in complete darkness. Latches clicked into place and electronics whirred. The rocket shivered and the force of the engines pushed from below. The rocket shook violently and my stomach seemed to detach from my body.

I felt a strong urge to pray. But praying hadn't gotten me this far.

Each Member Planet of the Planetary Alliance is allowed a single Senator who votes on behalf of that race. Each Member Planet is allowed to choose such a Senator by whatever means they deem appropriate. A Planet may not be considered for membership if the single Senator cannot speak for the entire Planet.

All decisions by the P.A. Senate are binding to Member Planets, and only a simple majority is required to pass a resolution.

The P.A. does not keep a standing army, though all planets are pledged to provide troops as necessary.

All Member Planets must adopt P.A. Standard as their main language and P.A. Credits, or PACs, as their primary currency.

The symbol of the P.A. is three concentric orbits around central 'P.A.' lettering, with eight dots on the inner orbit, ten on the central, and twelve on the outer, representing the Member Planets and the waves they joined in. Alterations of this symbol for commercial or other purposes are impermissible.

—From *A Primer to the Planetary Alliance*

CHAPTER TWENTY-EIGHT

"Fifteen hundred feet per second," Colonel Meer's voice echoed in my mind. "Twenty minutes to orbit."

The rocket threw me from side to side and I felt like I was steadily melting into the floor. My arms were glued to my sides and my chin was fixed to the bottom of the helmet, on my chest. I even struggled to keep my eyelids open; my eyelashes felt like lead rods. I could smell the sweat accumulating in the suit, even as it did its best to maintain humidity.

"Raider, you're about halfway now," Aseus said, his booming voice seemingly trapped in my skull. *Raider*—the code name we agreed to after I refused any of my father's. Separation in ten minutes, and rocket explosion in twelve. Only two minutes to get away. *Hope I can figure this flying thing out.*

Halfway meant I was just skimming the edge of the atmosphere—I was in space again. But I couldn't see anything, couldn't feel anything other than the giant pulling on my shoes. The inside of the capsule felt just like the air when we left. But I was *in space.*

Focus on the mission. My father had always said that was the key to success—be prepared, be focused, and execute. How did he feel, on his first mission? Was it as insane as this? *Okay, focus.* First objective—move away from the SAFA LM. Second objective—find the nearest ship and destroy it. Third objective...

"We're not alone," said a mousey voice in my head. That

had to be Analyst, the mission operator.

"Raider, you've been detected. We have to initiate separation early. One minute," said Colonel Meer. But I hadn't gone through all of the objectives yet!

I wiggled my fingers and toes with some effort, just to make sure they hadn't been crushed by the gravity. The great force pulling me down started to ease up. Then I heard a series of clicks, and the door burst open with a red flash. "Go, Raider!"

I pushed myself away from the rocket, but my foot tripped on the floor and I went tumbling out into the vastness of space. Dizziness and vertigo simultaneously assaulted my senses as Vastire below and the blackness of space above spun around and around my head. I put my hands over my visor and reflexively pulled myself into a ball, like you would if you had fallen out of a car. But then the tumbling sped up. Some part of my brain knew physics would ensure that happened, but my muscles weren't listening.

"You're panicking, Raider!"

"He's never going to pull himself out of this. Do something!" commanded Aseus.

Suddenly, the propulsive systems around me went to work. Each of the four thrusters fired the tiniest blast, then stopped, then fired again. I was slowing down, but it was taking too long. Vomit crawled up my throat.

"Extend your arms and legs, Raider!"

Reluctantly I obeyed with my eyes tightly shut. Each thruster started firing longer and longer bursts, and soon, I felt myself stabilize. Almost immediately, a blinding light penetrated my eyelids, and a shockwave pushed me away. I felt like a doll with my arms and legs being pulled by an aggressive child.

"SAFA LM detonated. Acceleration from the shockwave will push Raider into a higher orbit, but not high enough," said Analyst.

"Raider, fire your calf thrusters to increase your speed."

I opened my eyes, and though the dizziness was fading, I still felt the vertigo. At least now I could get a sense of my bearings. Outer space above me. Planet below me. I wasn't in control, just a cannonball circling the globe, but calmness washed over me. I was literally on the horizon, the edge of the universe, where it connected to Vastire. Though some clouds were below, Vastire couldn't hide from me—no secrets from where I was standing. Mostly, it was the mint green ocean, but I could see green and brown and gray and black, sometimes in orderly patches indicating man-made structures, and sometimes in natural, wild shapes. *Focus, Darynn!*

"Just pretend like you're walking, Raider. Send that signal from your brain to your feet," Dr. Shagod said. It was funny how odd it felt to think about walking. Walking just worked, from the time you were a toddler. *Okay, pick up this foot, using your thigh, and push it forward.* The thrusters on my right calf responded, and my foot moved forward.

But it overreacted, and I found myself turned sideways. *Okay, other foot.* Again, the calf thrust responded, but now I was turned the wrong way. I felt like a leaf in the wind, like I had no control at all. *Okay, both feet at once.* That felt ridiculous, but I started to right myself, and then I was moving forward uniformly. My feet jetted out in front of me, so I adjusted by putting my hands out like I was gripping a bar. Now my whole body propelled forward. "It's not graceful, but it works."

The first ship came into view.

It was a slender, eel-shaped ship, like a fighter jet, yellow and black. And heavily armed. My visor highlighted it in red and identified it as a Ter Slipt spacefighter. *Never seen anyone from Ter Slipt before.* My visor identified a few other ships that just looked like dots to my eyes. I must have been in Central Orbit, where the majority of the embargo ships were parked.

"First target, Raider."

"Destroy it," Aseus growled.

The intent, the will, the bond. Destroy the embargo with a blast of magic energy. I'm out here in space, risking it all for this. To save the people. The faces from the crowd drifted through my head. I didn't know them, but I recognized all of them. Starving, sad, desperate, dying. The ship in front of me became their oppressor, like it was bombing them from orbit. I could hear their frail voices floating up from the landmass below me, crying out in unison. *Help me.*

The will grew and my body responded. Two spheres of white energy formed in my hands, which bolted out from my shoulders, pointed at the ship. It seemed to smile cruelly, laughing at the Olan-Har's pain. My face went hot with anger, and black energy swirled around the white spheres. My wrists slammed together, and the spheres blasted away, swirling in a double helix. *Just like the Second Lady.* On a much bigger scale.

The spheres slammed into the Ter Slipt spacefighter, renting the hull with a huge tear. The spheres came out the other side and rocketed toward the nearest ship, which exploded into a blast of red and yellow fire. Three more dots exploded. My visor indicated them as targets no more.

I felt intoxicated with power. My arms surged and my eyes scanned desperately for the next target. *I'm invincible.* These ships were the fish, and I was the harpoon, and I could strike out again and again, and they would be clueless. New spheres of energy gathered in my palms, and I prepared to fling them at the next enemy.

Before I could, a body floated out of the Ter Slipt spacefighter. It was tall and gangly and a sickening yellow color, its lips purple, its eyes...missing, only strands of crimson tendon where they should have been. Its mouth was wide open, screaming, and though I knew I shouldn't be able to hear anything, I heard the awful, high-pitched wail. It sounded like Pavlar.

Another body floated out from the ship, this one with its eyes intact...and maybe still alive. Its arms and legs flailed wildly like it was desperately trying to catch onto a handhold.

As if it mattered—the pressure, cold, and airless space would kill it in seconds. His screams, too, reverberated in my head, and now Pavlar was screaming twice. I covered my ears in hopes of ending the screaming. Any power I had seeped away into space like there was a small puncture in my suit. I closed my eyes and turned away.

Another ship was zooming towards me.

"Raider, attack!" Aseus said.

"No, no, no, no."

"Damnit, he's losing it. We talked about this, Raider!"

"No, no, no..."

"Raider, prepare to evade. Ion cannons are locked onto you," Analyst said calmly. *How can she be so calm?*

A torrent of blue spheres erupted from the oncoming vessel. Instinct kicked in, and I dodged to my right, then over the destroyed ship. *No bodies on this side.*

I held fast to the ship, my hands locked onto an antenna. *What now?* Sweat dripped off my forehead and cheeks and floated through the helmet until it was sucked away by a hose out of view. I squinted hard and opened my eyes, desperately trying to focus.

"Raider, you can't turn back now. Either you kill them, or they're going to kill you," Colonel Meer said matter-of-factly.

"I...I can't. I'm not a murderer."

"That's right. You're a soldier."

"I'm not that, either. I'm just a kid!"

Aseus's booming voice overwhelmed Meer's. "You are a weapon. Fire!"

"I'm...I'm more than that." I thought about Fyra, and Kaylaa, and friends I'd made along the way. *Am I more than that?*

Then a scream—a *real* scream—echoed in my helmet. My heart fluttered. "What was that?"

"My Edge is on her neck. Act now, or I'll slit her throat."

"Don't do it! You're not a killer, Darynn!" Fyra screamed.

"I'm not afraid!"

"You bastard! You *will* regret this!" Another scream made my blood curdle. Burning rage engulfed me and I flung myself off of the ship. Three ships patrolled the area, searching for the weapon that destroyed their ships. *I'm right here.*

The power raged, black and white waves of energy swarming my body. My vision turned red, and every target around me turned into a threat to Fyra. Every ship pushed that blade further into Fyra's neck, rivulets of blood running down to her chest. Their fault. They needed to *die!*

"Temperature is high. The cooling system can't keep up. He's going to bake in there," Analyst said. But I didn't care.

I zipped forward, a huge sphere of burning black and white energy. My consciousness started to slip away, and I felt like a ghost watching my body act on its own. I saw myself crash into the first ship, which exploded instantly, like a firecracker thrown onto a campfire.

My head turned quickly, unnaturally, and like a heat-seeking missile, I locked onto the next ship. It cracked in half on contact. *Next target. Next target.*

I found it. Another ship, much larger than the others. A heavy hand holding the sword at Fyra's throat. I rushed towards it and broke through its skin. The hallways were vast, and the people inside were quickly sucked away towards the hole.

I smiled involuntarily, wickedly. I punched one of the people as I dashed by, tearing him completely in half, then kicked off the wall and punched another hole in the ship.

Bodies floated all around me, but they were nothing to me— each one was worth Olan-Har lives. And all of them, put together, still didn't add up to Fyra.

I rocketed from ship to ship, blowing holes in every one of them, setting them on fire, causing them to detonate. Silent screaming heads flew by. Corpses, hideously twisted into shapes of agony, floated around. I sailed through an orbital graveyard, explosions in my wake.

I thought I heard Fyra's voice echoing in my head, "Stop, Darynn! Stop!"

Why would I stop? I'm saving her; I'm destroying these monsters who are bringing her pain.

Out of the corner of my eye, I saw a flotilla of ships trying to escape. *No one escapes.* They were out of my reach, but that didn't matter. Instinctively, I crossed my arms on my chest, then flung my hands out. The ball of energy that had enveloped my body tore away from me at the speed of light and broke into a hundred pieces that attacked every escaping ship.

My body slumped in the suit. My chest heaved and my vision returned to normal. But it was still red—fires, blood, sunlight. Endless wreckage surrounded me, ranging from entire halves of ships to the tiniest specks of metal. Tears started to float in my suit and I could taste them in my mouth. Along with blood. At some point, I'd bitten my tongue.

I swallowed hard and the magnitude of what I'd done hit me. The absolute silence of space was deafening.

I destroyed everything. I killed everyone.

I ended the embargo.

Despite reports to the contrary, it was confirmed a single subject was responsible for the destruction of the embargo. The subject likely used Shard technology to reach orbit, but then acted on his own accord.

The overall rundown:

- *141 ships in orbit around Vastire*
- *71 ships destroyed*
    - *52 fighter class*
    - *19 cruiser class*
- *427 dead*

All 29 Member Planets lost at least one ship.

The subject attacked in three waves:

- *Wave 1: Destroyed 2 Ter Slipt Fighters and 3 other ships via magic blast*
- *Wave 2: Destroyed 20 ships by personally bursting through them with magic energy*
- *Wave 3: Destroyed 46 escaping ships with rockets of magic energy*

The subject stopped attacking at this point, unsure of reason, but likely exhaustion. Other small groups of ships escaped, theoretically within range based on the Wave 3 attack.

—From P.A. Report on the Destruction of the
Embargo Around Vastire

CHAPTER TWENTY-NINE

I sat in bed for hours the next morning—or at least what I thought was the next morning—staring at the paper scraps, dusty curtains, and cracked ceiling in Pavlar's room. My neck was stiff from laying on his lumpy pillow. The bed still smelled like him.

A strange image was trapped in my head. I was on one side of a wall, and Pavlar was at the top. He peered over the edge, shaking his head at me. If I could just get to him, I could explain to him what I did, why I did it. I would find a handhold or two, but then a brick would fall out or crumble beneath my hand, and I'd fall. Each time I fell, the wall grew until I could barely see him anymore.

Raucous cheering from outside jolted the image from my head. At first, the cheers were confusing, but then I understood. They were excited the embargo was gone, glad I had eliminated the source of their pain and sorrow. But the embargo was just a consequence, maybe—of a trap set hundreds of years ago. And now they were cheering for me—a killer. Worse. A mass murderer.

I covered my head with the lumpy pillow, but that was worse.

With the cheers muffled outside, all I could hear were screams, echoing louder and louder, repeating, drawn-out, overwhelming. I threw the pillow across the room and looked at Fyra's bed.

It was empty, but she hadn't been gone long. Her pillow was still damp with tears.

My arms wobbled as I lifted myself from bed. I took a few steps and stumbled into the wall. *Steady now.* I used the wall to steady myself as I staggered to the window. I wasn't hurt, but I was sore all over, like my whole body had been wrapped too tightly in a cast.

I drew the curtain aside just enough to peek outside.

The whole street swarmed with Olan-Har, their skinny bodies allowing hundreds to pack into a tiny space. Their arms sagged like the slivers and disc tattoo weighed down their skin.

But they were happy.

Huge smiles, most with missing teeth. The light glinting in their eyes. Laughing and cheering and real conversations. Holding each other up, swaying together, even dancing. Diterians and Maltans and the regular folk of Hargonla, all together in harmony.

I felt a smile cross my face. *This is why I did it.* It seemed like it had been years since I'd even seen one smile in Hargonla, and now I could see hundreds from my perch by the window.

The door opened and Fyra came through, her eyes sunken with exhaustion and her nails bitten until they bled. She wrapped one arm around my waist and said, "You're awake."

I nodded. Butterflies swarmed in my stomach. *She doesn't hate me.*

"They're here for the Savior of Vastire. For you." She smiled weakly.

I turned away from the window. "They don't know me for what I really am. I'm worse than my father."

"I won't pretend that the act won't haunt you, and me, but it is done. And the result is clear. The Olan-Har will find ways to survive again, something that just wasn't possible with the embargo overhead. You saved more than you killed." Her lips quivered and her voice cracked as she spoke.

From the corner of my eye, I saw her reach for my shoulder, but she pulled back. "I should've known Aseus might try something like that."

Aseus...I balled my hands into fists. I felt like a stove burner was under my feet, and steam was starting to rise from my ears. "He's next."

"You're not a killer, Darynn. You...did what you did out of love...right?"

"At first...but..." *No, I'm not going to tell her.* How the euphoric draw of power overwhelmed me, like an addict getting a fix. How hatred pushed me on. That could be my consequence, one of the oldest in the book. The corruption of power, unchecked. "Aseus loaded the gun, and pulled the trigger."

"You fought for Vastire. You fought for...me." Tentatively, she wrapped her arms around my back, and I held her soft hands in mine. I tried to live in the moment, but every time my consciousness slipped, another twisting, oxygen-deprived face seared my vision.

I turned toward her. "I care about you, Fyra. When he pulled what he did, I felt lost and helpless. I did the only thing I could." I held her tighter.

"I know." I felt her heartbeat quicken, but I couldn't tell if it was fear or love. "That's what is important. You did it out of a desire to protect, not destroy. You know..." She paused. "Maybe we've been looking at your magic wrong all along. Both the healing and the destruction. They're both powers of protection, though in different ways."

I hadn't thought of it like that. It made a lot of sense...but she didn't know about the mad rage I had gone into. Before that, yes, it was about protecting the Olan-Har. Protecting her. But after...I just wanted blood. And I got it.

She let go and opened a shabby drawer. She removed the Captain's Ring, polished it on her shirt, and handed it to me. "For the glory and honor of Vastire."

I wasn't sure about the glory and honor part, but my actions had served Vastire. I admired the ring and thought of Captain Madra, one of many who had helped me get here. One of the many who wasn't among the people outside.

The crowd swelled, and I heard a vehicle land outside.

"What's that?" I reached for my father's Plasma Edge, next to Pavlar's bed, and hobbled outside. The crowd stretched for miles, but they backed away from a familiar spaceship that had landed in the middle of the street.

Senator Shuka emerged from the ship and stood on a ramp. "Darynn Mark! How dare you? We sought peaceful means to save your people, and you repay me by killing my brethren?" His blue cheeks were flushed and his flabby arms flailed wildly as he spoke.

"You did nothing while my people starved!" I yelled. The crowd cheered.

"Nova Karr will hunt you like a rabid dog. You will not be able to sleep without an eye open, you will not be able to walk without looking over your shoulder, you will not be able to piss without worrying about a knife in your back!" He pointed a long finger at me, hate in his eyes.

I pointed my Edge back at him. "Then tell that coward to come out! I'll kill him now in front of all these good people." Another roar, and the crowd inched closer to the ramp.

"That would be too easy, an injustice to the innocent soldiers you killed above! No, he will haunt you like a specter."

"The only injustice was your embargo!" Another cheer, and this time, the crowd lurched toward Shuka, ready to tear him apart. But before they could, Kaylaa leapt from the ship and forced everyone back with her whirling Rapiers.

"Stop!" I commanded the crowd, and they froze. *She was with him again.* Of course she was; I killed who knows how many of her allies. I felt a flash of pain like an old wound.

Kaylaa pushed Shuka back into the ship, then saluted him. "I have completed my objective."

Shuka's mouth was agape, and then he snarled, "I should've

known better than to hire a busser, even a sharp tool like you."
Kaylaa flinched at the term *busser*. "I hope you're in the way
when Nova Karr kills him." The ramp slid in and the door
closed, and with a deafening blast, the spaceship launched out
of the atmosphere. Kaylaa cut through the crowd to stand at my
side.

I exhaled. "You scared me for a second there."

Her gaze lingered on the spot where the spaceship
disappeared. "I did my job. Always wondered why he hired me.
Guess I know now." She put a strong hand on my shoulder and
guided Fyra and me back into the house.

Kaylaa sighed. "I know why you did it. It's plain to see when
you look outside. When I first arrived, I'd distanced myself.
These people were just mission objectives. But now, when I look
at them as *people*, I get it."

Fyra smiled. "You're feeling empathy, Kaylaa."

Kaylaa nodded. "It makes me wonder what I'm going to feel
when I get home. I have people there I care about, including my
grandfather. It's time to do more for the Immigrants." She
looked distant, then focused on me again. "I'm still struggling
with what you did, Darynn. Part of me can't believe you went
through with it. Another part wonders if I would've made the
same choice...and had the will to carry it through. And if I
could've just beaten Colonel Meer..."

"I saw you fighting him," Fyra said, putting one hand on
Kaylaa's shoulder. "I think, with more time, you would've won,
but Colonel Meer is a master, even with just one arm."

"I struggled to focus. I never have that issue." Kaylaa shook
her head. "But I'm sorry, Darynn."

Part of me wanted to be honest and tell her even if she had
been able to free Fyra, it was probably too late—definitely too
late. When I turned...it was like I'd lost the part of me that made
me human. I had reveled in the chaos around me. *Like the
Vastirians did before the Rise of the Iveleen.*

I couldn't tell them because I was scared of how they would

react. "It's not your fault. I'm sorry if you lost some allies up there."

"I did but...my allies here are more important." She smiled, only for a second, before turning back to the stone-faced soldier.

Fyra's parents came inside from the courtyard. Lia held a tray full of smoking meats, crackers, and nuts. She placed it on the table and my stomach growled loud enough for the entire room to hear.

Lia smiled. "Glad you're awake. You must be starving! Eat. We've already eaten, so it's all for you."

"How is this possible?" I asked.

"Offerings on the doorstep," Makaro said. "For you." He seemed unable to look at me, which was somehow more unnerving than his hard stare. The two of them left the house.

Kaylaa, Fyra, and I sat at the table to eat. Kaylaa placed a data pad on the table. A live feed of a virtual gathering of the P.A. Senate played on it. A Vastirian man with a smooth voice and handsome face was speaking, conveying a message of unity and prosperity.

"That's Count Astar," Kaylaa said. "He, your King, and your Senator are on their way to Amicrux now, but while everyone was in transit, they started. His silver tongue has already started swaying the Senate to your side."

"So things will return to normal?"

"Don't be naïve. They're afraid of Vastire—afraid of *you* right now. But no one will like how Vastire bullied their way back into the P.A., and the wounds will fester. Senator Shuka is shrewd; he will pick at the wounds until they burst."

"And now Nova Karr is hunting Darynn," Fyra added.

"If I can..." I stopped short—I didn't want to talk about it. "I should be able to handle him."

"You can't take him lightly," Kaylaa warned. "He can't beat you in a fair fight, so he'll make sure the battle comes on his terms. He'll wait years if he has to."

"I'll be ready. And I have you two." I smiled, I think for the first time since waking up.

Fyra swallowed a politely cut piece of meat. "The embargo was only the beginning. Chasing the Great Secret to Yiptae will be just as taxing." She rubbed her shoulder. "I have this nagging feeling that there's...more. Much more to discover."

I wasn't sure I could take more, but we all knew it was there. "Aseus said to question everything. We'll find the answers. We'll find out about the ship. We'll find out why my father started a rebellion against the Virin-leen. We'll find out who really killed Kaylaa's father." My eyes turned to Fyra, "And maybe we'll just find out about your powers too, Fyra." They both nodded. "So what now?"

"I'll start gathering intel for Yiptae," Kaylaa said, chewing a bite.

"Darynn and I should probably help the Olan-Har get back on their feet before we go. In the meantime, I'll start looking into what I can find, even without access to the DataAxis," Fyra said.

It hadn't occurred to me yet, but she was right. It wasn't like a magic switch was flipped when I scared off the embargo. The Olan-Har will still take weeks, months, maybe years to get back to where they were before. "I wish Pavlar were here. He would know exactly how to get everything set up, how to get everything going again to help the Olan-Har."

Fyra said, "It won't be as efficient as Pavlar, but I think I can do it. We talked a lot about all of the things he did."

I put my hand over hers on the table. "I believe in you. I don't know what to do, but you tell me and I'll help." I felt a new kind of debt to the Olan-Har, even as it seemed like they should've been indebted to me. I couldn't let those lives lost up there—the ones I ended—mean nothing. The Olan-Har had to live, had to thrive. For now, that meant under the caste system, but maybe after Yiptae, it meant something else.

We were silent for a little while as we finished up our meals, consumed by our thoughts.

Fyra finally broke the silence. "I think we should visit Pavlar's grave."

"He has one?"

She smiled. "With some help from an unknown benefactor, my parents managed to get him a plot near the factories."

I smiled and wondered who Pavlar had helped that was repaying the favor. "Let's go."

We stepped out into the street, but we were greeted by eerie silence and hushed whispers. I soon knew why—Commander Aseus was waiting next to a Shard gyrocopter.

I blazed the plasma on my Edge. "Bastard! Coming here?" But before I could charge him, Kaylaa grabbed my arm and held me back.

"I did what I had to fulfill the Shard mission; to protect the people of Vastire. These people," Aseus said, sweeping his arms at the Olan-Har. The crowd cluelessly cheered. I gritted my teeth. "Invite me in so we can speak."

I mockingly swept my arm toward the door and let him walk past. I followed him in and plopped on the sofa. I kept my Edge close.

"Hate me if you like. But you need me." Aseus pointed at me like I was a child in trouble. "If you want to change things, you're going to need me. The royals won't support you. The GraCar won't support you. Besides, if you do let out the Great Secret, you're going to need the Shard to keep the peace. Listen to your girlfriend. She's smarter than you."

"He's right..." Fyra said. *No reaction to the word* girlfriend?

"So what do you want from me?" I didn't want to know the answer.

"Nothing, for now. You're a Shard now, whether you like it or not."

"You don't command me."

He crossed his arms. "However you want to think of it, I will call upon you when needed. Until then, enjoy your adoring public." He strolled out of the house and the swooping blades of the gyrocopter chopped the air until it was out of hearing range.

"I'm not sure who has the upper hand," I said, shaking my head. Images of my clones ran through my head. If they were capable of doing what I did to the embargo...and he still had the Eye of Deesa, and he knew the Great Secret. *Guess he has the upper hand.*

"We don't need to worry about him right now. Focus on recovery, then the mission," Kaylaa said.

I swallowed, then nodded. "Anyway, let's go to Pavlar's grave."

Once outside, we started pushing our way through the crowd. Everyone wanted to thank me, congratulate me, shake my hand, pat my shoulder, but it was exhausting. Even so, their joy nibbled away at my guilt. Each gesture was a reminder. *This is why I did it.*

After a while, Kaylaa started clearing the way with her Rapiers, scaring off anyone who wanted to get near. But the blocks were jam-packed with people, and the crowd followed us as we traveled southeast. I felt an eerie feeling of deja vu, like my father leading the people during his revolution.

My eyes drifted to the rooftops. "Follow me!" I said, taking the nearest staircase, ladder, and windowsills up to the roof of the nearest building. Kaylaa helped Fyra up, and I breathed in the fresh air. People hollered from the street, but we were safe from them now.

My view swept across the horizon. Nothing looked different, not yet. I wondered how long it would take things to get back to normal. If it ever did. Our trip to Yiptae may disrupt it forever. I shook the thought out of my head.

We traveled along the rooftops as best as we could, but we didn't make it long before the gaps between buildings were too wide. We made our way back down to the street, and fortunately, the crowd hadn't been able to keep up with us.

We found a break in the rusted fence that separated Hargonla from the rest of the city. Minutes later, it was plain to see why there was a hole. A vast graveyard—really just a collection of large rocks, stone bricks, and freshly turned dirt—had been built here. Somehow I wasn't aware of it before.

Today it was busy, with many families standing over the makeshift graves, lamenting the people they lost during the embargo. There were tears, but there was also joy, knowing that better days were ahead.

I looked to Fyra to see that she had tears in her eyes, but she was also smiling. "The people are finally feeling some semblance of relief. I am too," she said. I tried to smile, but all I could think was *at what cost?*

In the distance, Lia and Makaro stood over a grave, along with a third person.

"I leave you here," Kaylaa said. "I've got work to do. Try not to do anything stupid while I'm gone?"

"Okay," I said, and she was off, back into the slums.

"You really changed her," Fyra said.

"*We* changed her. But one thing hasn't changed: she's still focused on the next mission."

"That's true, but now, she has a reason to complete the mission, other than just for its sake."

"You've changed too. Before you wanted to help people, but you weren't sure how. Now you're still not sure how, but you're determined to do it anyway."

She smiled. "I think I'm stuttering less, too."

"Stuttering?"

"Come on, I know you noticed." She cocked her head to the side.

I thought back...and yeah, I guess she did stutter sometimes. "I never cared. It's just a part of you."

She responded with the widest, prettiest grin I'd ever seen from her. She took my hand, and we walked to the grave.

When we were close, the third person turned and came to speak to me. "The Grand Cardinal specifically asked for you to see him, as soon as possible," Father Ckoost said.

"Why me?"

"Does it matter?" He sighed. "He wants to know where you stand in your walk with the Iveleen."

"Oh, that. I'll go see him sometime this week, I guess."

Father Ckoost's eyes narrowed. "You should go today."

"I'm tired, and I have more important things to do right now."

"More important? I worry about your faith. And your pride."

"Worry about saving the Olan-Har for now, Father."

He crossed his arms. "I hope you do not think yourself to be as great as Nurka, like many are whispering."

Nurka, the Iveleen that sacrificed himself to destroy a fleet. *Maybe we are similar?* But I'm still alive. I smiled. "No, of course not, Father."

His body rocked like he wanted to slap me, but held back. "Come see me before you see the Grand Cardinal. I will go with you." He waved to Makaro and Lia and headed off in the direction we came.

"You should not ignore the Grand Cardinal, no matter how you're feeling right now," Fyra warned.

"I'm not ignoring him. I just don't have the energy today."

"Okay, but upsetting him would be unwise."

"Why don't you play politics for me?" I asked playfully. I clutched her hand tightly, and we continued to Pavlar's grave.

When we arrived, Makaro nodded to me, a tear in his eye, and pulled Lia away from the grave. There was no headstone, just a pile of dirt and sand.

"He deserves a great memorial," I said.

"He wouldn't want it," Fyra said. "All he wanted was to help people, and he didn't want recognition. You know, my father thought he didn't have a job at all. That was a partial truth, but Pavlar did so many favors, we were relatively well off in Hargonla. People would give my mother food and my father gifts, and they never knew why."

"Huh," I said. "I have a little secret too." Fyra turned to listen. "He never killed anyone, on any of our raids or otherwise. That took a special bit of skill, and I didn't really teach him that."

"He had the purest heart."

We silently looked at the grave, both lost in our thoughts. I removed the stone Gryphon from my pocket and examined it closely, like it was imbued with his spirit.

"You told me when you gave this to me that Pavlar would want me to protect the Olan-Har like a Gryphon protecting his pride. I hope he would be able to accept me for the way I did it."

"He wouldn't agree with how it happened, but you saved his people. He loved you, and he would forgive you, I think. He wanted you to take up his mantle, and you did."

Is she lying to make me feel better? Protecting out of love and loyalty...that's what this stone Gryphon really represented. I thought back to how I wanted to run away immediately after Pavlar's death. But I saved Captain Madra's little girl, and from then on, my responsibility had grown. Someone had to fill the gaping hole Pavlar left. Fyra was probably better suited to do that, but she would need protection, just like he had. But instead of going along for the adventure, I felt just as strongly that the Olan-Har were my responsibility, too.

I don't know that Pavlar weighed Olan-Har lives over others, but that merry crowd outside his house—he would've loved that. He would've traded almost anything for their joy.

"He'd be more proud of you, fighting through your fears to help people," I said. "Even as you struggled with your loss and your faith, you came out stronger in the end."

Even as she teared up looking at his grave, she held a smile on her face. I secured the stone Gryphon in my pocket. Part of me wanted to leave it on his grave, but I needed to carry that piece of him around with me, always.

Windoon's Star was setting on the horizon, but it lingered there, if only for a moment, not ready to set on this day. The very first stars peeked out above, and for the first time in years, I knew they were only stars, not ships. I wrapped an arm around Fyra's slender body and looked deeply into her sapphire eyes. Our shadows stretched out long across the earth, framing Pavlar's grave in light. Our hearts beat with the same rhythm, the rhythm of friendship, of love, of immortality.

ABOUT ATMOSPHERE PRESS

Atmosphere Press is an independent, full-service publisher for excellent books in all genres and for all audiences. Learn more about what we do at atmospherepress.com.

We encourage you to check out some of Atmosphere's latest releases, which are available at Amazon.com and via order from your local bookstore:

Saints and Martyrs: A Novel, by Aaron Roe

When I Am Ashes, a novel by Amber Rose

Melancholy Vision: A Revolution Series Novel, by L.C. Hamilton

The Recoleta Stories, by Bryon Esmond Butler

Voodoo Hideaway, a novel by Vance Cariaga

Hart Street and Main, a novel by Tabitha Sprunger

The Weed Lady, a novel by Shea R. Embry

A Book of Life, a novel by David Ellis

It Was Called a Home, a novel by Brian Nisun

Grace, a novel by Nancy Allen

Shifted, a novel by KristaLyn A. Vetovich

Because the Sky is a Thousand Soft Hurts, stories by Elizabeth Kirschner

ABOUT THE AUTHOR

Justin was born in Galveston, TX, and raised in the Houston area. In middle school, he fell in love with two life-long pursuits: space and writing. He knew he wanted to work at NASA and write science fiction/fantasy on the side, and lo and behold, that's exactly what he ended up doing.

He now works for the Center for the Advancement of Science in Space, who manages the International Space Station National Laboratory. He lives in the Houston area with his wife, daughter, and various small mammals.

Check out his website *starmarked.mailchimpsites.com* for more information on him, bonus material in the Star Marked universe, and upcoming releases.

CPSIA information can be obtained
at www.ICGtesting.com
Printed in the USA
BVHW071052110821
614085BV00005B/417

9 781637 528167